THE CONQUEROR'S PRINCESS

BOOK ONE
IN THE
PRINCESSES OF AELLOLYN
SERIES

ALICE CALLISTO

&

JEANETTE ROSE

ROSE & STAR

ROSE & STAR PUBLISHING

To Aisling & Amber,

Thanks for putting up with us talking about this nonstop, and Aisling enduring hours of edits including a re-write. You never gave up on us, and we never gave up on you.

Love,
Ally & Jean

THE UNKNOWNS

THE EM

KOLIA

FERROYN

THO

AILSA

JAROMIR

ABINGORA

RUSLAN

SASKIA

AELLOLYN

THE NORTH WARDENS

RAVARYN

GRIMMWING

ARCANUM

XANTHOR

ALYNTHI

KAMACHYA

VRUICA

MISTEYE

ABINEGRA

STEODIA

KESTRAMORE

ELLESMERE

ELWORA

AZRYN

TETHORIS

WINTERMORE

EHESSE

ALROWYN

TWYES

RAZAR

GREAT TEMPLE
OF VISHA

CANTRICK

KIKORO

EXINE

HIRAY

XIAPIA

ALABRAN

ANTLUR

ZEMIRA

ILIUM

CANDONIA

LYANA

VIELA

TYESK

SANCTIFIQUE

KAPINA

THE METAL MOUNTAINS

SUMMERISLE

WREN

RODRIN

CIRAL

THE SILVERCOAL ISLES

CABEN

LIVANE

INVART

THE MIST

SERODET

DOUR

DOLAN

STODDART

THE SEA OF HORRORS

MERITER

Trigger Warnings: Dubious Consent, Abuse of Minors
(Mentioned)

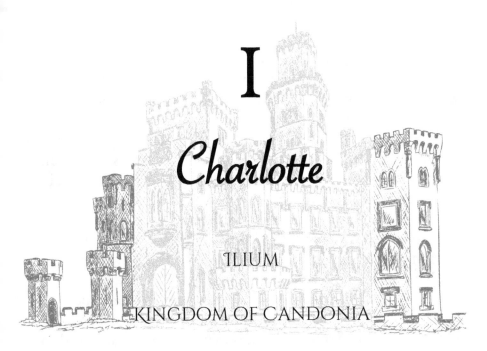

I

Charlotte

ILIUM

KINGDOM OF CANDONIA

He's here.

From the windows of the palace, I can see the banners of his army on all sides. Our city is surrounded by a sea of brutal soldiers following one man. A man we have spent years at war with, struggling to hold his horde at bay. He has made it all the way to Ilium, my home and a haven for thousands of people, the beating heart of our kingdom. Never have the walls of Ilium been breached, but they are about to crumble against the onslaught.

If the gates fall, there will be nothing to stop them. The conqueror's army will plow through the capital, burning, murdering, and pillaging everything they find. There will be nothing left. My gut twists, but my face remains calm as I watch the sea of iron surrounding the sandstone walls of my city. I know what will happen when they fall.

They'll come for us next.

My father will be first. The conqueror will wave his head on a stick through the streets, claiming victory. Next will be the queen and then me.

Any child I bear will have a rightful claim to rule. He will need to get rid of me to ensure my children don't take back what is rightfully theirs. Our blood beats through the heart of Candonia and has for over a thousand years.

This is the end. The end of my family, our legacy. The end of my country. My kingdom. My eyes well with tears, but I refuse to let them fall. Once I am gone, he will go for my sisters, Thalia and Eleanor. They will be next in line, and he would be foolish not to kill them as well. Having studied his tactics, victories, and methods at my father's side, I know this man—this *monster*—is anything but a fool. If only he were a fool, things would be so much easier.

He annihilates kingdoms, leaving nothing but ash and despair. They say he is nothing but a black shadow when he fights. You know your end is upon you when you see his dark figure pass by. He sets the cities on fire, skewering any that try to escape their fiery death. His joy? Is listening to their screams as the flames lick their skin, and they slowly burn to death. I hope he rots in *Ufelyn*, the realm of the dead.

I move from the window to sit at the desk, my normally bright room dark from the smoke hovering in the air. I twist the vial of poison in my pocket, and let out a sigh. A shiver runs down my spine as my mind continues to spin. It shouldn't have come to this. We made so many plans, so many ways to subvert this monstrous enemy. It only seemed to bring us one step closer to our demise. Instead of sending more troops to the borders of Vruica, we should have sent them east towards Steodia. We should have pulled back from the northern front earlier this year. *Would it have mattered? Would he have not found a way to fight a war on two fronts?*

I get up from my desk and walk over to a chest of drawers. From under one of my chemises, I pull out a thin dagger. I slip it into my pocket, letting out a shaky sigh. I will not go down without a fight. I may play the perfect princess for my people, but I will not surrender. He won't expect it from me. *Not from Princess Charlotte. Meek and mild, even-tempered Charlotte.*

That is the least I can do for my people. I will not be a coward and hide with my sisters and the queen in our safe room. Not if there is a chance of saving them. My hand tightens on the bottle in my pocket. I will not take the easy way out. I will face the conqueror and show no fear.

My door bursts open, and for a split second, my stomach leaps into my chest. *They're here? Already?!* I spin toward the threat, pointing my knife at Agatha, Eleanor's maid, as she rushes into my room. Years of being responsible for my sister have put deep wrinkles on her round face. No doubt the grey hairs are from her as well. Her brown eyes search the room, and my stomach twists. I can't remember the last time I was able to force food down.

Something's wrong.

"Your Highness," Agatha curtsies, still formal with the enemies around us, "it's your sister. We can't find her."

A part of me hopes she means Thalia. She has been practicing her combat skills since our mother died. She likely wanted a chance at the conqueror too. I made her promise she wouldn't do anything foolish if this day came. Eleanor needs one of us, and Thalia has been caring for her since Eleanor's birth.

"Thalia?" I ask, praying to see Agatha nod.

She shakes her head. "Princess Eleanor."

I curse to myself before heading for the door. My twelve-year-old sister is just as stubborn and intelligent but has yet to find her bravery. When frightened or overwhelmed, Eleanor will hide. On the day of our father's wedding to the queen, she hid away in our secret garden, and Thalia had to coax her out with cookies.

Agatha and I hurry down the long corridor. It is unusually quiet for this time of day. Typically, workers and maids pace the hallways, delivering items from one place to another and going about their duties. It is strange to see the grand halls of the castle empty. I'd ordered everyone to evacuate the palace unless they wanted to take up arms with the warriors and fight. Many of the men and a few women went to help as our last line of defense, hoping to give the people they love a chance at survival. There's no escape now. His army surrounds our city like an unrelenting sea, Ilium an isolated island about to fall beneath the onslaught.

I turn to the right and enter the east wing. The portraits of my ancestors stare at me as I rush down the hall. I can feel their silent judgment and disappointment. The walls had never fallen under their reign.

I grab the front of my ocean blue dress, holding up the skirt as I run up the staircase to the astronomy tower. Agatha is close at my heels as we reach the top. I fiddle with the old wooden door, hitting my fist against it. *Locked.* The wood is splintered and worn from use and age. I pull a bobby pin from my hair and stick it in the keyhole. I had a locksmith teach me how to do this the first time Eleanor locked herself inside. I dreaded not being able to get to her when she needed us. Or when danger approaches. *Like now.*

I hear the click as the ancient tumblers fall into place and tuck the bobby pin back into my hair before walking into the room. Dust motes dance in the sunbeams, white sheets cover the furniture, and the paint on the walls is cracked and peeling. A large telescope sits in the corner, pointing out the window, waiting to be used once more. The floorboards creak beneath my feet as I take a few cautious steps inside. I had always hoped to fix up the room and honor my great grandfather's memory, but that dream dies today. *As will I.*

A small sniffle comes from under one of the tables. I hold my hand up to Agatha, and she stays by the door. I lift the white sheet and find Eleanor. She has her face buried against her knees, her long platinum blonde hair flowing down her back. In the light, it looks almost white.

"El," I whisper, placing a comforting hand on her knee. She looks up at me, and I bite back a gasp. Her normally blue eyes are glowing violet. *If the enemy finds out what she is, what she can*

10

do... There are far worse things than death, and I can't let that happen to her. *I won't let that happen to her.* Eleanor's petite round nose scrunches as she sniffles.

"I-I don't want to," she whispers.

I sigh softly. "You have to, El. The queen and Thalia are waiting for you in the safe room."

"But what about you?" she asks, her eyes shining with unshed tears.

I tuck a strand of her hair behind her ear. "I will meet you there when I am done with my duties."

"You're going to face that man, aren't you?" she says, getting onto her knees. "You can't do that, Charlie! He will kill you."

I should have known better than try to keep the rumors of our enemy from her. Eleanor hides behind the wall during serious meetings. She reminds me of myself when I was her age, always curious, always wanting answers. Even when the answers, the *truth,* she seeks would devastate her.

I fight back my own tears, kissing her forehead. "I will be fine. Thalia needs you right now. She needs someone strong to look out for her. Can you do that?"

Stay strong. Stay strong. Don't break. Not in front of Eleanor. I had spent too many years forcing my own emotions down, protecting my sisters from the albatross of our kingdom that hung around my neck. I would not break now.

Eleanor nods, her brow furrowing. "I can protect both of you. I don't want you to—"

Loud shouts make us both turn to look at the largest window. We rush to it, and I try to step in front of Eleanor so she doesn't see.

My heart stops, freezing in my chest, and all air is sucked from my lungs. *Will it ever beat again? Will I ever breathe again?* The invaders have broken through the southern gates. Thousands of men are pouring through, rivers of black and red, twining through the cobblestone streets. The cacophony of swords clashing against the royal guard, metal grinding against metal, and agonized screams makes me want to cover my ears. The screams, I know I will never forget them. I grab my sister's arm and drag her to the brick wall. Agatha beats us there and lifts one of the lights, a secret passage appearing.

"Charlie! What's happening?!" Eleanor exclaims, but I ignore her. There isn't much time if I am going to save her. *I have to save her.*

"Take her to Thalia and stay with them. Do not leave the room unless you hear the code," I command.

"But, Your Highness—" Agatha begins, a worried expression crossing her face.

"Now!" I demand, lowering the light, locking both my sister and the maid behind the wall.

For a second, I stare at the blank space. That would be the last time I see them, the last I see of Eleanor. I place a trembling hand against the wall, a silent goodbye before I leave to face the enemy.

My heart pounds in my chest, and my hands are shaking uncontrollably. *This is it.* Even as my silk slippers glide over the carpet, I can hear my footsteps. They are the sounds of a woman heading towards her own death. My demise is in each breath and every beat is borrowed time. One moment closer to the end.

I sprint down the stairs to the entryway of the palace. I can't hear the battle raging outside, the sounds muffled by the thick walls. A lonely silence and preparation for what must come next. An icy calm suffuses me, muting everything else. I hide behind one of the marble pillars in the palace entrance, my dagger twisting in my hands.

For my father's smile. For Thalia's frown. Eleanor's sparkle. For every person who calls Ilium home. For every innocent who bled on his steel. For them, I will be strong. I'm ready for you, Evan the Black.

II

EVAN

ILIUM

KINGDOM OF CANDONIA

I didn't think I would ever be back here.
I glance up at the magnificent walls that surround the city.
Once, I thought they touched the sky, but I know better now.
Sandstone bricks are stacked high enough to keep the people
safe and are strong enough to keep their enemies out. Giant
steel doors open to the north, south, east, and west, ferrying
trade through the city and its famous market, where one of the
biggest commodities of all of Aellolyn passes through. Where I
once passed through.

Slaves. The major trade of the entire continent. I study the
bricks, thinking of all the men, women, and children sold within
these walls. *How many knew the horror that awaited them?* I hadn't,
but I was only a child. Ripped from my home and sold in this
very city to become the property of another. Now, I return as its
conqueror, its future in my hands. Hands that were once
clapped in iron before I was dragged through its streets.

I shift on my horse and pull my gaze from the walls. My men
slam the ram against the west gate, denting the steel and
splintering the wood beneath. It collapses with a boom, and the
city is mine. My lips curve into a smile, anticipation filling me.

I've dreamt of this day every night for the last twelve years. Dreams that nourished me during every long siege, every battle, and every day I went without food so my men could survive.

I tighten my knees and spin my horse, facing my warriors, shouting to be heard over the clash of the city guard and my men along the front line. "Today, we fight for each infant taken from their mother's breast! Each innocent sold like cattle! Never again will a child be born in shackles! Today, a new age begins!"

My men roar in agreement, thrusting their swords in the air, calling, "Black! Black! Black!"

The chant continues like a battle drum as we ride to the aid of those struggling with the Candonian soldiers at the wall. They are foolish if they think they can stop us. Twenty thousand of my men surround the city. Yet my skin prickles with awareness. I hear Wynonna's words in my head, *Never fight a desperate enemy. Desperate people will do anything to survive.*

I have made the people of Ilium *very* desperate. I have left them with no avenue of escape, nothing but a sea of death surrounding them.

I kick my horse forward, and we descend into the city, cutting down all who stand in opposition. Those who hope to end this with a stroke of their blade fall. How many thought that in the past decade? How many assassins or fools thought if they took my life, all of this would end? As if my life was the only thing standing in their way. As if I didn't know that each day could be my last. Like I didn't *prepare* for it.

With the gate down, my army floods into the city. The walls that once told me tales fall before the onslaught. Distantly, I hear more explosions, the other three gates likely meeting the same fate. My horse leaps over the shattered remains of the gate, his black coat gleaming with sweat and his nostrils flaring. He's as energized as I am for this. No nation, no matter how rich or trained, commands an army twenty thousand strong. *Only me.*

14

A long way from a slave with barely a name, I am what they made me. And now, they will see firsthand what they created. My heart pounds in time with my horse's hooves echoing on the cobblestone street. The homes of the citizens of Ilium are a blur, but I catch terrified faces pressed against windows and shutters slam as I ride past. A foreign invader is taking their once impenetrable city. I am the conqueror who burned a path from the north most tip of Aellolyn, through the snowy mountains of Grimmwing, the forests of Xiapia, the ocean cliffs of Vruica, and the hills of Steodia. They knew I was coming. The Jewel of Aellolyn is my last conquest and my new home. The one I never had. The one many of my men never had.

I know the path. Cobblestone streets slope into steps the closer I get to the towering palace. The Black flies up the stone stairs to another gate and two palace guards meet my sword when they unwisely try to stop me. Blood sprays over my armor, mixing with the mud and war paint already coating me. The last guard is smart. He opens the scrolled wrought iron gate for me, throws down his weapons, and bows deeply. I nod as I ride into the courtyard. My blood races, the thrill of the battle, the *chase* of dreams made true, is a fire in my veins. I want to celebrate, to cheer my victory, and announce to the world that I made them bow.

Unworthy, unclean, scum, nothing. Even amidst my victory, the voices of my past taunt me. I will not allow them to sway my course. Twenty thousand men depend on me. All the slaves south of Candonia I have yet to free. Their future, their lives, rest on my shoulders.

The Black's ears twitch, and he shifts to the side. I follow his motions, and the arrow whizzes past my head, taking a lock of my hair. My eyes narrow on the walls that separate the palace gardens from the rest of the city. They are lined with archers, and they were waiting for me. I got too arrogant and almost lost my head. And I'm rather fond of my head's current placement on my shoulders.

My bow is in my hands, and I release an arrow before my next heartbeat. My aim is true, and the archer drops. The rest scramble to fire, but my speed is unparalleled, my skill renowned. To be my target means *death*. I wouldn't have made it this far if it wasn't. The Black and I are in sync, the horse weaving and darting on his own, keeping me too mobile for them to get a fix on me.

The tips of my fingers crack and bleed, darkening the string of my bow as I nock and release arrow after arrow, taking out the archers on the walls. My movements are a blur, but my heart pounds a steady rhythm. I give them little time to respond to the volley. When my quiver is empty, I throw the bow to the ground and draw my sword from the sheath at my waist. I hit the two arrows hurtling toward me, redirecting them off the steel. Sweat drips down my face, mixing with ash and blood, and I squint my eyes as my eyes burn. Even over the roar of noise outside the palace walls as my men take the city, I can hear the shocked silence from the archers. They drop their weapons and run. *Smart.* If they don't pick up arms and try to fight against my men, they might just survive today.

I rub my face on my arm, smudging the war paint, smoke, and blood. But it's no longer blinding me, which is good enough for now. The courtyard remains immaculate even as smoke and ash darken the sky. The hedges are strictly manicured and form the royal seal of Candonia. At the center, crystalline water burbles in a fountain. I look up at the palace, the white exterior laden with golden accents. I sneer in disgust at the facade of beauty, knowing the rot that lies beneath. How many slaves died building it? The four towers at each corner, spiral to golden points, where the flags of the royal family fly flags raised means in residence, much to their demise. No longer will they hide behind walls, watching from above as their people give their lives for them.

A king waves his hand, and people die. No longer.

I kick the Black forward, and his hooves echo a warning as we climb the gleaming marble steps to the entrance. The doors are etched with the royal seal, two keys crossing behind a shield, topped with an obscene crown. The left key represents the Northern countries of Aellolyn, and the right key the Southern. Everything crosses through Candonia, including me. The lion in the center of the shield is a tie to their divine ancestry. There's an etching of words in Candonian at the bottom of the shield, which I know reads: *Our Light Thus Binds.*

My horse rears on command, hitting the doors and breaking the lock. Wood splinters and falls around us as we force our way into the palace. The Black's ragged breaths are the only sounds in the empty hall.

The bright red of the rushes on the floor cuts the blinding white marble of the entry. Two staircases flank the entryway, curling up on either side of the room, where they meet at the landing above. My gaze narrows on the archway below the balcony, the one that leads into the throne room. That's the one I need.

So close, I am so close to changing everything. No more children born in chains.

I dismount and pat the horse's side, dirt and ash forming a small cloud. My gaze moves restlessly, scanning the entryway, looking for something out of place. The way this space is designed leaves me vulnerable to an attack from at least five various directions.

Even weighed down in armor, my steps are quiet, muted by the rushes under my feet. I close my eyes and reach out with my other senses, waiting for an attack.

A sharp breath, out of sync with the silence, makes my head snap toward the archway to my right. I launch the dagger in my hand even as my eyes open. The blade embeds in the wall next to my enemy's head. The maid doesn't scream. Her eyes narrow on me, and her hand tightens on something in her pocket. No doubt a weapon. My next dagger lands in the wall on the other side of her head. She wisely pulls her hand out of her pocket.

The decision to run flashes in her eyes and I rush forward, my sword at the ready. I catch her right as she begins her sprint down the hallway and press the blade to her throat, cornering her against the wall. The light is too dim to make out her features or even the color of her gown, but it doesn't matter. She's an obstacle, and all obstacles must be removed.

Even in the darkness, I can see the hate burning in her eyes, but there is no fear. *Fascinating.* Seasoned soldiers have begged for their lives with my weapon at their throats, but not her. Her back is straight against the wall, her hands still at her sides and curled into tight fists. Her chin juts in defiance, the line of her jaw tense. There is not a trace of fear in her entire body. Her form is rigid and unyielding, refusing to submit.

"Visha take you," she snarls, spitting at me. My lip curls back, and I wipe my hand down my face, smearing the war paint, blood, and her spittle. I'm waiting for her to beg. They always beg. Even I had begged. Once.

Never again.

Her chin only lifts higher. "You won't win."

My sword presses a little harder into her neck, still no fear in her eyes. Absently, I wish it was bright enough to see their color. To get some hint of her thoughts, *are they sparking with bravery or with terror?* Despite what many believe, I don't kill women or children, but I will take advantage of my reputation. Many can be cowed by word of mouth alone, the fear in place before I even step into a room. *Words topple more cities than soldiers.*

I pat the pockets of her dress with my free hand, claiming the dagger I find with a raised brow. I put the knife in my belt and resume my search. My fingers wrap around the small glass bottle in her other pocket. I inspect it in the dim light before flicking the stopper off and lifting it to my nose, sniffing carefully.

Nightshade.

My eyes connect with hers, finally able to see the color in the low light. They are a deep, sapphire blue. The color makes me pause, a strange yanking in my gut. They remind me of the stormy sea that used to crash around the village when I was a child. The dark waves my dad used to fish and that once kept us fed.

Until they didn't.

I force the sensation down and away, along with the memory that I had thought long forgotten. I was too young to remember my parents, my home before being sold. I'll never have a last name, only a moniker. *The Black.* Carelessly, I toss the bottle of poison over my shoulder, shattering it against the stone. Her eyes never leave mine.

"The king," I grate out, my voice rough from battle. *Not* from this disconcerting female and her eyes that invoke memories I thought long dead.

"He's already gone," she sneers, reaching up to yank one of my daggers out of the wall.

I check a look of victory when the knife doesn't budge, no matter how hard she pulls on it. She growls low and continues to try. She is a stubborn thing. What was her plan once it was free? I still had her pinned, my sword at her throat.

"You're a terrible liar," I say. She gives up on the first dagger and tries the second. It was amusing at first, but now it wears on my patience. Lowering my sword, I grab her throat, tightening my grip. "Unless you want me to leave this palace as nothing but ash, you'll take me to the king."

"That won't be necessary," comes a new voice, cool and cultured.

Both things I'll never be.

I don't like being taken unawares, and usually, I'm on high alert. The girl had distracted me, and no doubt that was her plan. I yank her forward and spin, keeping my hand around her throat. I press her back to my front, using her as a shield. "Finally decided to stop hiding behind a woman's skirts, Antias?"

The King of Candonia stands in front of me, his hands tucked behind his back. Grey laces his black hair, and his eyes are the color of sapphires. *Sapphires...*maybe my captive is more than a maid. His form is still fit for his age, only a couple inches shorter than me, but not nearly as wide. He commands attention with a magnetism that comes with being royalty.

The woman's hand reaches up to mine, trying to pry my fingers from around her throat. Her nails dig into my skin, drawing blood. She snaps at the king in Candonian. It is a language I do not know well, but she is no mere servant based on her tone. In the better light, I can see the color of her hair. It is dark, rich mahogany, and her dress is silk, not wool.

The king ignores her, remaining focused on me. "What do you want?"

I keep her pressed tightly against my chest, even as her nails claw at my hand. "I have a proposition for you. You'll find it to be quite generous."

She winces and tries to throw her elbow into my stomach, and the king snaps, "Enough, *Friglia!*"

Friglia. A Candonian word I did know. *Daughter*.

King Antias has three daughters, Charlotte, Thalia, and Eleanor. Eleanor is a child, barely twelve summers, which narrows things down. I'm looking for Charlotte. She's the pawn I need. Thalia is the spare, but Charlotte is the heir.

"We can't let him win!" she says to her father.

I smirk at the king and raise a brow. Keeping the precarious nature of power apparent, one little move from me, and she dies. "So, this is your daughter?"

He ignores me, his gaze flickering between me and the hold I still maintain on his precious child's throat. Indecision is clear in his eyes. "What is your proposition?"

My hand drops, deliberately taking a slow detour down her body. Not as curvy as I typically prefer, but her hips and breasts flare nicely and are enough to grab and hold on to. She tenses and makes a sound of disgusted outrage. I wrap my hand around her throat, pressing her back against me, stopping her from fighting me again. Never breaking eye contact with the king, I lower my face to her hair. I sniff the silky strands loudly, even as she throws her head back, trying to bash in my nose.

20

Honey and chamomile.

There's a reason for everything I do, even this. I doubt he knows I was handled exactly like this when I was first sold as a child. Now, I am subjecting his daughter to the same humiliation. The same degradation every slave sold in the Grand Market endures.

"You'll remain as king, living out your life in peace and prosperity," I say, my lips twitching with amusement at the confusion on his face.

His eyes narrow at my enjoyment. "In exchange for?"

"Your eldest daughter's hand."

Charlotte. His heir. The vulnerable key to the throne of Candonia. *My key.* Antias's face flickers with shock, his cool mask dropping to horror, then to disgust, and finally resignation. He has no choice. My army surrounds the walls of his city, a snap of my fingers, and everyone he protects will die. The power is with the once powerless.

"No! I would never marry a monster like you!" she exclaims.

Thought that was you.

I wrap my arm more tightly around her waist, my lips lingering at her ear. "You'll marry me, or your father dies. Then you'll marry me, anyway. Your choice."

"It is your choice, *Friglia.* I will not force you to marry anyone." His voice has lost its cool and cultured tones, the edge of hatred leaching through. He hates that I have put him in this position, a place without choice. *How many people did you rob of the same, Antias?* I expected him to force her to save his pathetic life. Perhaps he's not as cold-blooded as I thought.

Charlotte's body trembles slightly against mine before her spine turns to steel. She hisses, "You are a monster. One that I will never love. You will be hated by my people. They will never accept you as their future King."

"We'll see about that," I growl into her ear. I drop my hand from her throat and shove her forward, forcing her father to catch her or watch her fall. "Have her ready in an hour." My voice chills, my gaze locking on him. "My men have orders to destroy the city if anything goes wrong."

Charlotte looks up at her father, but his eyes remain on me. "She'll be ready."

I spin on my heel and walk to the wall, easily removing the two daggers. I return them to their holsters in my armor as I walk out of the palace, leaving the royals to process their new reality.

III

Charlotte

ILIUM

KINGDOM OF CANDONIA

Evan the Black. He is everything the rumors say about him. A cruel, barbaric monster that takes what isn't his. I caught his stench even before he entered the room, his body caked in sweat, dirt, and blood. *The blood of my people.* My stomach twists at the thought, and my hate for him grows. It did surprise me that he hadn't killed us. An intelligent man would have rid himself of the entire royal family and taken the throne. Then again, he knows our people love us. If he killed us all, there would be resistance and an uprising. The only way to prevent that is to marry into the royal family.

Marriage. I have been fighting my father for years on the subject. I never wanted to marry a man that I did not love, and now here I am marrying my worst enemy. Though I understand why it must be done. I can't let him kill my father or torture my people. If I am married to this monster then I can still be there and hopefully put a stop to whatever plans he has. I won't let this conqueror think he has control of my country. Not while I am alive.

Evan. His name sends shivers down my spine, and I feel myself grow cold. He is to be my husband. The man I shall grow old with. Will he abuse me? Harm me like he has my people? Take me even when I beg for him to stop? Crush my spirit and force me to submit to his every command?

Well, I have a little surprise for you, Evan. I will not be easily broken.

Before my mother died, she taught me many things. One of the most important is that women have a say in this world. Insane, right? She honored the Ancient of Magic, Kalliste, who wrote in her book of commands that all women have the right to their own opinion and have a say in the law. Other than Vruica and Candonia, the kingdoms banned the book. During my thirteenth year, I read it over ten times, its words inspiring me to become a better woman and ruler.

Since then, I have not let the men in my life make my decisions, and surprisingly my father accepted my stance. He was madly in love with my mother and admired her for her strength and passion. When I spoke my mind about specific laws and issues pertaining to our people, he didn't dismiss me.

We walk up the stairs to my room, and my father wraps his arm around my back, giving me a comforting pat. I appreciate the gesture, but it does little to soothe my rising anxiety. I shake my head and look up at him but have no words for what I am feeling. This is my decision. My father would never force me into a position of no choice. He would have laid down his life for me if I had said no.

I have looked up to him throughout my life, and his wisdom has given my life stability. Antias became king at sixteen when his father was assassinated during the war with the Kingdom of Vruica. The war went on for another two years until my father finally agreed to marry the Princess of Vruica, my mother, Clara. The two of them did not get along at first. They hated each other, in fact. My mother did not like being told what to do, and her stubborn attitude gave my father headaches. She had her own opinions and wasn't afraid to speak them, which was a shock to him. He'd been raised to believe that only men had a say in certain matters. She showed him a different way, and he became the man I admire so greatly. He allows my sisters and me to make our own decisions as long as our safety isn't at risk.

Now, looking into his eyes, it breaks me to see the defeat and sorrow. His face looks older than a few days ago. The war has given him more grey hair, and the wrinkles on his forehead truly show his age. It terrifies me to see the tears building in his eyes. We never give up. It isn't in our blood.

"We can't let him win, Father," I say, the determination in my voice cracking. I can't accept defeat. Not yet.

My father presses his lips together into a thin line. "There is nothing we can do now, *Friglia.*"

I open my mouth to say something but close it again. *He is right.* Evan's army surrounds our city. I look out the window and can see the white canvas tents being set up beyond our walls. The blood of my people and his men stain our streets. His warriors patrol the market, dragging the bodies of the dead outside the city for burial. My fists clench and unclench at the sight. How can one man be so cruel? Murder those who don't deserve it? I wish I'd said no to him, but he'd left me little choice. It was my freedom or the lives of my family. I can't lose my father. I will need to suck it up for now and put on a brave face. Maybe there will be a time when I can take my revenge.

"I love you, Father," I whisper as we stop outside my room.

Antias grabs my shoulders, turning me to look at him. His usual smile of pride has been diminished to a sad smile. "I love you, too. I know you can do this, *Friglia.* You have so much of your mother's strength in you."

I smile at him, my eyes tearing up. Princesses are taught to hide their emotions. If you openly show your weaknesses to others, they will abuse it. If they know what makes you tick, they will use it to batter you until you are bloody and there is nothing left.

I learned this at a very young age when the queen married my father. She knew how I felt about one of the younger maids, Lara. I considered her my best friend. We would play around the castle grounds, hiding from the workers when we would get into trouble. The queen discovered my fondness for the girl and turned what should have been my strength into a weakness. The queen used it to her advantage and threatened me, saying that she would hurt Lara if I didn't do what I was told. I was never very good at doing what I was told, and one day, Lara disappeared. I never asked my stepmother what happened to her, but I later found out that the queen had exiled Lara and her family. When I tried to speak to my father about Lara, he seemed distant and uninterested. It was as if he could not see what the queen was doing. My father started changing the day he married the queen, but it was still strange that he would dismiss my concerns. That was only the beginning of my list of grievances toward my stepmother.

My father pulls me close, holding me tightly in a bear-like hug. Who knows what will happen after tonight? After a few seconds, he releases me and turns away. His shoulders slump in defeat as I watch him walk down the corridor. The knowledge that his eldest daughter is to wed a cruel and monstrous man weighs on him. The thought makes my hands shake. I take a few deep breaths, calming myself before entering my room alone.

The maids are still in the safe room along with my sisters, which allows me some time alone with my thoughts. I let out a small sigh, trying to pull myself together. *Stay strong, Charlotte.* My emotions are trying to get the best of me, and I struggle to control them. My sisters will come straight to me as soon as they hear the news. They will need me to be their anchor and to reassure them that everything will be alright. I am doing this for them, for Father, and our people.

Tears sting my eyes, but I forbid them to fall. Instead, I blink them away and walk to my wardrobe. I look at all the dresses, trying to decide which would be most suitable. There is nothing white like the traditional wedding gowns, but this entire marriage is against tradition, anyway. Does it even matter what

I wear? It's not like the man I am to marry will even look at me. He will probably be drunk, dirty, and celebrating our defeat.

I pull out a pastel pink dress. The material is light, and it has a slit along one side, which will help with a getaway if I get the opportunity. It covers both of my shoulders and drops into a scooped neckline, the loose, flowing sleeves draping to my forearms. It is elegant, tasteful, and modest. I will not be giving this monster a show. I toss the gown onto my overly large bed and slowly undress. Thalia burst into the room, her caramel hair wild. She looks beyond angry, her honey golden eyes blazing with ire. Thalia has a quick temper and is never one to be calm in difficult situations. Even as a girl, she had trouble controlling herself when something threatened those she loved. Thalia once flew into a rage when the queen was going to send Eleanor to Vruica for etiquette training. Thalia received ten lashes from the queen for that incident, but in the end, she was victorious, and Eleanor stayed with us.

I study her face, and my own anger flares when I see the bright red handprint on her right cheek. My father doesn't know about the harsh punishments Thalia endures at the queen's hand. The day I discovered what she was doing to my sister, Thalia made me swear on the Ancient of Truths, Blyanna, not to say a word. I reluctantly promised never to speak of it to Father. After such a binding oath, even if I wanted to, I wouldn't be able to tell. My mouth would magically seal shut if I ever tried to utter the truth to him.

Eleanor lingers behind Thalia, just inside the door. Her big sea-blue eyes stare at me sadly. There are small rips in her dress from running behind the palace walls, the front of it wet from the tears pouring down her face.

Don't break down. Stay strong for them.

"This isn't right," Eleanor whispers. "This isn't love. You can't marry someone you don't love."

"I don't agree with this either," Thalia hisses. "Are you sure I can't just..." Thalia pulls out her silver dagger, the tip shining as she twists it in her palm. I shake my head, giving her a look of disappointment, and she tucks it away.

"I must do this. It is my duty as the eldest," I say as the maids enter. They help me into my corset and start the process of tightening the thing. I wince from the pain and pressure in my chest. *I hate these things.*

Thalia throws her hands in the air. "Then we kill him!"

I glare at her. "We have tried, Thalia. If we kill him, his men kill everyone. I will not allow my family to die."

My sisters fall silent, and the maids slip on the pink dress. I run shaky fingers down the silky material.

Be brave. Don't show weakness.

Eleanor smiles sadly. "At least you look beautiful."

I smile at her, walking over and kissing her on the head. "Thank you, El."

She takes one last glance at me before one of the maids ushers her out of the room to prepare her for the *surprise* wedding. With her gone, I allow my emotions to show on my face. As much as I want to, I can't hide anything from Thalia. Her anger morphs into sadness, and she wraps her arms around my neck. My throat clogs with built-up tears, and I fight to keep them down.

"You know...I could have done this," Thalia whispers, rubbing my back soothingly.

I shake my head. "No, I would not have let you."

Thalia sighs, slipping something into the pocket of my dress. I tuck my hand in, fiddling with the object she placed there. A cylinder of glass with a cork. *Nightshade.*

"A way out," Thalia whispers to me.

"Thank you," I whisper back, and she pats my arm before leaving my room.

I am left alone with my thoughts again. My heart races in my chest, and sweat makes my hands sticky. *There is no running from this.* Yes, I could drink the nightshade and escape before the real torture begins. But if I do, he will only marry one of my sisters, and I can't leave them to the mercy of a monster. They still have a chance to find their happiness.

28

I let out a shaky sigh, looking at myself in the mirror. My face is red and blotchy from the pent-up tears. I dab a bit of powder onto my cheeks, hiding any sense of weakness. The maids tied my hair into a half-up, half-down style, the curls reaching down my back. Nothing extravagant. This man doesn't deserve it.

Closing my eyes, I concentrate on numbing the pain and putting up my walls. When my lashes lift, my face is back to its normal rosy state, although I cannot muster a smile. I doubt I will ever smile again.

Be brave.

I turn from the mirror, ready to face this nightmare.

It is time to get this over with.

IV
EVAN

ILIUM

KINGDOM OF CANDONIA

The Black is waiting for me, prancing at the entrance to the palace. I rub his snout in greeting, and the massive warhorse bows, lowering enough for me to swing my leg over his back. My gaze sweeps over Ilium as I get settled. The sun is close to setting on the horizon, and from this elevated plateau, I can see the white canvas tents popping up outside the walls surrounding the city. The sounds of armor and steel clashing still rings in the smoke thickened air. I am relieved to see that my men followed my orders, and the fires burn outside the gates, sparing the city. This will be their new home. Today, a new age of Aellolyn begins.

The Black tosses his long mane and prances impatiently. I pat him soothingly, the bond I share with him more than man and animal. From the moment I climbed onto his back at a gangly sixteen, the massive midnight warhorse and I have worked as a team. I use my knees to guide him when necessary, never having put a saddle or a bridle on him. I doubt either of us would enjoy the experience if I tried. Despite the rumors, my warhorse is the origin of my title, Evan the Black.

A black blur is the only thing you see before you die. At least, that's what they used to say. Over the years, words warped, the stories becoming more and more monstrous as they passed from town to town.

Carefully we make our way down the steps, and I am unsurprised to see my generals waiting for me at the base of them near a bubbling fountain. These four men and one woman came to me in various ways, some of them of noble and even royal birth, yet they follow me. *The slave.*

All five of their faces display varying forms of disapproval.

"You shouldn't have gone alone, Black," Lorcan, my youngest general, snaps from astride his armored mount. His hair is a platinum blonde, his eyes a dark, almost fathomless brown. His frame is lanky, and he specializes in long-range weaponry. He always watches from a distance, but when he disapproves, he is vocal.

Wynonna, Lorcan's mother and my mentor, snickers before leaning over to hit her son's shoulder. "You should know by now, that the Commander listens to no one. Not even himself."

Wynonna is a gruff, hard woman. Her hair is matted from her ride and her eyes match her son's. The glow of youth is gone from her face, her skin leathered from years on the road.

Niklaus frowns. "You ordered us to wait for you, and then you go off by yourself?"

Niklaus and Kian are polar opposites. Niklaus's stern ice-blue eyes are unyielding, and he's built like a brawler. His dark hair touches his broad shoulders, but his face is clean-shaven. Kian is lanky, with dirty blonde hair cropped close to his head. His skin is darker, marking him as a man of Steodia. His dark blue eyes glitter with amusement, and his lips are almost always quirked in a wry smirk, finding humor in everything around him. Especially Niklaus.

Kian laughs. "He wanted to see his new prize. I've heard she's gorgeous."

My eyes fall to the last man, who remains silent, watching the rest of us. His frown is intimidating, and his grey horse looks as mean as he does. At six and a half feet, he towers over the rest of us, every inch of his frame wrapped in muscle. His hair is a dark red, and his eyes are a bright green, sparkling like emeralds. Even though he can't speak, he makes his opinion known.

He looks up at the castle, then at me, raising a brow. Usually, he communicates using hand signals. All my men are fluent.

I nod in response. "They'll follow instructions."

He nods silently and turns his horse away, trotting back toward camp. His contingent of my army will disentangle from the town and follow him. They'd breached the south gate, and from my perch atop the steps of the palace, I could see there was little left standing.

My lips twitch with satisfaction, and I dismount from the Black, turning to the four remaining generals. "Any other problems from the locals?"

They follow my lead, swinging off their massive warhorses. I take the Black over to the fountain and rip a piece off the banner hanging nearby. I dip it into the water and start scrubbing down my horse. The task is always soothing to me, even as it covers me in more filth. The horse only allows me close, rearing up or snapping at all who dare to come near. It has been this way since I first got on his back. I slept in the woods with him, waiting for him to approach. He threw me seventeen times, and still I stayed. Besides my stolen sword and dagger, he was all I had at the time. I needed the horse to trust me, to let me ride him. I needed hope.

Twelve years later, he remains with me, my warhorse, my symbol of hope. Through all the battles, all the trials, he remains, as do I. The repetitive movements of grooming him allow my mind to wander as more of my troops congregate in the courtyard. Several men carry large sacks of commandeered food and ale. They are eager to celebrate the victory over the Jewel of Aellolyn. My men are not smooth like royal armies. They are coarse and rough. Most come from a life like mine, hoping to find some sort of normalcy.

Warriors drag large wood slabs in, propping them up on empty barrels, using the once meticulously groomed hedges as chairs. They tie their horses to the fountain, keeping away from the Black out of habit. I've never been the type to celebrate a victory. I am always thinking of the next conquest, the next fight, the next city. Tonight, I think I should make an exception.

The party only escalates the darker it gets, and the more men make their way into the courtyard. This was a long time coming. Many days we went without food or water, and now we are here, surrounded by bounty. This is our final campaign.

From the start of this conquest, I have waited for this single moment. To stand in front of the palace, prepared to marry into the royal family. In an hour, I'll be a prince. Though the battle is over, the next step will be even more difficult. It will be a completely new action, foreign to me after twelve years of war. I'll be staying. My camp will remain outside the city walls, but the gates will remain open to us, allowing my men and the city of Ilium to weave themselves into a single entity. It will be our new home. And a home is something most of us have never had.

The occupation of the capital city will remain until I have a steady handle on the politics and a sturdy grip on my wife. I have to give her some credit. She is fierce and not what I expected, but even with her fiery strength, she can be broken. Anyone can be broken, even me.

The last time I was in this city, I was a slave. This is where I was sold as a boy of five to my first master. He kept me until I was too old for his *tastes,* and then he sold me to another man in Vruica. I wasn't with them long. He felt his wife liked me *too much.* The last owner I had was in Steodia when I was sixteen. He was trying to rape one of the young slaves, and something in me *snapped.* I was moving before I even registered the intention, stepping up behind him, I sliced my dagger across his neck. His blood spilled over the slave, and she screamed in horror, even as she scrambled away. I knew the sound would draw the other slave owners, and they would kill me before hanging my body as an example.

I grabbed the master's sword from his waist and ran into the woods. I believed I was on borrowed time and that the men would be after me at any moment. Later, I learned that the girl I'd saved had enlisted the help of others to hide the body. They fed him to the livestock and pretended he'd run off. They were the first group of slaves I went back and freed, but I was a month too late. The master's wife had whipped the girl to death. I remember the rage, the red in my vision. I remember dragging the woman out of the manor, tying her to a post, and whipping her to heal what they'd broken inside me. Wynonna stopped me from killing her, but just barely. I hadn't harmed a woman since.

I grew my army, cutting a swath through Aellolyn, freeing every slave we found. And now, over a decade later, I'm finally going to have somewhere to call home. My men will have a place to call home, even if it does come with...*conditions.*

She'll learn her place soon enough.

The men alert me when it's time for the ceremony. I am ready to usher in a new age for the entire continent, for all of Aellolyn. An age of freedom, where no one, no matter their birth, will be born into shackles. All I have to do is bind my life to a stranger. *A princess.* Someone who's never known struggle or strife and is no doubt spoiled and cruel.

I nod my head to my men, whistling sharply to my generals. All but the Mountain, who never returned from camp. The four remaining nod back at me, looking up at the palace. Though my men have made themselves comfortable in the courtyard, no one has come in or out of the castle. Now, the massive doors swing open, pushed by two doormen in gold livery, announcing the wedding with trumpets.

I should have washed up for the event, I suppose. But despite the show they seem determined to put on, it's a farce, a sham, and we all know it. So I didn't bother. I will go to her with war paint smeared across my face, covered in blood, ash, and dirt.

My generals glance at me, flanking me on both sides, as we silently walk back up the steps to the palace. The doors stand open, but the entry is now filled. The nobles who took refuge in the castle during the siege watch my men and me with morbid fascination, but I pay them little mind. If they know what's good for them, they'll obey my orders and stay out of my way.

I make my way into the throne room, stepping over the red rushes. The king stands at the end, with the Bishop of the Ancients at his side. The bishop's ceremonial robes are embroidered with the symbols of the twelve Great Ancients. Antias's shrewd eyes watch me carefully as I make my way to the throne, and take my place in front of the bishop. My generals fan out, their hands resting on their weapons, waiting for someone to take a step out of line.

The bishop is sweating, wiping his forehead nervously with his silk handkerchief. He stutters, "Sh-Sh-Shall we-e-e begin?"

I nod at him and turn, looking down the aisle. I cross my hands over each other in front of me, waiting for my bride.

Time to get this over with.

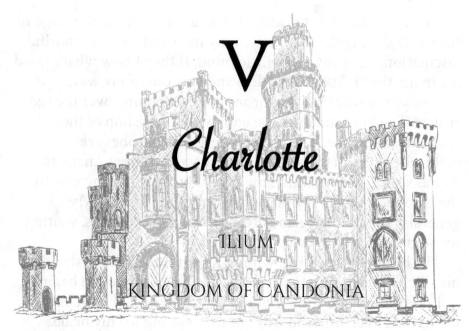

V

Charlotte

ILIUM

KINGDOM OF CANDONIA

Tick-tock. Tick-tock. The grandfather clock outside the dining hall taunts me as it counts down my last few minutes of freedom. At the back of my mind, thoughts of escaping tempt me to run. It would be easy. Just turn away from this and disappear deep into the forest to never be seen again. *No.* I need to stay strong and push the temptation from my mind.

I twist the bouquet of pink and white peonies in my hand. One of my maids insisted I have them during the ceremony, as the flower represents good fortune. She told me that the Ancient of Luck, Faylen, would be by my side during the ceremony if I carried these flowers. I need all the blessings I can get marrying this monster.

The doors in front of me open slowly, and I let out a breath. I look everywhere but at him. The room has been rearranged for the wedding. Long benches have been placed along the walls, although most of them are empty. There are no decorations, the nobles attending are fearful, and I can feel their pitying stares. *Pity.* I dislike that emotion intensely.

I finally lay my eyes upon my future husband. He hadn't even bothered to clean the grime from his body. Blood smears his chest plate, and dirt covers his face and hair. I realize I don't even know what he truly looks like.

I lift my chin and walk down the aisle quicker than a bride should. A woman should enjoy her wedding day, savoring each step toward her true love. But I just want this done. As I get closer, he holds his hand out for me, and I glare at him in response. Is this an act for the crowd? That will not work for me. I know what he has done. I know who he truly is.

I take my place beside him, keeping my focus on the archbishop as he begins the ceremony that will tie my life to this monster. Evan lifts my hand and presses his lips to the back of it. I sneer at him in contempt.

"Behave," he whispers. I yank my hand away from him, staying silent for the rest of the ceremony.

"You may now kiss the bride," the archbishop announces.

I gulp, shuddering in disgust and focus my eyes elsewhere. There is no way I will be kissing him, touching him. The very thought makes me sick. Evan grips my chin and turns me to face him, dragging his thumb gently along my cheek. His steel-grey eyes are glowing as they connect with mine, and for a moment, I'm lost. *Why does the monster have such pure eyes?* An unwelcome spark of interest flares into heat as he brushes his lips against mine. Nothing like I expected. I thought he was going to be rough, claiming, but his gentleness makes me melt. My entire body goes warm, and a soft moan escapes my throat, flavoring the kiss. I snap my eyes open, shocked at my response, and push away from him.

What in the name of the Ancients was that?

Evan clears his throat before turning to the people. "To the feast!"

Heat rises in my cheeks as I turn away from him with a frown. I feel something change inside of me, as if my gravity has shifted and is tugging me toward him. I shouldn't be feeling this warmth, and I try to push the feeling away, but it stubbornly remains.

I step away from my *husband,* not waiting for him to escort me down the aisle. I may be married to him, but I will not show him any form of respect. He catches up to me, slipping his fingers between mine. My heart leaps in my chest as he lifts my hand, pressing a kiss to the back of it again.

"Behave, lamb," he whispers, and I frown for a moment, trying to figure out why he would call me such a name. My curiosity gets the better of me, and I break my silence.

"Lamb?" I question, looking at him in confusion. I try to tug my hand from his to stop my racing heart, but his grip only tightens.

"Yes." He smirks, not looking at me. "My little lost lamb."

I am not yours. I will never be yours.

We step outside the castle into the large courtyard, and I feel my tension ease a bit. A huge feast has been prepared, and the men are already celebrating. One large table has been set in the middle with the food, while smaller tables are scattered throughout the space. Mead drips from the cups the men are holding, and something about the atmosphere relaxes me. As soon as we make it to the front steps, all of Evan's men look up and let out a massive cheer.

"*To the Black!*" They chant it repeatedly, their voices filled with joy.

Evan allows them to cheer for a few minutes, a bright smile lighting his face. I find myself admiring him a little more than I should and turn away, looking back down at the feast. *He is the monster who invaded your home and stole you away from your family.* I keep repeating the words in my head, trying to snap myself back to reality.

"This has been many years in the making. We have finally found a place to call home. We will stay and put down the roots that so many of us have never had!" Evan announces before looking down at me. My cheeks heat a little beneath the intensity of his gaze. "I would like to formally introduce my wife and your future queen!"

A loud roar of celebration meets his words as they cheer for both of us. I give them a genuine smile even though millions of

38

questions cloud my thoughts. None of this makes sense to me. I was their enemy. I still am. They should be booing me, throwing food. Why don't they hurl insults at me? *Why would he introduce me in such a friendly manner?* I look up at Evan as he leads me to our table, his focus on everyone around us. They must respect him and his choices if they are alright with this union. My brow furrows as I think of the beginning of his speech. *They've never had a place to call home?*

My husband pulls out my chair, and I take a seat. *Another act of kindness.* There is no need for him to continue these gestures of respect, yet he does. The conqueror is more confusing the longer I am in his presence.

The staff brings out the food, placing it in front of us. There is an array of meats, cheeses, and a few vegetables. My stomach grumbles from the smell, but I ignore it, looking at the warriors around us. They all eat like ravenous animals, patting each other on the back and yelling loudly.

From the corner of my eye, I see Evan cut into his food with his dagger like a barbarian. I fold my hands on my lap, focusing on my breathing. *Stay calm. Stay calm.*

"Eat, lamb. You'll need your strength," he says.

I raise my chin, defying his order. "I am not hungry."

He grabs my chin, turning me to look up at him. I am captured by his eyes once more. They spark with annoyance, and I take that as a small victory, smirking at him. *Not so easy, am I?*

"We don't need to be enemies," he says, his grip on my chin loosening.

"You didn't need to invade my city," I hiss.

Evan scoffs, pointing at the food. "Eat. Now."

"No," I say, crossing my arms to hide my trembling hands.

"Don't disobey me," he growls. "I can still change my mind."

My entire body tenses at his threat. *Would he really change his mind over me not eating?* The idea is so insane. Why is he so intent on me eating? It is not like I matter to him. Our marriage is a farce. Why would he care if I eat or not? Unless this is him trying to demonstrate his control over me, reminding me of my place in his world by forcing me to do something so simple.

I look down at my food, my hands dropping to my lap. How do I know if the food has been poisoned? There are going to be many times I doubt my meals now, and I will probably be on guard for the rest of my life. I pick up a piece of cheese and nibble on the corners.

"Good lamb," he says with a smirk.

"I'm not your little lamb," I hiss in response.

He picks up another slice of meat. "Yes, you are. You are mine."

Another shiver runs down my spine as I pick up some more food. *His.* Never. He doesn't realize how stubborn this princess can be.

"I may be yours on paper, but you'll never have my heart," I say under my breath.

"Who says I want your heart?" he asks, raising a brow.

I tense again, forcing myself to stay seated. "Without my heart, I never will truly be yours."

"You are my wife, and tonight you'll be mine. You'll bear my heirs and be my queen. You can keep your heart to yourself. I'll take the rest." I feel his gaze on me as he drinks a huge flagon of mead before standing. "It's time for the bedding!"

My eyes widen as Evan's men let out another huge cheer. *No, no, no. I can't allow this! I won't allow this! I don't want this!* My mind goes into panic mode, and my hands shake as I lose control. Evan leans over, and my stomach twists with nausea.

"Don't make me wait too long," he growls into my ear before walking away. I look back down at my food, grimacing. *He is right.* I will need my strength to fight against him.

It takes a few minutes, but I manage to finish most of the food on my plate. My stomach is content with the amount I have eaten, and I feel a little better. I push from the table, mentally fighting with myself as I head back to the castle to prepare. Every inch of me wants to run away, forget everything about this life and start anew. I need to get these thoughts out of my head. Running away would do nothing but destroy my family, and that I cannot do.

The servants I pass as inside the castle look at me with sadness before bowing their heads. I fake a smile before continuing to my room. The hardest part is pretending that I'm alright and assuring everyone that everything will be fine. I must be strong for so many people, but I am shattering on the inside.

Once inside my room, I allow myself to break down and crumble to the floor. My sobs are silent, but they tear through me, coldness seeping into my bones. Everything he did tonight was a show, his kindness, the gentleness. He dangles the very things I crave in a husband, teasing me with what could have been. Why would he be so cruel?

He is probably waiting for me in his tent now, conjuring up all the ways he will torture his new prize.

Pull yourself together, Charlotte.

I struggle to my feet, wiping the tears from my face. I undress and toss my gown onto the bed. There is a small thunk as something falls to the floor. My heart thuds as if in fear as I pick up the small vial and stare at the liquid nightshade. I still may need this. I clutch it in my hand as I loosen my corset and pick up the new royal blue dress. It has a lower neckline, thinner material, and is very light, making it easier to run and fight. I slip into it and tuck the vial away in the pocket before fixing my hair and washing my face.

I silently slip from my bedroom and make my way down the stairs. I do not want to run into my family. Not right now. I couldn't stand to see the look in their eyes before leaving them to be with our enemy.

On the main floor, I see my father at the entrance. He is pacing back and forth as Thalia screams at him. I lift the hood of my cloak and walk in the opposite direction. My father can handle Thalia's rage. He will probably have guards stationed outside her room for months until she settles.

The cook doesn't even notice me as I sneak out through the kitchen. The cool summer air greets me, and I lower my hood, making my way to the gate. There is a huge hole in the east wall where the invaders broke through. I run my fingers over the ruined stone, sighing sadly.

I can't hide behind the safety of these walls anymore.

I pick my way through the rubble and into the camp of my enemies. The warriors don't even look at me as they walk from one area to another, and I stop, unsure where I am supposed to go. I clear my throat awkwardly and approach a small group of men. They look down at me with something akin to hatred, and I feel my entire body tense.

"I am looking for Evan the Black." I lift my chin defiantly.

They look at each other and laugh, and my cheeks flush a bright red. One finally points toward a tent. It is the largest one, right in the middle of the camp. I should have known.

"Thank you." I gulp and step away.

It's time to get to know my husband.

VI

EVAN

It's strange to have an actual tent in camp. I usually sleep under the sky, ready to uproot and leave at a moment's notice. Someone prepared this new home for me and...my wife. The giant white tent sits on a knoll, raised above the rest of camp, and filled with treasures from past conquests.

The bed frame is something we plundered from a nobleman's home in Vruica. Valuable goose feathers fill the mattress, and the furs that cover it are from Xiapia. A vanity with a small mirror sits to the side. Several trunks for storage take up floor space, and valuable rugs cover the cold ground under my feet. Someone had even brought in a small table and a nightstand. I am very unfamiliar with this level of comfort.

My squire helps me out of the heavy metal armor, placing it on the wooden stand. I only wear the chain mail and steel during battle, preferring my molded leather breastplate, vambraces, and shin guards.

I roll my shoulders in delight and shoo the Boy away. I tear off the soaked jerkin that was beneath my chain mail. Toeing off my boots, I toss them to the side and strip out of my breeches. I sigh with relief as I climb into the steaming tub, allowing the heat to relax into my muscles and release the tension. I'm still energized, as I often am after a battle. Normally, I would utilize a local brothel, expending the excess energy that way, but now things are different. Now, I'm married.

The grime and blood leech into the water as I sink beneath the surface. I come up for air and use some of the soap we bought in Xiapia to wash. I rinse my golden hair with the jug of water left to the side of the tub and slick it back from my face. It is longer than I usually allow it to grow, and I make a note to cut it. I grab the pumice stone and use more of the soap to scrub my scarred body. My movements are methodical, allowing my mind to wander.

Wynonna was at my back when the arrow sliced through my thigh during the ambush. I shouted shortly in pain, even as I looked for my attacker. There were thieves throughout the forests of Steodia, hoping to catch travelers unawares. Lorcan, just fifteen, let loose his arrow, killing the bandit hiding in the trees. Wynonna and I gaped at him as he executed a short bow.

Her eyes are like sapphires.

The stone freezes along the scar on my upper thigh. Where did that thought come from? She's a means to an end, nothing more.

Her eyes shimmered when I cradled her face in my hands, my rough, calloused thumbs rubbing over her flawless skin.

I shake my head and resume my bath, scrubbing even harder at my skin. *What is it about her that has me so intrigued?*

It's her eyes. Even sitting next to her at the feast, I couldn't help but notice her. Conscious of every movement she made, her every breath as the revelry continued around us. She sat with a rigid spine, displaying her disgust for me openly, refusing to eat what I offered. I wonder if she knows I saw her hand shake ever so slightly. The almost imperceptible tremor confirming she was not as calm and collected as she wanted to appear.

My squire comes running when I order the dirty water to be cleared, and a fresh bath brought in. I want to relax my muscles in the heated water as I wait for her. I settle back into the clean bath, my senses on high alert, and every sound in the camp outside making me twitch. Will she push through the tent flap as if she owns it, faking a bravado I know she doesn't feel? Or will she linger outside the tent, trying to summon the courage to enter, hoping some assassin has offed me in the tub?

I tense slightly, hearing harsh breathing outside the flap. *Finally.*

"Come in, lamb."

The heavy canvas makes little noise as Charlotte pushes it to the side, taking a step inside. I turn slightly in the tub to look at her. The firelight from the metal brazier flickers over her features. When she walked down the aisle to me, the torches in the throne room lit up more of her, and for a moment, I forgot to breathe. If her eyes arrested me, the rest of her left me spellbound.

Charlotte's skin is porcelain, unmarred by strife. There is a slight flush along her cheekbones, and her chin tilts stubbornly at me. Her lips are full, almost too full, a perpetual frown on them when looking at me. The gown she's wearing reveals even more of her curves than the one she wore at the ceremony, and it matches her eyes.

Her hands are clasped together, the knuckles white, and she keeps her gaze high, avoiding looking directly at me. She's at my mercy and surrounded by men loyal to me. None of them will lift a finger to help her, no matter the sounds that come from my tent tonight. Yet, she still refuses to cower.

"Come here."

Charlotte's breath catches before she obeys, taking a few steps closer but staying just out of reach. Her gaze is still high, refusing to look at me, her jaw clenching and unclenching.

My lips twitch, and I hold a hand out to her, just as I did during the wedding. It's an impulse, a need to draw her closer.

"I won't bite, lamb."

"I'd rather you not touch me," she hisses.

That won't do. I will touch my wife. In fact, pretty much all I can think about at the moment is touching her, kissing her, taking her. There's the slightest tremble in her lower lip as I watch her, and I find myself saying, "I won't force you."

I stand and step from the tub, ignoring the drying cloth. I ease closer to frame Charlotte's face and force her eyes up, locking our gazes.

"Kiss me."

To my surprise, she presses a gentle kiss to my lips. Her voice is unsteady when she pulls back to whisper, "You...you won't force me?"

I shake my head, pressing closer to her, leaving almost no separation. Something is pulling at me, ordering me to close the distance, and I can't seem to stop myself.

"Never. I have never forced a woman, and I don't allow it in my men. If they do, they will meet my blade."

I saw too much of that growing up as a slave, and I would never tolerate it. Let alone ever do so myself. Choice is essential to me. For many years of my life, my choices were not my own. No matter the height of battle fervor, my men know that if they dared to take a person against their will, their life was forfeit.

"Yet, you forced me to marry you," Charlotte asks. I like the sound of her voice, smooth and elegant. Each word formed and thought out, weighed carefully. Her words should strike my temper, which I am forced to keep under a tight leash, yet I'm too focused on her eyes to care.

My thumb trails along her cheek, and I lean down to kiss her again. "I did."

Charlotte's soft moan flavors the kiss, her body relaxing against me before she pushes away. I drop my hands to my sides. Her eyes glow in the firelight, the blue of the sea crashing along the shore as she analyzes me. "Why are you doing this?"

"Kissing my wife?"

Her eyes narrow, and she shakes her head. I reach over and grab the cloth, wrapping it around my waist.

46

"No. Why are you being...kind?"

My brows furrow, and I scowl at her, not sure if she is mocking me. I'm many things, but *kind* has never been one of them. "I'm not kind."

Her beautiful eyes widen, and she tilts her head. "You insist I eat when you could have just ignored it. You say you won't force me to lie with you."

I turn my back on Charlotte, heading to the bed. Why am I so concerned with her? Why am I so focused on her movements? Her breaths? Her thoughts? I don't know her. She's a pawn, but I can't seem to remember that. Not while she's here in this tent with me, not when I'm thinking about her mouth against mine. Her body against mine.

I drop the towel and slip under the furs. "I won't force you. One thing you can take comfort in, lamb, is that I *never* lie."

She shakes her head, looking away. "You never lie?"

The bed is soft and decadent. I settle in and tuck one arm under the pillow, my eyes locking on her. "Never. Undress."

Charlotte shakes her head, crossing her arms over her chest, the movement drawing my gaze to her breasts. My mouth goes dry. She truly is beautiful. *Too* beautiful. *Too* distracting. *Too* elegant. *Too...everything I'm not.* I snarl silently at myself, the thoughts horning in. Born into shackles, I spent my formative years being told I was nothing. That I was no one. Sometimes those thoughts still lingered and even took control. Everyday I struggle against them, the seeds of doubt have sunk their roots deep inside me. *I refuse to be consumed.*

"I prefer to keep my clothes on."

I doubt she understands how telling her actions and words are. "Scared I can seduce you?"

Her eyes snap to mine, her cheeks flaming. "No."

"Then undress, I won't force you, so you have nothing to fear."

Charlotte studies me, considering my words and no doubt wondering if she can trust me. She drops her arms to her sides and turns to give me her back as if she needs to preserve some modesty. Her hands shake as she pulls at the ties on the back of her dress. It slips down her body in a wave of silk, pooling around her feet. She's in nothing but a chemise and corset, allowing me to see even more of her form. I can't swallow, unable to take my eyes from her. Her hands move to the ties of her corset, her fingers fumbling.

In the next breath, I'm covering her hands on the ties, whispering, "What are you scared of?"

She startles, not having heard me move. Her breathing quickens, and her hands tremble beneath mine. "I...I have never..."

Innocent. Another thing I'm not. I wish I could rip out the part of my mind focusing on our differences. I am not who I was.

I undo the laces of her corset, focusing on my task, savoring each inch of skin revealed. "I know this is all new to you." The tension and fear in her are living things, and I hate it. I hate that I brought her to this point.

"Can we... Can we wait?"

No. I won't have my claim to the throne ripped away by a technicality. But I also don't like to see her like this. I want the brave woman who stared me down across the steel of my sword, who looked at me with disdain even when she trembled. I don't like how terrified she is, and I have to force myself not to offer her what she wants. There are lives on the line, the lives of my men, and all the slaves in the south that I hope to free. But the sight of her fear is making me forget them, forget everything but her. A conundrum.

I lean down and press a kiss to her bare shoulder, noticing that she relaxes beneath my touch. "You'll only build it up in your mind."

The corset falls to the ground, and the dam breaks, tears rolling down her face. "B-but... I'm..."

I turn her to face me, brushing away the tears on her cheeks. I drop my hands to the edge of her shift and lift it off her, leaving her naked in front of me. Her cheeks are wet when I cup her

48

face and gently press my lips to hers, hoping to soothe her. I can't seem to stop kissing her.

Her body tenses, and she tries to cover herself. "Please..."

I lift her into my arms and carry her to bed. She doesn't resist when I slip under the furs with her and pull her into the cocoon of my arms. "I won't force you."

Silent tears flow down her face, wetting my chest. My arms tighten around her, pressing her into me, one hand rubbing her back. "Let it out, lamb. Let it all out."

I hate that I made her cry, that I pushed her into a situation I swore to never be in again. *A place without choice.* Yet, stealing her choice now will give it to the rest of the continent. One person in exchange for the rest of the world. But at this moment, it's hard to remember that. Not when she's crying. Not when I'll do anything to get her to stop.

Charlotte balls her fists, landing ineffectual hits against my chest. "I don't want to be here. I don't want to be with you!"

I allow her to vent her frustration on me. I deserve it, don't I? I made her marry me. "Look at me."

She continues to sob, but her gaze lifts to meet mine. I kiss her. I'm helpless not to. My body aches with need as I say against her lips, "It's just you and me here. No one else. Just you and me."

Her fists uncurl, her hands lying flat against my chest. Charlotte stares into my eyes, searching for something.

"Just you and me," I say, holding her gaze steadily. My hand moves from her back to cup her head, and I take her mouth in a deep kiss.

Her crying tapers off, her body relaxing against mine, her soft curves molding against me. Her hands move from my chest to my neck.

I pull away and sprinkle gentle kisses across her face. "Sleep, lamb, you're safe."

She nods without saying a word and closes her eyes. Pressing against my warmth, she slowly drifts off.

I don't know how long I wait there, keeping her in the haven of my arms, the salt of her tears lingering on my lips. Sleep eludes me, and although I want to remain with her, I still have too much energy. I disentangle myself, careful not to wake her, and slip out of bed.

I dress and stomp into my boots before stepping outside. My squire and the Mountain are outside, and I order them to guard the tent. I'll sleep under the stars like normal, giving her time to adjust to her new life.

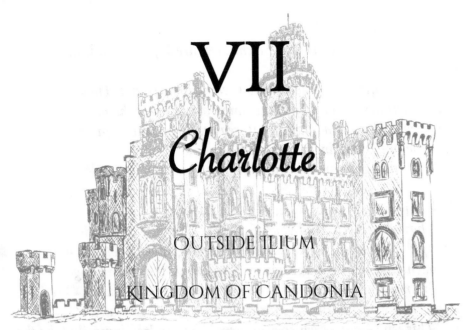

VII

Charlotte

OUTSIDE ILIUM

KINGDOM OF CANDONIA

I run down the streets of the city, laughing loudly as the maids try to catch me. At age six, I am wild and uncontrollable. Something my sisters and I all have in common. I've practically given all my maids heart attacks from the amount of times I have gone missing. My parents don't mind, though. They think it is wonderful that I want to explore the city. We have one of the safest capitals in Aellolyn, and there is no reason for them to fear that anything will happen to me.

I duck into the alleyway as the maids scurry by and giggle when I realize I have lost them. I lift my hood and make my way to the bakery, one where no one will know me. Although I am a child, I can be smart and sneaky. If anyone recognizes me, they will summon the guards, and that will be it. They will send me back to the palace before I can do what I came out here to do.

At the bakery, I pay for the bread and sneak off into the shadows. I weave my way through the back streets, arriving at a mansion just outside of town. There in the garden, a few children work to trim the bushes and shrubs. They are only a few years older than I and sickly looking, yet they work tirelessly for their master. Mother always told me that children should be out playing with their friends during the day. It makes me sick that these children are kept in chains and not allowed.

A few months ago, I decided to become their friend. They told me that sometimes the master of the house doesn't feed them, so I bring them food. There is no harm in it, really. I wait until a guard walks away before appearing in the garden.

"Ta-da!" I announce, holding out the bread.

Troy, the oldest of the boys, smiles and steps forward, brushing his dark hair from his eyes. "Charlie. How have you been?"

"I have been well. And you?" I ask, frowning when I notice the younger girl, Gwen, has bruises on her arm. Rage bubbles in my stomach, and I glare at the house. "I will have that man hanged."

Gwen walks over to me, placing her hands on my cheeks. "We appreciate your kindness, Charlie. But we are fine. Really."

"This isn't right," I whisper to them. The children hungrily take the bread from my hands. "I will do something about this. I promise."

Troy doesn't take his piece of bread, giving it to Gwen instead. "Charlie, if you tell your father, the worse he will do is slap our master on the wrist. Then our master will turn his anger on us."

I frown. "One day. I will change the world, and you will be free."

Troy kisses the top of my head. "You will move mountains, Charlie. We can wait until then."

A crack of a whip gets all of our attention, and the younger children's eyes widen with horror. The man holding the whip is none other than Lord Demetrius, their master. I step in front of my friends, raising my tiny chin.

"You will not touch them. By order of the princess," I announce, crossing my arms.

"The princess?" The lord laughs. "I don't see a princess here. Just a meddling child who doesn't know her place."

He has a point. I am not wearing my princess attire, but some rags that I stole a while back to blend into the city. I keep my chin high, unafraid of the lord. He will pay for what he has done to my friends.

"I would suggest you walk away, sir," I say. "These children will accompany me to the palace and will be my new maids and gardeners."

The man laughs at me, and his eyes turn deadly as he storms toward me. He grabs my tiny wrist and pulls me forward, forcing me to the ground. I land on my hands and knees with an oof.

*"I will teach you how to behave properly, **princess**," he snarls. I hear the crack of his whip as he lands a skin-splitting lash on my back.*

I sit up quickly, gasping for breath with my hand on my chest. I must have stopped breathing at some point while I slept. There is a sharp pain in my back where the scars are forever etched into my skin. I haven't dreamed about that day in a few years. It only comes to me when I lose control of my emotions.

Evan the Black has been wreaking havoc with my emotions, and I can't stop thinking about him. I am confused by his display of affection and care toward me. I expected him to take my innocence without permission, force himself into me as I silently screamed for help. Yet, he didn't. He assured me he wouldn't do that to me, and what was even more surprising was that he kept his word.

He allowed me to hit him. Although my punches were weak and ineffectual, he should have stopped me. I am supposed to be an obedient wife. He told me to behave, or he would change his mind about allowing my father to live. Yet, I acted poorly all night with no consequences. If I were to hit some other man, he would have corrected me with a firm hand. He would have taken me without my permission just so I learned my place in my new world, but Evan hadn't. Why didn't he?

I rub my temples and my heart thuds in my chest as the memories of last night fill my mind. I kissed him. Why would I obey his command and touch my lips to his without a fight? Why did I slip off my clothing and sleep beside him? My own actions confuse me. It is like I am in a trance every time I look into his steel-grey eyes. Like they call to me. Like they are familiar.

Ba-dum.

Stop it. I command my heart, pressing my hand against my chest, but it doesn't listen. It hasn't stopped thudding since he comforted me. I was vulnerable and weak, easy to manipulate, and he still didn't touch me when he could have.

I lift the furs, covering my naked body as I look around the bright room. Where is my husband? Did he change his mind? Has he gone to take care of the rest of my family?

No.

I blink a few times at the voice in my head. It's so clear and loud that I believe it. *Am I going crazy?*

I cover my face with my hands and lie back on the bed. I am not sure what to believe. My mind and heart are telling me two different things. I need some time alone and a chance to breathe. Maybe then I can sort my thoughts. I get out of bed and slip on my chemise. Ignoring the corset, I pull the dress on over my head. It is considered improper for a princess to go without one in the Kingdom of Candonia, but I couldn't care less. The things only cause discomfort, and it will lead to a bigger headache.

After tying my hair back into a high ponytail, I step out of the tent. Soldiers glare at me as they walk by, coldly looking me up and down before continuing on their way. They dislike me, and they have no fear of showing it. I am their enemy, but this hatred seems personal. What did I do to make them hate me this much? I take a deep breath in, but it does little to calm me. More questions crowd my mind, making it hard for me to figure out an answer for any.

Before I can spiral completely out of control, a boy steps in front of me. He can't be older than fourteen, but he is taller than one would expect for a boy his age. His shaggy brown curls almost fall into his eyes as he looks down at me. He flicks his head, his hair moving to the side.

"My lady!" the boy says.

"Yes?" I watch as he shifts from foot to foot. His dark brown eyes focus on mine, and he tries to form a sentence.

"I mean princess? My princess? No, that doesn't sound right. My Commander's wife," he stumbles over his words. It's cute, and he seems harmless enough. He has a different vibe about him than the other men in the camp. Maybe it is because he is still a kid, but there is a glimmer of hope and understanding in his eyes. Children tend to be more trusting than adults.

"Your Highness," I smile, correcting him. Though, I couldn't care less about titles at the moment. "And what is your name?"

"Boy is my name while I am your husband's squire. It is a great honor to have," he says.

"Oh." I continue to frown. It is an odd quirk of mine that my father has tried to train out of me. I prefer to call people by their names and not their titles. I understand there is an honor that comes with titles, but using their names is my way of showing respect. Titles separate my people into different classes, and I don't particularly like that.

The Boy can see the disappointment in my face before he looks around frantically, his voice becoming a low whisper. "You have to call me that, but my name is Ben, Your Highness."

I smile at him. "Thank you for telling me your name. I will be sure to call you by your proper title."

Ben smiles toothily at me as a man appears behind him. The newcomer has short, dirty blonde hair that shines in the sunlight. His skin is a dark gold, and he is just a bit taller than Ben. He is thinner than most of the men at the camp but is still wrapped in lean, hard muscle. From the smirk on his face and the glint in his eyes, I can tell he must be playful. His entire outfit is black, including the scarf tied loosely around his neck, and his belt holds an array of weapons.

"Is the Boy talking your ear off, my lady?" He smirks, continuing to study me with his piercing blue eyes.

"No. Not at all." The boy's smile is infectious, and I grin back at him. I already have a soft spot for Ben. I don't know why as I just met him, but he seems pure and is one of the few people in the camp who has been kind.

The man smiles, ruffling Ben's hair before turning his attention back to me.

"It is an honor to make your acquaintance, Your Highness. I'm Kian of Steodia, one of your husband's generals," he says, bowing deeply. Kian. He is the prince of that kingdom, which explains his complexion. I'd never had the opportunity to meet the man, though. My father and his uncle tend to disagree on policies, so my father never brought me on trips to Steodia. A couple of years ago, the King of Steodia, Kian's uncle's son, passed away, making Kian the last heir of that bloodline. There were rumors that Kian had run off to join the conqueror's army. I guess those rumors are true.

I curtsy in return. "A pleasure to meet you, Kian."

Kian nods, the smile never leaving his face. "Are you looking for Evan?"

"No. I was going to go for a walk," I say.

Kian looks around, whistling, and another man joins our small group. His forest green eyes look me up and down, and I frown. He is intimidating with his height, and I assume they use him to strike fear into their enemies.

"This is the Mountain. He'll serve as your escort," Kian says. In the sunlight, I can see the Mountain has dark reddish hair contrasting against his olive complexion. Those who are pure-blooded from the Kingdom of Ciral have this trait. I wonder how he would have met Evan, but that is a question for another day.

"No," I shake my head, "I prefer to go alone."

Kian clears his throat. "I'm sorry, my lady. We have strict orders not to let that happen."

I open and close my mouth, shocked. "From whom?"

"There's only one man whose orders we follow." Kian laughs as if my question was a stupid one. The Mountain grunts in agreement.

My eye twitches. First, he forces my hand in marriage, and now he continuously takes away my freedom? What else is he going to take from me? I cross my arms in defiance, glaring at the two men and the boy. They have no idea who they are dealing with, but I have and will never go down without a fight.

"Well, I won't be following his orders. Now, if you excuse me," I say with a huff, attempting to get around them. They close in, narrowing my escape path. I can't help but be a tad nervous as they loom over me. *So much for my confidence.*

"My lady," Kian says, his tone less playful and more serious. "We have orders."

I look at each of them before sighing softly. There will be other ways for me to escape. Perhaps I can cut a way out through the back of the tent. They would underestimate me, never believing a woman could have those ideas.

"Fine," I say in defeat.

The two men relax their shoulders slightly while Ben dances nervously from foot to foot. He opens and closes his mouth a few times before something finally comes out. "Do you want to go up to the palace?" Ben asks me. "I have to go, anyway. I could escort you?"

I smile at Ben, his words strangely comforting. My intuition was right about him. The men here seem to dislike me, but this boy, sensing that I need time away from the camp, came up with a solution.

"Please," I say, trying to keep the desperation from my tone.

Ben looks up at the Mountain, signing to him before looking back at me. "Are you ready now?"

"I am." I nod.

Kian bows again. "My lady, before you go, the rest of the generals want to formally introduce themselves to you tonight."

"I will prepare myself for introductions while at the castle then. Thank you." I curtsy, chewing my bottom lip. My stomach and mind are spinning again. There are too many things happening at once. I am having a hard time keeping it all sorted in my head. Knowing that I will be in a room with all the men who possibly hate me makes me feel uncomfortable as well. *Suck it up, Charlotte. You can do this.*

Kian looks at the Mountain, nodding to him before walking away. Ben looks down at me, smiling.

"Shall we?" he asks.

"We shall." I nod before turning toward the palace. Ben and the Mountain flank me, preparing for the moment I run. They don't trust me. Then again, I wouldn't trust me either. A part of me was hoping I could sneak away from them and lose myself in the forest.

We walk to the castle in silence, my thoughts going back to Evan. I am still conflicted, and I am sure I will be until I see him again. He is supposed to be my enemy, yet when we are together, I am drawn to him. It is strange. What is he doing to me? Am I falling under his spell? I have asked myself that question a million times since last night, and I still have no answer.

VIII

EVAN

ILIUM

KINGDOM OF CANDONIA

I can feel eyes on me, even as I help three of my men lift the massive beam into place. We are placing the framing that will support the new dining tent. It rains often in Candonia and eating outside won't be feasible much longer. With the beam in place, I slap the captain on the shoulder, gifting my men with a rare smile before moving on to the next task that demands my attention.

The blacksmith holds out the small armor I'm having custom-made for the Mountain's squire, Khrys. The boy turns sixteen in a few months and leaves for his quest. If he survives, he'll return to be knighted and join my army as a captain. The armor is meant to be a surprise. Each time one of our squires ages out, I try to present them with a gift that will aid them on their quest.

My brows furrow over the shape of the breastplate, inspecting it in the light. I hold out my hand, and the blacksmith gives me the hammer, allowing me to slam out the small dent. As he takes the armor, the feeling of being watched intensifies. I spin and lock eyes with a pair of terrified sapphire ones.

She's outside the tent.

She cried, and I can still hear her words in my head when I close my eyes. *I don't want to be here! I don't want to be with you!* I forced her into a position I actively fought to prevent another from remaining in. She's my wife, she'll be freer than any slave, but I still took her choice. To marry or not, to choose the man she would spend her life with, both are massive life decisions. Choices which will affect the rest of our lives, and I gave her no options. Even the knowledge that so many more will be given that precious gift does little to soothe me.

I started this new age of Aellolyn, an age of freedom and choice, by stealing someone else's. What does that say about me? Do I really care about the choice if I robbed her of it?

I'm a hypocrite. I take a step forward, hoping to close the distance between us. The camp's cook blocks my path, demanding my attention, and when I look back, she's gone. The second horn for morning drills rings, and I'm forced to head for the training grounds instead of following her.

The knoll that my tent sits atop abuts the sunken practice field, and a small hill off to the side allows my generals and me to watch over the drills from a higher vantage point. All my troops gather below, breaking into their various specialties to train. My men have used this field for practice only a handful of days, and already they have stripped it of any grass and turned it into mud.

Niklaus raises a dark brow at me as I storm up the hill, making me want to plow my fist through his face. Ancients, I need to get my temper back under control. Niklaus hits my shoulder, and I bite back a snarl before turning to look over the men as they run drills. Lorcan is pacing through the ranks, correcting posture, and instructing several of our new recruits on the proper way to hold a sword.

So many of my men never touched a weapon before they came to me. Slaves are not allowed to hold a sword because they got *ideas*. Some of my men were once knights, even of noble birth, most were slaves freed by us. No matter what a man was

60

before coming to me, he is treated the same as the next. Birthright and lineage make no difference to me, and neither does gender. My army is filled with women in well-tailored armor, many fought even more viciously than the men they fought beside. If they can hold a sword, they are welcome.

I growl at Niklaus, "What did I miss?"

Niklaus frowns at me, unaccustomed to me expressing displeasure without a source. The downward twitch of his lips is one of the few ways that he expresses emotions, his face normally a completely impassive mask. His ice-colored eyes make his blank face even more unnerving. The way they focus on you is reminiscent of a predator sighting prey. Typically, I find his lack of expression a sign of trust, but today it only irritates me.

The fuse of my temper is shorter than ever.

Another way that woman is affecting me. Niklaus holds out the scrawled note, patiently waiting for me to read it. My stomach rolls as I struggle to make sense of the scratches and lines on the small piece of parchment. The back of my neck flushes as it always does when my generals go quiet when I read. I hate the looks of patience my men give me.

"Kian is rooting out dissent in our new home," Niklaus adds, waiting for me to finish.

"My ears are burning," Kian says, strolling up to stand on my left side, the generals flanking me. They are identical in height, but their looks and attitudes could not be more divergent.

"What news do you bring?" I'm in no mood for his quips.

Kian pauses, his head swiveling, and I can see him assessing me out of the corner of my eye. My hands tighten into fists at my sides, even more irritated than I was before. "Shouldn't you be more cheerful after spending the night with your wife?"

My gaze snaps to him, and he takes a step back involuntarily at what he sees in my eyes. Kian clears his throat before continuing his report, "We spread word through the city that slaves should rise up and that all slaves are welcome in your army as equals. Just as we have done in every slave city we've come to."

I nod and look out over the field, not really registering the activity. She keeps invading my thoughts, and I can't forget the way her eyes looked away, her thoughts as loud as if she'd said them. *You've made me your slave.*

"However, the king banned slavery in Candonia two years ago," Kian adds, his voice cautious and measured, very unlike him. *Is my lack of control that apparent?*

"What?" I demand, glaring at him, my focus solely on him now. How had this not reached me?

Kian nods. "I was surprised too. It seems that someone convinced him it was a loathsome practice, but it's unclear who had the king's ear."

Ilium is the largest slave market in the world, and someone outlawed slavery? That was their major trade! Their lifeblood and my source of outrage toward this nation and its king. How could I not know?

It was a night of storms, and the wind buffeted the cottage, water pelting the small door. My ma was holding me tight, my Da screaming as he tried to keep the waves out.

I shake my head, pulling myself out of the past to focus on the now. What are these memories? I don't remember growing up. The only thing I remember is being sold as a child. I don't remember before, or at least, I didn't *used* to.

"Finally, seeing the light after years of evil means little to me. How many slaves passed through his gates unnoticed? How many of them did he abuse himself? How many bodies are buried in shallow graves never to be found?" I grind out, my irritation making my vision waiver and a knot of tension coil in my neck.

"No one is saying we should forget," Lorcan says, coming up behind me. I see Kian nod as I turn to glare at Lorcan over my shoulder. My generals all know that I hate people at my back. The young general is lucky that he still breathes after approaching me from behind.

Lorcan smirks and taunts, "You would think after fucking that princess cunt, you would be a bit more relaxed."

I see red.

I don't remember moving. But suddenly, Niklaus is yanking me back, his arms beneath mine, and his hands locking behind my head. Lorcan's face is a bloodied mess. I can feel the throb in my knuckles, and I know they are bruised and torn.

My generals stare at me in shock. My body moved on impulse, wailing on my trusted general. His comment about my wife, who I've known for a day, made me forget more than a decade of friendship.

I pat Niklaus's arm, signaling my return to my senses. He slowly releases me, prepared to intervene again should I lose control, a precaution I have never needed before. My temper may run rampant at moments, but I can focus it, using it in battle. Never taking it out on someone undeserving.

What is she doing to me?

I step forward and hold my hand out to Lorcan, offering to help him back to his feet. He allows me to pull him upright and pinches his broken nose with two fingers, trying to stem the bleeding.

I mean to say *I'm sorry*, but what comes out is, "I won't tolerate anyone speaking about my wife in such a way."

He drops his hand and hisses at me, "She's just a means to an end, isn't she?"

Wynonna moves between us, slapping a hand on each of our chests. She snaps to her son, "Lorcan, that's the man's wife and your future queen. Show some respect." Wynonna hits her son's chest again. "Or I'll teach you some."

To me, she orders, "Go cool off."

Cool off. I stalk down the hill, heading for the lake, needing to swim.

I walk instead of calling for the Black, not even bothering to remove my clothing before I jump into the cold water. The icy shock washes over my head, and my rage ebbs, giving me the clarity I need.

I breach the surface and wade from the water, pulling off my sodden clothing. I hang them to dry on a tree branch before reclining on the shores of the lake. The peace of this place soothes me as I try to organize all these new foreign thoughts and feelings.

My wife has me twisted up inside. By forcing her to marry me, I have taken away her choice, her power. She's nothing like I expected. She's not cold or cruel, and the more I fight this strange pull toward her, the more out of control I feel. I sit up and tunnel my fingers into my hair, resting my head in my hands.

It's been barely a day of marriage, and already she's turned me inside out. What is it about her? From the moment she walked down the aisle to me, I haven't stopped thinking about her. I can't afford a distraction like this, especially not one that makes me attack one of my generals.

I grab a fistful of dirt and hurl it into the lake, wishing the small, petulant action provided some clarity. My most trusted advisors, the ones I would normally lean on to explain this to me, are useless. The only one who's been married is Wynonna, and she's been a widow as long as I've known her.

What if there is something greater at work here? I pull a knee up to my chest and wrap an arm around it, glaring at the lake. What if she's my reward for years of anguish? Have the Ancients finally felt I've provided enough blood, sweat, and tears that I deserve something *good*? Could she be that? My prize? I stare out over the water, mulling the idea over in my mind. What if she could be mine in truth? What if we could share not only a bed but a life? Something we build together as partners.

I stand with a deep sigh and pull on my still damp clothes, a shiver running through me from the chill.

Maybe I'm being fanciful and dreaming far more than I should, but I can't help but wish that this marriage could be something more than just a way to secure the crown.

IX

Charlotte

ILIUM

KINGDOM OF CANDONIA

Stormy, pale grey eyes clashing with mine across camp. Frozen moment in time. Everything faded, the sounds, the smells, the people around us. *Just you and me.* But it was only for a second, a breath, before the world forced its way back in. I think about what I saw back at the camp as we walk toward the palace. Evan's men admire him greatly. He isn't like most Commanders who would leave their people to set up on their own. He is approachable and works alongside them, making himself available to all. Someone so adored by those he commands must be doing something right, and my respect for him grows.

We arrive at the palace, and even though I have only been gone a day, the home I grew up in suddenly feels less familiar to me. I pause at the bottom of the stairs, Ben and the Mountain standing patiently on either side of me. I study the castle, trying to imagine it as if I were seeing it for the first time.

Four narrow, square towers are connected by high, thick walls made of pale stone. Together they create a protective barrier around the palace. The gate is formed from iron bars and guarded by two warriors. In the front courtyard, large trees and manicured shrubs provide shade to animals and the guards who patrol the grounds. Tall windows are scattered along the light grey stone walls of the castle, allowing enough sunlight inside to keep the gloom at bay. It is a stunning sight, but it feels as if it is not real to me now. As if I no longer belong here. As if I am a stranger.

I start up the large white stone staircase, holding up the front of my dress. I wonder if my family will be waiting for me. My question is quickly answered when I push open the large wooden doors that lead to the foyer. Eleanor is standing just inside, wearing armor that is two sizes too big for her and wielding a wooden sword. Two of her maids are trying to calm her down as she swings the weapon through the air, yelling something about coming to save me. I try to hold back a laugh as her blue eyes fall on me.

"Charlie!" she exclaims, her eyes narrowing on both Ben and the Mountain. She steps forward, pointing her sword at Ben. "Release my sister!"

I look up at Ben, who only smiles, pulling out his dagger. "Prepare yourself!"

Eleanor's expression changes from something serious to playful as she giggles. She charges Ben and hits his blade weakly with her wooden sword. Ben makes a dramatic flourish with his knife and exclaims, "You fiend!" Which earns him another giggle from Eleanor.

"I believe you are the fiend!" Eleanor says. "You have my sister captive."

The words pull me back to my reality. *Captive. Prisoner.* I will be nothing more than a tool to him, a backdoor to the throne. I take one last look at the children before sneaking down the hallway to my room.

The walk through the castle is slow and quiet. I can feel the stares of the servants on my back, making the hair on my neck stand on end. Their pity drowns me in more guilt and pain. I know they would help me if they could, but there is nothing they can do. There is nothing anyone can do. Even my father couldn't stop what happened.

I stick my hands in my pockets and frown as my fingers trail across a glass object. I pull it out and stare at the small bottle of nightshade that I'd forgotten I had. My heart pounds. Unlike Evan, Thalia had given me a choice yesterday. Live my life with a husband who could never love me, always feeling like I do not belong, or I could end it.

The torches in the hallway appear to dim as I arrive at my bedroom. The heavy wooden door used to be so welcoming, but now it feels like the end. Tears sting my eyes as I enter, the dark colors in the room coming down on me as I close the door, making it hard to breathe. I feel like all the air is being pulled from my lungs as I take a seat at my wooden desk.

My chair creaks under me as I take the vial from my pocket and stare at it. I could end it. Evan wouldn't care. He would probably be happy to be rid of me. If I end it, I wouldn't have to worry about what my heart and mind are telling me. I wouldn't have to feel this confusion anymore, and I wouldn't be in this loveless marriage.

I cradle the vial in my hands, running my thumb over the smooth glass as I stare at the purple liquid. Something about that thought feels wrong. Evan cared for me last night. He could have taken me against my will, but he hadn't. He kept his word and showed me kindness when there was no advantage to him. Perhaps my husband isn't the monster I thought he was.

I am no fool. I know he forced me to marry him, but the way he held me as I wept gives me hope that our marriage might become something more than a means to an end. He is waiting for me to be ready to lay with him. He ensured I felt comfortable with him in his tent. That isn't cold or heartless. Those are not the acts of a monster.

My parents' marriage started out like mine. They were forced to wed to end a war, and at first, they hated each other. Over time, they fell in love, cherishing one another and facing the world together. When I was a child, I wanted a love like my parents. They were the best of friends and always laughing. My father looked at my mother as if she was the only woman in the world. It destroyed him when she died, and he tried to stay strong for us, but he was never the same. He became more absent toward my sisters throughout the years, forcing Thalia and me to look after Eleanor. The only time I felt close to him was when we discussed the kingdom. We were shocked when he remarried, and I never understood why he did it. But as I am now all too aware, politics can force a person to do crazy things.

I look down at the vial of nightshade, sliding my fingers over the glass. Maybe this marriage won't be what I expect. He has already shown me a side of him I did not predict. I will give this a chance, and hopefully, he can prove me wrong.

Perhaps this man will surprise me, and his final conquest will be my heart. I smile to myself, placing the poison on the table.

A big hand swipes the vial from the table. I jump, and my face pales as I look up to see the Mountain looming above me. He flicks the top and sniffs the contents, his teeth baring in a silent snarl. His hand whips out, and I flinch, cowering away from him as the glass shatters against the wall, spilling the deadly contents. He is beyond angry, and I fear for my life as I realize why. *He thinks I plan to kill Evan.*

"I-I can explain," I stutter.

The Mountain's dark green eyes flare, and he grabs my arm tightly, forcing me to stand. I wince from the pain, my heart pounding in my chest. My fingers claw into his hand as I try to escape his grip.

"I wasn't going to do anything!"

He only glares at me, making my stomach twist with nausea. The Mountain starts to sign at me, but I shake my head. "I-I don't understand."

He drags me back to the desk, writing on a spare piece of paper. *You will explain this to your husband.*

I shake my head, the sickening feeling making my heart go numb. "N-no."

I can't let him know I contemplated ending my life. Who knows what he will think?

The Mountain crosses his arms, glaring at me again with distrust and anger in his eyes. He really thinks I am planning to kill Evan. I can't blame him. We are still enemies. And why does that thought make me ache? I place a hand on my stomach, trying to suppress the pain.

"I wasn't going to do anything," I lie. The Mountain looks at the shards of glass, and I let out a shaky breath, tears building up. "I was contemplating taking my own life."

The Mountain gapes at me in shock before writing. *Why?*

I look away from him, guilt eating me alive. The Mountain grabs my arm again, pulling me toward the door as I try to squirm from his grip.

"Because I do not want to be trapped in a loveless marriage! I do not want to be used as a pawn, only to be summoned to satisfy his needs!" I yell.

The Mountain growls at me, releasing my arm to write. *You don't know anything about him.*

Tears roll down my cheeks as I nod. "You're right. I don't. That is why I have decided to give this a chance."

He narrows his eyes at me again before writing. *Turn out your pockets.*

He still doesn't believe me. I look away from him, allowing the tears to flow down my face, but do as I am told.

The Mountain grabs my arm again, dragging me to the door and opening it. To my surprise, Thalia is waiting with a menacing glare. She lifts her sword and points it at the Mountain. She has tied her hair back into a fishtail and is wearing her sparring gear. A short, thin brown dress with splits on the side and a pair of skin-tight breeches.

"Unhand her," my sister says, venom in her voice.

The Mountain scoffs, hitting the sword away with his hand. Thalia hisses back at him, whacking him with the flat of the blade.

"Thalia!" I scold, but she ignores me, her gaze focused on him.

"I said unhand her," Thalia says.

The Mountain grabs her sword, bending it with one hand. Thalia swiftly knees him in the groin, and he hisses out a pained breath, releasing me. I whack Thalia on the arm.

"What are you doing?" I hiss.

Thalia pushes me behind her, raising her bent sword. "I will not allow some brute to manhandle my sister."

The Mountain's eyes snap up, and he grabs Thalia's sword, yanking it from her grip and tossing it to the side. She rolls her eyes and cracks her knuckles.

"Fine," Thalia scoffs. "If that is how you want to fight."

"Enough. Now," I command, but Thalia only shrugs me off and throws a punch at the Mountain. He steps out of the way, grabbing Thalia around the torso and trapping her arms against her sides. Instead of trying to pull back, she drops low, escaping from his grip. Thalia swings her leg in a clockwise motion, tripping him, and he lands on the ground with a massive thud. My sister moves to straddle him, locking his arms and body between her thighs as she lifts her arm to punch him.

I grab her arm just in time. "Thalia, enough!"

Thalia glares down at the general. "You can't be serious, Charlotte."

"Deadly," I say. "Leave this issue alone."

She huffs, rolls off the Mountain, and reluctantly holds her hand out for him. He smirks, spinning his legs and knocking Thalia onto her back. He gets up while my sister gasps for breath, and I shake my head.

"Jerk!" she shouts. To my surprise, the Mountain holds out his hand to her. Thalia glares at him, her golden eyes nearly glowing with fury as she takes his hand. He pulls her up a little too hard, and she lands hard against his chest. I hold back a snicker as Thalia looks up at the Mountain, her face turning bright red.

"Touch my sister like that again, and I'll kill you. Understand?" she says, pulling her hands away.

The Mountain snorts, and my sister slips a dagger from the slit in her dress, holding it against his inner thigh. In a flash, the Mountain's own knife appears in his hand, and he presses the tip under Thalia's breast.

She tilts her head. "Hm."

He smirks at her, both putting their daggers away. I stare at them in confusion as the Mountain looks at me with a raised brow.

I nod. "Yes, back to camp."

The Mountain sidesteps my sister, who looks at me.

"I'll see you soon, Lia," I say to her. She scoffs and shakes her head as she walks away. The Mountain and I make our way to the courtyard, my nausea growing as we walk down the steps. From the corner of my eye, I spot Eleanor and Ben. He shoves my littler sister to the ground, and I frown.

"Should we interrupt them?" I ask the Mountain.

He shrugs as my sister stands up, preparing to shove Ben back. *Oh no, not another one.*

"Eleanor!" I scold. She quickly turns to look at me, her face flushing red.

"Sorry, Charlie," she whispers, looking down in shame.

"Are you ready to go home, Your Highness?" Ben asks me.

I nod. "I am."

Eleanor grabs Ben and whispers something to him. I turn to the Mountain, and he meets my gaze with ice-cold eyes.

I let out a deep sigh. "Let me talk to Evan. Please?"

He frowns, pointing at the sun and then lowering his finger to the ground. *He's giving me until sunset.* I nod and look at the children. Ben is frowning at Eleanor, his arms crossed over his chest, and my sister is...crying? I clear my throat, and Eleanor walks away as Ben joins us. The Mountain gestures us forward, and I decide not to ask questions. I walk ahead of them, keeping my head low and chewing my lower lip as I try to figure out what I am going to tell Evan. Will he believe me?

I hear a gasp behind me, "Poison?!"

My entire body tenses at the word, and I stop, turning to look back at the Mountain.

"You told him?" I ask, my eyes tearing up again.

"He told me you have until the sun sets to tell Evan, or he will," Ben informs me as the Mountain continues to scowl.

"What else did he say?" I ask.

Ben crosses his arms over his chest. "That he doesn't believe you intended only to poison yourself."

They will never believe me. Why would they? Their Commander forced me to marry him and live in the camp, away from everyone I love. It makes sense for me to want to poison him, even though that is not the truth. Evan might kill me for this himself. My heart sinks deeper into my chest as dark thoughts crowd my mind. *Maybe I should have drank the poison and saved him the trouble.*

I turn away from the both of them, angrily brushing away tears as I start back to camp. Ben grabs my arm, turning me to face him again.

"But, did you?" he asks.

"Did I what?" I reply, completely defeated.

"Intend to kill him?" Ben frowns. "Truly?"

I shake my head, trying to pull myself together. "No. My sister gave it to me last night before the wedding, so I had a way out."

Ben's eyes lock onto mine, and we stay silent for a minute as he studies me. "I believe you."

My lip trembles, breathing out a sigh of relief. Did I hear him right?

"You...you do?" I ask.

The boy releases my arm, nodding. "Yes, I do."

Someone believes me. The boy truly believes me. Maybe I'm not alone. The past two days have been insanely crazy. Knowing that the boy is on my side feels like a blessing.

"Thank you," I say. Ben nods, looking up to the Mountain and signing something to him. I turn around, slowly continuing along the path to the camp.

"The Commander will be back soon," Ben says as we arrive back at the tent. I nod and look at the boy one last time before

72

entering. As soon as the flap closes, my emotions overwhelm me, and I collapse to the ground. Only one thing repeats in my mind as I sob silently.

Give him a chance. Give him a chance.

X

EVAN

OUTSIDE ILIUM

KINGDOM OF CANDONIA

I went straight to drills after my time at the lake, and already I feel more in control. I push open the tent flap, my eyes scanning for her to find her curled up in bed. Did she fall back asleep after her walk with the Mountain and the Boy? For some reason, I doubt it. Despite her lineage, my wife does not seem the type to laze about in bed. *Now, where did that assumption come from?*

Over my shoulder, I snap at the Boy for the tub and a hot bath. As he jumps to the task, I unbuckle my forearm braces. The molded leather drops to the ground, the sound muted by the rugs.

"Lamb?" She doesn't respond, remaining in a curled ball on the bed.

She lets out a shaky sigh, making my brows knit and my stomach drop. She stands, keeping her gaze down as she walks over to me.

I frown and wrap my arms around her, pulling her into a kiss. I have noticed that her mind tends to wander, and she is always thinking, but something is different. Her lips are cold and stiff, and I can feel her hands shaking against my chest. I break the kiss, looking down at her and scanning her face. "What's wrong?"

Her eyes are not sparkling. They are dull and distant. She's standing right in front of me, her hands on my chest, but she's not here. Her mouth repeatedly opens and closes, and tears pool in her eyes. "Th-the Mountain. He found me with a vial of poison..."

"What?" I must be hearing things because it sounded like she said *poison*. Was she that desperate to get away from me? Have I forced another to consider the same choice that haunted me every day as a slave?

Could death truly be worse than this?

She steps away from me, her breathing becoming even more ragged. "M-my sister gave it t-to me last night before our wedding...for a way out..."

"A way out." I know those words. I thought them often enough once. Whatever thoughts of hope and happy endings I had today are so far from the truth, it makes my stomach roll.

"I wasn't going to drink it!" she insists, confusing me.

My jaw tightens and loosens. "Why not? I've trapped you, haven't I? Forced you?"

I step closer, looming over her. She lifts her chin, her eyes connecting with mine. "You have. But you are not what I expected."

I grab her upper arms, my jaw tensing. My eyes scan hers for something, anything to tell me I wasn't wrong earlier. "What? A monster?"

She winces slightly from my grip, and I stop myself from releasing her. "I thought you were one, but you've proven me wrong. When she handed me that poison, I thought you would take the last choice from me. That you would force me."

My grip loosens, but I still don't release her. "What?"

She wrings her hands together. "You showed me you aren't the monster I once believed you to be. You have been nothing but caring towards me since I arrived at camp. I...I should not have judged you as quickly as I did."

I release her as my squire and several other men bring in the copper tub. They dump steaming water into it, and she glances at the Boy, eyes watering before looking away. *What else is happening in my camp?*

I look at the tub and shake my head. "I'm going to the lake."

She blinks up at me, hurt flickering in her jewel eyes. "Why?"

"Do you care?"

"I do," she says, deflating my anger. I study her, tension coiling through me. She said she doesn't think I'm the savage my reputation makes me out to be, but is that enough?

I turn my back on her, strip down, and step into the tub. The hot water relaxes my muscles and eases some of my tension. When my eyes lock back on her, I see she's wringing her hands again and looking away. The knuckles of her elegant fingers are turning white from the strain.

"Come here."

Charlotte obeys, keeping her head low. Meek. I hate seeing her meek. When she pauses next to the tub, I take a deep breath, looking her up and down. I'd decided that I want us to be more, hadn't I?

Are we more or less?

Partners or strangers?

Without warning, I pull her into the tub on top of me. I catch her squeal of surprise as I cover her mouth in a kiss. The water soaks her clothing and laps over the edges of the tub, spilling onto the rugs. She giggles against my lips, softening into my hold, even as she demands, "What are you doing?!"

I kiss her again, then frame her face with my hands, so her eyes lock on mine. Hopefully, she can read the sincerity in them. "Promise me, if such a thought crosses your mind again, you'll talk to me."

I know those dark thoughts, some days they lurk just out of sight, waiting for me to fall. I never had someone understand. If she lets me, I can be that for her. I want more from her, and I've made the first step forward. Now, I can only hope she joins me.

76

She places her hands on my chest, nodding. "I promise." I press my lips to hers, my hands fiddling along her back, searching for the soaked dress ties. Her hands shake as she shyly explores my chest. I break the kiss, giving up on the laces, and reach over the side of the tub. I find my boot and the dagger inside.

The dagger glints in the low light as I flip it in my hand and carefully saw at the soaked ties. She remains silent as I cut her out of her dress and pull it off her, dropping it to the side in a sodden heap. She looks away from me, her cheeks red and her body trembling. I slide my hands over her, easing her out of her shift. It's as if her clothing presents a facade between us, creating the division I hope to erase.

She crosses her arms over her breasts and worries her lower lip, her eyes focused on my chest. I open my mouth to speak, but she buries her face in the crook of my neck, letting out a shaky exhale. *My lost little lamb.*

"I'm not going to take you for the first time in a cramped tub, lamb," I whisper against her head.

She pulls back just enough to lock her gaze with mine, her hands dropping slowly from her breasts. Her eyes fill with more gut-wrenching tears. "P-Promise?"

I nod solemnly. "Promise. You're safe with me."

She lets out a breath, slowly relaxing against me. I wrap my arms around her, feeling the tension ease from her. Taking a cloth, I rub some scented oil into it. I slide it over her back as I kiss her forehead, accustoming her to my touch. I clean us both in silence until she relaxes fully against me.

When the water cools, I lift out of the tub, cradling her in my arms. I set her gently on her feet before wrapping her in a towel.

She fidgets with the ends, looking everywhere but at me. "I suppose we sh-should prepare for th-that meeting."

She only stumbles over her words when she's truly terrified. Otherwise, her words are slow and thoughtful, even and cool. Stepping closer to her, so there's barely a breath between us, I lift her chin with a light brush of my fingers.

She gulps visibly. "Y-Yes?"

My eyes roam her face, caressing her features. "You never have reason to fear me. You are the only person in the world to claim that."

Her sapphire eyes widen, and she blinks repeatedly. "B-But we a-are enemies."

I trail my thumb along her lower lip. "No, we were enemies. No longer."

She takes half a step closer to me. "Then what are we?"

My lips twitch. "Married."

Her eyes scan mine before she stands on her tiptoes, kissing me softly. I smile and say against her lips, "Like that, do we?"

She pulls away, her cheeks burning red. "Perhaps."

To my surprise, I let out a loud laugh before I catch myself. When was the last time I laughed?

I clear my throat and take a step back. "We should get ready," I say, moving to my trunk. I grab a pair of black breeches and a white lawn shirt, tossing my towel onto the rack by the brazier to dry.

"Is something the matter?" she asks.

Yanking on my breeches, I turn back to look at her. "I laughed."

"Is that not usual for you?"

Another laugh bubbles in my throat at the question, and I shake my head. "I'm surprised my men didn't think you were killing me at the sound."

"Oh…" Her hand tightens on the towel as she watches me pull on my lawn shirt.

I look her up and down when she makes no move to get dressed. "Are you planning on wearing that? It will be the shortest meeting in history with all my generals dead."

Her cheeks glow red. "Evan!"

I gesture to the three trunks next to mine. "The first of your things were delivered from the palace."

She smiles in delight and opens one, pulling out clean clothes. Her little huff of displeasure draws my attention, and I recoil when I see what she is holding.

A corset. Monstrous things.

I grab the offending garment and toss it to the side. "You don't need that."

She blinks at me a few times. "It's not proper."

Another laugh forms in my throat, but I keep it from breaching my lips. "So?"

She gives me a small smile before picking up a dress. "Oh, nothing."

Charlotte slips on the gown and tries to reach around to yank the ties closed. I come up behind her and trail my fingers along her spine, feeling her tense beneath the caress. I slowly tighten the dress, leaning down to press a kiss to her shoulder when I finish. "We might have to cut you out of this later."

"You better not. This is one of my favorite dresses."

Her scent is intoxicating as I hover at her shoulder and whisper against her ear, "No promises, lamb."

"We have a meeting to attend." She shivers but doesn't look back at me before heading for the exit of the tent.

XI

Charlotte

The general's tent is big enough to hold at least fifteen men. I can feel the anxiety building inside me. I am about to be in a room with men who probably want to kill me, but they aren't going to be like Evan. For some reason, he has been kind and caring, but there is no reason for these men to show me the same respect. For all I know, the men could have voted to kill me and put my head on a spike.

The generals go quiet when we enter, and all eyes fall on me. Among them, I notice Ben and the Mountain, and my gaze skips away from them. They are probably still disappointed, and I know the Mountain will never trust me again. I wonder if he has told the others. They stare, waiting for me to do something, and the room starts to close in. Evan's hand tightens on mine, and I feel a little more confident.

It's just you and me. The words Evan said on our first night give me enough courage to look up. I take this moment to study the room, avoiding looking at the men a moment longer. A large round table sits in the middle of the tent, with six chairs surrounding it. On the table are a few books and a map that has little figures placed on it. Looking up, I see there are multiple shelves along the tent walls that are stuffed with books. There is a stand for their swords in the corner, although, at the moment, it only holds one.

My attention circles back to Evan, and I smile as he gestures to the only other woman in the room. Her blondish-grey hair is neatly woven into a braid along the side of her head, and her eyes are dark but kind. If it weren't for the braid, I wouldn't have known she was female. Her armor conceals her shape, and her face is hard.

"Lamb, this is Lady Wynonna of Arcanum in Grimmwing," Evan introduces.

The lady bows deeply. "Your Highness, an honor."

I curtsy in return. "The honor is mine, Lady Wynonna."

The older woman smiles, stepping back, and I feel the tension in my body ease. Kian steps forward, and I smile. He didn't seem too horrible earlier. In fact, he appeared kinder than I expected. He takes my hand and kisses the top of it.

"Enchanted, as I was earlier, Your Highness."

My lips twitch slightly and I relax even more. "Pleasure to meet you again, Kian."

Evan takes my hand from Kian's, glaring at his general before kissing the same spot. I tilt my head at him, confused. *Is he jealous?*

Another man steps forward. His dark brown hair is long, and his eyes are the color of ice. There is a shadow of a beard on his strong jaw, and his cheekbones are prominent. His face is young, but his expression is closed and unchanging.

"Niklaus," he says with a nod.

"Pleasure to meet you," I say before looking up at Evan and smiling. I find I am looking to him for comfort and direction in this situation. It is intimidating being in a room with the men who only yesterday invaded my city, but I feel oddly calm with Evan at my side. This is going much better than I thought it would. They all appear friendly, or at least have the decency to act it in front of me.

A scowl slowly forms on Evan's face, and I turn to see the cause. The man looks like a younger, more masculine version of

Lady Wynonna. His blonde hair is cut short and swept to the side. He glares at me with his dark eyes, his jaw clenching and unclenching. *He doesn't like me.* It is plain as day from his expression that he detests everything about me.

"That is Lorcan," Evan says, his eyes narrowing. "He is Wynonna's son."

"An honor to meet you," I say, curtsying again, but he only glares.

Evan gestures to the last general. "And you've already met the Mountain," Evan says. The Mountain bows before signing something. "He says you have permission to call him by his given name."

My lips curve in a small smile as I look up at the Mountain. "I do?"

The Mountain nods, watching me carefully.

"Lord Seamus Demir," Evan says.

I blink. He has given me permission to use his given name. A man who I thought hates me has given me permission to something that many people have to honor. I didn't expect this after all that had happened this morning. He may not trust me for now, but this shows me he does respect me. It gives me a small glimmer of hope and heat radiates through my chest. *I don't want to be their enemy anymore.*

"It is a pleasure to meet you again, Lord Demir," I say, curtsying.

Demir signs something to Evan, and my husband looks down at me. "He says if you would not be averse to learning sign language, he could teach you so that he can communicate with you more efficiently."

"I would love to learn," I say, smiling brightly. Another step closer to becoming someone they may eventually trust.

Demir nods, looking at each of us before exiting the tent. Evan waves his hand, and the rest of the generals exit. Lorcan trails behind them but pauses to glare at Evan.

"You would be a fool to trust her," he hisses.

"Don't presume to know my mind," Evan says, his eyes narrowing.

"She is still an enemy." Lorcan sneers at me and my stomach twists.

"Goodnight," Evan says, pointing to the opening of the tent.

I look down at my hands as Lorcan exits. These are strong warriors. Men that would die to protect Evan. It is their job to see threats where he may not. It will take time to earn their trust and prove myself, but I am up to the task.

Stay strong, Charlotte. Show no weakness.

"He doesn't trust your intentions, and he doesn't know you," Evan says.

"None of them do," I whisper.

Evan looks down at me. "You were the enemy."

"They think I still am," I say, lifting my chin. *What is stopping them from convincing Evan to kill me? That he doesn't need me?* I am nothing but a pawn, a tool, something that they can sweep off the general's board at the snap of their fingers.

"Give them time," he says.

I press my lips together as a heavy weight falls on my shoulders. "I'm tired."

Evan brushes my hair over my shoulder. "Too tired for a ride?"

"No," I say, looking up at him. The idea of going for a ride sounds wonderful. Perhaps some time away from the camp with him will clear my mind. Evan takes my hand in his and leads me out of the general's tent. He places two fingers in his mouth and whistles so loudly that the sound has me covering my ears.

A few seconds later, a black blob comes charging through the camp. My eyes focus on the thing, and I realize it is a horse. The horse that Evan used to break down the front doors of my palace and it's coming straight toward us, nearly running over several of the warriors. I shift behind Evan, my heart pounding in my chest. I have never seen such an intimidating-looking horse in my life. Its shoulders are a mass of muscles, larger than any of the horses in my stable. I can only imagine how many battles this horse has seen. How many men has it taken down on its own?

The sound of the animal's heavy breathing in front of us has me holding my breath. Evan picks me up and swings me onto the animal's back before mounting behind me.

"Hold on, lamb," he says.

I blink a few times before grabbing his arms. "A-Alright."

Evan kicks the horse's flanks, and I squeal in surprise, my hands digging into his arms as the horse bolts into the forest. We leave the camp behind, and exhilaration fills me. There are no walls, no warriors, nothing but him and me.

The moonlight shines off the surface of the lake, casting everything in silver. The water is undisturbed, not a ripple or a wave marring the mirror-like surface. Evan dismounts and quickly strips down to nothing before running to the lake and jumping in. I laugh as I slide off the horse, my legs a little wobbly from the ride.

"What are you doing?" I ask him.

"Swimming," he says, his gaze on the stars as he floats on his back. I stand on the shore, warmth curling in my belly as I watch him. This man is full of surprises.

XII

EVAN

The water is cool, but not cold, even this late at night. The lake is far enough away from Ilium and the camp that it's almost another world. A world where we can be alone, just her and me.

There's a reason we're not taking up residence in the palace, despite our marriage making me the crown prince. My camp is full of men loyal to me, and I want her away from those who would turn her against me. I hope she will come to see me as her safe port in a storm of the unfamiliar. It would be the opposite in the palace. Instead of her adapting to fit my needs and my life, I would change for hers. Not knowing how to be royalty, I would look to her for answers, and that's unacceptable to me. I won't let others lead me through this transition. I will never be *ordered* by another. Not again. *Never again.*

She was supposed to be a pawn, a faceless chess piece moving into place. But then her hands trembled, then she cried, and she became more. Even now, swimming through the lake, my strokes cutting cleanly through the water, I'm aware of her. I can feel her gaze on me, watching me intently. No doubt she is trying to figure out my motives for bringing her here. *Why did I bring her here?*

I wanted somewhere neutral, somewhere we could be different. Here, I'm not the man who conquered the kingdom, and she's not a princess. We're man and wife, just her and me. *Just you and me.*

My eyes lock on the sky, cutting through the water on my back. I don't remember learning to swim. It seems like a skill I have always known. Yet, that flash of memory when I looked into her eyes, of the sea crashing on cliffs, seems to have unlocked something. I have been remembering a small fishing village on the coast. Did I grow up there? I'm having the strangest impressions of a woman's face, a man's hands, my parents? For years, I've searched my memories for some glimpse of my past before being sold without success. Now just gazing into Charlotte's jewel-bright eyes has brought forward lost impressions.

I look up at the sky, marveling at the cascade of dark colors streaking across the midnight canvas. I love stars. They have always represented a freedom I once thought impossible to obtain. In my hovel with my first master, I ripped a hole in the patched roof so I could look at them while trying to sleep. It didn't matter if it rained or snowed. I never closed the hole. I got wet, or I shivered, but I never stopped watching. My life is charted by the stars and the imaginary designs I made up as a child. They were my escape, the place my mind would wander when I was too slow, and the master caught me. *"Little Evander,"* he would whisper in my ear as tears silently fell down my face. I would look for the stars, detach mentally and physically, imagining I was among them and floating in the sky. It was enough until he sold me.

I slow my strokes enough so she can hear me and murmur, "You're lucky to have grown up in such a beautiful place."

The lake is beautiful, the water close to clear. Even now, with only the light of the moon and stars, I can see the bottom. Colorful fish skate along, wary of me as my kicks disturb their homes. The small meadow is the only place at the lake's edge that isn't thick forest, allowing us privacy.

I swim closer to where she stands on the shore. Her voice is so soft that even in the complete silence of the meadow, I almost miss what she says. "I was never allowed out of the palace."

That can't be true. This fierce woman, who had looked at me with disgust, even with a sword at her throat, could not have been so sheltered. Where else had she learned such courage, if not on the battlefield?

"Never?"

Slowly she comes closer to the edge of the lake. She chews her bottom lip, and her sapphire eyes focus on the ground between her feet.

"After an incident when I was young, my parents forbade me to leave the palace without a full guard." She shifts her weight from foot to foot, her slippered feet digging into the ground.

An incident? What could have possibly forced Antias to keep her so well guarded?

"An incident?" I prod, swimming closer.

She stiffens, and I can almost see her emotional walls coming up. "Yes."

I can tell I will not be getting any more information now and decide to change the topic. I will send Kian into the city to find out more, there is little he cannot ferret out.

"Do you know how to swim?" I ask, watching her carefully, analyzing every shift in her expression.

That gets her attention, her eyes snapping to me. She scans my face, looking for something, weighing her answer. "No, I do not."

The water laps at my waist as I stand. The soft mud sucks at my feet, and plants wrap around my calves, working in concert to pull me in. "Would you like to learn?"

She takes a step closer to me, her eyes remaining locked on mine. Her words are slow and measured, as if each one is carefully thought out. "I would."

Lifting my hand, I hold it out for her to take, holding my breath. I have offered my hand to her twice, once at our wedding and in the tent last night. She spurned me both times, and this time will be the last I offer it.

Heat flickers in her eyes, and then she yanks at the ties of her dress, letting it fall to the ground. In only her chemise, she proves her courage once more and steps into the water, slipping her hand into mine.

I release the breath through my teeth as I slowly coax her forward. Soon she is a few steps away from me, and the water is at her shoulders. Her dark hair floats on the surface in a halo around her. The moonlight reflecting in her eyes reminds me of the night sky, making her even more alluring. She is entrancing and hypnotizing. Does she know the effect she has on me?

My thumb draws a small design on the back of her hand before I release her. I give her an encouraging smile. "First, you float."

Her hands grip my shoulders, squeezing slightly. "F-float?"

I nod and grip her hips, pulling her deeper into the water as I step back.

Her hold on my shoulders doesn't loosen, making me readjust until she's cradled in my arms. My voice is gentle as I encourage, "Let go, lamb. I have you." She studies me for a moment before her hands drop, and I lower her onto the top of the water. I support her lower back and between her shoulder blades. "Let go, just let everything go."

Her gaze remains locked on mine, taking a long breath in and out before she slowly closes her eyes. I am her enemy, the man who conquered her country, who forced her to marry him, and she is trusting me to keep her afloat. She's trusting me.

"There you go," I whisper.

She giggles softly, and immediately, I know I love the sound. I'm going to make her do it as much as possible. Such a simple, innocent sound, yet it warms me. "I'm doing it?"

"Yes, you're floating."

Her soft, full lips curve into a gentle smile, and she relaxes. "This is...nice."

"I like to swim to clear my mind."

She opens her eyes before lowering her feet to the mud. Looking up at me, she says, "I can see why. It's so peaceful out here."

I raise my hand to brush her hair out of her face, whispering, "You're so beautiful."

Her cheeks flame, and her words stumble, but not from fear this time. "Th-thank you."

I step closer to her, my fingers caressing the soft curve of her shoulder. "You look like my little water nymph."

She laughs, and the soft, innocent sound warms me, even as she splashes me. "I am no water nymph."

The moment is so pure, playful, and innocent, but then something changes. For a moment, I can pretend we met under different circumstances, married because we fell in love. It's not the truth, but I wish it were. Lifting both my hands to her face, I look down at her. She truly is beautiful, and she is mine.

Her hands cover my much larger ones, holding my touch close. She goes to her tiptoes and hesitantly presses her lips to mine. I'm so surprised that it takes me a moment to respond.

I wrap my arms around her and take command of the kiss. She melts against me, her arms twining around my neck. My tongue plays along the seam of her lips, a question that she answers by granting me entrance. I pull her in tighter, fitting her closer to my body, trying to consume her.

I lift her feet off the sand and carry her back to the grass, our tongues dancing the entire time. I allow my hands to explore, smoothing down her curves.

XIII

Charlotte

OUTSIDE ILIUM

KINGDOM OF CANDONIA

More. That is the only word I can think of as our lips clash together. Evan lays me under him on the grass, his calloused hands catching on the fine material of my chemise as he explores the shape of my body. Everything about him is intoxicating, his smell, his touch, his warmth. It overwhelms me, lust taking over my thoughts, and I don't fight it. I want this. *Need this.*

I shift beneath him, goosebumps forming on my skin in the wake of his touch. He grips the wet fabric between my breasts and pulls, ripping it down the middle. He trails kisses down my chest, the heat of his mouth forcing away any chill. A moan escapes my lips, and my hands grip his shoulders as he takes my breast into his mouth. His tongue swirls and flicks over my nipple, and I feel each suck tug at my core.

More. Need more. My breath comes in soft pants, and I can't control my moans as Evan moves to my other breast. He slides his hands down my body, lifting my thighs and wrapping my legs around his hips. He shifts, pressing his rigid cock against my clit.

He continues to move from one breast to the other, increasing my hunger with every lick, flick, and bite. I tremble with pleasure, my core aching and begging to be touched. I arch my back as he slowly makes his way down my body, leaving a path of gentle kisses along my stomach. He settles between my thighs, slowly easing one finger inside of me as he presses kisses to my clit.

"F-Fuck," I gasp, rolling my hips against his mouth as his tongue slides over my soft folds. Waves of heat flow through my body as my breath shudders and my hands tighten on his shoulders. I've never felt such pleasure. *I never thought he would be this gentle and caring with me.* My heart pounds in my ears as unfamiliar sensations build, my body on fire with hunger and need. He slips another finger into me, earning him another loud moan as my body stretches, and he readies me for more.

"Evan."

"Evander," he growls, attempting to work a third finger inside of me. The heat of his breath against me makes me shiver. "Call me Evander."

"Evander." I moan his name, biting my bottom lip. *Evander.* I like it. Evan the Black is the monstrous conqueror, but Evander is someone else. He is the human part of this man.

At the sound of his name slipping from my lips, he covers my clit with his mouth and sucks. My cheeks burn, and my heart flutters, all my thoughts fleeing. Nearly unbearable pressure builds inside me, and I writhe beneath him. He grips my hip tight with his free hand, keeping me where he wants me. One last flick of his tongue and my eyes cross as my legs press against his shoulders.

"Fuck!" I scream. He continues to lick and suck even after I have come, causing me to squirm more. He pulls his fingers from me, moving to hover over my body. A soft kiss greets my lips, and I taste myself on his tongue. I'm already addicted to this sensation, these feelings, and I want more. *I want him.*

"There will be pain for a moment, lamb, but it will be brief, then only pleasure," he whispers, comforting me with his words.

My eyes connect with his glowing ones, my hands petting his chest. "P-pain?"

He nods, pressing his forehead to mine. He shifts above me, and I feel his tip pressing at my entrance. He feels big, almost too big. With a quick thrust, he is inside me. Evander presses his lips hard against mine as I scream, tears filling my eyes. My nails dig into his arm as he holds himself deep inside me. He presses soft kisses down my neck as my body stretches and adjusts to his invasion.

"I know, my lamb, I know. It will pass," he soothes, even as I feel his body tremble with the effort of staying still. I relax under him, clinging to his arms, my breath coming in small pants. My grip loosens as the pain subsides, and all that is left is a fullness. I lift my hips experimentally, and that must be what he was waiting for, because he kisses my shoulder as he starts to move slowly inside me.

He is so gentle, each thrust sending a wave of pleasure through my body, eliminating the pain. I moan in his ear as he lifts my hips, angling them to hit deeper inside me. My hands slide to his back, digging my nails into his skin, hard enough to leave marks.

"Evander," I moan again.

He gathers me close and flips us so that he is on his back, moving me on top of him. His hands grip my hips and he smirks. "Ride me."

I smile at him, placing my hands on his chest as I slowly roll my hips, grinding against him. He leans up to kiss me, his tongue exploring my mouth, tasting my pleasure, claiming all of me. Evander's grip is tight on my hips, but he allows me to control the speed and movements of our union. I press hot kisses down his neck, sucking on his skin as my pace quickens, becoming more frantic as the heat tears at me.

Evander moans something in his native tongue, his hands sliding up my sides to cup my breasts. A shiver runs down my spine as I feel the pressure building inside me once more. My eyes connect with his, and he thrusts up, his hips meeting my thighs. My orgasm rips through me, and I scream out in pleasure. Evander groans as he finishes, his back arching and his body shaking. He falls back, and I collapse onto his chest, my breathing heavy. I moan softly, wrapping my arms around his neck as he holds me close. Evander presses soft kisses over my face and along my neck, soothing me with his touch. *Addicting. This feeling with him is addicting.*

My heart flutters in my chest from the display of affection. I am shocked at how kind and considerate of a lover Evan is. I expected him to be rough and demanding, to show no mercy when taking my innocence. But this was warm and gentle. I felt safe and comfortable the entire time, and I enjoyed every second.

"Th-thank you," I whisper, closing my eyes. Exhaustion is quickly taking over as I relax in the safety of Evander's arms.

"Thank you?" he questions, massaging my arms and kissing my skin. I can feel his tongue lick my shoulder and I shiver.

"For being gentle," I say, rubbing my cheek against his chest. His heart is beating heavily, and I wonder if he feels this pull as well. This strange need to never let go?

"I should have waited to take you in a bed, like you deserve," he whispers.

Ba-dum. He cares? He really cares about my well-being? Why would the conqueror who supposedly hates royalty care where he takes me? To him, I should deserve nothing. Yet, here he is, surprising me with his words. I smile to myself.

"I…liked this," I whisper.

"You did?"

"Yes, I did." I nod. Though his chest is covered in scars from battle and his hands are coarse from wielding a sword, he was intimate, careful, and gentle. Everything I dreamed my first time would be. For a moment, I can pretend that the two of us came together in love. That we aren't a conqueror and a princess but a farmer and his wife, celebrating a wedding that we'd imagined for years. I can dream that he is my soulmate.

Ba-dum. As soon as I think that word, my heart leaps in my chest. Soulmates are a very real thing, despite what most people believe. The Ancient of Love, Devika, fell in love with one of the Ancients of Fate, Taerel. Their relationship was forbidden, as the Ancients of Fates could never marry. Their duty came above all, but the two of them did not care, and they married in secret. When Basilius discovered what they had done, he banished them to separate realms. Devika was sent to Xeollerene to live with the other Ancients forever, while Taerel was sent to Ufelyn with Visha. The two were never to see each other again. Before they separated, they created soulmates. Each mortal was to be born with one, and it is rumored to be the truest love. Once soulmates meet, their hearts are bound, connecting them for the rest of their lives. Is that what I am feeling now? Is that what this strange tugging sensation toward Evander is?

Evander sits us up, moving me off him before standing. I lay in the grass, continuing to catch my breath. My body feels heavy, and I am finding it hard to stay awake. I watch as he picks up my ruined chemise, dipping it in the cool water. He returns to me, cleaning the blood from between my thighs. My face burns red with embarrassment, but at the same time, I feel cherished. He is taking care of me. A monster wouldn't do this, would they? After all, he has gotten what he wants from me. There is no reason for him to treat me with such care.

Evander helps me up from the ground, reaching for my dress and slipping it on me. His fingers trail down my spine as he ties the back, and I wobble slightly, trying to keep myself steady as he dresses. My legs feel like seaweed, and I want to melt back to the ground. A breeze rushes across the lake, and the sudden rush of cold air sends shivers down my spine. He looks up, seemingly attuned to my every move.

"Are you cold?" he asks.

"Y-yes," I whisper, shivering once more.

Evander walks over to me and picks me up, cradling me in his arms. He kisses my head and whispers, "I'll keep you warm tonight."

I smile to myself, resting my head on his chest. "Thank you."

Maybe this won't be so bad.

XIV
EVAN

OUTSIDE ILIUM

KINGDOM OF CANDONIA

With a shrill whistle, the horse trots over to me, and I gently place Charlotte on his back. The Black prances slightly, not liking her up there alone. I pat his side and mount behind her, resting her against my chest. "We'll be back in our bed soon. Just rest."

My arms wrap around her, keeping her against me, warm and safe. Even with her hair still dripping wet from the lake and her dress soaked through, she's curling into me. She doesn't seem to care about her clothes or anything else at the moment. She just wants to get closer to me. I brush my lips against her forehead as she nods. Her eyes close, again showing her trust in me as I gently nudge the Black toward camp.

I didn't take Charlotte out to the meadow intending to seduce her, and I didn't offer to teach her to swim to do so either. I did both because I thought she would like it. The idea of seduction and consummating our marriage was the furthest thing from my mind. All I know now is that I want more. More of her touch, her taste, her skin, her moans. I love how she cursed when I took her, that I drove her so mad with lust that all those proper rules and etiquette drilled into her from birth fell from her head.

My back will be marked from her nails digging into me as I claimed her, breaking her fragile maidenhead. The first wounds I will wear with pride, although they will probably blend into the numerous raised scars on my back. I'll just have to repeat the process. I never expected a princess to be so...passionate. Her walls of ice crumbled under the onslaught of the heat between us. Her cries of pleasure and the sound of my name on her lips still ring in my head.

Evander.

Why did I ask her to call me that? No one has said that name since I killed my master. It's my slave name. When anyone has said that name in the past, I was once more a young boy trying to evade his master's grabbing hands. *Little Evander, you cannot escape me.*

My next two masters used the same name. When my third master died at my hand, I became Evan. Evander died that day. *Evander* was a slave. *Evan* was a conqueror. Or so I thought.

I asked her to call me Evander.

Why? Is it because I want her to have something of me? Something no one else has? Or is it to remind me of my past and that I am just a slave? Yet, when she screamed my name, I didn't feel the burgeoning hatred churning in my gut, the disgust with myself for what I was forced to do to survive. Instead, I felt...new. As if the second the name dropped from her lips, it was a new name, one that was not chained to years of regret and pain. Even now, I can't wait to hear her say it again. Take her again.

I look down at her as the Black weaves his way through the trees. Her cheek is pressed against my chest, and her soft lips are parted in sleep. Locks of wet hair are sticking to her face and neck, and I can't help but carefully push them back. Her hand is curled against my chest, a fistful of my shirt locked in it. A fanciful part of me hopes that she's doing it to keep me close, as if she can't bear to part from me. But the logical side knows that she's merely trying to stay warm.

She's going to hate me even more in the morning. When the lust and passion of our coupling clears, she'll realize I took her innocence on the ground like a common whore. She's a princess, and she should have had an actual wedding night with candles and flowers, or even an actual roof over her head. There should have been a ceremony and a long list of traditions to be followed before I had the privilege of calling her my wife.

We would have needed to go before the bishop and recite our sacrifices to each of the twelve major Ancients. Since we were married in Candonia, they would expect the sacrifice to Basilius to be the biggest. Each of the royal families claims a bloodline as close to divinity as possible. Candonians are supposedly linked to the King of the Ancients, Basilius. It's been their claim to the throne for the last thousand years, the same with the seven other regents. Visha, the Ancient of Death, belonged to none, and all at the same time. There is no escaping her. The three unclaimed Great Ancients are rumored to have left Aellolyn for parts unknown, and we are awaiting their return.

But there were no traditions for us. I didn't even wash the battle off before we were married. Even now, she lives with me in camp, away from everything familiar to her and everyone she loves.

Another reason for her to hate me.

The edge of my sleeve rides up, exposing the scars around my wrist. It is a reminder of where metal cuffs once lived. The tan of my skin makes them appear even paler in the moonlight. She shifts in sleep, her hand resting against mine, and the comparison of our lives is even more stark and apparent. She's perfect, porcelain skin unmarred by strife and toil. As we slowly make our way back to camp, the differences between us could not be more obvious.

A princess, my wife grew up and lived as a princess in a palace. The only way I could ever have a princess is by force, by giving her no other option. I needed that connection which only marriage could provide. All of my generals objected to my plan of leaving King Antias alive, allowing him to live out his life on the throne. They thought it would breed dissent and rebellion, but they didn't understand. I don't know how to be king, Antias does, and his people love him. That is what I want. I don't want to be the foreign invader for the rest of my life. Commanding an army comes as easy to me as breathing, but I need to learn to be king. I could have no better tutor than Antias. And the princess? She was meant to be a means to an end.

The torches that mark the boundary of the massive camp swim into view, and I nod silently to the sentries as we pass. We weave through the numerous white tents that compose many of my men's homes. The smell of campfires and the sound of carousing reach me, making me smile softly.

My men go quiet as they see the sleeping princess in my arms, choosing to bow their heads in respect instead. The Black's heavy hoof falls are the only sounds as we move forward into camp, heading for the raised knoll.

At my tent, one of my men reaches up to take my wife from me, but my dark glare makes him immediately think better of it.

I lift her into my arms and swing my leg over. I drop to the ground, bracing myself to keep from jostling her. The Black snorts at me, moving on his own to the small round pen set up for him. Someone had placed hay and a water trough inside for him. One of my more daring men darts forward and shuts the gate. The paddock is more of a formality. Everyone knows that nothing and no one can contain the stallion if he has a mind to get free.

I carry Charlotte into our tent and remove her wet clothes. She doesn't wake up the entire time. I tuck her under the furs and strip myself before slipping in next to her. I turn her into my chest and brush her hair back from her face, tracing my fingers along her cheek.

What is it about her that has me so spellbound? I am fascinated by every breath she takes in and out. On that thought, an extremely indelicate snore rips from her diminutive frame.

Fuck.

I should go outside and sleep under the stars, but I can't make my muscles move. I don't want to leave her, and my eyelids are heavy, weighted with exhaustion.

Sunlight slashes into the tent through the slit of the canvas door. My eyes squeeze shut, and I pull her back against me, kissing along her neck. I trail my hand down her spine, my lips sliding along her shoulder. Her skin is so soft and smooth, the scent of honey and chamomile making my usual hatred of the morning lessen. My eyes slowly pull open, and the morning light shows me something I missed before.

Five slashing lines mar her back, faded and thin with age. My fingers trail along the first one, trying to reconcile exactly what I'm seeing. I know those markings. I have many on my back and chest.

Sitting up in shock, I push her hair forward, trying to analyze the scars more carefully. My voice cracks with emotion, "You were whipped?!"

She tenses, trying to pull away from me, yanking the furs to block my view. "It was nothing."

I pull the furs off her and trace my fingers over the very thin marks. "Did your father do this?" I throw my legs over the side of the bed, standing. "He'll pay dearly for this." He'll beg for the blessed release of death by the time I'm through.

She crawls over the bed, grabbing my wrist. "It wasn't my father."

My breath comes ragged in and out of my mouth, my body shaking uncontrollably. The need to commit violence is free, and I need to expend it. "No one hurts my wife and lives."

Her fragile alabaster skin, flayed open by a whip. The scars are light and almost invisible on the top layers of her skin, and my stomach rolls in realization.

A child. She was whipped as a child.

100

"The man is already dead," she whispers.

I close my eyes, trying to calm myself. If she's telling the truth, and the man is already dead, then I can't be upset or outraged at this. Justice has been dealt. Still, I can't stop seeing her as a little girl, screaming for her parents when the first lash landed. I remember my first whipping all too well.

Her hand releases my wrist, and I open my eyes, seeing her pull the furs up to cover her back. It doesn't matter. The damage is done.

"Explain. Now."

She shakes her head, standing with the furs wrapped around her, looking around for her dress. "It doesn't matter."

I skirt the bed and grasp her chin, forcing her to look at me. "Tell me. I need to know. Please."

Please. A word I haven't said since I was a slave.

She lets out a shaking sigh, chewing her bottom lip. "When I was younger, I would sneak out of the castle dressed as a servant. My father and mother were always busy, and no one suspected a thing."

My stomach rolls. "But you got caught."

I make sure my touch is gentle as I guide her back to bed, settling her in my lap and wrapping the furs around us both. She closes her eyes, bracing herself. "I met some children who were slaves," my entire body goes rigid, "and I would sneak them food as often as I could. One of those times, I got caught by their master." My hands shake ever so slightly as I rub her back soothingly. "On the fifth slash, some guards made their way to the commotion, and one of them recognized me. My father had the master's head by the evening."

It's not enough. I want to decimate the family, the friends, everyone who ever came into contact with the man who dared to harm my wife.

"How old were you?"

She presses her lips together tightly. "Six."

"A child." My hands tighten into fists. "I only wish he was alive, so I could make him live through that punishment every day until his body gave out. Only then would I grant him death."

She glances up at me, nodding. "He was worse to those children than to me. I...I saw," she clutches her chest as if the memories physically pained her, "horrible things."

"I know," *better than she could ever understand,* "many of my men were slaves before we freed them."

Her lips curve in a small smile as she relaxes against me. "They were?"

My origins are a closely guarded secret, and it could be grounds for the bishop to grant an annulment between us. A slave, even a former one, cannot be a prince and cannot marry a princess. The Church and the Slavers Guild's history were so entwined it was often impossible to separate them. The Church claimed the rule was to ensure the divine blood of the royals was not tainted by the blood of the unclean. "Every place I conquered, we went because there were slavers. We took any who were too old to start over and offered them food, a place to sleep, and decency. In exchange, they come with us and help make all of this work. Many jumped at the chance."

Most never had one of those things, let alone all three.

"That is very kind of you."

There's that word again. *Kind.*

"It's not. Sometimes I'm not sure I'm any different. Am I just enslaving them to my cause? To my pursuit of a world of freedom?"

My darkest fear. *Am I just another master?* I've never said the words out loud, yet with they tumble forth.

"No. You gave them a choice, and they chose to follow you. You aren't forcing them here against their will."

She tenses, and I can read her thoughts as loudly as if she said them aloud.

"Like I'm forcing you," I provide, breaking the silence. Charlotte doesn't deny her thoughts, glancing away as my chest tightens. What we have shared the last two nights doesn't change how we began. Not for her.

102

I shift her off my lap and get up, hurt making my shoulders knot. Grabbing my clothes, I yank them on, putting on my lighter training armor. "I should get to morning drills."

"And what shall I do?"

I don't look at her, stomping my feet into my boots. "Whatever you wish, you're not my slave. No matter how much you believe yourself to be."

I don't look back, storming out of the tent.

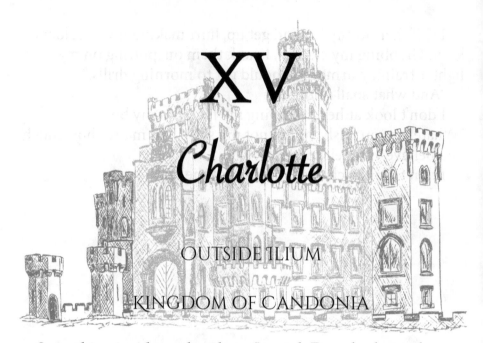

XV

Charlotte

OUTSIDE ILIUM

KINGDOM OF CANDONIA

Something inside me breaks as I watch Evander leave the tent. I shared a part of my past that only a few people know, and it ended up with us fighting. At least I know one rumor is true. He has a quick temper. Instead of talking things through, he stormed out and left me on my own to try to process everything. He stole me away from my family, the life I know, and brought me here. I am nothing but a tool for him, or at least that is what I thought. His reaction to seeing my scars was unexpected. That he was willing to kill someone who would ever lay a hand on me has me curious. But I have no answers for the ache in my heart.

I don't like this feeling of helplessness. Whenever I feel hopeless or upset, I confront the problem. I want to go after Evander and talk this out, but I can't move. One thing is true. *He forced me to marry him.* He took away my freedom and choice. Two things I have fought for since I was a child. Even when my father forbade me from going into the city on my own, I didn't listen. I enjoy having my own voice, something that most women are not allowed. I should hate him for taking this all from me, but I find myself wanting him more and more.

The unanswered questions weigh on me as I slowly stand and go to my trunk. I slip on my chemise first, then a navy blue dress with a modest neckline. I tie my hair back into a messy ponytail before sighing softly. We were starting to get along. At least, it seemed to be the case. I felt like I could begin to let down a few of my walls. Was it all a lie? The gentleness, the kindness, the caring. Did he only show me those traits to seduce me? I frown to myself. *No, that doesn't seem right.*

My mind and heart are sending conflicting messages again. It is giving me a headache, and my breathing becomes harsh as I start to feel trapped. I need to clear my mind, and I can't do that sitting in his tent all day, waiting for him to return. Looking in the long mirror placed beside a vanity, I spin to check my dress before observing my face. My pale complexion has come back to life, and there is more color in my cheek. My eyes aren't as sunken compared to the last few months, and they are shining with vitality. The specks of grey mixed into the blue irises, almost sparkling in the sunlight.

What is he doing to me?

I turn away from the mirror, running my trembling hands down my dress. A walk should help me sort my thoughts, and I can figure this out. I pause at the desk to scribble a note informing Evander of my whereabouts. I shouldn't be gone for long. Leaving the note on the bed, I walk to the tent flap and pause, Lorcan's words from last night echoing in my ears.

She is still an enemy.

The sting of those words stays with me as I step from the tent. I am surprised by how busy the camp is. Warriors and camp workers walk back and forth, some carrying supplies and others laughing and talking together. A group of warriors stop their conversation to glare at me, and I gulp. Their stares are lethal, and I shudder at the thought. If I weren't Evander's wife, they would have jumped me by now and have done Ancients know what.

I look forward, letting out a shaky breath and lifting my chin before walking away through the city of tents. To my surprise, neither Ben nor the generals stop me from leaving. Perhaps they don't even notice I am gone. I smile to myself, stepping into the forest and letting out a breath.

A little time for myself.

XVI

EVAN

She thinks she's a slave. The idea burns me. She doesn't know what it means to be a slave and truly have no choice. Yet, she is right. I forced her into a position I actively fought to prevent myself and all others from having to face. She's my wife, and she'll be as free as all my people. But unlike them, she still won't have made the choice of her own free will. She can never walk away from me. Even as I run through morning drills, it makes my stomach twist to think about it.

Have I made her my slave?

No. Charlotte's my wife. She'll be my queen, and she'll give freedom to all the countries south of Candonia. She's not a slave, but her worries are valid, and I shouldn't have lost my temper. Neither watching the conclusion of drills or even participating helps my mood. My mind is on her, and I retreat, finding a quiet spot to clean my weapons. My gaze falls to the scars on my wrists, and without conscious effort, I remember how I got them.

I'd hung suspended for three days, forced to lift myself every couple of hours to get air. The metal cuffs rubbed and bit into my wrists until they finally lowered me to the ground.

I trace the thick scars thoughtfully. The wounds were not deep enough to nick my arteries, but there had been no skin left beneath the steel. Now I wear permanent shackles made of white scars, and all who see them know the trauma of my past. Every mark on my body tells a story of an injury, a punishment. There is no escaping my time as a slave. A person without choice. A prisoner. *The exact thing I've made my wife.*

I need to speak with her. Resolved to sort this out, I don't even alert my generals before storming back to my tent. I yank the flap to the side and call out, "Lamb, we need to—"

Silence.

On the empty bed is a piece of folded white parchment. With a frown, I pick it up and open it. I scowl, trying to understand her curving scratches of ink on the page. I am a grown man, a Commander, and a child taught me a basic skill. Even with all the work I have put into it, I still have not perfected it. I dread every letter I open, knowing that someone is watching me patiently, waiting for me to finish. Charlotte doesn't know who I used to be, only who I am now—conqueror, warrior, husband.

E...V...A...N..D...E...R

My lips twitch of their own accord. This is the first time I've ever read my entire name. I'm Commander to most, General to others, Evan to a few, but to her, I'm *Evander*. At least I know that it's not a ruse or a ransom letter. I pause for a moment, tracing my fingers along her elegant script, mouthing my name.

I try to focus on the letters, the scratches swimming in my mind, recalling all the lessons the Boy and I went through. I take a deep breath and reach for patience, forcing myself to continue reading.

Gone...for...a walk. Return...by...nightfall.
-Princess...Charlotte

I trace my fingers over her name, a soft smile curving my lips. *Charlotte.* I suppose I should call her that. Most married couples use each other's first names, at least those with any sort of familiarity do. But she won't be Charlotte to me, not yet. Right now, she's *lamb, my* lost lamb who might be a tigress in disguise. Wait. She went for a walk? Alone?!

"Boy!" I shout, crushing the note in my fist. My squire bolts into the tent a moment later, his shirt on backward and struggling to get his eyes open. I know he tries to catch an extra nap after morning drills before continuing his chores. Squires learn early on to get sleep when they can, where they can. It is the sign of a good squire and a better knight to sleep lightly.

Last night when I slept with her in my arms, I had to adjust. I woke at every slight movement, to every change in her breathing. I was not used to sleeping in a bed, let alone with another person, but I will adapt.

My squire blinks his eyes again, trying to pull up his eyelids, and yawns so big his jaw pops. "C-Commander, you called me?"

Right, the note.

"Have you seen my wife?" I snap at him. Two days of marriage, and she's already changing me. I don't know enough about her to tell if she's changing with me or if this metamorphosis is one-sided. What if she's not changing? What if I'm changing for the worse?

I understand the idea of change, the necessity of it, and I plan to change the entire continent, but myself? I hadn't planned on my marriage having any real impact on me at all. It was something that needed to be done. Now, I'm stuck with a wife I'm developing an unhealthy obsession for, and is currently missing.

"N-no, I haven't seen her. Is she missing?" He stumbles through his words, still in the process of waking up. His light brown hair is hanging into his barely open eyes, and his features are disproportionate on his face, having yet to grow into them. He grew over a foot in the last year, and he's still attempting to get a handle on his overly long limbs. He often runs into things, like low-hanging tree branches, not used to his new height. It is a source of mirth for the generals, who enjoy ribbing my young squire.

Missing. What if she ran? What if she had been manipulating me, hoping for me to lower my guard enough for her to run?

Did she write that note to distract me and throw me off the scent? Could she have sensed my need to keep her isolated from her family and make her cling to me? Is this her way of telling me that my words meant nothing?

Ancients above, this woman is turning me inside out. I don't question myself like this. I make decisions, act with surety, and I know the next step and the ten that follow it. I do not waiver on my actions.

My hand tightens on the note. "Summon the generals. We need to plot an assault on the palace. I'm getting my wife back."

He stutters in shock, "Are you...you sure?"

My eyes narrow on my squire, and his gaze darts to the ground as he bows. "I'll notify them right away."

With him out of the room, I tilt my head to either side, trying to calm myself. But the panic and anger only grow, twisting inside me, reaching out to poison my thoughts and breath.

I'm going to get her back. She's mine, and no one will stand in the way of that.

No one.

XVII

Charlotte

OUTSIDE ILIUM

KINGDOM OF CANDONIA

The forest is peaceful and quiet. It reminds me of the palace gardens where I used to do most of my best thinking. The fresh air and silence of the woods give me the chance to examine all the questions shoving at my mind. The sound of the wind whistling through the leaves and the birds twittering in the trees are the only things to disturb my solitude. I can pretend to be whoever I want to be in the forest, not the person everyone expects me to be. A perfect princess who has her life together. The one who knows everything about the kingdom. The one who has answers to every question and problem that arises. There is no one to impress out here other than myself.

I sigh softly and take a seat on a log in a small clearing. The sunlight shines on a meadow, the wildflowers vibrant beneath the golden rays. I look up at the clouds, counting them as I try to sort my thoughts and calm my mind.

Nobody stopped me from leaving camp, which I thought was strange. Every time I have tried to leave the tent, someone was there to stop me. Although, there is no need for anyone to watch the tent when Evander is with me. He'd stormed out in a fit of anger and must not have told anyone that he was leaving me alone. Or does he trust me not to leave now?

I bury my face in my hands as I continue to think. Lately, I feel like my mind is not my own. I am overwhelmed with all these changes in my life, and I have barely had any time to myself, let alone time to process it. In the weeks leading up to the attack on our city, I was always with my father. There were new developments daily, and in most cases, we needed to make decisions quickly. It was so stressful, and we hardly ate or slept. We knew our end was coming. When Evan the Black set his sights on you, it is only a matter of time. Though, I never pictured this.

I thought my mind would be at rest once the war between my country and Evander ended. No one else has to die, and there can be peace in the kingdom again. I can still feel the tension that hangs in the air above the camp. There seems to be none between Evander and me anymore, but I can feel it with the others. Lorcan, the youngest of the generals, seems to have the most issues with me. The others were all polite, most likely reserving judgment, but Lorcan spoke his disdain of me to my face. The purpose of it? To ensure I know I don't belong and that they will never trust me. It burns me.

But who could blame them? We have been at war for years. How many of their men killed my own? How many of mine killed their friends? There is no reason for these men to like me or even trust me. *I am their enemy.*

Then I think of Ben. He told me he trusted me when I said I didn't intend to hurt Evander. He didn't have to say that to me. There is no reason for Ben to believe me at all, but he sounded genuine about it.

I sigh. There is no way out now. I should be trying to make this marriage work between Evander and me. Yet, I keep looking for other things to focus on, away from the true issue. *What is wrong with me?*

I focus on my breathing, my eyes drifting close. When I was a teenager, my father taught me to look for issues in the smallest things, preparing me for the day I become queen. If you don't think of every possible outcome, you will surely be blindsided by one.

I have always had to be on my guard, trusting no one but my father and sisters. When I'm with Evander, I don't feel like I have to be anyone but myself. His touch and kiss clear my mind, and I feel more like myself than ever before.

Ancients, I should hate him. He was my enemy, but I never felt a connection like this to anyone. I tried to attack him the moment we met. He knew I hated him, but he has shown me another side of him. I wonder if it is fate that we met, and this experience is meant to change our paths. The only question now is, will it be for the better? For both of us?

My parents. They were like Evander and I. Enemies for years. Their marriage mending the damage our ancestors created. They managed to fall in love. Soulmates woven by the Fates. But the Fates don't always work in someone's favor. This thing between Evander and I could be just some sort of sick amusement. To let me believe that there could be loved stemmed from the deep hatred we have for one another.

I sigh and look up, watching the sunlight filter through the leaves. I gasp as a small bird lands on a branch and studies me. The dove has a blue streak that runs from the tip of its head to its tail feathers. It is a dove of Devika. Rumor has it that if you pray to the dove or ask it a question, she may answer. I have never tried it, mostly because I never went searching for the bird, but Eleanor has a few times. She asked questions about our parents, and apparently, Devika answered her. Eleanor would not tell me what the Ancient said.

I place a hand on my chest, looking into the eyes of the little bird. *Might as well give this a shot.*

"Ancient of the Love and Heart, Devika, please answer my prayer. Tell me why my heart continues to pull towards the conqueror, Evan the Black. I am supposed to hate him, yet I feel like I am starting to fall in love with him. Is he my soulmate? Please tell me. I need to understand," I whisper.

Silence. There is nothing but the wind and the sound of birds chirping in the trees. I should have known better than to think the old wives' tale was true. My sister has abilities that I have seen no one else possess. Maybe that is how she got her answers. That, or it is not time for me to know the truth.

If only it were simple.

There is a rustle in the bushes, and I sit up straighter, my attention snapping toward the sound. Is it an assassin? Did someone follow me into the woods? The hairs on the back of my neck stand up, and I brace myself for what is coming.

Suddenly, a small rabbit hops out from the bushes, and I tilt my head. *Wonderful Charlotte. You're scared of a bunny.*

I look down at the little creature. Its grey fur shimmers in the sunlight as it nibbles on the grass. Rabbits are the animal of the Ancient Taerel, and after asking for a sign from Devika, I can't help but think that maybe this is fate answering my question.

"Hello, little guy." The bunny only blinks, its whiskers moving back and forth. I can't help but feel a twinge of jealousy. This rabbit gets to be free, out of the palace walls and away from the eyes of others. It can come and go whenever it wants. "You have it so easy. All you need to worry about is shelter and food."

A wolf howls in the distance, and I frown.

"You have enemies as well." I have enemies like that, ones who will do anything to kill. They steal everything and leave you nothing but bare bones. It is exhausting.

"I don't want to fight anymore. I just want peace. How do I show Evander I mean no harm?"

Silence. This is pointless. Why send me a sign when there is no actual answer? Then again, the Ancients are known to be vague and speak in riddles.

I look back at the bunny and smile. "Thank you for listening, little guy."

The rabbit blinks a few times before jumping back into the bush. I stand from the log, brushing the wrinkles from my dress.

"I should get back to camp. I have already been away long enough," I whisper to myself, turning away from my spot. On the walk back to the camp, I feel lighter. Now that I have had time to think and organize my thoughts, I am calmer, and although I don't have a plan, I am ready to move forward with Evander. It is almost like a weight has been lifted from my shoulders.

When I arrive, the men are running around camp, preparing for something. Half of them look confused, while others are stretching their arms, hungry for a fight. My stomach twists as fear grips me. Something must be wrong. Men are strapping on their armor while others are gathering supplies. Is there an attack on the castle? Has someone attempted to attack the camp? More worries crowd my already busy mind, and I knit my brows as I rush to my tent. As I get closer, I can hear the commotion from inside. Opening the tent flap, I am not surprised to see my husband with his generals.

"What is going on?" I ask.

XVIII

EVAN

OUTSIDE ILIUM

KINGDOM OF CANDONIA

My body goes rigid at the sound of her voice. I grip the edges of the desk, stopping myself from whirling around and castigating her publicly for worrying me. All of my generals look at me, varying expressions on their faces. They filter out of the tent, and wisely none of them speak, at least not loud enough for me to hear.

"E-Evander?" she stutters, and my shoulders coil tighter. Normally, the sound of my name on her lips makes me happy. Right now, it infuriates me. Doesn't she know what she is coming to mean to me? Doesn't she know that I just might need her?

My hands fist at my sides as I slowly turn to her, stopping myself from closing the distance between us. I want to slam my lips to hers and then lecture her repeatedly. *Gods, when did I become such a swain?* I need to break this hold she has on me. I'm losing myself with every passing minute in her presence, and I don't know what I am becoming.

"Where were you?" I grind out through clenched teeth.

The tent flap falls shut behind her, closing her in with me. Her sapphire eyes are frantically scanning my face, no doubt looking for some hint of my mood. "Th-the forest."

I cross my arms over my chest, trying to control my need to grab her and never let go. *What is happening to me?*

She chews her lip. "I-I left a n-note."

It's strange to hear her stutter. I'm used to her carefully formed thoughts and sentences. She must be terrified of my reaction if she is stuttering. At the moment, I'm not sure how I will react.

The realization that she was, in fact, walking alone in the woods tempers my need to grab her and hold on. "Do you have any idea who you are now?"

Her lips press into a line, and she shakes her head. I grind my teeth. By the time a month passes with her, I'm going to have pulverized them into dust. Does she not know the target resting on her back? How many enemies would kill or torture her just to get at me? "You are my...weakness."

Fuck, I meant *wife*, not weakness. Though she's both now, isn't she? Already I'm plagued with constant thoughts of her, guessing at her thoughts and feelings. Involuntarily, I step closer, hovering above her.

She looks up at me, her brows furrowing. "Y-your weakness?"

I run my hands through my hair.

I have no weakness. Except you. Never have I held so tightly to something, hoping to keep it. Never have I been so decimated at the mere *thought* of losing it.

She chews her lower lip again. "W-why me?"

I have no idea, but it's you, "You're...my wife."

Ancients, that is brilliant. I can't come up with anything better?

She blinks slowly, her sapphire eyes locked on mine. "And if I died tomorrow. You would still have a claim to the throne."

My hand grips the back of her neck, and I growl, "You will not die on me."

Her hands go to my chest. "You...you really do care about me."

Fuck, I think I just might. I don't know how it happened so fast, but I do care. I don't know how she feels, but I can only hope I am not alone in this. Could she possibly be caught in the same tumultuous hurricane of emotions?

"I was preparing to come for you in the palace." *I was prepared to burn the world down to get you back.*

"Why?" she asks with a frown, and I don't have an answer. I can't explain what I'm feeling or even begin to understand it. "Evander?"

Evander. The sound of her saying my name is a balm to my lingering anxiety. Only she calls me Evander, the name I used to shudder and recoil at, instead fills me with warmth. The tension in my shoulders and jaw eases.

"Every time you call me that..." Her hands drop from my chest, and the words tumble from my lips unbidden, sharing the monstrous truth with her. "It was my slave name."

Her face pales. "What?"

I squeeze my eyes shut, regretting the words the moment I say them. I hadn't meant to tell Charlotte that. Over the years, I've had various reactions to the truth, the most common being horror. I don't know if I am ready to face her disgust. Disgust that she allowed me to touch her, that she's wed to me. That she, a princess, was forced into marriage with a former slave. I open my eyes in surprise when she takes my hand, glancing down at the smooth alabaster of her skin against mine.

"Why would you want me to call you that name?" Charlotte asks, her voice gentle.

"I thought you could reclaim it for me." The truth slips from my lips, and I flinch back slightly. Is that why? I want her to reclaim the name I shed twelve years ago? A name that usually fills me with self-disgust makes me melt when she whispers it.

I'm losing my mind.

She goes onto her tiptoes, kissing me softly. "I would be honored to reclaim it."

I dig the fingers of my free hand into her hair, slamming my lips to hers. Her hand releases mine, moving to the back of my neck, keeping me close. Yet that doesn't ease the gnawing anxiety in my stomach. She is so vulnerable, a glaring weakness waiting to be exploited by any of my numerous enemies. Pressing my forehead to hers, I order, "You cannot go out on your own anymore, lamb. Promise me."

"I promise."

I kiss up and down the soft skin of her neck, whispering into her ear, "It's for your own safety."

She moans, tilting her head to the side, exposing the vulnerable line of her throat. "I understand."

Fuck, this is a serious discussion, not a time for seduction. It would be easier if she didn't smell so incredible. What is she using on her skin? It has to be some kind of addictive substance.

I pull away from her and shake my head to clear the lingering scent of her, trying to focus. "I have many enemies who would delight in getting their hands on you."

She nods, "I know."

"You will be a target for them."

She buries her face against my neck. "I um..."

The weight of her is comforting as I lift her into my arms and carry her to bed. I just need to hold on to her. I toe off my boots and demand, "Tell me."

She gazes up at me from our bed, and my mind blanks for a minute. "I have enemies of my own in the kingdom."

"You do?" She's the princess. Are there anti-monarchy groups after her? More people who will try to take her from me? *Never.*

"I passed a law two years ago that made many people angry."

I pull my shirt and breeches off before crawling onto the bed with her and slipping under the furs. She wraps her arms around me, nuzzling my chest. I love that she already clings to me, that she crawls into my arms without me having to do anything. We are enemies forced into a marriage and should still be at odds. Yet, I'm delighting in her wrapping her arms around my chest.

"A law?"

She nods against my chest. "Yes. It enraged those who it affected, but many others were happy. I don't regret it."

"What was the law?"

She pauses for a moment and then whispers, "I outlawed slavery."

A sudden roaring blares in my ears, and I'm not sure I heard her correctly. "What?"

Her eyes go wide. "I, um, outlawed slavery."

I must have heard her wrong. I sit up, looking down at her, my ears still ringing. "You outlawed slavery?"

She nods, sitting up beside me. "I know that there are people who aren't following the law. I have been trying to track them down, but I have had little success since we had to spend our efforts on the war." My cheeks heat, and my body tenses. She feels the change in me and looks up. "Have I said something wrong?"

Wait, did she say that they would have been pursuing slavers if not for me? "I stopped you from going after them?" I think I'm going to be sick.

Her mouth opens and closes. "Sort of."

My body stiffens. "So I might have made more slaves?"

"No!"

She wraps herself around me. Her legs go around my waist and her arms around my chest, locking me to her. "Evander."

I try to disentangle from her, but she clings to me. She refuses to let go. "We will free them together."

My throat works as I try to swallow. Charlotte did more with a single law reform than I did in twelve years of conquering.

The true reason for taking Candonia. It is the center of the entire continent of Aellolyn, between the North and South countries, and all trade funnels through it. If you make an enemy of Candonia, you are cut off from essential supplies. Every country has a major export, Ciral provides most of the fish to the rest of the continent; Grimmwing provides steel and timber; Vredour is where coffee, tea, and spices are grown;

Steodia provides the grain; Vruica exports a majority of livestock; Xiapia is famous for the pelt trade; Kolia's fruits and vegetables are cropped out. It all comes to market in Candonia, The Jewel of Aellolyn, which made it the perfect place to install myself as king and institute widespread change, abolishing slavery. But apparently, I'm too late, my ambitions and dreams already completed by another.

She whispers, "Yes, I outlawed slavery, but there are those who continue to do it. I need you."

She doesn't, though, not truly. I'm two years too late. Although, no other country has followed Candonia's example, except for the ones coerced by me. The enforcement of these laws will fall on my shoulders but could easily be done by royal patrols.

"You don't."

She places her hands on my cheeks, our eyes connecting. "I do."

I cover her hands with mine and ask, "Why? Why do you need me?"

"I can't do this alone."

You already have. I'm not needed. Charlotte doesn't need me. Nobody does. I'm nothing, and I'm no one. Nothing but a slave trying to change a world that doesn't care.

She kisses me again, crawling around my body to my lap, never releasing her hold on me. Her touch grounds me, pulling me back to the present. I fall back on the bed, pulling her on top of me. She straddles my hips, her lips finding mine. "People don't believe I can do this."

You think a slave can make a difference, boy? You will always be tainted by your origins, no matter how many you kill or free. You will never be more than a slave. Unclean. Worthless. Scum.

I frown into her kiss, pulling away to ask, "And you think we can? Together?"

"Together." Something about the way she says it, so matter-of-factly, makes me believe it a bit more. Ancients, I can't believe I ever thought her weak. I must have forgotten how strength is not just the physical, but the emotional as well. In that, Charlotte has no equal. Her determination to change the world shines like a star inside her, eclipsing even the biting insecurities plaguing me. She may have outlawed the practice, but enforcement is lacking, and that is an area where I excel.

Her hands roam my chest. She grabs the ties of her dress, pulling them roughly, loosening them. She stands and undresses before straddling me again. Her hands tunnel into my hair, keeping me locked to her.

I wrap my arms around her and roll, pinning her beneath me. I kiss down her neck, growling, "You're teasing me."

Her sapphire eyes are hazy with lust. "Am I?"

I nip at her shoulder and along her arm before kissing her hand. "You know the effect you have on me."

Already. The effect you have on me already.

She bites her lip, shaking her head. "Tell me."

"How about I show you instead?" I say with a wicked grin and grab her hips roughly, yanking her higher until she's straddling my mouth. I'm aching to be inside her, but I know she's sore. I'll have to settle for making her writhe against my tongue. My eyes roll back, and I growl at the first taste of her.

"Evander!" she screams, throwing her head back.

I take long, slow licks, growling at the taste of her, pausing to look up wishing I could say, *all I can think of is getting inside you, kissing you, touching you.* A thousand other things. But mostly, making sure that every inch of her belongs to me and is touched by me. I want her to need me.

She grips my hair as I pull her tighter against my mouth, almost tearing it from the roots. "I think I'm addicted to you," she pants between moans.

Charlotte keens in pleasure as I suck harder on her needy clit. I pause, blowing cool air onto her swollen folds. I bring her close to release, then level her off, again and again, not letting her fall over the edge. My hand lands hard on her ass, leaving red outlines on her alabaster skin. Primal instincts driving me to leave some part of me imprinted on her, marking her as mine.

"Never stop," Charlotte pants, riding my mouth frantically, pushed past any kind of control. The sight of her so lost in the throes of pleasure is my undoing. I fist my cock, pumping it hard, wishing I was inside her.

My heels dig into the bed, my back arching. I can't stop, and I need to take everything brimming inside me out on her body. I flick my tongue over her clit and then graze my teeth against the sensitive nub. Her entire body shakes and she screams, tightening her thighs around my face. Her orgasm bows her back, and she presses hard against my mouth. I'm right behind her, losing control as she comes, my seed shooting from me.

My body feels empty and hollowed out, but I don't think I have ever felt such peace. I release her, and she slips off me, collapsing on the bed. Charlotte drapes herself over my chest, our bodies damp and our limbs lax. Will I ever get enough of her? Will there ever be a time I'm not an untried youth around her?

Silence falls between us, punctuated by the sound of our shallow breaths.

XIX

Charlotte

OUTSIDE ILIUM

KINGDOM OF CANDONIA

Silence. The only sound is our breathing, ragged and heavy. The more we connect, the more I crave him. He is like a sickness in my mind, and a part of me doesn't mind. We are different when it is just the two of us, not a princess or a conqueror, just two lovers. The bond between us continues to grow with each touch and kiss, and I am not fighting it anymore. Our goals are aligned. We are two people constantly doubted by the perceptions of the people around us. For me, people see my gender and assume I have nothing of value to contribute. For him, they learn of his past, and he's ostracized. I want to welcome this feeling of kinship and pray it never fades away.

"What are you doing to me?" he asks, his breath shaking. His question has me smiling to myself. So, he feels it too, this strange need to be with each other constantly. These ties are growing stronger, binding us closer with each day that passes.

I open my eyes and turn to look at him. My chest is still rising and falling heavily as I try to catch my breath. "You? W-what are you doing to me?"

He laughs shakily, propping up onto his elbows up, but he collapses back into the bed within seconds. "I have to leave tomorrow."

The idea makes my heart freeze in my chest. Leave? What does he mean, leave?

"Why?" I ask.

"Why what?" he asks, raising a brow.

"Why do you have to go?" I move closer to him. Perhaps there is a chance I can convince him to stay. After all, the war is over. There shouldn't be any reason for him to leave.

"I do have other duties," he says. He wraps his arms around my back, pulling me into his side. I place my hand on his chest, his heart still beating quickly under my fingers.

"But we just started to—" I cut myself off, my heart aching more. *Why does it hurt me so much that Evander is leaving?*

"Started what?" He frowns, his perfect brows knitting together in thought.

"Getting to know each other," I whisper. There are so many questions I have for Evander. Simple ones like his favorite meal and what he likes to do when he isn't conquering? Then there are the complicated ones, like what made you choose Candonia? What made you choose me? That one question has been at the back of my mind since our wedding night. *Why me?* And then there is that unexplained connection between us that keeps pulling me closer to him.

"I'll be gone for a month, maybe two," he says nonchalantly.

"A month?!" I sit up.

"Not that long."

Not that long? My heart sinks, and I press a hand to my chest, trying to stop the pain. How does he think a month without seeing each other will work? Am I still just another tool to him? A pawn to be used and discarded? Does he not want to get to know me like I want to get to know him?

He frowns at me, obviously confused. *Will he not miss me?* "I doubt you'll even notice I'm gone."

I blink, tearing up. "I will."

"You will?" he questions, brushing the hair back from my face. I lay back down on him, sniffling. *Do you not feel this pull to me like I feel to you?*

"I will," I whisper, rubbing my cheek against him. The thought of being alone in camp is dark and lonely. Not only will he be gone, but I will be surrounded by men who hate me. Some may even do anything to see me dead.

"Lamb," he says. He sighs heavily, running his fingers through my hair. "I'm just going to check on an alliance we haven't heard from in a while. I'll be back."

I inhale deeply, taking in his scent. I close my eyes, struggling to come to terms with my emotions. Every time something happens between us, the bond seems to strengthen. He conquered my kingdom, forced me into marriage, and surrounded me on all sides with men loyal to him. Yet, a part of me no longer wishes to change any of it. Our goals seem to be aligned. With him, I know I will be able to implement my plans once I become queen. With him, I know that when I pass a new law, he will support it because it is something he wants as well. I know we will make a good team, and he will protect me and our kingdom with his life.

Our union might be what is best for both our people. Maybe it is what is best for me as well. When he calls me lamb, my heart flutters in my chest. When he looks at me, my entire body feels warm. Even now, in his arms, I feel safe and protected. That is something I haven't felt since my mother died and my father married that woman, then disappeared from my sisters' lives.

Evander fists his hand in my hair and gently tips my head back, interrupting my thoughts. I peek at him from beneath lowered lashes, his lips brushing against mine as he says, "Shh, you are thinking too hard. Sleep, lamb."

He kisses me deeply and then tucks me tighter against his body, holding me close. My mind is always running, always working. I hardly sleep because of it, but Evander manages to

126

calm my thoughts with a simple kiss. My leg rests on his thigh, and the heat of him relaxes me more. He kisses the top of my head, and I am at peace, exhaustion finally taking over.

I sit in the garden, waiting for my mother to meet me. She often spends a few times a week with me, going over lessons she learned when she was a child. Though I am only seven, she wants me well prepared for the day I become queen. After all, one never knows when the people they love can be taken from them. I only hope that it won't be for a long time.

Picking a daisy from the grass, I start to pick one petal off at a time. I repeat the phrase "He loves me" and "He loves me not". Something one of the younger maids taught me. They say if you land on "He loves me" at the last petal, then the person you are thinking of has to love you back.

I am thinking about Greyson. He is the son of a lord from Vruica. The boy is just a few years older than me, and rumor has it all the girls my age have a crush on him. I met him a couple of times, and I thought he was quite handsome. I promised myself that he would be my husband when I reach the age of eighteen.

Pausing at the final petal, I frown. "He loves me not."

I sigh, allowing the last petal to fall to the stone walkway. I guess he will not be my husband then. The sound of someone clearing their throat makes me jump, and I turn to face my mother. She is smiling brightly at me, her eyes filled with love. Her long blonde hair is tied back in an elegant updo like always, and her crown rests on top. Her facial features are soft and small, and some would call her delicate. My mother is only five and a half feet tall compared to my father, who is several inches over six feet. Though that doesn't stop her from gaining the room's attention. She always manages to have all eyes on her, her soft voice the most powerful I have ever heard. My mother takes a seat beside me.

"You know, Charlotte," she says, "you shouldn't settle for anyone who doesn't truly love you."

I tilt my head. "I shouldn't?"

She shakes her head and rests her hand on my cheek before she looks out at the garden.

"You should marry for love." She sighs. "Many men will want to strip your power from you, all the while claiming to love you. Do not believe them unless you feel it in here."

My mother looks down at me and points to my heart. I frown and place my tiny hand on my chest, thinking.

"How will I know?" I ask.

She laughs. "Always a thinker, aren't you, my daughter?"

I nod, moving closer to my mother. Her presence is always comforting. "Well, there will be a pull to them. It is something you can't deny, no matter how hard you try. Your soulmate should feel the same and should want to give you the world."

"My soulmate?" I ask.

"The one who will love you until the end of time." She looks up as my father enters the garden.

"How are my two favorite girls?" he asks. Thalia runs up behind him, frowning. She is only five years old but has the sass of a teenager. My father looks down at her and laughs. "You are my favorite too, Thalia."

Thalia smiles brightly, hugging our father before running to me. She looks at the torn-up flower and frowns.

"Why did you do that?" she asks.

My face burns, and I hide the stem of the flower behind my back. "It was nothing!"

Our mother laughs before getting up from the stone bench. She walks to our father, wrapping her arms around him. For a moment, I see it. A red string that loops around them, pulling them closer together. I sigh softly, placing a hand on my chest. Thalia makes a vomiting sound, crossing her arms.

"Gross." She shudders.

My mother looks back at us. "You will get married one day, Thalia."

My sister shakes her head. "Never! I will never, ever, ever get married."

128

We all laugh, and she pouts to herself. Her stubbornness is as strong as ever. I look back up at my mother and father, hoping that I will find what they have one day. I vow not to marry anyone but my soulmate.

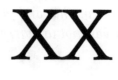

XX

EVAN

OUTSIDE ILIUM

KINGDOM OF CANDONIA

My eyes open slowly, the sound of raised voices pulling me from sleep. I *napped*. I didn't know that was even possible. But I was so exhausted from the worry over my wife that my eyes closed, allowing me to drift off. Whoever just woke me better have an excellent reason for doing so. My wife is curled against my side, her hand resting on my chest, and I hold my breath, waiting to see if the shouting will wake her. The smoldering fire in our tent casts shadows on us but provides enough light to see the lines of her face. Why didn't anyone come to wake me? Even in rest, her brow is furrowed, likely trying to work out some complicated problem in her dreams. Does she wonder about this connection we have? This pull?

The shouting continues, and I try to disentangle myself from her. It's only an annoyance to wake me, but if they wake her, someone is going to die.

Charlotte's hand twitches, her elegant fingers digging into the hair on my chest, trying to keep me with her.

That's it. Someone is going to die.

"What is it?" she mumbles, her eyes blinking open. Even hazy with sleep, her gaze sears me.

I sit up and glare at the tent flap where the voices filter in from right outside. The tent is composed of a main support pole at the center and a wooden frame, all embedded into the ground. Thick canvas drapes the structure, held taught by steel stakes at the edges. Though it's usually enough to dull the sounds of the camp outside, sometimes a very unwise soldier would make too much noise, and I'm reminded of how not alone I am. When you sleep light, anything wakes you, even the sound of a soldier's drunken carousing a few tents over. It is even more shocking that I fell asleep in the middle of the day when the camp is at its loudest. *What's happening to me?*

The shouting continues, and I pull Charlotte's fingers from my chest, whispering, "Go back to sleep, lamb, I'll take care of it."

I'll kill them.

She sits up, rubbing her eyes and yawning big, her jaw popping. "It sounds like kids?"

I lean over and kiss her hard. "Go to sleep."

I swing my legs over the side of the bed. I find a pair of breeches in my trunk and pull them on. One of the trunks, the well-worn one which has clearly seen better days, keeps my clothing, all of them stitched and restitched from wear over the years. The Boy learned how to sew as part of his duties as my squire and often mends my clothes.

The three other trunks, all shiny and new, belong to my wife, and I seem to be on a mission to empty the gowns and chemises within them, tearing them to shreds when we are intimate. Along with her clothes, more of her things were delivered from the palace. A privacy screen and another tub, along with an array of fresh-smelling soaps and perfumes, fill the tent with her feminine scent. There is a writing desk, a stack of books already leaning against one of its legs, and hundreds of quills.

Our tent is becoming cluttered, and I grumble as I search for my boots. I find them drying next to the embers still burning in the brazier. My gaze falls on a pair of her delicate blue slippers, and I make a mental note to get boots made for her. Those tiny things she calls shoes will be worn down living in camp. She's not walking over expensive carpets and gleaming marble anymore.

Charlotte sits up, reaching for a new chemise in one of her trunks, slipping it on. "Why are you grumbling?"

"I don't like being pulled away from you even for a moment." I shoot a glare at the tent flap. "Especially when it sounds like my squire is the culprit."

The Boy is going to be doing chores until he drops to the ground from exhaustion. He knows better than to wake me up.

A loud female scream rips out, making me touch my ears at the pitch. That could not be human. Only dogs are supposed to be able to reach that level of howling.

I storm out of the tent, and I find my squire with his hand wrapped around a young girl's arm, dragging her out of camp. She's screaming at him, flailing ineffectually in his grip, and digging in her heels. The platinum hair tells me immediately who the girl is.

"Boy!"

My wife comes out behind me, having slipped on a robe over her chemise. "Eleanor?"

My squire freezes, releasing the young princess, who falls back onto the ground. At the sound of my voice, he whirls around, bowing his head slightly to me. "I was just getting her back to the palace, Commander."

The young princess lets out a large oof, glaring at my squire. "Jerk."

I step forward and glower down at the young princess. "And why are you here?"

She points her finger at my squire, sticking her tongue out at him. "He promised to sneak me in so I could see something!"

My squire lets out a snarl that makes my brows shoot up in surprise. I have never seen the Boy express such vitriol towards anyone. His youthful face turns completely savage when he's angry, and I can, for a moment, see the man he will become.

The young princess snaps her teeth back at him, and my wife steps to my side, frowning at her sister. "You know better than to sneak away from the palace."

The young princess gazes up at us. For a moment, I think her eyes change color but it must be a trick of the torchlight. She scrambles to her feet, her breeches and shirt clearly stolen and covered in mud. Half of her ethereal hair is in a braid, the other half completely wild, as if she sprinted away from whoever was attempting to tame her.

My eyes narrow on them both. I did not need to have my sleep interrupted for this. "Get her back to the palace, Boy. I don't want her in camp again."

The young princess's big eyes tear up before she storms off. My squire pauses for a moment before chasing after her.

Charlotte touches my arm and sighs, pulling my gaze back to her. "I'm sorry about that."

"What was that about?"

She glances at her sister's back and the Boy chasing after her. Her hand drops from my arm. "Nothing."

I cross my arms over my bare chest and turn to face her with a frown. It's clear she is keeping something from me. It practically vibrates in the air between us. "Tell me."

Her gaze locks with mine, and she worries her lower lip before whispering, "In private."

She takes my hand and pulls, leading me back to our tent and closing the flap behind us. She keeps her hand locked on mine, pressing closer to me. "You cannot tell anyone what I am about to tell you."

"I do know how to keep a secret." Though, all my closely held truths seem to tumble from my lips in her presence.

Her hand drops from mine. Her gorgeous face is pale, and she is wringing her hands together. "Evander. This is serious."

I cross my arms again and raise a brow, waiting for her to continue. Whatever she needs to tell me can't be as bad as she's making it out to be.

"We believe Eleanor has powers," she says, her eyes locking on my face and scanning my features. Did she think this was a secret?

The young princess emits a low hum from her aura. Even a cursory glance at her indicates she is more than most. Likely she's more attuned to the *Old Ways* as I am. Since I was a child, I could move faster, hit harder, see farther than most. In the time of the High Sorcerers, I would have been considered one of the *Blessed*, touched by one of the Ancients, and gifted with unique abilities. At one time, the Blessed were revered, but now we are simply oddities of a past era of magic. "And?"

Her hands continue wringing, her knuckles white. "Lately, she has an obsession with one of her abilities. She looks for soulmates. Her belief is that if you don't marry someone that is your soulmate, you will suffer."

I can't hold my scoff at that. "Soulmates? There's no such thing."

"You don't believe me?"

"I don't believe in soulmates, but I know your sister has powers."

The latter is undeniable, but I have yet to see any proof of the former.

I've been to the North Wardens' sanctuary in Grimmwing, the last remaining sanctuary left of the Great Magic Age, and seen things there that have been lost to time and reduced to myth. I've traveled all over Aellolyn and even met other Blessed, like myself. I have seen the little bit of magic left in our world. But never have I seen evidence that when a person is born, their soul is tied to another's. A decision, a *choice* made for you.

She shakes her head, her eyes going wide. "You don't believe in soulmates?"

"I've been all over Aellolyn, and I've seen nothing to make me believe in soulmates."

She turns away from me sharply, her hands going to her mouth. Her entire body is rigid, and her shoulders slightly

134

slumped. If I didn't know any better, I would say she looks *defeated,* but that doesn't make any sense.

"What?"

Why is she so upset? I don't have much experience with deciphering emotions. I have experience with battles, sieges, and soldiers, but my wife's emotions leave me...lost.

She crosses her arms, still facing away from me. "I happen to believe it."

"You said yourself you've never been outside of the castle. You haven't seen the things I have."

She shoots a dark look over her shoulder at me. "I've seen enough."

"Lamb..." She hasn't seen what I have, the horrors I have. She would know if she had. The more fanciful tellings of the Ancients are just tales. Only evil is real.

She looks away from me again. "I would like to be alone."

I flinch back at the coldness in her voice, icy tendrils reaching out across the small distance between us. She thinks I'm punishing her, that I'm wrong for not believing what she does. She doesn't want to look at me? Fine. I'll leave. I grab my shirt and leather training armor, snarling, "Fine."

I storm out of the tent for the second time today, leaving my wife behind and trying to figure out what exactly went wrong.

XXI

Charlotte

Soulmates. A concept I have believed in for so long and the thing that has stopped me from marrying on countless occasions. I feel the tug toward Evander, just as my mother described. She told me that once you find that other person, your bond strengthens, and the Ancients of Fate will continue to weave your futures together. You will find yourself thinking of the other person constantly, and time apart will make you feel as if you are less. Any fight will leave you sick and drained. If your soulmate dies after the bond has been established, you will never be the same, a piece of you lost.

Not everyone believes. Many think that the Ancients have abandoned us, but I don't believe that. I have seen things that prove to me they are still out there, their magic flowing through Aellolyn, and that soulmates exist. Evander scoffing at the idea has me heartbroken. It was the one thing I'd clung to when all the suitors pressured my father to take the choice away from me. I thought I was being rewarded for being patient, even if my soulmate arrived in the form of the hated conqueror. But he doesn't believe in soulmates. He thinks I'm a foolish girl, just like all the other men who wanted to take my choice from me. There is no way he feels for me what I feel for him. It's as if I need him to breathe, like a spell was cast at our first kiss. He is mine.

I sigh, scribbling away on a piece of paper as I work in his tent. Evander hasn't returned, and it is almost time for me to turn in for the night. He leaves tomorrow. Maybe he won't come back tonight. Would he go without saying goodbye? My heart twists in my chest at the thought. I place my quill down on the table, sitting back in my wooden chair. There is a trade deal with the Kingdom of Kolia that I need to work out. Queen Seraphina is notoriously ruthless and I need to focus, but I can't stop thinking about our fight. Maybe I should go find him? Will he be mad if I interrupt his drills with the men? Will he even want to talk to me?

Suddenly, the tent flap opens, and I smile to myself, excited to see him. It fades into confusion when I turn to find my sister. Thalia is wearing her training gear like always, plain brown pants and a fitted white shirt. Her brown hair is wild, and worry creases her brow. She looks at me in concern as Demir enters the tent behind her, his squire, Khrys, at his side.

"What are you doing here?" I ask, my heart leaping in my chest. There is only one reason she would be here, and I pray it is not the case.

"I'm looking for Eleanor," she says.

My heart sinks in my chest. *Damn it.* "I thought she was back at the palace? Ben escorted her back?"

I look at Demir, who nods at me. Yet, why do I have the feeling that something went wrong?

"Let's go talk to Ben." I frown, getting up from my chair.

Thalia nods, and we follow Demir to the boy's tent. It is empty, but we spot Ben at the edge of the woods. He is punching a tree, doing little damage to the trunk, but blood drips from his knuckles. That doesn't stop him, his eyes are on fire, and he is focused inward, not even noticing we are here. Something has set him off, and I would bet that Eleanor is to blame. Thalia storms over to the boy and pinches his ear.

"Where is my sister?" she growls at him. Thalia, subtle as ever.

Ben hisses, batting at her. Thalia dodges, anger turning her face bright red. It is strange to see the boy like this. He seems mature for his age, always level-headed. Then again, I haven't known him long.

"Answer," she hisses, not letting go of his ear.

"Thalia, let him go," I demand, and she does so reluctantly.

Ben frowns, rubbing his ear. "She's home."

"She's missing." I sigh, shaking my head.

"She must have run off as soon as you left her," Thalia says, rubbing her chin in thought.

Ben frowns for a moment before turning towards the forest. "Shit!" he says and takes off, sprinting between the trees.

Thalia huffs, looking up at Demir. "I'm going to need a sword and a torch."

"And what are you going to do with that?" I ask her, scoffing. As much as I want to go find my sister, I know that there is uncertainty in these woods at night.

Thalia walks in the direction of the camp, shouting back at me, "I am going to find our sister."

Demir steps in front of Thalia, signing quickly to Khrys, who translates. My sister knows sign language. She began learning the day she found out one of her maids was deaf. Thalia dislikes anyone in the palace feeling unwelcome, and it was her way of making the girl feel at home. The two of them are now close friends. The question, though, is why didn't she tell him she could understand him?

"Oh, no. I am not going back to the tent! I am going to look for her, and you can't stop me!" Thalia shouts and steps around him. In a quick movement, Demir pinches Thalia's neck, and she collapses onto the ground. I raise my brow as he meets my gaze, the question in his eyes clear. *Nope.*

"I'll just walk back to the tent," I say before turning and hurrying in that direction. He picks Thalia up, throwing her over his shoulder before following behind me. I hold the tent flap aside for Demir, and he steps inside. He drops my sister and she groans as she lands on the rugs. Demir looks at me and points to the ground, indicating that he wants me to stay here before he walks out. I throw my hands up in frustration and begin pacing the confines of the tent. Thalia's eyes slowly open, and she rubs her bum.

"Asshole," she mutters.

"He is only trying to protect us," I say, crossing my arms.

"I don't need protecting!" Thalia shouts.

I sigh. "Thalia, if Eleanor hasn't returned to the palace by now, then something is wrong. It will do no one any good for you to run off and get lost as well."

Thalia shakes her head before looking away in stony silence. I close my eyes and take a deep breath before continuing to pace. The two of us are falling apart. When did we become this distant? We used to tell each other everything. Help each other out in times of distress, but I know she has been keeping secrets.

I turn toward the entrance a moment before Evander steps into the tent, Demir at his heels. Sweat drips from his body as he yanks off his armor. His hair is sticking to his forehead, and his face is serious.

"How long has she been gone?" he asks, stripping off his clothes. Thalia turns her back with a sneer.

"No one has seen her since Ben left her at the palace."

Evander grabs a fresh set of clothes, dressing quickly before splashing some clean water on his face. My heart pounds in my chest, and I can't tell if it is from fear for Eleanor or desire for my husband.

"The Boy is the best tracker I have. He'll find her," Evander says. He signs something to Demir, who hurries from the tent. Evander must have ordered Demir to do something and used sign language so I wouldn't understand.

I step closer to Evander and take his hand. "You'll find her?"

"I will," he says, rubbing his thumb along my knuckles. His touch soothes me, and for a second, all my worry dissipates. Evander turns to glare at my sister. "Stay here."

Thalia scoffs, crossing her arms, turning back around. "I'm coming as well."

His eyes lock with Thalia's. "You will remain here even if I have to bind you."

Thalia glares at him, mumbling curses under her breath. Evander ignores her, looking back down at me and kissing me softly.

"We will find her," he reassures me, his hands tightening on my waist.

"Promise?" I ask, my eyes filling with tears I refuse to let fall.

He nods. "Keep your sister here. She'll only get in the way."

I look back at Thalia, who is nearly vibrating with fury, before turning back to him. "Alright."

Evander kisses me again before storming out of the tent. As soon as he is gone, the anxiety creeps back into my soul. I let out a long sigh before walking over to my bed and taking a seat. My mind is racing as Thalia paces back and forth, her hands fisted and her breathing quick.

"If they don't find her…" she begins, her voice cracking.

"They will." The words leave my mouth before I can process them, but part of me knows them to be true. Those that dare face my husband most often meet their death. If he promises to find her, he will.

Thalia shakes her head, looking over at me. "How can you trust them? Don't you remember? He stole you! He forced you to marry him, and now you are on his side?!"

I look up at her. "Evander isn't that bad, Lia."

Thalia blinks at me. "Are you listening to yourself right now?!"

"I know it sounds crazy, but give them a chance. It is no use continuing to be their enemy. They aren't as barbaric as we were led to believe," I say. Thinking about everything the past few days has shown me about Evander and his men.

Thalia stays silent for a moment, looking me up and down. "Fine. But if you're wrong—"

"You can tell me I told you so." I smile weakly at her.

Thalia sighs before walking over to the bed and wrapping her arms around me. Her hug is comforting, and I hold her tight. either of us is used to sitting and waiting for something to happen, but at night, in a camp full of men who wished us ill, it is wise to wait for Evan and the Mountain to return. Just because it's the wisest course of action does not make it the easiest. Thalia and I sit in tense silence, our thoughts on our younger sister alone in the woods.

XXII

EVAN

OUTSIDE ILIUM

KINGDOM OF CANDONIA

I throw myself onto the Black, and the horse bolts toward the woods, his nostrils flaring. I guide him along the path left behind by the Boy and the Mountain. The trees fly past me, the horse and I working together, listening for sounds out of place within the forest. It only takes me a few minutes to find them. Eleanor is clinging to the Boy's hand, and the Mountain is moving silently behind them, all of them coated in blood. The little princess's eyes are glowing an ethereal purple. She gazes up at me, her hand digging into the Boy's arm.

Shifting on the back of my horse, I glance at my squire. His jaw is held tight, his knuckles are shredded, and I notice a strange burn on his boot. "Any survivors, Boy?"

Ben shakes his head. "No, Commander."

It's enough for now. They will tell me more when we are back in camp. Most squires are not trained to fight until they leave for their quest, but I've always prepared mine for anything. Even at a gangly fourteen, the Boy is a scrappy fighter.

Kicking the Black forward, I hold my hand out to Eleanor, ordering, "Come, I'll take you back to the palace."

Eleanor hides behind my squire, clutching his shirt. Her eyes are flickering, and blood soaks the ends of her platinum hair. The Boy doesn't move out of the way, remaining as a human shield for the young princess. His eyes flicker between her and me, his loyalties clearly divided. Pulling my hand back, I frown at her. "You have to go back to the palace." She shakes her head fervently, her jaw setting in that stubborn line that is all too familiar. I sigh. "You can talk to your sisters in camp."

I shoot a look at the Boy, and he winces before stepping closer to hand Eleanor up. She chokes back a sob, even as I settle her in front of me on the Black. Her voice is broken and hoarse as she begs, "Please...Please..."

This strange bond between my squire and the young princess is becoming a source of concern. I kick the Black forward and ride with her back to camp, cutting off any response the Boy could form. Severing their connection now will prevent a greater evil. My squire leaves for his quest in two years and will be gone for another two before returning to be knighted by me. The fewer attachments he has before leaving, the better. I've lost squires before on their quests. Their thoughts too focused on what they had left behind rather than where they were. I won't let it happen again. I can't.

I know I am right, but it doesn't make the young princess's distress any easier to endure. Eleanor hits her small fists against my chest, sobs wracking her body. The camp comes into view, but she never stops crying. Shouldn't the girl have run out of tears by now? Even as we near my tent, and I dismount with her in my arms, she continues. No doubt, just to make me feel wretched.

The second we enter the tent, the young princess screams and kicks her legs, struggling in my grip. I try to contain her in my arms, but it's difficult when I could seriously hurt her with my strength.

"Eleanor!" my wife scolds.

Thalia glares at me, her golden eyes shimmering with accusation as she demands, "What happened to her?"

My squire appears behind us, ducking inside the tent. He must have sprinted the entire way back to camp. He murmurs to Thalia, "She's alright, it's not her blood. Some," his voice softens even more, "bad people got a hold of her. We took care of them."

Charlotte shoots me a look of concern, a question in her bright sapphire eyes. I nod solemnly, silently communicating that the threat was eliminated. She nods back at me, returning her focus to her sister.

The young princess shakes her head, screaming hysterically, "I don't want to go back!"

My ears ring with the pitch of her screams. My wife sends me a pleading look while Thalia rubs her face tiredly. "We have to, Eleanor."

I narrow my eyes on my wife over her wailing sister. "A military encampment is no place for her, and I leave tomorrow."

Eleanor sobs louder and struggles even harder against my hold. "But Charlie has to stay!"

I shoot a questioning look at my wife, trying to keep from hurting her sister as she wails. "Charlie?"

She points to herself. "Me."

Charlie?

Thankfully, Thalia comes forward, holding her hands out for Eleanor. I happily relieve myself of the burden, even as she continues to wail and scream. My squire's eyes remain locked on his feet, shuffling side to side. The young princess continues to beg, her arms wrapped around Thalia's neck, reaching out for my wife. "I don't want to go back, please. Please. I want to stay with Charlie!"

My wife shoots me another pleading look. Crossing my arms over my chest, I frown at her. "Don't even think about it, lamb."

"Then I need to go back with her," she retorts, crossing her own arms.

"Go back?" I hiss.

Thalia drags the little princess from the tent as she continues to cry, and my wife walks over to me, whispering, "To the palace."

Out of the question. Why would Charlotte want to come back to me after being there? They'll convince her I'm a monster that should never be allowed near her.

The Boy suddenly speaks up, "She can stay with me."

My head snaps to him. "What was that?"

Charlotte looks at him too. "Are you sure?"

I cover my wife's mouth with my hand, trying not to wince when she bites my palm, and address my squire, "You would be responsible for her." He nods. "Her mistakes would be yours." He gulps but nods again. "Her punishments, yours."

"Understood, Commander."

"She will bunk with the female squires. Take her and tell them about their new roommate."

Charlotte slaps at my arm, and I drop my hand from my wife's mouth. She storms from the tent, running after her sisters. Thalia is already down the camp aisle, hurrying toward the city. Eleanor is still sobbing and fighting her sister. My squire moves in a flash around me, quickly passing Charlotte to stop Thalia. She glares at him, but he ignores her, speaking softly, "Elle?"

Elle? This attachment is worse than I thought. Something will need to be done.

She immediately stops crying, looking at the Boy and sniffling loudly. "B-Benji?"

The look on her face makes me forget all the reasons I should insist that she return to the palace, all the reasons she can't stay in camp. I know that look. She's reaching out for a lifeline, something to hold on to, and it's not her fault that the mooring she found was Ben. At least she'll get to spend time with Niklaus and Wynonna's squires, and maybe she'll mimic some of their independence. If she doesn't break her friendship with Ben, so much pain and strife will lay ahead of them both.

He holds out his arms for her, speaking softly, gently, keeping her focus on him. "You're my job now."

Eleanor willingly moves from her sister's arms to his, wiping her tears on his shirt. She hiccups, wrapping her arms around his neck, pressing her face against his chest. "I am?"

He smiles down at her. "Yes. You can stay in camp with the other female squires until—"

"Six days," I growl. "We need to leave for the North." It's the most time I can give them, the longest I can delay our departure. Hopefully, they can make the most of it.

Eleanor rests her head on his shoulder, her tears finally stopping. My wife threads her fingers through mine. Thalia frowns at the squire and princess, but I see the flash in her golden eyes. I glance at the Mountain, gesturing with my head toward Thalia. "The Mountain will escort you back to the palace. Inform your father that Eleanor will be in camp for the next six days under my protection. No harm will come to her."

Ben doesn't even ask for permission to leave before turning on his heel and taking Eleanor to the female squire's tent. Thalia looks at Charlotte and speaks rapidly in Candonian. The flurry of their conversation slips past me, and I make a slashing motion with my hand. "Common tongue," I demand.

Thalia sniffs at me, turning on her heel and walking back toward the palace, the Mountain at her side.

Looking down at my wife, I frown and ask, "What did you two speak of?"

Charlotte shoots one last look after Thalia and pulls me back into our tent. She carefully closes the flap and knots it before answering, "She was saying the queen is going to kill her."

I expected a lot of things, but not that. I really need to learn Candonian, but it's a difficult language for outsiders. I'm fluent in Grimmish, Vrucian, passable in Xiapian and Vrucian. I even know a phrase or two in Vredu and Cirii, but Candonian eludes me.

"What?"

She releases my hand, sighing audibly, before sitting on our bed. "The queen isn't the nicest person..."

"Did she ever raise a hand to you?" If she did, she would die today.

She shakes her head, sparing the woman's life. "I am always with Father, or I used to be."

Does the king not know of his queen's mistreatment of his children? Another injustice to lay at his feet. My jaw tightens as I gaze down at her. "I do not like this."

She sighs heavily, pouting up at me. "I do not either, but she prefers dealing with it on her own."

Perhaps, I should reconsider killing the king for being so unaware. How could he not see the suffering under his nose? *But then, the man once owned the largest slave market in the world, am I truly that surprised?*

I sit beside her and take her hand. I lift it to my mouth, pressing a kiss to the palm, then her inner wrist right over her frantic pulse. "You get me for another six days."

She sighs, smiling softly at me, practically glowing. "Is it selfish that I am happy?"

Laughing, my hands drop to her hips. "A few more days with your husband makes you happy?"

She nods, wrapping her arms around my neck. "Yes." She tenses slightly, her fingers twirling the hair at the base of my neck. "I'm... I'm sorry about this morning."

My hands tighten on her hips, lifting her. She wraps her legs around my waist and buries her face against my neck, holding me tight. "This morning was this morning."

Tonight, I just want to hold her, be with her, smell her. It's hard even to remember why we fought. It feels like it was days ago.

She pulls her head back, pressing her forehead to mine, whispering, "And tonight?"

I sigh heavily and sit down on the edge of our bed, the wood of the frame creaking from our combined weight. "We should sleep."

It is late, and even though we napped, I need rest to be ready to train tomorrow. She nods silently but pouts, her hips rocking against me. I know she has no plans on either of us sleeping anytime soon.

XXIII

Charlotte

OUTSIDE ILIUM

KINGDOM OF CANDONIA

Six days. I get six more days with him, and the idea makes the butterflies in my stomach dance. All I want to do is get to know my husband and explore this strange attraction I feel toward him. I want to discover why the fates intertwined our lives together.

Thank goodness for Eleanor and Ben. It is so kind that the boy offered to take care of my sister. After all, the two of them only met yesterday morning, and when I saw them then, they were in the middle of a fight. Why did Ben offer to care for her? Even as I wonder what is going on between those two, I can feel the connection between them. Eleanor has never had any friends. With her unique abilities, Thalia and I have been hesitant to let her out of our sight. Perhaps it is Thalia's glare, the energy that Eleanor gives off, or that she is royalty, but other children tend to avoid her as well.

My focus turns back to my husband, and I look up at him, nibbling my bottom lip. I want to stay up longer and spend time with him. Evander's eyes soften as he looks at me, his lips twitching.

"Unless..." he says, his voice deepening.

"Unless?" I ask, a small smile tugging at my lips.

Evander wraps his arms around me, his hands drifting down my back to land on my bottom, squeezing it tightly. "You're not tired."

"Scoundrel!" I gasp, my eyes widening as a shiver runs down my spine.

"Not normally." He laughs, continuing to hold me. I am overwhelmed with his scent, and I push closer to him. The dreaded conqueror, my enemy, and I'm trying to press even closer to him.

"Oh?" I ask, sliding my hands beneath his shirt and over the heavy muscles of his chest. His heart pounds beneath my fingertips, and I smile as he pulls me closer, fitting me against him.

"I'm not a scoundrel, but I can't seem to keep my hands off you," he growls, his grey eyes glowing.

"I feel the same way," I whisper, kissing his jaw.

"Is that why you're happy I'm staying?" He groans. I can already feel the hard length of him pressing against me. Another shiver runs down my spine, and I roll my hips in a slow sensual rhythm. Something about Evander has me begging for more of his touch, his kisses, him.

"No, I am happy you are staying because I want to get to know more about you," I whisper, trailing my lips along his jaw before kissing him, my tongue teasing and tempting. I am so far from the young woman who cried at the thought of him touching me.

He takes command of the kiss, his fingers sliding into my hair. His hand fists, and he pulls my head back, flicking his tongue over my lips before asking, "What do you want to know?"

"Your favorite meal. Your favorite thing to do. Your favorite color." I kiss Evander between each sentence. *Why can't I stop kissing him?*

He pauses for a moment, nipping at my lips as he thinks. "Favorite meal? You. Favorite thing to do? You. Favorite color? Sapphire."

I tilt my head, my cheeks heating from his answers, even as I gently slide my nails over his chest. "Sapphire?"

He nods. "The color of your eyes."

"You flatter me too much." Warmth tingles through my entire body, and I kiss him again.

"And you? Your favorite things?" he asks, kissing my chin.

"I enjoy reading, learning new things, and," I roll my hips against him, "you."

His hands trace my curves in a slow exploration, moving to my ass. "I suppose I enjoy learning things."

I place my hand over his heart. "Perhaps we can learn something new together?"

"I'm...not as learned as you," he says, his neck turning pink. I stop grinding against him, placing a hand on his face as I look into his beautiful steel-grey eyes.

"What do you mean?" I whisper, my thumb caressing his cheek.

He looks away from me.

I turn his head, capturing his gaze once more. "Tell me."

"I just recently learned to read," he says. His hands tighten almost painfully on my hips as if he is afraid I will pull away from him. He is the most feared man in Candonia, and he conquered the entire North of Aellolyn. That he didn't possess this important skill and was still able to accomplish all he has is astounding. And then he had the strength to seek someone to help him learn.

"That is a wonderful accomplishment."

"I'm not very good at it," he says, shaking his head.

"I can help you if you would like," I say, kissing him again, the warmth from his lips beckoning me. I can't keep away from him. Not even for a minute.

"I'm sure you have more important things to do," he says.

"I will always have time for you," I whisper. I want to teach him, I want to share my knowledge, I want to spend more time with him. There is still so much I don't know about him. It would give me a chance to be with him and only him. I ache to understand this connection between us.

He shakes his head. "It's nothing."

"If you want to learn more. I can teach you," I say against Evander's lips.

He pauses for a minute, considering my words, before whispering, "Will you teach me Candonian?"

"Of course! I'd love to teach you." I smile at him. He flicks his tongue against my lips, which has my hips rolling against him once more.

"I have many things to teach you," he whispers huskily, grinding his hardness against me. His eyes glow, and our breathing becomes heavier. I ache for him.

"Like what?" I giggle.

"The delights on the flesh?" he says, falling back onto the bed. "I've only begun your education."

"I'm listening," I say, my hands resting on his chest as my hips continue to move in instinctive invitation.

He leans forward, his teeth sinking into my neck. I gasp, and my hands grasp at his shoulders, my core going liquid. The sensation is pain that morphs into pleasure, and I'm quickly becoming addicted to this feeling. A shiver runs down my spine, and I tug impatiently at his shirt.

"Evander..." I moan as he rolls us, my back landing on the bed. He undresses me, placing soft kisses on each part of my body as he reveals it before settling between my thighs.

"Time for my favorite meal," he growls.

I grip the furs, my entire body burning with need. "Do enjoy, Husband."

Everything becomes a haze of pleasure as soon as he touches me. He continues to take me to heights that I didn't know existed. By the end, we are both panting, sweat misting our bodies. The only sound I can hear is my thundering heartbeat and our heavy breathing.

"I didn't scare you?" Evander looks at me cautiously and gently rubs my arm, searching my gaze.

I shake my head, my face flushing as I think of what we just did. It was different, something I never expected, rougher, more urgent, *frantic*. "I…I um liked it."

"I thought you might," he says with a smirk filled with male satisfaction.

"What does that mean?" I ask, looking up at him, embarrassed. The heat in my neck and face only grows, and I fight the urge to bury myself away in the pillow.

"You have that look," he growls, shifting on the bed. His fingers trail low on my stomach, and I hold my breath.

"W-what look?" I ask.

He rolls with me, laying me across his chest. His heart is pounding under the palm of my hand as he says, "Of wanting more."

"Explain," I whisper, tracing one of the scars on his chest. There are so many of them. They decorate his entire torso, his arms, his legs. The only untouched part of him is his face.

"That one is from a crossbow bolt," he murmurs, watching my index finger trail across one just under his ribcage.

I scrunch my nose. "You ignored my question."

He raises a brow. "Did I?"

Oh, don't give me that look. You know perfectly well you did.

I pout at him. "Yes."

"You're not more interested in how I got my scars?"

My curiosity is piqued, and I run my fingers down his chest, looking at the marks. *He is starting to figure out my weaknesses.* There are a few things that can distract me or divert me off my path. Sharing knowledge about things that have roused my interest is the main one. It was the year that Eleanor was born that I became more curious about everything. Once I learn something, it sticks in my mind forever, easily accessible when needed.

"Tell me," I say, biting my swollen bottom lip. My eyes scan his chest before I place a finger on the white scar on his shoulder. "This one?"

"I was chained," he says flatly. The words make me tense, and I look up at him, my stomach twisting.

"I hate that you had to go through that." Each time I think of what he would have suffered, it makes me want to vomit. It haunts me that anyone could be that cruel to a child.

He sighs, kissing my hand. "Every scar is something I survived."

"Doesn't mean I like it," I say, my eyes becoming heavy, exhaustion finally winning.

He kisses my head. "Every scar brought me closer to you."

"I'm grateful for that," I whisper, closing my eyes and yawning. *Truly grateful.* "Goodnight, my husband."

"Goodnight, my wife," he whispers, and they are the last words I hear before I fall asleep.

XXIV

EVAN

OUTSIDE ILIUM

KINGDOM OF CANDONIA

The morning horn for drills is an unwelcome intrusion into my sleep. I pull Charlotte tighter against me, kissing her shoulder, reluctant to leave her soft warmth. When boots sound outside my tent, I groan softly and disentangle myself from my wife. I get out of bed, my eyes barely open as I get dressed. I can't help but pause for a moment and look down at my sleeping wife. She stirs and frowns in her sleep, reaching out for me. I push my pillow into her grasping arms, and she settles, wrapping herself tightly around it. With a grin of satisfaction, I lean over, kissing her forehead.

With a soft sigh, I brush a lock of hair out of her face before tearing myself away. The men are waiting on me, and I'm running late. I never run late. I'm always the first there and the last to leave. But that was before I got married, before I started changing, before Charlotte.

I jog down the hill toward the training fields. Several of my captains, lieutenants, and even my generals raise a brow at my late appearance. Kian is the first to say something, coming to my left side as I survey the troops. The army's hierarchy is divided. The lowest level of officer is a captain, and they lead a unit of ten to twenty men. Those who excel as a captain move on to lieutenants, overseeing four to seven captains and their units below them. My generals are equally responsible for one-fifth of my army. It is something I explain in each promotion, that no person is higher than another based upon rank, there are no added benefits for officers that the men themselves do not also enjoy. The only perk granted to my generals is that their tents are slightly bigger. Solely, so they are easily identifiable. The biggest tent isn't even mine. It's the one we use for strategy meetings, large gatherings, and to serve meals when it rains.

"I can't remember the last time you were late to morning drills," Kian says, smirking. He cocks his head to the side, eyeing me up and down, lingering on my neck. I barely stop myself from covering it self-consciously.

My eyes narrow, and I cross my arms over my chest, surveying the men. "Hoping to match Lorcan, Kian?"

The generals all snicker, except Lorcan, who touches his still bandaged nose. I feel a twinge of remorse for having broken it. But at the same time, he needed some more scars to be taken seriously. He was far too pretty to be intimidating, and a broken nose will help him fit in.

"Not at all, Commander. I'm just concerned that you might be slacking in your own training. You're looking...fat." Kian glances down at my stomach with a wince. I pat my stomach self-consciously.

Fat?!

I snarl at him and slice my hand through the air, and all my lieutenants, captains, and soldiers freeze in their spots. Twenty thousand men pause, holding their breath, waiting for my next command.

Without looking at Kian or any of the other generals, I raise my voice enough to carry across the field, "A special treat for you all. A chance to see your Commander take on one of his generals. I'll let you pick my opponent!"

A moment passes in silence before the cry goes up, *"Mountain! Mountain! Mountain!"*

156

I suppose I had that coming.

I rotate my shoulders with an anticipatory smile and glance at the Mountain. He grins as we walk down the hill to the center of the troops. The men give way, parting to form a circle around us. The Mountain is famous for his height and width, towering over even me by at least three inches and weighing a whole stone more. To the casual observer, there is no contest, especially as the Mountain's broadsword clicks on its way out of the scabbard. One downward stroke from overhead can cleave a man in half.

I face him and crouch slightly, not bothering to draw my sword or dagger. The Mountain moves his hands behind his head, gripping the hilt of his broadsword, about to bring it down in an arc. My hands remain low, and I dart to the side as the sunlight flashes off metal at the very top of his swing. The sword impales the ground from the force of his blow, disorienting him enough for me to move forward and slam a hard kick against his hands. He's forced to release the grip on the weapon or break his fingers. A crushing fist slams into my solar plexus, knocking the wind from me and freezing my lungs.

Instead of trying to regain the air I'd lost, I fall back with the hit, reverse somersaulting, until I'm back on my feet and the air is back in my paralyzed lungs. The Mountain takes the moment to tear his sword from the ground and swing it at me as I rush forward. I hit the ground, sliding under his sword feet first. My momentum carries me between the Mountain's firmly planted feet, his stance wide to force power into his strike. I grab the dagger from his boot and hold it to the artery on his inner thigh, not even getting up from the ground.

He growls at me, throwing down his sword and signing, *"You move too fast to be human."*

I smile up at him and say, "I don't know why you're always surprised by that."

He steps to the side, holding his hand out. I take it, allowing him to pull me to my feet. I flip the dagger over and hand it back to him. There is an exchange of money amongst the men, and I bestow a rare smile on them before clapping my hands, ordering, "Back to drills!"

The men scatter, and two figures on the outskirts of the field catch my eye. My squire looks out of place, but the lilac dress stands out even more.

I raise a brow at the pair as I move toward them. "Lamb? What are you doing here?"

My wife whispers something to the Boy before turning her full attention to me and stepping forward. She gives me a warm smile, whispering, "I came to see you."

I snap my fingers at the Boy, and he leaps forward, unbuckling my leather training armor. The weight nearly takes him out, but determination keeps him from falling over. His face turns red with exertion as he carries the armor over to the table set up for the other generals and me. All of them are removing their training armor for the strategy session. I should be over there, leading the meeting, but I can't seem to pull myself away.

"Me?"

She nods with a slight pout. "You left without saying goodbye this morning."

I step closer to her, pulling off my lawn shirt, which is sweaty after the short battle. I twist it and say, "And...I'm supposed to?"

She looks down at her feet, moving some dirt around with her slippered toe. "I would have liked that."

She has a terrible habit of looking away when she talks to me. I lift her chin, meeting her brilliant gaze. "How would you like me to say goodbye, lamb?"

Her sapphire eyes heat, and she licks her lips. "With a kiss."

I smirk and press a soft kiss to her lips. I am stopped from taking it farther by the sounds of cat-calling. Various cheers and boos come from my men as they enjoy the show. She ignores them, kissing me harder, her hands sliding over my chest. When the sounds from my men only grow louder, I'm forced to break away from her, turning to scold them, "You're supposed to be training!"

They ignore me, continuing to cause a ruckus. She laughs softly, again a sense of glowing contentment radiating from her. "Are you busy now?"

I shoot a wistful glance at the general's table, finding that they are already in a heated discussion. Niklaus has his fist slammed on the table, and Kian's leaning back in his chair, suspended on two legs. Wynonna is stroking her long braid in thought while Lorcan flips a dagger around his hand, and the Mountain watches the rest of them.

I kiss her again. "I don't have to be."

There is little that will pull me away from my wife. *Very little.* And the list is growing shorter and shorter by the day. My generals will survive without me. I tasked them with being my advisors and to function as a replacement if I were to fall in battle. They don't need me. At least, not at the moment.

"I was wondering if you would like to join me for breakfast?"

I smile brightly at her and lock my hand with hers. The rest of the day passes by in a blur as I savor stolen moments with my wife.

The next morning I nudge her awake before I leave to claim my kiss and then push hard through morning drills so I can return to her side. She's still in bed, stretching, likely just about to get up and start her day. She's cuddling my pillow, which I tucked into her arms again.

"You know what I have come to realize?" I ask her, coming to the bed and kissing her nose. "Camp food leaves much to be desired."

She laughs and stretches slow and languorous, turning from side to side before getting out of bed. "How has your morning been?"

I grunt in response, helping her get dressed. Lacing up her dress is becoming one of my favorite pastimes, second only to unlacing it. She looks over her shoulder at me, letting her hair fall down her back. "You haven't answered the question."

I smirk, take her hand and exit the tent. "My morning? Infinitely better now."

She smiles, happiness radiating from her. She rests her head on my shoulder as we walk through camp. "I was thinking we could go to the lake tonight after dinner."

The men stop as we pass by, nodding their heads in respect to me, then bowing formally to Charlotte. I wonder if she's noticed the difference in their behavior towards her. Bowing is a significant improvement from outright displays of mistrust and hostility.

"Oh? Why?" I ask, continuing our slow walk out of camp and into the city. I notice the construction already underway to replace the gates damaged by my men. I'd tasked several of my regiments with the repair, working side-by-side with Candonians to build better defenses, ones that might keep the next conqueror out.

"I thought we could continue my swimming lessons," she whispers. Charlotte blushes, no doubt thinking about the last time we swam together. As am I. It feels like I never stop thinking about her.

"Swimming? Or what happened afterward?"

She buries her face against my arm as we continue to the city, leaving the world that's familiar to me behind and moving into hers.

"Both."

XXV

Charlotte

ILIUM

KINGDOM OF CANDONIA

Hand in hand, we make our way into the city. The buildings tower over us as people walk back and forth between their homes and the market, gathering the supplies they will need for the week. A few stop when they recognize Evander and me, gossiping to one another in Candonian. I am sure Evander notices. He is an observant man, after all.

Since being in my husband's camp, I haven't had much time to ponder what my people could think or what they assume happened. To the best of their knowledge, a conqueror has come into the kingdom and stolen their princess. They must think he is torturing me or something far worse. I need to show them that that is far from the truth. My people should not fear their future king when there is no need. He is here to help make a better Aellolyn. Hopefully, this walk through town will be a step in changing some of their opinions or at least have them doubting their negative thoughts of our union. I want to build a future for them with the help of the man at my side, my *former* enemy.

Evander and I end up in front of a clothing shop. We step inside the large store, and I glance at all the different clothing on display. The outfits are simple and tasteful but beautiful. The tailor walks over to us as Evander presses his muddy hands to a pair of clean black breeches. I snort to myself. It is considered rude to touch clothing that another might wear. If you handle something, it means you are planning to buy it. I will need to teach him the customs of Candonia.

The tailor's eyes widen, and he scurries to my husband, any fear he might feel overridden by the thought of a sale. I tug on Evander's hand, and his eyes go wide as the tailor leads us to a raised dais. The man's nimble fingers shake as he measures my husband's chest and arms. Evander looks at me, and I smile as the tailor grabs him a matching set of breeches and a lawn shirt. My husband laughs when I stick my tongue out at him, and the tailor frowns before looking at me.

"Are you alright, Your Highness?" the tailor asks in Candonian.

I nod, and even I can hear the happiness in my voice. *"More than alright, thank you."*

I pull out some crowns from my bag, handing him more money than necessary. *"Will this do?"*

The tailor continues to frown at me, confused by my relaxed behavior. *"Are you sure?"*

Evander looks between the tailor and me. "Lamb?"

"I'm sure," I reply to the tailor before walking over to Evander. I stand on my tiptoes and kiss him softly, reassuring him.

The tailor nods at us before offering the new clothes to Evander. He gestures to the back for my husband to change. I let go of Evander's hand, and he walks behind a partition. I impatiently rock back and forth on my heels, trying to take a peek at him.

"Evander?" I question after a few minutes.

"Yes?" he asks. My heart stops in my chest. He is wearing a black doublet and formal black breeches. Gold embroidery covers the stitches, and the colors of Candonia are on his breast pocket. *By the Ancients.* There is something about him in traditional *lord* attire that takes my breath away. That I want to rip it off him doesn't even concern me. My mouth goes dry, and I crave his lips to help quench my thirst. *I'm addicted to him.*

"I-I-I..." I stutter.

"Is it too much?" he asks, his cheeks turning pink. He pulls at the neck of the doublet. "This is more suffocating than I thought."

Unable to stop myself, I step close to him, fixing his cuffs. "You look quite handsome."

Evander's face goes from pink to red before looking at the tailor. "Do you have something for her as well?"

"It would be my honor to clothe the princess." The tailor beams. The queen only allows her dressmakers and tailors from Steodia to create our wardrobes. I protested this, wanting to give our local merchants a chance to design clothes for the palace, but I lost that battle.

"Do you have anything that would match his outfit?" I ask him.

The tailor nods excitedly. "Yes, Your Highness."

"I would love to try it on, please," I say, biting my bottom lip.

The tailor nods, gesturing for me to follow him. He shows me a black gown with slits down the front of the dress, revealing a white underskirt. The seams are embroidered with the same golden design as Evander's shirt. I like the idea of matching him, making us a single unit. I want to show everyone we are working for the future of Candonia *together.* I slip it on, taking a few minutes to tie it up before stepping out to show Evander.

"What do you think?" I ask him, twirling around.

His mouth drops as he looks me up and down. He turns to the tailor, pointing at him. "I would like you to send at least ten various sets of these to my tent."

"I-I..." The tailor gapes in shock before looking at me. "Princess?"

My face burns hot, and I laugh, Evander's excitement warming my soul. I give the crowns to the tailor, nodding. "It is beautiful. I love it."

Evander holds his hand out to me, and I take it, holding the dress out to the side.

"By the Ancients…" he whispers.

"Do you like it?" I ask.

"Too much." He nods, kissing my knuckles before looking at the tailor. "I would like you to come to camp."

The tailor pales, his hands shaking slightly. "W-what?"

"You are going to give this man a heart attack," I whisper to Evander. No citizen of Candonia is ever invited to camp. No doubt rumors abound about what happens to those who dare cross into the territory of the monstrous conqueror.

"I would like to hire you to clothe my men," Evander says.

"Y-your men?" The tailor blinks.

"They deserve the chance to have an actual decent set of clothes." My husband nods. I smile at him before looking at the tailor.

"I will cover the costs," I say, raising my hand slightly.

"No, I will," Evander says. I look up at him in admiration. He is clothing his men with his own crowns. That is very selfless of him. Most people do not care about the needs of others. Yet he does. How else will he surprise me? Again, the feeling of fate wrapping around us shoots down my spine. It doesn't even matter if he doesn't believe.

"I would be honored, si— Your Highness." The tailor nods. Smiling brightly, I turn to look up at Evander, and I kiss his cheek. The first citizen to recognize him as royalty. More are sure to follow suit. He smiles at me and opens the door.

"Thank you," Evander says. As we leave the tailor's, he looks down at me. "Breakfast?"

I nod, squeezing his hand. "Let's go."

There is a place I want to show him. It is my favorite spot to get breakfast when I come into the city, and the owner is one of my favorite people. Evander tucks my arm in as we stroll along the street.

"These clothes are a bit more restricting than I thought," he says, pulling at the doublet again.

"Why do you think I dislike corsets so much?" I snort.

164

He snorts. "What would you like for breakfast, lamb? I'm hoping to get some stable provisions and supplies to camp."

A group of children run down the street beside us, laughing loudly, and I smile. My thoughts go to the future and the children Evander and I will have— Wait, when did I start dreaming about this? I blink a few times before looking up at my husband to answer his question.

"How about Leonardo's Bakery? He usually has some fresh sweets around this time," I say.

He kisses my hand. "Lead the way."

I nod and can't wait to see the look on his face when he tries one of the delicacies. They are the best in the city. Even the cooks at the palace can't make pastries as good as Leonardo's.

We turn the corner and see Leonardo walking out the bakery door with a fresh pan of bread. The baker is a jolly man with a round belly, his apron stained with various baking ingredients. His hair is slowly turning grey from his two sons and their rebellious ways. Through it all, I can always count on seeing a smile on the older man's face.

"Princess! It has been too long, and...is this him?" Leonardo asks me in Candonian.

"Yes, this is my husband, Evan the Black." I nod, smiling.

Leonardo looks my husband up and down before putting the tray on one of the tables. *"He is as intimidating as they say."*

I laugh. *"He isn't that bad."*

Evander crosses his arms over his chest. "I would prefer it if we speak the common tongue."

I look up at my husband, smiling apologetically. "Evander, this is an old friend of mine, Leonardo. He makes the best sweets in all of Candonia."

The baker blushes. "You flatter me, princess."

"It is an honor to meet anyone who is known to my wife." Evander nods to Leo. "And if your pastries are as good as she claims, then I would like to hire you to feed my men one night soon. As a special treat for them. I will pay handsomely."

"I would do it for free, Your Highness." Leonardo smiles toothily. "Now come in! I have a fresh batch of apple strudels that need tasting."

I take Evander's hand, following Leonardo into the bakery. The small shop brings back memories of when I was a girl. This was one of the spots I would get food for the children in the city. Leonardo would keep my secret while I went around feeding the underfed children and those who were slaves. He supported me through it all.

The scent of bread and strawberries tickles my nose, and sunlight streams through the large windows. There are shelves and shelves of breads, pastries, and other sweets. The bakery is always busy and one of the most popular spots in the city for both residents and visitors.

"I could not take advantage of your hospitality in such a way. I insist on paying you," Evander says to Leonardo before looking around. "You take great pride in your work, as you should."

"Thank you, Your Highness," Leonardo says as he pulls a fresh batch of strudels off one of the shelves. He places them on the oak counter, picking up two of the pastries and holding them out to us. I take one of them, taking a bite of the sweet-smelling treat. The apple tastes a little bitter at first, but the sugary icing sweetens it. I look over at Evander as he takes his pastry, biting my bottom lip as I wait for his reaction. His moan of pleasure sends a shiver through me, and I laugh softly.

"You and your men must have been on the road for so long," Leonardo says.

"We have been on the road since many were too young to know the difference," Evander says, taking another bite of the strudel.

Leonardo looks around the bakery in thought before his eyes brighten. "Well. I had someone cancel their order of croissants this morning. I could have them at your camp within the hour? Give those men a taste of their new life."

166

Evander tilts his head to the side. "You would do that?"

"Of course!" Leonardo beams. "They need to be eaten, and I'd hate for them to go to waste."

"They would be very grateful. Camp gruel leaves a lot to be desired." Evander hums in pleasure as he takes another bite.

"Markus, Albert!" Leonardo calls out. Two younger boys walk out from the back and look up at their father. Markus is taller than Albert by a foot, and they are younger, brown-haired versions of their father.

"Grab four of the boxes from Lady Camilla's canceled croissant order. You will be taking them to the camp with the prince and princess," Leonardo instructs, and the boys run to the back.

My husband's cheeks turn red as he whispers to me, "Strange to hear that."

"Well, you did marry a princess," I say.

He raises a brow, lifting my hand to his lips. Leonardo turns his attention to us, muttering to himself, "Young love. A beautiful thing."

I blink, caught off guard. *Love?* The word has crossed my mind a few times. Well, mostly the idea that Evander could be my soulmate, but love? Is that why my heart pounds when I see him? The emptiness I feel when he is not with me. The warmth his kisses provide late at night.

"This is too good," Evander says, taking the last bite of his pastry and ignoring Leonardo's comment.

Leonard picks up a raspberry danish, holding it out to Evander. "If you like the strudel, you will love this."

"I'm going to have to do another round of morning drills after this," Evander mutters but still accepts the pastry.

I pat Evander's stomach, giggling. "I love your pudge."

The danish falls from his hand, his jaw dropping. "Pudge!"

"Oh yes! It is perfect." I snicker, poking his stomach more. His face turns redder, and he pulls away. "It is only a joke, my husband."

Evander touches his flat stomach, his brows furrowing, and I feel bad. Before I can apologize, I hear something fall in the back room, and I sigh.

"I should go help the boys," I say, leaving the men behind in the shop.

XXVI

EVAN

ILIUM

KINGDOM OF CANDONIA

I watch Charlotte leave until the door to the back closes behind her. I raise a brow and cross my arms, taking the opportunity to gain some intel. The baker visibly gulps at being left alone with me. I know that both the tailor and Leonardo interrogated my wife about me. There is no other reason for them to speak in Candonian, knowing I don't understand. "How is morale in the city?"

He pauses for a moment at the question, packing the pastries away in a little box for us. His thoughts clear on his face, he was trying to decide what to say. "It has been low since the occupation. I cannot lie about that."

Smart man. I will always trust an enemy who tells me the truth over a friend who lies. He watches me from the corner of his eye, far more shrewd than I think my wife credits him with. From the windows of his pastry shop, I can feel the gazes boring into my back. If looks could kill, I would have been dead thrice over by now.

"Understood. I know I will not have a favorable image here." Many will always see me as the foreign invader, the conqueror, even when I'm their king. It's something I'm prepared to live with.

The baker holds out the box for me, but he pulls it back out of my reach. I cross my arms as he says, "Most of the people love the princess. We were all concerned for her after finding out about the wedding."

They love her. They worry about her falling into the clutches of some evil monster. I don't know if I've ever encountered such devotion to the royal family before, even in Grimmwing.

"I would never harm her." I know many believe I keep her in line with a harsh hand. They don't understand, and they likely never will. I would decimate anyone who raised a hand to my wife. And if that person were me? There would be no suitable punishment.

He nods, placing the box on the counter instead of handing it to me. His hands are covered with flour and various colors of jam. "She has never looked at another the way she does you." That's slightly comforting. One side of his mouth tilts up, wiping his hand on a rag. "It looks like our princess has fallen in love."

All the air in my lungs vanishes.

"L-love?" I stutter.

The baker's back is to me, so he doesn't see my stunned expression. My mouth just opens and closes repeatedly. "Do you know how long the king has tried to get his daughter to choose a husband?"

Air returns to my lungs, but it takes a moment for my breathing to regain its regular rhythm. I knew she was older than normal for an eligible princess. Most royals were married the moment they reached maturity. Yet, my wife is twenty-four, not eighteen. Why did I never consider this? Why have I never wondered why she was still single? She never had the coming-out balls, the courting, and traditions because she valued her choice that much. She wanted to marry for love, a dream she must have clung to for the better part of a decade. I had robbed her of that choice.

You stole her.

I would never have been one of those suitors. Given a choice, she would have never chosen me. I'm a former slave whose power comes from the army I command, not the blood that beats in my veins. I have no ancestral estates or titles. If I hadn't stormed the city, the king would not have let me through the front doors of the palace. I wouldn't have set eyes on his daughter, let alone married her.

Leonardo continues, not noticing that my hand shakes as I fist it against my chest. "He has been trying for years, but the princess is a stubborn one. She was only going to marry someone she truly loved."

I took that from her. She married because I gave her no choice. Years of waiting for love, all taken from her in a blink of an eye. *By me.*

"Until I arrived," I whisper, my eyes focusing on the pastry box so I don't have to meet his gaze. The box is a pale pink, and the bow on the top is meticulously tied. Leonardo must have performed the task a hundred times before.

Leonardo places his hand on the box, breaking my gaze and returning my focus to him. "And now she looks happier than ever. I wonder why that is?"

I don't have the answer to that, so I stare at him, holding his gaze. I will not give Charlotte up. She is *mine.* I will find a way to make her happy. *I have to.*

Leonardo hums loudly, and I have the feeling he may see much more than I want him to. I take the pastry box from the counter, my hands still shaking a little. I lift it carefully as if it is something that requires every ounce of my strength.

Charlotte returns from the back room, the two young boys following her. She's glowing, her happiness infectious. I've never smiled or laughed as much as I have since she entered my life. The two boys are each pulling carts stacked high with identical little pink boxes. She meets my eyes, and her smile is filled with a warmth I am not sure I understand. "We are ready to go."

I nod, focusing on the pastry box, turning away from her.

Leonardo's shrewd eyes look back and forth between my wife and me. "I hope to see you both again soon."

That baker sees more than I think even Charlotte realizes. I look back through the windows of the bakery, and almost fifteen Candonians turn away. They frantically go back to their business, acting as if they haven't been watching the entire exchange from the moment we walked inside. Without looking at Charlotte, I offer her my arm, waiting for her to take it. I look over my shoulder at Leonardo. "Yes, you will."

She loops her arm through mine, smiling at the baker, waving. "Take care!"

Many Candonians call out to my wife in greeting as we walk down the cobblestone street, though they pull back when they see her arm in mine. Likely deducing who I am.

She can't love me. She told me herself that I would never have her heart. I stole her, and I took a choice she had fought to maintain. She would never have picked me. I'm not enough. I'm not titled or purebred. *Nothing. Worthless. Slave. Scum.* The words scream in my mind, over and over. I do nothing to quiet them, letting them grow louder and louder.

A block away from the baker, she gazes up at me. "Are you alright?"

I glance down at her dismissively before looking back at the street. "Me? I'm fine. How are you?"

"You don't seem fine," she says, tightening her hand on my arm. I know if I look down at her again, her sapphire eyes will be scanning the lines of my face, trying to read the thoughts racing through my head.

"Do you remember what you said to me on our wedding day?" I ask suddenly.

Her hand tightens slightly, the only hint of her mood. "Yes..."

I lock my gaze on the street ahead and not on her. "You said I'd never have your heart."

She pauses and yanks me to a stop as well, spinning me to face her. I can feel the eyes on us. Together in our ridiculously

172

nice clothes, we stand out, drawing even more attention. I stop myself from yanking at the doublet again. No one needs to be wearing tight clothing unless it is going under armor to keep it from chafing.

"I did say that."

I watch her closely, the two boys stopping a short distance behind us. She keeps rubbing her lips together, formulating something more to say. "Is something wrong?"

Her sapphire eyes continue scanning mine. "Why are you bringing this up?"

I look away, something about her eyes searing me. They force me to reveal all the inner truths I've buried deep inside. "We should get back to camp."

I signal the boys to go ahead, and they continue toward the gate. The wheels of the carts squeak as they wobble over the stones, the boxes in them teetering side to side.

"Evander." Does she know what it does to me when she says my full name? That I'm helpless to deny her so long as she uses it? A weakness I never knew I had.

"Yes?"

"Something's bothering you."

I clear my throat, very aware of the gazes that remain on us. They are searching for a weakness, a crack in the armor of my marriage. "It's nothing."

I need to escape this conversation. If I'm not careful, I'll end up confessing the whole truth to Charlotte and tell her I want what I can never have. *Her heart.*

Her hand slips off my arm as I turn away, pulling out of her hold and yanking on the oppressive doublet again. I need to get back to camp, back to normal. I need to figure out why she has this hold on me, but her words make me freeze. They are a soft whisper, almost lost in the continuing clamor of the city, "I was wrong."

I don't turn around, my eyes remaining on the gate, wishing we were outside the walls. The whispers of the Candonians lingering along the street are louder, practically shouting. Spewing all the twisted stories of me, weaving truth and fantasy so tightly together, they become indistinguishable. "We should get back to camp."

"Evander."

I can hear her confusion and pain in that one word, and I reach back for her, still facing away. "Lamb…"

I hold my breath, waiting for her to take it. When she does, she whispers, "What's wrong?"

"It's nothing. We can discuss it later." I pull her against my side and release her hand, wrapping my arm around her waist.

She presses her face against my chest, leaning heavily against me. The walk back is silent, both of us wrapped around each other. When we get to camp, the baker's boys are already there, passing out the croissants. The men fall on them with excitement at the rare treat. I pull away from Charlotte. "I should finish up evening drills with the men. Do you still want to go swimming later?"

I can feel her eyes on my face, even as her arms drop from my waist. "Of course I do."

"Later, then."

Her voice barely carries over the sound of the men, "Later…"

XXVII

Charlotte

OUTSIDE ILIUM

KINGDOM OF CANDONIA

We were so happy exploring the city and then his mood suddenly changed. It aches when we fight, and flutters when he returns after drills. I didn't realize it until he mentioned my heart never belonging to him. But it already does, and he doesn't realize it.

I make my way back to our tent, my thoughts in turmoil. I will tell him the truth tonight when we go for our swim. He needs to know that my feelings for him are changing. For now, I will work on a new project. The idea came to me this morning while we were at Leonardo's bakery. I want to throw a celebration, something to display the future Evander and I could create, but the details are still undecided in my mind.

The rest of the day passes in a blur, but Evander doesn't return. I frown, looking down at my papers, my fingers tracing over his name. *Did I say something wrong? Do something wrong?* The sun set an hour ago, and I am having a hard time keeping my eyes open. I get ready for bed and slip under the furs. Perhaps something has happened. The drills could be going longer than usual. He is staying a little longer than he intended. Maybe something else came up? I sigh, staring at the tent flap and waiting for him to return. He doesn't, and with my soul aching with his absence, I fall asleep.

My head hurts when I wake the next morning, and I know before I even open my eyes that he is already gone. The side of his bed is dented and warm. He came back sometime last night, but snuck out before I awoke. I need him to tell me that everything between us is alright. Did he sneak out on purpose before I awoke? Was the sight of me too much?

I get out of bed but don't bother getting dressed. Slipping on my robe, I belt it tightly around my waist before taking a seat at the desk to continue on my project. I find myself stopping to stare at nothing, thinking about him constantly throughout the day. I don't eat much at breakfast or lunch, my stomach twisting and turning with uncertainty.

The sun is setting, orange and red light peeking in through the slits of the tent. I don't turn around when I hear the tent flap open. It is only someone bringing dinner, and I can't face the disappointment of it not being Evander.

"Lamb?" The sound of Evander's voice makes my breath catch.

"E-Evander?" I stutter. My eyes fill with tears from the pent up anxiety. I spin in my chair, looking at him. He is coated in grime from the drills, and his blonde hair looks brown from the mud. Sweat and dirt cover his training armor, but I don't care about any of that. I am just happy to see him.

Evander smiles and says, "Who else would it be?"

I run to him, wrapping my arms around his neck. "I thought you were mad at me."

"Mad at you?" He frowns, holding onto me tightly. "I've just been worn out from all the extra training we've been putting the men through before we leave."

Evander leaves in a few days and my lip trembles at the thought of him being gone for an entire month. It is selfish of me, but I am trying my hardest not to beg him to stay.

"Oh. You said that we were going swimming last night," I whisper.

Evander shakes his head. "I am sorry, I should have sent word. I'm missing this evening's drills to go with you tonight."

"Truly?" I ask him with a small smile. I hadn't realized how cold I felt.

He nods, tucking a piece of hair behind my ear. "Are you ready now?"

I nod, but then I remember my project, and my eyes brighten. "I must show you something first!"

"Show me something?" Evander asks, raising a brow. I nod and take his hand, guiding him to my desk. There are multiple papers covered in cursive writing sprawled on it, along with ink and quills. I'd neatly stacked the final drafts, while my brainstorming notes have scratches and lines crossing out words on them. Many have doodles drawn in the corners, including Evander's name written in a heart. I chew my bottom lip, hoping he doesn't notice that one. I quickly pick up the final sheet, holding it out for him. He takes it, looking it over slowly.

"I have an idea for a new festival," I say, wringing my hands nervously.

His brows furrow as his eyes slowly scan the paper. I don't rush him, knowing that he only learned to read recently. My handwriting can be a bit difficult to read with the loops and the size, but I tried to make it as clear as I could for him. I made the letters bigger and spaced them out. When I was twelve, I held classes for a few of the slave children I'd saved. They admitted they didn't know how to read or write, so for Eiramus I gifted them classes. I was surprised by how excited they were. The smiles on their faces made it all worth it.

"A festival for freedom?" he questions.

I nod, chewing my lower lip. "The anniversary of the law I passed happens in about a month. I thought it could be a time for everyone to celebrate the lives they have now."

"The lives they have now?" He tilts his head at me, and regret fills his eyes. "I won't be here for it."

I fiddle with the bottom of his shirt as my stomach twists. "It will be the middle of next month. I was hoping you could be home for the day."

He catches my hand, looking down at me with that glow in his eyes that has become intimately familiar. "Don't you want to go swimming?"

He is changing the subject, something I have noticed he does when he doesn't want to disappoint me. I bite my bottom lip, nodding at him.

"I do."

He puts the proposal on my desk and tugs me towards the exit. "Let's get going."

I follow him out of the tent. As much as I want to push him for an answer, I know I can't. It is something that will be in the back of my mind until he returns.

"How were drills?" I ask him.

"Good." He clears his throat. "I kept thinking of you."

"You did?" I ask.

"Couldn't seem to stop," he says, his cheeks turning red. I press a kiss to his lips, smiling to myself.

"I couldn't stop thinking of you either," I say.

Evander whistles and his horse trots to us, his black mane shimmering in the moonlight. There is something magical about this horse that I can't quite put my finger on. He appears loyal to my Evander, and they are definitely in sync. If you look hard enough, you can see the similarities between the two. Both seem angry, stern, and rough. Evander grabs my hips, lifting me onto the stallion before swinging up behind me. He presses his lips hard against mine, and I sigh softly.

"What were you thinking about?" he asks. Has he finally figured out my thinking face?

"Oh, things." I blush.

Evander's legs tighten, and the Black trots forward. "Things?"

178

"Things that would be improper for a lady to think," I whisper, leaning back to kiss him. Evander turns me around on the horse, so I am straddling his hips. "Evander!"

"Yes?" he says. He looks so innocent, like nothing about this will lead to something intimate.

"I care deeply about you," I say, smiling at him. My fingers trace little shapes on his chest as I bite my lower lip. Evander looks at me, smiling but not responding. I press against him, savoring the feel of being held in his arms until we arrive at the lake. The water laps quietly along the shore, and the only other sound is the leaves rustling the trees. It is like a different world out here, so peaceful.

Evander dismounts and holds his hands out to me. He helps me down from the Black before walking over to the front of his horse. He whispers softly to the big warhorse and kisses him on the nose.

"What did you say to him?" I ask.

He looks over at me, rubbing down the Black's neck. "I told him he's a good horse."

"How did you find him?" I ask, biting my bottom lip.

Evander presses his face to the side of his horse's cheek. "I don't really remember. As far back as I know, he's always followed me around. I used to see him outside the slaver's camp."

I look at the horse, thinking. There have been rumors of familiars, but they went extinct when the High Sorcerers were killed. At least, that is what everyone believes.

"He sounds like a familiar," I say.

Evander tilts his head at me, looking me up and down. His eyes glowing as he slows his gaze over me, his eyes close to a physical touch.

"Evander!" I scold, my face burning red.

"What?" he asks, pulling his shirt off and tossing it aside.

I turn away from him, trying to calm myself. "You're a scoundrel."

"Only for you," Evander says as his hands drift to my hips. A shiver runs down my spine, forming little goosebumps on my skin.

"I thought we were going for a swim?" I ask him.

"We are," he growls, his hands gripping my dress.

I turn my head slightly to look up at him. "Help me undress?"

Evander yanks at the ties of my dress, only knotting them more, and I laugh.

"I am going to have my new tailor make you a dress without ties," he growls.

"Oh? You know ties are essential for a dress," I whisper.

Evander frowns and reaches into his boot, pulling out his dagger. He cuts the side of my dress.

"Evander! What am I going to wear back to camp?" I exclaim.

He shrugs. "Me?"

I turn fully to face him, my dress falling to my ankles. "And if your men look at me?"

He only growls, his steel-grey eyes turning stormy. They seem to shout one simple word at me. *Mine.* Evander drops to his knees in front of me, his fingers flicking my nipples.

I gasp, my fingers tangling in his blonde hair. "Evander!"

He doesn't reply as he kisses my lower abdomen and hooks my knee over his shoulder. His eyes gleam in the dark, and I bite my bottom lip. *You're an addiction I never want to end.*

XXVIII

EVAN

OUTSIDE ILIUM,

KINGDOM OF CANDONIA.

Her eyes lock on me, glowing with desire. "You are so good to me." I lick her slowly. Her hips lift, and her head falls back as she moans softly, "Fuck..."

I keep her locked against my mouth, preventing her from squirming away from me, no matter how intense the sensations. Her other hand drops to my hair, gripping the strands. She moans louder, almost ripping it from the roots. It would be a worthy loss.

"Evander!"

Her leg muscles are shaking around my ears, even as she begs, "More..."

I pull away from her suddenly, stopping her just on the cusp of coming. She whimpers, "Why'd you stop..."

I fall onto my back beside her. My shaft is painfully hard, aching at every one of her moans and whimpers. I crook my finger at her. She crawls on top of me, teasing her core against my shaft.

I'm in no mood for games. I want her body, her soul, and her *heart,* everything she has to give. And then I want even more. I want her to feel like I do, as if I'm hollow without her. It's as if she's crawled inside my skin, my very soul, and I no longer know where I end, and she begins.

"Show me how much you love my cock inside you."

Only me.

Show me I can give you something that you could never have gotten from another. I need to know that whatever faceless man who was meant to be hers could never have given her this.

She impales herself on me with a low, husky moan. "I love this so much."

My back arches at the feeling of her hot sheath gripping me. "Just like that."

Charlotte rolls her hips against me, a slow sensual grind. She leans forward, her small hands braced on my chest as our eyes connect. "Like this, Husband?"

"Just like that...just like that." She doesn't speed up, continuing at the slow and passionate pace, kissing my jawline, then my lips.

"I need you," I whisper against her lips, "always."

I sit up with her, wrapping her legs around my back to seat myself even deeper inside her and take control. Our eyes lock, a line of intangible tension connecting us, something electric, emotional, and touching. Something deeper than I've ever felt during a night of passion.

Her words are mostly moans as she presses her forehead to mine. "You'll always have me."

My eyes roll back as I come inside her, her sheath squeezing me tightly with her own climax. Her nails drag down my back, leaving a trail of raised skin. I couldn't care less. She could take a whip to my back at that moment, and I would bear it with a smile.

The only sound that makes it to my ears is our heavy breathing. I press my face into her neck, struggling to form words. "That...that was more."

She nods, kissing the side of my head, her body trembling. "I loved that."

She did? It was nothing I'd ever experienced before. I kiss her shoulder, my mind still reeling. "It felt...different."

182

She whispers, her voice shaking, "Like...love..."

She looks at you like she's never looked at another. She refused to marry for anything short of love.

I clear my throat, and the first thing that comes out of my mouth is, "Swimming."

She disentangles from me, frowning. "Evander?"

"Swimming. You wanted to swim." I stand up and hold my hand out for her to take, even as I try to look everywhere else.

"Yes..." She takes my hand, allowing me to help her to her feet. I slowly walk backward into the lake until the water is chest deep for me and chin deep for her. She places her hands on my shoulders for support.

I kiss her head absently and ask, "Do you remember how to float?"

She nods. "I do."

She's looking away from me, and I frame her face in my hands, making her look up. "Do you not want to learn anymore?"

"I do."

I stroke her cheeks with my thumbs and ask, "Where are you then?"

You're not here. At least not mentally.

Her eyes scan mine, searching for something. "It's nothing."

I break eye contact with her, looking over her head. "If you don't want to be here..."

She wraps her arms around my neck, stopping me from pulling away. "I want to be here. With you."

Why did she pause? I swear I need an actual book to decipher my wife's emotions and thoughts. She flickers from one thought to the next and won't tell me what's wrong.

I meet her gaze again. "Are you sure?"

She kisses my chest, and it soothes some of my ragged emotions. I'm still feeling raw from what just occurred between us. I'm exposed and vulnerable.

"I'm sure. I—" I interrupt her by lifting her into my arms. Charlotte's hair fans out around her as I settle her on top of the water. I smile down at her, supporting her back with one hand

and her legs with the other. Her eyes lock on me, her body tense and sinking like a stone. "I need to tell you something."

"Soften your body," I whisper, brushing a kiss across her cheek. I am sure whatever it is can wait, but she doesn't listen. If anything, she tenses even more. "I...I..." She closes her eyes, almost forcing herself to release the tension before continuing, "I need to tell you something about earlier."

I move my hand lower in the water and smile when she remains floating. "You're doing it!" She sighs and starts to sink. I quickly return my hand to its place of support. "You need to soften."

"I can't." She stands up in the water, her feet meeting the sand beneath her.

"Why not?"

"Because I..." She chews her lower lip, and I tilt my head, waiting for her to confess what's on her mind. She whispers, making me strain to hear her, "The night of our wedding...I was wrong."

My heart stops in my chest. "Wrong to marry me?"

She shakes her head, and the simple motion allows my heart to restart. "No! That my heart could never belong to you."

"What?" I ask, my voice breaking.

Her cheeks flame and she looks away. "My heart...it's yours."

"Charlotte," I say hoarsely.

I don't deserve you. I stole you. Forced you to the altar, took away your choice. You should hate me. Why don't you hate me?

She presses closer against me. "Yes?"

My throat is dry, and I'm having trouble breathing. "There's a lot you don't know about me. Things I've done." I pull away from her, backing deeper into the water, looking for an escape. So much she doesn't know of the terrible, *evil* things I've done. My hands are dripping in blood with the lives of men who did nothing more than defend their homes. Acts that would make her shudder to know. Things that make me shudder to remember.

184

She paddles to me. "I don't care."

I move away, even my feet leaving the ground. "One day you will, though."

One day you'll look at me and see the monster, just like everyone else.

She continues after me. "Evander."

I hold my hands out for her, smiling wanly and forcing a topic change. "You're swimming."

She takes my hand, treading water with me. "I am?"

I nod at her, pointing to the shore, which is farther than it's ever been. She glances down at the water, and a look of pure delight crosses her face. "I'm doing it!"

I release her again and pull away a bit. "Swim to me."

She smiles proudly, paddling to me slowly. I catch her against me when she makes it. She kisses me, her delighted giggles teasing my lips. "Thank you."

The water ripples around us as I spin her in the water before pulling away again. I hold my hands out. "Again."

She paddles, her voice a little ragged from the unfamiliar exercise. "Come back!"

When she makes it to me this time, she locks her legs around my waist, and I growl, "I like you swimming to me."

"Why is that?"

I tread water for the both of us. "I like anything that ends with you wrapped around me."

"It's a good thing I can't keep my hands off you, husband," she says and kisses me again.

I glance up at the sky and see that the night is growing darker. "We should head back. I still have to leave the day after tomorrow," I say with regret.

She sighs sadly, releasing me. "You're right."

I pull her back to me and wrap her around me as I wade onto the shore. She buries her face into my neck but doesn't lower her legs.

She shivers, and I find my shirt, draping it over her. I pick up my breeches and debate a way to put them on without putting her down. I sigh and finally let her slide down my body until her feet touch the sand. She slips into the shirt, looking away as I yank my breeches and boots back on.

I whistle loudly, and the Black trots over. I lift her onto his back before swinging up behind her. "You look fetching in my clothes."

She gives me a soft smile and leans against my chest as I guide the Black back to camp. "Thank you, my love."

"I suppose I should regret cutting your clothes off."

I can hear the smile in her voice as she says, "Do you not?"

My hand settles on her thigh, drifting up the smooth skin. "I don't."

She shifts, wiggling her ass back against my groin. "I don't either."

My hands draw a design on her upper thigh as we ride through camp. At our tent, she shifts in my arms, whispering under her breath, "Evander!"

I slide off the Black and help her down, holding her close against me. "Are you surprised?"

XXIX

Charlotte

OUTSIDE ILIUM

KINGDOM OF CANDONIA

Not at all." I shake my head, grabbing his arms. Evander helps me to the ground, and I move closer to him, craving his warmth. In all honesty, I can't keep my hands off him. All I want is to be in his arms, curled against his chest, listening to his heartbeat. I'm becoming unhealthily obsessed with this man.

Evander brushes the wet hair out of my face, smiling down at me. His beautiful grey eyes stare into my own, and it makes my heart flutter.

"You're a sickness I hope to never recover from," he says before scrunching his nose. "That didn't sound right."

I giggle as we walk into the tent. "No, it doesn't."

We both get undressed, and I crawl into bed first. Getting under the furs, I hold my arms open for him. Evander slips in beside me, pulling me close to rest his head between my breasts. I gently play with his wet hair, twirling a strand around my finger.

"I'm going to miss you," I whisper.

He wraps his arms around my torso. "I'm sure you'll find some way to occupy yourself."

I shake my head, my fingers continuing to run through his hair. "You'll be gone for an entire month."

"How did you occupy your time before me?" he asks, kissing the side of my breast. The action sends shivers down my spine, and for a second, I don't remember what I did before him. It feels like I have been with him forever. How is that possible?

"I would spend time with my father and work on new proposals for the kingdom." I sigh. As the heir, there were countless other duties, but that was something I did every day. I was training to become the Queen of Candonia.

"You'll be able to spend time with him." Evander sighs. "Since you'll be going back to the palace while I'm gone."

I frown in confusion. "Wait, what?"

"Hm?" Evander yawns loudly, nuzzling me. Not even his touch can pull me away from this subject. There is something about the camp that makes me want to stay. Like it will feel like he is still here, even though he isn't.

"I want to stay here," I whisper.

"No," he replies.

"But why not?"

He looks up at me. "You are not to stay in camp without me. The Mountain will escort you and Eleanor to the palace after we leave. He will remain behind as your personal guard."

I don't like this. I don't want to go back to the palace without him.

"But I want to stay," I pout stubbornly.

"Absolutely not," he says.

"And the reason?" I question.

"Do I need a reason?" he asks, narrowing his eyes on me.

"You do." I nod.

Evander sits up. "No, I don't. I am your husband. You go where I tell you."

Oh no. That isn't how it's going to work. Our marriage will not be a dictatorship. The queen has tried to control me before, thinking that she has authority over me. When I am determined to do something, I don't take no for an answer. I will sneak back here with or without his permission, and he won't be able to stop me.

188

"I have a mind of my own, Evander," I say, sitting up beside him and crossing my arms across my chest. "I can make my own choices."

"Not in this," he says, his jaw tightening. "You'll go back to the palace while I'm gone. As will Eleanor."

I open and close my mouth, anger bubbling my stomach. "You are not the boss of me!"

"Yes. I am," Evander grits out between his teeth.

My entire body tenses and I lie back down, turning away from him. *No, you are not.* Though, I will not fight with him tonight. Tomorrow morning we can continue this conversation when I have cooled down. His words are still ringing in my ears, and I can feel my blood pumping from the frustration and anger. It is normal for a man to think he owns a woman. It was written long ago in our history, decided by past kings in different kingdoms that we have no say. When you become a wife, you become property. My mother and father didn't install that same idea into my head, though. Thalia, Eleanor, and I were raised to have a mind of our own. Much to the distaste of the queen and many others. I hear Evander sigh.

"You're not safe here," Evander says, turning his back to me.

"I'll have the Mountain," I whisper, fiddling with the furs, still bristling at the idea of him controlling me

"To many of my men, you are still the enemy," he says, grinding his teeth.

I take a deep breath and let it out slowly before saying, "They'd kill me? Wouldn't they?"

Evander hisses out a breath. "My men are rougher than your palace guards."

I sigh, my body nearly vibrating with frustration and pain. I know that respect is earned, and that takes time, but how will I ever earn their trust if I don't have the opportunity? If they don't give me a chance to show it? Evander rolls over, wrapping his arms around me and pulling me against his chest.

"They'd never touch you sober. I just don't want to take the chance," he whispers, running his fingers gently through my hair. "Is that so bad?"

"I trust your decision," I whisper, moving closer to him. Now that I know the real reason he wants me to go back to the palace, I understand. It was not about controlling me as much as it was *protecting me.*

"I'm not used to explaining myself to anyone." He sighs. "I also don't want you to be scared."

I turn to face him, placing my hand on his cheek. "I'm not scared when I'm with you."

"But I won't be here, and I need…" He pauses, searching my eyes and brushing my hair from my face, "I need to know you're safe."

I nod, looking up at him. "Can I visit the camp during the day? It's nice out here."

He huffs. "You cannot be here after dark. No matter what. Promise me."

"I promise." I give him a bright smile before kissing him. Now, I can work on a plan to show Evander's men that I am not their enemy. I am not sure how, but I will have a month to figure that out, and ideas are already swarming my mind.

"I can't imagine you wanting to be in camp rather than the palace," Evander says, his arms tightening around me.

I draw shapes on his chest. "In the palace, I feel like I need to prove myself. Here I feel…"

I frown as I try to think of the right word. I feel like I can be myself. There are no eyes on me other than Evander's men, but they judge me for different reasons. Not how I hold myself. Not how I act. They only believe I am the enemy and that I am determined to change.

"Safe?" Evander says, lifting my hand to his lips and kissing my fingertips.

"Free." I nod, looking at him. *I feel free.*

He blinks at me. "I never thought a princess would be anything but free."

I sigh. It is funny how many people think royalty equals freedom. We do get perks like food on the table and warm baths, but there is a duty to our people. It weighs on our soul, and often I can't sleep peacefully at night. *Am I doing the right thing? Should I be doing more? Is this right?* Those questions circle through my mind constantly, and it is exhausting.

"There are duties a princess must fulfill daily. I hardly get time to myself," I say.

"Like what?" He frowns.

I take his hand in mine. "I usually spend the morning with my father, listening to the concerns of our people. Then I insisted on joining in for the war meetings, even though our generals disagree with a woman being present. In the afternoons, I would take time to learn a new language or read up on history. Then if there are foreign delegates, I must entertain them. Prepare parties and other small events."

The list goes on.

"My poor lamb," Evander says, yawning.

I sigh softly. "Yes…"

His lips twitch. "Would be hard to work with me needing to bend you over every available surface at least three times during the day."

"Evander!" I blush and hide my face against him.

He smirks, closing his eyes. "I can't help it."

"Sleep," I whisper as a shiver runs down my spine.

"Well, you can be sure that our first child will arrive in roughly nine months," he says, pressing me against him.

"You think so?" I ask, my face warming and stomach tingling. The idea of children had been far from my thoughts since I had yet to marry. Now it is a possibility, and I could be pregnant even now. Surprisingly, that doesn't scare me.

"Did I say that out loud?" he asks.

"You did." I giggle, biting my lower lip. I am already thinking of possible names, imagining the sounds of an infant crying and childish laughter in the palace halls.

"Let's just forget about that," he mutters.

"We will find out when you return if I am," I whisper, kissing his chin.

Evander clears this throat. "I wouldn't want to rush you. I know you want to get to know me better."

Kind. Considerate. Caring. He continues to surprise me. I softly press my lips against his before laying back down. "Thank you."

"Though, I know many will expect an heir immediately," he says, his lips twitching.

I kiss him softly. "Then we can start as soon as you return."

"I don't...maybe we should wait longer." He gulps and tenses under me. He sits up, his body hot and sweat dripping down his back. His breathing is harsh, shallow, and frantic.

"Look at me," I say, sitting up beside him. I place my hands on his cheek, forcing him to face me. His breathing remains frantic, and his eyes are glazed over. I feel my own widen with concern as sweat drips between his brows.

"Lamb," he mumbles.

I rub his cheek with my thumb. "I'm here. It's just you and me."

The same words he'd said to me on our first night together. It's just the two of us, no one else. At the time, the thought was comforting. Maybe they will help him come back to me. Evander's breathing slowly calms, but his body is still covered in a slight mist of sweat.

"I just realized..." He shakes his head, silencing himself.

"Tell me," I whisper.

"I don't even know who my parents are. I don't have a father," Evander gulps, his face turning red, "or a mother. I had masters. I don't...." He pulls away from me. "I need to go for a walk."

"I think you'll make a wonderful father," I say, grabbing his arm. If there were a way to go back into the past and change it, I would. I hate knowing he was taken from his family. His life and everything he loved ripped away from him. It breaks me.

He only shakes his head. "I don't know how to be one."

"I don't know how to be a mother," I say, taking his hand in mine and squeezing it. "We can learn together."

"You have a mother," Evander says, closing his eyes.

"She died when I was a girl," I whisper.

"What?!" Evander looks at me in surprise. "You have a mother."

I shake my head. "The queen is my stepmother."

"She is?" Evander asks, his brows furrowing. I am not surprised he doesn't know my mother died. My father had not made an event of it. We had a quiet ceremony that only family attended.

"My mother died giving birth to Eleanor," I whisper. I still remember her pale skin and how cold she felt the last time I saw her.

"Oh, lamb, I'm so sorry," he says.

I move closer to him, wrapping my arms around his torso. "I've accepted it."

"I suppose it's better that I will never know my parents," he whispers.

An idea strikes me, and I look up at him. "Maybe we can find them."

Evander chokes. "Lamb, they don't keep records for what I was. And no one can know, or they'll petition the bishop for an annulment."

"Then I'll find them in secret," I whisper, determination in my voice.

He turns to me, his expression serious. "Swear to me now that you will never, ever go looking for them."

"But—" I begin, my brows furrowing.

"Now," he says, his voice as stern as ever.

I sigh. "I promise never to go looking for them."

"Thank you," he says, hissing out a breath of relief.

"Sleep?" I say, sighing sadly.

He nods, and we both crawl back under the furs. I move close to him, cuddling up to his body. Something in the air doesn't feel right. We are both tense from the conversation. I don't like how I can't look for his parents. What if they are alive? What if they are looking for him? It doesn't seem fair that he can't find them, that they can never be reunited. It makes my stomach twist.

Evander gets out of the bed at some point, and I stay as still as possible, waiting to see what he will do. He slowly gets dressed before exiting the tent. I sit up as soon as he leaves and stare at the tent flap for a long time before laying back down. I pull his pillow against my chest, keeping my eyes open.

I will find your parents Evander, and you will make a wonderful father.

XXX

EVAN

OUTSIDE ILIUM

KINGDOM OF CANDONIA

The sea crashes on the shore as my ma cradles me to her chest, her scent that of clean linens and honeysuckle. It soothes me as the storm rages outside the small shack. My Da is gone, but his scent lingers on the rough sheets of their bed. Smoke and the sea air envelop me in comfort, in familiarity. But when I look up at my ma, her face is nothing but a blur, her features impossible to distinguish. Even searching my mind, they only become hazier.

I can't remember her face or his, but I can remember the feel of the cheap sheets on their bed. The smell of our house, but everything else is a blur.

I don't remember any of the lessons I should have absorbed from them. The knowledge I'm supposed to pass on to my children. The children I could have in ten months. Fuck, why didn't I think about it? Until I threw that off-handed comment to my wife, I never really considered the consequences of constantly taking her.

Ancients above. How can I expect to be king and change Aellolyn when I don't even know the most basic things? How can I be a king and a father? I circle the camp and nod at the sentries as I pass them, remaining within the torchlight.

Will I be a good father? A good king? Or will I be like all the rest? Forgettable? Lost to history? A conqueror who should

have never been king. A man who should never have been a
father. A slave who should never have been more than that.

Nothing.

Scum.

Dirt.

The voices of my past scream in my head now, and I do
nothing to quiet them. I circle the camp for a couple of hours
before I feel ready to return to the tent. I fall face-first onto the
bed next to Charlotte. She's face down and curled around her
pillow. I settle deeper into the mattress and pull her back
against me, my body aching for sleep. She shifts, opening her
eyes and looking at me. "Evander?"

"Why are you still awake?" I whisper, brushing her hair back
from her face. I wouldn't have left if I thought she would wake
up.

Her sapphire eyes shine at me. "I woke up a few hours ago. I
can't sleep without you now."

Nor can I sleep without her. Already our lives are wrapped
around each other. I can't make myself care as I trace my hand
over her cheek. "I'm sorry."

She scoots closer to me, moving from her pillow to mine. She
curls against me, closing her eyes slowly. "It's fine."

Her scent wraps around me as I kiss her forehead and wrap
my arms around her. "I just needed some air."

"I understand," she whispers, nuzzling my chest.

"I didn't know kids scared me so much." The idea of an heir
was always an abstract, a necessity, not an actuality. But when
we spoke about it, I saw a little girl with dark curls like her
mother and eyes a steely grey. And a boy with a mop of blonde
hair and sapphire eyes. It all seemed so real. I had never
considered that I would feel anything more than a sense of duty
toward my wife. But now, everything is different.

"You've never thought about it before."

"The concept of an heir, yes, just not...I have never had a father." My breathing escalates again. "I don't know how to be a father."

Her arms tighten around me, pulling me back when I try to distance myself. "We don't need to think about this now." She kisses the side of my head. "It's just you and me."

The exact words I'd said to her on our first night together. A sort of talisman for our marriage.

"Just you and me," I repeat, kissing her.

"Let's get some rest, husband."

I close my eyes, relaxing. "Yes. Sleep, my love. Sleep."

She rests her head on my chest, and we drift off wrapped around each other, our hearts slowly syncing to beat as one.

Light wakes me before the morning drill horn. I keep my eyes closed as I feel Charlotte shift and her fingers slide through my hair.

I quirk my lips in a lazy smile. "You're supposed to be asleep."

She continues playing with a lock of my hair, whispering, "Can't I admire my husband?"

"Nope." I keep my eyes closed, moving down her body to rest my head between her breasts. "These are my new favorite pillows."

Her hands twirl a lock of the hair at my neck. "Are they?"

I kiss the side of one of her breasts, more content than I can remember being. "Easy access to my second favorite place in the world."

She laughs. "And your first?"

I shift so she can feel my hardness.

"D-don't you have training?" she stutters huskily.

The morning horn for drills goes off, making me groan and pull away. "You're right."

My eyes open, and I kiss the curve of her breast again before sitting up. I stretch, lifting my arms over my head.

Her fingers dance down my spine, making me shiver. "You may have me tonight."

It takes a moment for me to stop focusing on her and get out of bed. "I have to get ready for tomorrow."

"Oh, I forgot..."

Her eyes are downcast, and she is tracing an edge of the furs. She nibbles her lower lip, dreading our separation.

"I have something to show you," I say, pulling on fresh clothes from my trunk.

The sound of the sheets rustling tells me she's sitting up even before I turn around. "You do?"

I walk back to the bed and sit on the edge to yank my boots on. I lean over and kiss her hard before saying, "Get dressed and meet me outside."

Charlotte pushes me back and jumps out of bed, slipping on a fresh shift. "What is it?"

I laugh and stand up, watching her scrounge around under the bed for her delicate slippers. "You do know what a surprise is?"

She opens her trunk, pulling out a pastel blue dress. She slips it on and faces away, waiting for me to lace it up. I'm not sure why, but I love this task. The palace even sent a lady's maid to camp the other day, and I dismissed her before my wife could see her. I like this simple task, and I will not let anyone take it away from me.

"No, I don't. Remind me?" she asks coyly, dropping her hair down after I finish.

I kiss her shoulder and say, "Something you will not get if you keep mouthing off to me."

She smirks over her shoulder. "I am doing nothing of the sort."

Deliberately, I trail my fingers along her neck, lifting her hair to tie with one of the pale blue ribbons on her vanity. "You are."

The bow in the ribbon is more like a knot, but it is enough to keep her hair out of her face.

She turns to face me, a hand resting on my chest. "I think you're mistaken. I'm an obedient little princess who does exactly what she's told."

I pinch her chin playfully, smirking down at her. "Oh? If that's true, you can't possibly be my wife."

My hands drop to her hips, guiding her back against me. She purrs, "Are you sure?"

I nod at her. "My wife is definitely not obedient. She is strong, powerful, and speaks her mind, so you can't be her."

She scoffs and lifts to her tiptoes, offering her lips. I dip my head to accept, but a horse whinnying from outside stops me from going any further. I step back and take her hand, interlocking our fingers so I can guide her to the tent flap.

We step out, and the light from the sun is momentarily blinding, making me blink for a moment. My vision adjusts when a massive shadow blocks the sun's rays. The white horse rears, tossing its head as it drops to the ground, prancing side to side in the soldier's grip. She is not a fan of being controlled, just like her brother.

The Black moves between the soldier and the White, forcing him to release her or get trampled. The soldier wisely picks life and drops the reins. My men linger, unsure what to do. It is always this way when it comes to the Black. My men know he has a mind and will of his own, and the only person he listens to is me.

I turn to my squire and order him to let the men know I will not join them for morning drills and to continue without me. He sends me a sly smirk before running off.

I let out a short whistle, and the Black's head comes up. He locks on me, nudging his sister toward us. When he comes closer, I hold my hand up for him, and he presses his nose to my palm in greeting. "You're excited she's here, huh? You missed her?"

The Black lets out a soft huff of air, and I rub his face in praise. I look back at Charlotte lingering at the edge of our tent and smile at her. "A wedding present."

She steps forward slowly, holding her hand out for the mare to inspect. The White looks to her brother for direction, and he watches her, as do I. It takes a moment, but she cautiously sniffs Charlotte's hand, then retreats. My wife is patient, waiting for the horse to come to her of her own accord. When the mare presses her nose against Charlotte's palm, my lips twitch.

"She was supposed to be here before the wedding, but she got stuck on the trip down from Grimmwing." Charlotte pets the softness of the mare's muzzle, and the horse presses closer to her, lowering her head to inspect her new mistress from head to toe.

"You got her for me before our wedding?" she murmurs, her eyes brightening.

I rub the Black's neck as he inspects my breeches for treats. He huffs in disgust when he finds nothing. "We think she's the Black's sister." We couldn't be sure, but she is one of the few animals or even general creatures I've ever seen the warhorse express any kind of attachment to. "And I didn't intend to come completely empty-handed to our wedding."

My wife's hand trails along the mare's gleaming neck as she murmurs to the horse, "Oh...I love you." She pauses for a moment, her cheeks turning pink before she whispers, "I think I will name you Snow."

I hate the pang of jealousy that hits me. I wish Charlotte were speaking to me, that she loved me. To distract myself, I move behind her, patting Snow affectionately. "She is a beauty, isn't she?" As is her mistress.

"She is," my wife says reverently.

I move to the horse's side and hold my hand out for Charlotte. "Would you like to go for a ride?"

Unlike her brother, Snow is outfitted with a bridle and saddle. My wife slips her hand into mine and bounces in place. "Yes, I'd love to."

I lift her onto the mare's back, and she settles into the saddle, gathering the reins.

XXXI

Charlotte

OUTSIDE ILIUM

KINGDOM OF CANDONIA

A horse. He has given me a horse. Her brilliant white coat nearly sparkles in the sunlight. She shakes her mane, and it shimmers, almost glowing. There is a connection I feel towards this animal, an unexplained bond. I bite my bottom lip before looking at Evander.

A gift for our wedding. I didn't think he would have thought of getting me something for our marriage. The idea is endearing, and it makes my heart flutter in my chest. Even though he forced my hand, he thought of giving me a gift. I was so pleased by the gesture that I even whispered under my breath that I love him. Luckily, I was looking at the horse when I muttered those three simple words. They have me thinking. I know my heart beats for him, but do I love him? So soon?

"Ready?" Evander asks me, snapping me from my thoughts. I know he is taking important time away from his men to be with me. My first ride on Snow and some time with Evander away from camp and the city. I would never give up an opportunity like this.

I gather the reins and look at him. "Yes. Where to?"

"Would you like to go check on a nearby village with me?" he asks, turning the Black and kneeing him closer.

I nod, biting my lower lip. "Which one?"

He smirks and leans toward me. "First, a kiss."

I lean over, pressing my lips softly to his. "Now tell me."

Evander sighs, pulling away. "Slavers had overtaken Ghynts. We freed it on our way to the capital, but we haven't heard anything from them since."

My brow furrows in thought. Ghynts is a village southwest of Ilium. There should be no slave activity at all in that region. At least I thought there was none. Then again, there has been significant resistance to the laws against slavery. I'd received reports of slavers caught in the act. However, the efforts towards catching them had to be paused when the war got more intense.

"That's strange," I say.

"It's my squire's hometown," Evander says, clearing his throat. He presses his heels against his horse, and the Black breaks into a gallop. I follow behind him, the wind in my hair and the sound of hooves on the road clearing my thoughts. I love this feeling of freedom.

We are still a distance away from Ghynts when I smell the distinct scent of smoke. It takes us another thirty minutes to reach the village, and my breath hitches in my throat when I see the state of it. The entire town is charred, the buildings as black as coal and barely standing. Small fires crackle in the middle of what is left of the homes. I grip the reins, my eyes tearing. The smell of burnt wood and stone makes my nose burn, and I cover it with my cloak. *Who would do this? What kind of monsters would burn the entire village?*

Evander dismounts and strides to the middle of the village. His cold gaze scans the skeletal remains of the town, his shoulders stiff and his hands fisted in rage. I feel my heart squeeze in my chest as I slide off Snow and slowly walk up behind him. I have never seen anything like this, though I have heard stories. It makes me sick to my stomach, and I can feel my entire body shake. *Whoever did this will pay for their crimes.*

"No bodies," Evander whispers icily. "Slavers."

"How?" I choke.

He looks back at me. "As you said, outlawing and enforcing are two very different things."

A young boy emerges from one of the burnt houses. He looks no older than five, and his entire body is covered in soot and ash. His bright blue eyes are the only color on him. He runs to us, throwing himself at Evander's legs, clinging to him tightly and trembling. How long has he been alone? Where are the others?

"Mister Black, they took my mommy! They took them all!" the boy cries, his body shaking with sobs.

Evander crouches, brushing the soot off the boy's cheek with his thumb. "Which way did they go?"

The boy points to the woods in the south. "That way, less than a day ago."

Evander looks back at me. "Will you take him back to camp? I have to take care of this."

"I will, but you'll need help. Who should I send?" I ask, walking over and picking the child up. The thought of him going to deal with this on his own scares me. I can't lose him.

"I won't need help," he says as we walk back to our horses. "Don't stop until you get home."

"You better come back to me, Evander."

Evander doesn't respond, just kisses me hard before helping the boy and me onto the mare. She paws the dirt, shaking her head anxiously. I rub the side of her neck, though it does little to calm her.

"Don't stop," Evander says, slapping Snow's rump. She rears before galloping toward the camp. The boy buries his face against my stomach, and I hold my hand to his head, keeping him close. He is still shaking, and I know he is in shock and needs comfort. He saw everyone he loves taken, and who knows what the slavers did to them in the process. The home he grew up in burned to the ground, and he watched as his world was destroyed. I know Evander will save those the slavers took and bring them back, but I can't help but worry.

The further from Evander I get, the more my heart struggles to beat. It is an actual ache in my chest. My mind spins with thousands of questions. What if I don't see him again? There are things I still want to tell him, things I have yet to say out loud.

I let out a shaky breath, looking down at the child who is clinging to me. *Breathe, Charlotte. The child needs you, and you have to be strong for him.* I tighten my arms around the boy as the camp comes into view. The men go about their duties as if everything is right with the world. Only a few of them look up at me, raising a brow but not asking questions. I need to find Demir.

Snow trots into camp, and I can feel the anxiety radiating off her body, mixing with my own turbulent emotions. Demir is laying out his armor by his tent. His squire is there beside him with a cloth tied over his eyes. It is traditional for all squires to spend their final year blindfolded to heighten their senses. He looks up as he hears my horse. His frown deepens when he sees the bedraggled child trembling against me but no Evander.

"Where is he?" Demir mouths clearly to me.

I slide off the horse before helping the boy down. "The village we went to check on has been b-burnt to the ground by slavers." I choke back a sob. "Evander w-went after them. W-we have to help him."

Demir looks me up and down before pointing to the ground, indicating that I have to stay here. He does not look concerned, and that should comfort me, but it doesn't. I watch as he mounts his smoky grey horse and digs his heels into its sides. My eyes stay on him until he is no longer in sight before I look down at the boy. I see blonde curls poking through the soot and grime.

"Are you hungry?" I ask, crouching beside the boy. I wipe away his tears with my thumb, clearing some of the dirt from his cheeks. The boy only breaks down more, throwing himself at me and wrapping his little arms around my body. I pick him up, walking over to the cook's tent as he sobs into my shoulder.

"Evander will bring them home," I whisper. *He has to.*

204

XXXII

EVAN

OUTSIDE GHYNTS

KINGDOM OF CANDONIA

The rage simmers through me as I launch onto the Black and follow the trail left by the slavers. The deep imprints from a cart cut into the dark forest surrounding the remains of the smoking village. They took everyone, including the old and sick, which means they'll be moving slowly and stopping often. It will be easy for us to close the distance.

The Black flies along the tracks, and it takes me less than an hour to catch up with the caravan. Twelve heavily armed slavers surround the people of Ghynts, kicking at them when they stumble, forcing the villagers forward. My hands tighten on the Black's mane, my lip curling back from my teeth. I scan my surroundings, noticing the slavers are heading into an even more densely wooded area, forced off the beaten path because of Candonia's law. The perfect opportunity for a one-man ambush, isolate the slavers and pick them off one by one.

Once I'm close enough, I dismount and move into the trees. I pull out my bow and arrows and start picking off the men at the end of the caravan. They drop with a shaft through the side of their heads, crumpling silently to the ground and not drawing attention. One of the villagers sees me at the edge of the trees. She opens her mouth to scream but pauses when I send an arrow through the second slaver's eye. I hold a finger to my lips, and the young girl freezes. Our eyes connect, and she nods before pretending to stumble and fall. Another slaver drops back to grab her and yank her up. He pulls his hand back to slap her, and my next arrow goes through his forehead.

She covers her mouth, muffling her yelp of fear. She can't be more than fifteen, her straw-colored hair matted and her face covered with soot. The girl takes a few steadying breaths before she grabs another slaver. When he opens his mouth to yell, my arrow goes through his throat.

By the fifth body, they catch on, and the leader orders his men to surround the *merchandise*. The slavers stare into the trees, looking for the threat. I cover my mouth with my hands and emit a whistle mixed with a bird call. The Black charges forward, rushing through the circle of people. Their defenses break as they scramble to get out of the way of the stampeding horse. Amid the chaos, I lunge out of the forest and grab another slaver. I drag him back into the trees and break his neck.

Six to go.

The Black runs off, and I straighten, firing another volley of arrows from the trees. They ping off their shields when they manage to yank them up in time. Now that they know I am here, it is time to make my presence known. No more hiding.

I whistle again, and the Black weaves through the trees, galloping toward me. I grab a fistful of his mane and swing onto his back, nudging him with my knees. The warhorse whirls in the other direction, darting between the slavers and their path forward. He rears, his hooves slashing at the air, and the men flinch back.

The slavers grip their weapons, fear radiating off of them. The leader steps forward, looking me up and down. "Out of our way, stranger."

My lips twitch into a smirk, not moving out of his way or introducing myself. The villagers' eyes all lock on me, and they whisper to each other.

"It's *the Black.*"

"*Evan the Black.*"

"He's returned."

The other slavers shift from foot to foot at the whispers, and some tighten their hands on their scimitars. The head slaver ignores the murmurs, focusing on me, puffing his chest out. "You are between me and my payday."

Payday, that's all they are to him. All I once was. All I swore never to be again.

"You are between me and my people. I'm going to let you live so that you can spread the tale. The Kingdom of Candonia is under the protection of Evan the Black." The slaver pales and drops his weapon, his men following his lead. "And one more thing," I yank my bow up, letting the arrow fly, landing right in between the lead slaver's eyes, "I'm coming for them all."

The other slavers scream and flee into the trees, leaving their weapons behind. Word will spread, and as it does, the number of those who disobey the laws of Candonia will drastically reduce.

I holster my bow and dismount, unsheathing the sword at my waist. Grimmwing steel is special, the ore mystical and drawn from deep within the mountains. I swing down at the chains, and it slices through the iron with a small spark, freeing the villagers. I whistle loudly to gain their attention, raising my voice so all can hear me. "Your homes were burned behind you, but you all may take refuge at my camp outside the walls of Ilium. It won't be what you are used to, but you will have a place to sleep, food to eat, and work if you want it."

An elder comes forward, leaning heavily on a gnarled staff to support himself. "We would be honored to accept that request, Your Highness."

He bows his head with a knowing grin. My marriage must have spread throughout all of Aellolyn by now, the repercussions of it remaining to be seen. I nod at him in acknowledgment and begin helping the elderly of the group into a cart the slavers had forced them to drag. I whistle the Black over, hitching him up to it, despite his reluctance.

The horse refuses to wear anything, including a bridle or saddle. I once tried to put a pouch around his neck, and he rubbed it off at the next tree. He also refuses to be ridden by another, no matter what. Even if I wanted to, I couldn't put any of the villagers on his back unless I rode with them.

The Black twitches at the cart's harness, and I hold my breath, waiting for him to do something. It takes a moment before he decides to trot forward with the old and sick, whinnying as he does. My hand drops to my sword when I hear hoofbeats, and I move to stand between the villagers and the approaching horse. My sword makes a soft click as I pull it partway from the scabbard.

My hand relaxes when the Mountain rides into view on his fat, dappled destrier. "What are you doing here?"

The Mountain signs, *"Your wife."*

I shake my head and say, "I told her I didn't need reinforcements." The Mountain snorts, rolling his eyes at me as he dismounts and wordlessly offers his horse to a woman and her children. We work together, getting everyone organized and turned in the right direction. The Mountain and I walk side-by-side, leading the villagers back toward camp.

The sentries patrolling the edges see us coming and step forward to help the villagers get settled. I unhitch the Black, who rears and snorts at me in disgust before trotting off. Likely to find his sister. The pair are practically inseparable when in the same country.

I start snapping orders at my men, and they scramble to set up more tents, get fires started, and distribute food. As I turn to issue another command, my wife collides with me, her arms wrapping around my neck. I whisper into her hair, "Lamb." She clings to me, and I pull her closer. "Were you worried about me?"

She nuzzles her face against my neck. "Terribly worried."

I would normally take it as an insult that she worried, as if she doubted my skills in combat. But I like the greeting when I

208

return too much to say anything about it. I'd allow any insult to my abilities so long as it ends with her throwing herself into my arms and clinging to me like ivy.

"I do have some experience with this."

I killed my first slaver at sixteen.

"I know. I just…" Charlotte trails off, not finishing whatever she had to say. She just kisses my neck and the side of my head instead.

"I'm sorry our ride had to end so abruptly." I had hoped to help her explore more of her country…*our* country.

She tightens her arms around me even more. "I'm just happy you are here."

The Black neighs loudly, prancing around Snow. I sigh at the sight as I pull away from her. "I wish your present wasn't tainted like this."

"It isn't tainted, Evander. I will cherish her forever."

I clear my throat slightly. "As I will…cherish you."

Ancients, this woman is turning me into a total swain.

I can't bring myself to care, though. So long as she is the way she is, I'll whisper her praises until I'm blue in the face. Especially when she looks at me the way she does now, tears flooding her sapphire eyes. "You cherish me?"

I rub the back of my neck, eyes darting away. "Maybe."

She grabs my leather breastplate, yanking me to her, and kissing me hard. "I truly love you, Evander. I hope you know that."

Blink. Blink. Blink.

"What…what did you just say?"

I must be hearing things because it sounded like she told me she loved me for the first time. Maybe this is all a dream. Maybe I was injured when we first took Ilium, and I'm lying in the healing tent, dreaming of some better world. A dream where she could love me, where even if she had the opportunity to choose from a bevy of suitors, she would still pick me.

"I-I love you."

Not a dream.

My hands shake as I lift them to frame her face. I search her gaze before asking in disbelief, "You love me?"

She nods, even as her cheeks flush. "I love you."

I smile and grab her around the waist, lifting her above my head and spinning her around. It takes me a couple of spins before I am ready to put her feet back on the ground. She laughs, kissing me again.

"Would you like to help me settle the villagers? I offered to let them stay and rebuild their lives."

She nods. "Of course. I'd love to help you."

I link my hand with hers and squeeze it gently. "Thank you, lamb."

"Thank you?"

"For trusting me with your heart."

The one she swore I would never have. The one I don't deserve. The one I stole. This isn't a dream world where she got to choose. In this world, I robbed her of the choice she fought for years to have.

"Just take care of it?"

"I will." I lift her hand to my lips and kiss her knuckles. She smiles up at me, her blue eyes nearly glowing with happiness as she walks toward our tent. Out of the corner of my eye, I notice the looks of indecision my wife is receiving. Clearly, the feelings of hostility toward her are lessening.

"There is abandoned farmland to the northwest of here. It could be a good place for the villagers to rebuild."

Charlotte constantly surprises me with her valuable insight into politics and how deeply she cares for people. She thinks in ways I never expect. I understand why her father used to rely so heavily on her opinion. I'm coming to rely on it as well.

"That is an excellent idea."

She smiles up at me, resting her head on my arm. "I am sure my father will be alright with it. The land is unused, and the city will eventually need more food with its sudden growth."

"Would you like to go speak to him? Together?" This will be the first time I have a conversation with the king that isn't at sword point. It is probably better my wife is present to run interference.

"Yes, let's do that."

I lift her onto Snow before grabbing the Black's mane and swinging onto his back. She shoots me a look. "Race you?"

I kick the Black hard without agreeing, racing toward the city.

"Cheater!" she squeals.

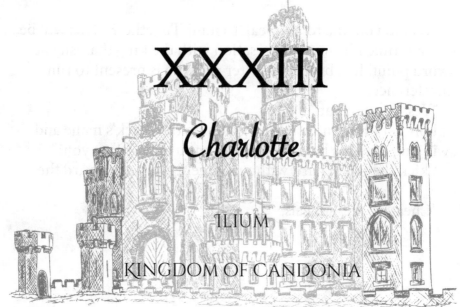

XXXIII

Charlotte

ILIUM

KINGDOM OF CANDONIA

The wind blows through my hair as Snow and I try to catch up to Evander. The Black is too quick, blocking us each time we get close. Winning or losing, it doesn't matter. Our laughter fills the streets of the city as I try to pass him again, people stopping to stare as we race by them.

In the distance, I see the palace, the home where I grew up. Its towers reach high into the sky, looming over the city. It feels foreign to me. Has a week away really changed me this much?

I lower my head as we make our way closer to our destination. At the last second, the Black slows down, Snow and I passing them. I laugh and throw my hands up in the air.

"We did it!" I cheer to Snow as I bring her to a stop.

Evander rides up beside me, pulling me off Snow and onto his lap. "You did," he says and kisses me softly.

I turn around to face him, laughing as I press my body close to his and deepen the kiss. *True bliss.* He pulls away when someone clears their throat behind us. My stepmother looks down at us from the top of the stairs with a glare of disapproval. I wonder if she is feeling well. Her cheekbones are so sharp they look carved from stone. She narrows her chocolate brown eyes at us, and I notice that her hair is not in its usual tight bun but loose and messy.

"I thought you forgot about us," she says, her voice monotone and unchanging.

"My apologies, Your Majesty." I sit up and raise my chin slightly. *I never call her mother, only Your Majesty.* Evander lowers me to the ground before dropping down behind me.

"I was guarding her jealously. The fault is mine," Evander says. The queen ignores him, her gaze focused on me.

"Your father has been worried about you and Eleanor," she says, clasping her hands behind her back.

Evander grabs my hand, lifting his chin as he responds for me. "We are here to speak with him."

The queen finally snaps her eyes to him, looking him up and down. She stays silent for a moment as she studies him, and I squeeze Evander's hand. Although the woman has never done anything to me, I still get the shivers when she gives someone *the look.*

"Hm," she finally says, "he is in his study."

Evander holds her gaze a moment longer before gesturing for me to lead the way. I lower my head as we walk up the stairs and past the queen. I'm just about to open the large doors to the palace when the queen clears her throat again.

"Charlotte? You will be wearing your corset the next time I see you," she scolds.

Evander's body snaps straight, and he slowly turns his head to look at the queen. "You will not be ordering my wife. Is that clear?"

The queen remains unfazed. "I will be as long as she is a Princess of Candonia. She knows the rules."

I squeeze Evander's hand, tugging it lightly as I try to avoid the confrontation. He ignores me, pulling his hand from mine and resting both hands on my shoulders.

"And as future King of Candonia, I dictate what the rules are," he says.

The queen tilts her head. "You are not king yet, boy. The princesses know better. Isn't that right, Charlotte?"

"Yes, Your Majesty," I say, trying to finish the conversation.

This only makes Evander stiffen more. "I would be cautious, Queen *Mother*, who you cross. Without your husband, your position is *tenuous*."

The queen goes silent, glaring down at me. The look in her eyes is deadly, and I know she will be on the warpath once I leave.

I gulp and look up at Evander. "Let's go."

Evander nods and follows me inside. I am greeted by the familiar smells and sights of the palace, but something about it feels different with Evander here. Servants are going about their duties, preparing the castle for fall. Red carpets have been laid out on the marble flooring. Summer flowers have been replaced by autumn ones. Even a few of the paintings have been switched over to fit the season. The house staff lower their heads as soon as they get close to us. There was once a rumor that if you look into the eyes of the conqueror, he will melt you with his glare. My husband doesn't have the best reputation here.

I spot Thalia rushing through the hall, and my stomach twists. The queen will surely take her wrath out on my sister if they cross paths right now. I look up at Evander, chewing my lip.

"Evander, I need to speak with Thalia for a moment," I say.

He raises a brow, crossing his arms over his chest. "Why?"

"I may be protected from my stepmother's anger, but she is not," I say.

"She would target your sister?" he asks, his lips tightening into a grim line.

I watch Thalia from the corner of my eye as she turns down a hallway. "She doesn't have anyone to protect her."

"I don't like that. Not one bit," he says, narrowing his eyes.

I look around, lowering my voice, "There is nothing we can do about it right now."

"No one would stop me from killing her, would they?" he growls.

"My father might," I say. "Don't do it. Thalia has been waiting for her moment to get revenge. I don't condone the idea, but..."

Evander's hand drops to my lower back, pulling me closer. "But you won't stop her."

I shake my head. "I will allow my sister to do what she needs to do."

"Why is it not something you have to deal with?" he asks, kissing me.

"My stepmother has always avoided me, but I know what she does to Thalia, even if Thalia doesn't admit it most of the time. Thalia is in charge of Eleanor, and if something happens with Eleanor, then Thalia is *punished*."

Evander goes silent, and I look up at him. It is the first time I have admitted that to anyone. Anytime I spoke to my father or even hinted at the queen's abuse, his eyes would go blank. It was as if he didn't even hear me. It was frustrating, and I tried my hardest to help Thalia when the queen would search for her. I hold Evander's gaze and can see the calculation in his eyes. I tilt my head, raising a brow. "What are you thinking?"

He frowns, looking around. "We need to see your father."

"I should speak to Thalia first. I can meet you in my father's study?" I suggest.

"You want to leave me alone with your father?" he asks with a smirk.

"Yes?" I look up at him, confused when his lips twitch. I frown at him. "What is so amusing?"

"You do remember the last time I spoke to your father?" he asks.

Closing my eyes, I think back. The last time I saw my father was...oh. The wedding. My father hasn't seen me since then. How could I have forgotten? "Right..."

He crosses his arms. "Go speak to your sister. I'll wait."

I nod before turning away from him and racing down the halls. I dislike leaving him alone in the palace, but I know he will be fine. He is Evan the Black, after all. Nothing scares my husband. My sister is just stepping into the courtyard when I stop her, tugging her arm.

"Lia," I say.

She turns to look at me, frowning. "Charlotte? What are you doing here?"

My eyes widen when I notice the purple bruise forming on her right cheek. The sight makes my stomach twist and rage consumes me. One day, the queen will get her karma, whether by Thalia's hand or my own.

"I want you to go to camp."

Thalia frowns. "What?! Why?"

I place my hand on her swollen cheek, and she winces, pushing away my touch. "The queen is going to be searching for you. She and Evander just had words, and she is furious."

"Then I will deal with it like I always have," she snaps, looking away.

I grab her arm before she has the chance to walk away. "Please. Just for the day. Then the three of us will return together tomorrow."

"Fine." She frowns.

I breathe a sigh of relief. "You remember the Mountain?"

"I do..." my sister says, her cheeks turning slightly rosy.

"Find him and tell him I sent you to camp, alright? Wait in my tent until I return. I shouldn't be long," I say.

Thalia nods once more, looking down at her feet. She wraps her arms around me, embracing me quickly.

"I will see you soon, Sister," she whispers before pulling away and hurrying across the courtyard. I wait a few minutes, watching her until she is past the bushes and out of sight. Letting out a steadying breath, I return to the throne room. Evander is pacing back and forth, his head low as he waits for me.

"Evander?"

He looks up. "That was quicker than I expected."

I raise to my tiptoes and kiss him, whispering against his lips, "I sent her to camp."

"I'm going to end up with all of them living underfoot."

216

"It is just for tonight," I whisper. "Then the three of us will return together when you..."

"Leave," he says, finishing my sentence. He presses his hand against my cheek, and I lean into it, covering his hand with my own.

"We should speak to my father," I say. *Then I get you to myself again.*

He nods, and I take his hand and lead him to my father's study. On the door, the words *King's Study* are written in flowing gold lettering. It is worn and faded with age, but memories come flooding back to me every time I look at it. It is like I am eight again and walking into an important general's meeting. My father didn't care. He told me to sit with him while they planned their next battle. It is a treasured memory.

I squeeze Evander's hand as I knock on the door. Soon, the meetings would include the three of us, working together to change our world.

"Enter," my father's voice booms. I step inside with Evander and smile warmly at my father.

"Father," I say.

"*Friglia.*" My father smiles back at me, opening his arms for a hug. I let go of Evander's hand and run to him. I jump into his arms, hugging him tightly. The familiar scent of cherries surrounds him, soothing me. I hadn't realized how much I missed him.

He pulls back to place a hand on my cheek and study me. He looks like he has aged in the last week, the lines on his face deeper and weariness darkening his eyes. No doubt he has been worried about me, but today I will show him that there is no longer any need.

"*Has he been treating you well, Friglia?*" he asks in our native tongue.

"*Yes, Father. He has,*" I reply.

"Common tongue," Evander says from behind me. My father turns his attention from me to my husband. I can see his cold glare and my stomach clenches. I don't want them to fight. There is no need for it now that we are all on the same side.

"How may I help you, *Son?*" my father asks him.

"Lamb?" Evander says, his body stiffening.

I look up at my father, who looks back down at me, his face instantly softening. "I have a proposal for you."

My father raises a brow, smiling at me. "Do you?"

I nod, smiling back. "Slavers raided the village of Ghynts. Luckily, Evander was able to save them all."

The king looks at Evander. "Alone?"

"Don't sound so surprised, *Father,*" Evander says, crossing his arms over his chest.

My father nods for a second before looking back down at me. "And what are you proposing?"

"There are some farmlands to the northwest that were abandoned years ago. I was hoping we could give it to those villagers to rebuild their homes. I think it would be a great use of the land, and with all the new people in the city, we will need more food for next winter, anyway. What do you think?"

My father stays silent for a minute, tilting his head as he thinks. I already know what he is going to say. The twinkle in his eye gives him away.

"I think it is a wonderful idea, *Friglia,*" he says, smiling at me. I move back to my husband's side.

"She is incredibly creative," Evander says, running his fingers down my spine. I shiver, my cheeks warming.

My father narrows his eyes on Evander's hand. "My daughter has always had a talent for problem solving."

Evander continues to trace his fingers along my back. "I suppose I am lucky to have stolen her."

"Yes." My father tenses, pausing. "*Friglia,* leave us."

Evander stiffens beside me. "She doesn't take orders from you anymore."

I turn to look at Evander, kissing him softly. This needs to happen. They need to talk. Maybe then my father will see what I see in Evander.

"It will be alright," I whisper.

"I don't want you to leave," he murmurs

I smile softly at him. "Do this for me?"

"Fine," he hisses.

I kiss him again, squeezing his hand before exiting the room. Now, I wait. Hopefully, they won't kill each other.

XXXIV

EVAN

ILIUM

KINGDOM OF CANDONIA

The tension in the room immediately escalates without Charlotte here to run interference, and I feel Antias's eyes on me. Even now, knowing I've won, and I'm now crown prince, I can't help but feel the creeping nature of intimidation from this man. He has a magnetism, a *presence* that comes from knowing that you've held the world in the palm of your hand since birth. It is something I'll never have.

Even now, he sits while I stand, and I know he still maintains the power in the conversation. The office is sumptuous. Finely embroidered silk covers the seats of the chairs, a deep sapphire blue laced with golden threads, the wooden frames lacquered to a high shine. Lush tapestries cover the walls, no doubt worth more than everything in my entire camp. I look closer, and my lips twitch as I realize they catalog the great battle that gave the King of the Ancients, Basilius, his crown. Golden threads form his crown, cutting through the darkness, and fighting back the swirling void that once threatened to swallow the entire world. My eyes drift over Antias's desk, and I notice several discarded teacups off to the side. A strange purple residue stains the fine white porcelain, and something about that nags at me.

"She cares about you," the king says, raising a brow at me and pulling my attention back to him. I keep my face impassive, crossing my arms over my chest, glaring at King Antias. It's hard to remain unmoved when he looks at me with her eyes. They are the same deep sapphire blue that entrances me when Charlotte gazes at me. It's disconcerting, to say the least, and I have to fight not to fall into the same trap that I do with Charlotte. She works magic with those eyes, and I always feel the need to spill my darkest secrets. I can't do that in front of Antias. *I won't do that in front of Antias.* Though his eyes are more vacant than his daughter's, what I once interpreted as calculating and thoughtful appears almost *lost* when we are alone.

"What did you wish to speak to me about?" I ask, trying to cover how unbalanced I feel in his presence. Even knowing that I'll one day be king, that one day this office will be *my* office, I can't help but feel like an imposter.

How many former slaves have stood in this room? None, I'm sure. As far as I know, I'm the first, and I'm willing to put crowns on it. Now I sound like Kian. My assassin and spy was constantly wagering.

"My daughter," he says, his hands moving to his desk slowly, as if monitoring my every move. We are two predators circling each other, waiting for the other to stumble and fall or show any weakness before they attack.

I rest my hand on the back of the chair I refused to sit in, my grip tightening slightly. "She is not your problem anymore."

She's mine. Even within the walls of the palace, where she was born and raised, she's mine more than she will ever be theirs. They lost her to me, and I will not be giving her up. It is why I took her away from the palace in the first place. I will not let her loyalties be divided, torn between the life she knew and our future together. In camp, she clings to me. Here? Everything is jumbled.

"She is still my daughter. If anything happens to her, I am not afraid to kill. Even if it costs me my kingdom."

If anything happened to her, I would do more than just *kill.* My hand clutches the silk seat, and I feel the wood of the chair groan beneath my grip. "I would destroy anyone who tried to take her from me."

I will destroy everything, leaving nothing but ash behind. If someone dares to take her from me, I'll show them how true the rumors are.

"So we're on the same page?" His voice is slow and steady, even as we discuss his daughter. There's no hitch in his voice to give away his emotions, and his hands haven't tightened even slightly on the desk between us. He could be telling me about the weather. But his eyes. They're a storm, just like hers when her emotions are riotous and uncontrollable. Despite his ability to keep up appearances, he's holding it together by a thin wire. Something about speaking about his daughter is making him focus. I wonder if he's the same when he discusses his other two daughters, or if it's just my wife?

I nod slowly. "We are."

Antias watches me carefully, opening a drawer and dropping a stack of paper on the desk, along with several scrolls. His hands are neatly folded on the desk again, but his eyes grow even more wild. "Then, if you care for my daughter, you might want some information."

"Information?"

He gestures to the papers and scrolls on the desk. "There have been a few attempts on her life over the past two years since she passed the law."

I circle the chair and sit, a sweet, sickly smell making me sneer. It takes a moment for me to locate the teacups as the source. What is he drinking? "A few?"

I pick up one of the reports and try to decipher the scratches on the paper before realizing they're in Candonian. As if reading and writing were not already a struggle.

"They hired assassins," the king adds while I pretend to read the document in front of me. "I have narrowed it down some, but I am stuck."

I lower the paper, locking my eyes on his across the desk. "She doesn't know, does she?"

He shakes his head slowly, the lines on his face revealing his age and weariness. He looks *tired*. It's hard to see. For many years he has been my hated enemy, the king who profited on the backs of slaves. Now, he seems so very human. "I didn't want to worry her."

My eyes narrow. "She is far stronger than you think."

"When you have a daughter, you will understand. You want to protect them from the world."

A daughter. A little girl with a mop of unruly blonde hair and stormy eyes that ensnare all who glance at them. Yet this man in front of me is careless with his younger daughters. He never demanded Eleanor's return to the palace, and he hasn't stopped his wife's mistreatment of Thalia.

"You've made her ignorant!" I snap. "Why didn't you tell me this during the wedding?"

"You were the enemy at the time. I didn't think you would care much for her safety."

Neither did I, but things changed. She changed everything. She's changing me, and I don't know what I'll be when she's done.

"At the time?" He should still consider me the foreign conqueror, the man who stole his treasured heir and married her, the beast who occupies his city. And yet, he's talking as if he knows that our feelings have changed.

"I see the way she looks at you, Son."

I hiss out a slow breath. "I can't reciprocate what Charlotte feels for me."

I can't love her. Love makes a soldier weak, a man weak. Unable to make the choices he needs to make. I have more than my men's lives weighing on my shoulders. I have the lives of every slave in Aellolyn and every future slave that could be, waiting for me. They are waiting for me to change the world. Love can't happen for me. I can't love my wife *and* change the world. There must be a balance, and I will do what I have to for the future of the continent. Even if it means I can never feel for her what she does for me. Even if it means I'll break her.

"Oh?" he asks, raising his brow.

I won't have my weakness for his daughter analyzed by Antias. I stand, gathering the papers and scrolls, tucking them under my arm. "She is already enough of a weakness."

"And your enemies are aware of this?"

My body stiffens slightly. "They are aware I am married, yes."

Hopefully, word will *never* get out that I am brought to my knees by a sapphire-eyed slip of a woman. I'm not sure my reputation can take such a blow. The target on her back will only grow if they know I cherish my wife. She is safest if people believe she means nothing to me, just a pawn I am using, someone of no use to anyone else.

He frowns at me. "That doesn't make Charlotte a weakness. You could be married to my daughter and not care what happens to her."

I scoff at him, moving towards the door, "I don't have the luxury of political enemies. My enemies are brutal. There is no delicate dance with them, a blow for a blow. They will do *whatever* it takes to hurt me. They will search for any soft target, and she's a soft target."

He fiddles with a quill on his desk. "You still haven't explained why my daughter is a weakness. She is a *soft target*, as you claim. If something were to happen to her, you could marry my other daughter, and your claim to the throne would remain intact."

It makes my hackles rise to hear his careless words about Thalia, the disparate treatment of his affections. It doesn't make any sense. That tea's sickly smell is making my head spin. I don't want his other daughter. Charlotte is mine. In just a handful of days, she's wound my soul around hers. I don't want anyone else, and I doubt I ever will. So long as she draws breath, I will crave her.

"You would offer Thalia up so easily?" I demand, covering my own thoughts.

"Still avoiding the question, hm?" he asks, smirking.

I'm done with this conversation. He reads me too easily, and my usual evasion tactics are doing nothing for me. I grit my teeth and grind out, "I'm going to go find my wife."

"Be sure to look over those reports. I am sure you will find it useful, *Son.*"

I growl at him and exit his office, slamming the door shut behind me for good measure. Prick. He thinks he knows everything, does he? He doesn't know anything about me. Or about Charlotte. Or about our marriage. So he can choke on his snarky little comments and his elegant evasions. I will work on concealing my own mind and emotions for my next encounter with him. I need to be less of an open book to his analytical gaze.

Charlotte is in the hallway, pacing back and forth. Her brow is furrowed in thought, and she is gesturing with her hands as she mutters to herself. The light illuminates the marble hallway behind her, flickering off her mane of dark hair, hinting at threads of red.

"Lamb!" I call.

Her entire face brightens as she sprints toward me, and my heart leaps in my chest. "Evander."

I catch her against me, dropping the reports and scrolls on the ground as she wraps her arms around my neck. I lift her against me, and the anxiety gnawing at my stomach after the conversation with her father eases. Her effect on me is that swift and powerful.

She kisses the side of my head, her hands digging into my hair, keeping me locked to her. "You survived."

I slowly lower her back to her feet, releasing her. "You have no faith in my abilities. I *let* him live."

She smiles up at me, going on her tiptoes to kiss me hard. "Thank you."

I sigh at her. "It was difficult. Are you ready to go back to camp?"

"It means the world to me that you did that, and yes, I'm ready."

Charlotte helps me gather the papers and scrolls I dropped. She hands them to me, asking, "What's all this?"

I tuck them back under one arm, my other hand linking with hers. "I'll explain when we get home." It's not safe to discuss it in the open. Not when any of those who made attempts on her life could be lurking.

She nods, wrapping her arms around mine and resting her head on my shoulder. "I'm going to miss you."

My time with her is limited, and I want every single moment, every single breath to count. So I forgo riding back to camp, preferring to walk in companionable silence. The Black and Snow follow behind without being led. The closer we get to camp, the tighter her hold on my arm becomes. Kissing the top of her head, I whisper, "What's wrong?"

She holds me even tighter. "I don't want you to go."

I stop in my tracks, turning slightly to face her. "It's only for a couple of weeks, a month, maybe two."

Maybe even longer. Can I last that long without her? Can she? Will I even make it to the border of Candonia before turning back for her?

Her sapphire eyes turn to twin pools of despair. "It will feel like forever."

I brush a lock of her hair back from her face. "Will you write to me?"

She presses her cheek into my hand. "I will. Will you send letters in return?"

My neck heats slightly. "I'm not very good at it."

She kisses me again. "That is alright, my love. Any letter from you will mean the world to me."

I clear my throat, feeling the blush creep into my cheeks. "We need to talk still."

XXXV

Charlotte

OUTSIDE ILIUM

KINGDOM OF CANDONIA

We need to talk. Those four words can make anyone panic. For a person who overthinks, it is like the end of the world. My palms become clammy, heart racing in my chest. I rub my hands over my wrist until they glow red from irritation.

Instantly, thousands of questions start racing through my mind. Was it my father? What did he say? Is it something to do with the scrolls? Is he going to be away longer than he expected? The look in his eyes tells me it's something serious, and I feel like all the air has been sucked from my lungs. I lead him into our tent, trying to pull myself together, though my breathing and hands are still shaky. It takes me a moment to realize that Thalia is not in the room. I did tell her to find Demir. Hopefully, she is still with him, and they haven't killed each other.

"What's wrong?" I ask. He sighs, gesturing for me to sit on the bed, and there goes my heart. It becomes still in my chest as I take my seat, and I feel lunch trying to crawl back up my throat. I look him up and down, trying to figure out what could be going on in his mind. When he doesn't respond, I say, "You're scaring me."

He frowns, pulling the scrolls out from under his arm and unrolling them for me to see. They are reports from the palace. I have seen many of them before, but I don't recognize these.

"Your father has been keeping secrets from you, lamb," he says.

"Secrets?" I frown.

He taps the paper with his knuckle. "Read."

I take the scroll from him, clearing my throat before reading out loud. "Report Eleven. There has been another attempt on—"

I stop when I see my name, reading the rest in silence as I try to digest this information.

Report XI

There has been another attempt on Princess Charlotte's life. We found the suspect roaming the hallways of the palace, heading toward her room. He had a dagger dipped in liquid nightshade when apprehended by the guards. One guard claims that the man was an ex-slaver who disagreed with the princess's new laws. He was muttering that he was going to put things right once and for all.

My hands continue to shake and the words become muddled. The thought makes me sick. How close was this man to taking my life? This is report eleven. That means there are at least ten others who have tried to kill me. How many more were there after this one? My stomach twists as I lower the scroll. I have enemies in my kingdom, as well as Evander's men disliking me. *Will I ever make a good queen?*

I gulp, looking up at Evander. "I-I figured there would be attempts, but I had no idea."

"Your father kept them from you," Evander says, his face unreadable.

"Why are you telling me this?" I ask, placing the scrolls on the table. I wrap my arms tightly around my stomach, trying to calm the nausea.

He watches me carefully before saying, "Because I want you to be aware. I am leaving tomorrow, and you're going back to the palace. The Mountain can't protect you every minute."

I nod again, whispering, "I will keep a dagger with me at all times."

"I will send the Boy with messages from me. Don't trust anyone else," he says.

I take a deep breath and reach for his hand. "I think my sister will like that."

"Who? Thalia?" Evander frowns in confusion, moving to sit next to me on the bed.

"Eleanor," I say, shaking my head. "She hasn't come to me once since being here in camp."

Evander's thumb traces along the back of my hand. "Come to you?"

"Eleanor doesn't have many friends. She comes to Thalia and me when she feels alone. Which is quite often." Eleanor often sneaks into my room in the middle of the night. Nightmares plague her, and the only time she is free of them is when she is with Thalia or me. Two nights rarely go by without her coming to find me.

My husband frowns, pulling me close. "And who do you go to?"

I fit my body close to his as I think about how to answer his question. I have Thalia and Eleanor, but I try not to bother them with my troubles. They both have enough of their own. My father is busy running the country, and I would never go to the queen. I realize I have been alone for a very long time, always caring for others, never myself.

"No one," I finally say, rubbing my cheek against his chest.

Evander lifts my chin to look him in the eyes. "You have me now."

"Just you and me?" I ask, holding his gaze.

"Just you and me," he says, nodding. I kiss him hard, the warmth from his lips calming my vibrating body. His smell overwhelms my senses, and I feel at peace, comforted. I nibble at his lower lip with a sigh of contentment.

"You'll be careful? While I'm gone?" Evander asks, his tongue flicking at my lips.

I tug at his shirt, continuing to kiss him. "Yes."

"And I'm the insatiable one?" He laughs.

"Oh, hush and kiss me." He laughs again, pulling me onto his lap. I straddle him, placing hot kisses down his neck. My addiction to him only grows with each touch and kiss.

"So demanding! You do know I'm the Commander, not you?" he says.

"I am your wife." I snort, sucking on the skin at his neck, leaving little red marks. He is mine. I smile as he tilts his head, allowing me better access to his throat. I grind against him, and from his reaction underneath me, he wants it as badly as I do.

"So that means you should follow my orders to the letter," he growls, his hands gripping my hips harder, sending shivers down my spine.

"And what are your orders, Commander?" I ask.

"I want you to strip for me," he says. "Slowly."

"Yes, my husband," I whisper in his ear.

I pull away, my eyes heavy with lust, and stand in front of Evander to undo the ties of my dress. Making the process painfully slow, I allow the fabric to roll down my body. It pools around my feet as I lift my chemise over my head and drop it to the side. I bite my bottom lip, watching Evander's pupils dilate as he looks me up and down.

"By the Ancients, you are too beautiful," he says with reverence, shifting on the bed.

I slide my fingers over my body, taking a step toward him. "Am I?"

"Too much for my sanity," he says, his hand covering my own. His tanned skin is stark against the pale porcelain of mine. Goosebumps form on my arms as I admire him.

"You are so handsome," I whisper, running my hands down his arm.

He shakes his head. "I am scarred."

"That has never mattered to me," I whisper. He is one of the most handsome men I have ever laid eyes on, scars and all.

"But," he guides my hands to rest over his heart, "what if I'm scarred here too?"

"That I would be happy to help you heal," I say, kissing him softly. Evander deepens the kiss, swinging his legs onto the bed and shifting to his knees. I moan against his lips, pressing myself closer to him. "I love you, Evander."

"I need you," he says huskily, pulling me onto the bed. He rolls with me until I am under him.

"I'm yours," I moan. Evander grabs my arms, pinning them above my head with one hand, the other working the front of his breeches open before he takes my mouth again. He settles himself between my thighs and thrusts inside me. I arch my back to take him deep, unable to stop the cry of pleasure that seasons the kiss.

"All mine?" he pants against my lips, holding himself deep and still.

"All yours, Evander." I moan louder. He grunts in response, biting my shoulder and keeping my hands trapped under his. I wrap my legs around his back, breathing heavily, and press closer, needing him to move. "Fuck...Evander. Please!"

He presses his forehead to mine. "You love me?"

"I love you." I nod, my eyes connecting with his. He hooks his free hand under my knee and lifts it higher. He pulls back and then slams deep, and my eyes cross. The pressure builds as he sets a slow, steady rhythm. "You care for me?"

"I..." he rotates in me, and I gasp from the pleasure, "I do. Fuck."

His words make me smile, and I whisper, "Come for me."

"That's my line." He laughs shakily, sweat dripping from his body onto mine.

"I love you." I lift my hips, arching into his thrust, taking him deeper.

He roars, and I release the pressure, climaxing at the same time as him. My body shakes, and I moan his name. Evander collapses on top of me as we try to catch our breath. He rolls to the side, pulling me against his chest. He presses kisses to my forehead, nose, chin, and cheeks. Everything about this moment with him is perfect. My heart has never felt this full, and I have never felt this much peace. Within minutes, I am fast asleep in his arms, a content smile on my face.

XXXVI

EVAN

OUTSIDE ILIUM,

KINGDOM OF CANDONIA.

I barely slept, trying to memorize every line and angle of her face. The soft sounds of her breathing as she sleeps, how she wraps herself around me, and how her hand curls against my chest. I want to remember it all. Her eyes slowly open as she nuzzles her cheek against me. I shift, lying partially on top of her, my head resting between her breasts. I'm clinging, and at the moment, I'm probably smothering her. Again, I can't bring myself to care, especially as she whispers, "I'm going to miss you so much."

I kiss each of her breasts again. "I'm going to miss my new pillows."

Not exactly the most eloquent of prose or declaration of love, but it's what I have. I'm not the smoothest of men.

She giggles, looking down at me. "Perhaps you should take my chemise with you."

I place my chin on her chest, looking up at her. "Oh?"

Her cheeks turn red, visible even in the low light.

I smile and sit up, lifting her discarded shift off the floor. I bury my face in it and inhale deeply. It still smells like her. "This one?"

She crawls to me, pressing against my back and kissing my shoulder. "Whatever one you like."

"I like this one, and I'll sleep with it in my palm every night." I will ache for her every single time I do. Each time I close my eyes, I'll know I'm one day closer to holding her again. It will be a link to her until I'm right back here in our tent, with her scent overwhelming me and her hair trailing along my skin.

She cuddles closer, wrapping her legs around my waist, pressing her soft breasts against my back. "And what about me?"

I look at her over my shoulder, shocked by the question. I have nothing of value to give her, and it didn't occur to me she would want something of mine. She's already *commandeered* several of my shirts. I'm not a sentimental man, and I don't feel an attachment to material things. It's too easy for possessions to be stripped from you as a slave, and you learn not to get attached. But there is one thing. I gently disentangle from her and pull the dagger out of my boot. It's nothing special. It isn't Grimmwing steel, but iron and its hilt is chipped and well worn. But it is the only thing I've held onto all these years. It's the only trace of my life as a slave that isn't painted on my skin. "This is the dagger that I used to kill my last master. It is very special to me, and I carry it with me everywhere." I hold the hilt out to her. "I want you to keep it on you. At all times."

She glances from the dagger to me. "But, it's important to you."

"As are you." *More than you can ever know.* The looming choice still lingers, the fate of Aellolyn or the future of one girl. I can almost hear the Ancients of Fate flipping a crown in the air, waiting to see where it lands. Which will I choose? Heads for heart, tails for the world.

She crawls into my lap, demanding, "Kiss me."

I oblige, pulling myself away from the future, focusing on the now and her. I lick along her tongue, tasting her pleasure as she grinds against me. She breaks the kiss to say, "I like being important to you."

I frame her face, my thumbs sliding over her cheekbones. "You are the most important thing to me."

"I am?"

"You're my wife." *But you're also so much more than that.* I can't form the words. They refuse to make it past my lips, getting stuck in my throat.

She chews her bottom lip. "Just because I'm your wife doesn't mean you have to care."

My eyes scan hers, searching for some guidance on what she's thinking at this exact moment. "But I do. I shouldn't, but I do."

Her gaze clouds with confusion and maybe a touch of hurt. "You...you shouldn't?"

"I can't have weaknesses." I also can't stop kissing her, can't stop touching her, thinking about her.

"It's alright to have weaknesses."

I shake my head, trying to clear my thoughts. "My enemies will exploit it. They will do horrific things if they get to you."

Charlotte rests her forehead against mine. "Then I'll become stronger."

"You will only trust the messages when the Boy delivers them," I say.

"I told you I would."

I let out a soft sigh and look at the dagger on the floor. "You'll keep my dagger on you at all times?"

She nods. "I will."

I close my eyes, admitting, "I don't want to lose you."

I can't lose you. Even thinking about a world without her makes my throat close up.

"You won't lose me, Evander."

I open my eyes and lock my gaze with hers. "Will you think of me?"

"Often," she says, her cheeks flushing.

"At night? Home alone in your palace?" I ask, and drop my hands to her ass with a wicked smirk.

She bites my bottom lip and then soothes the small sting with a kiss. "In my bed..."

I massage her curves and press her closer, fitting her against me. "Will you scream my name? I'll hear you if you're loud enough."

"Then I'll scream so loud the entire palace will hear."

"I need you like I have never needed another," I growl into her ear.

She wraps her arms even tighter around my neck as she shivers. "Don't ever leave me."

"I have to leave sometime."

She pouts. "No."

I can't help but laugh at her adorable, pouty face. "Oh?"

She keeps kissing me with her pouting lips. "How much longer do we have?"

"An hour, maybe two." She ignores me, her tongue sliding against mine, letting me taste her passion and need. She makes it difficult to remember what I'm supposed to be doing. "I'm going to miss you."

She grinds against me. "I'm going to miss you too, my love."

My cock is aching and hard as steel beneath her. "Me or my cock?"

Her moan is low and throaty, and I swear it vibrates through me. "How about both?"

"Commander?" Kian's voice intrudes from just outside the entrance to the tent.

"Someone better be dead!" I snarl back.

Charlotte shifts off my lap, covering herself in the furs. She is always careful of her modesty, except for the moments when I have my hands on her. She seems to forget everything then, and to be honest, so do I.

Kian laughs. "No, not yet. We have a message from the North."

I check on Charlotte, making sure she is covered, before saying, "Come in."

Kian walks in, his hand covering his eyes. He hits a trunk with his knees, having to navigate around it, holding out a letter

236

for me. I stand and snatch the letter from his hand before turning him around and shoving him out of the tent. "Someone better be dead next time."

Kian chuckles and closes the tent flap. Turning back to her, I walk toward the bed, smiling as she holds her arms out for me, opening and closing her hands. "Miss me?"

She nods. "I want you for as long as I can have you."

The first few words of the letter make me frown, stopping me mid-stride.

"What is it?"

I walk closer to her, holding the parchment out. "My eyes are swimming. Someone rode all the intelligence out of me. Read it to me?"

She takes the letter from my hand, tucking the furs tighter around her as she reads. "The letter is from a mother superior. Slavers are encroaching on some territory near the North Wardens in Grimmwing." She glances up at me. "I thought the North Wardens were no more?"

"You know of the North Wardens?" It wasn't a common area of knowledge in the current day.

"A few tales, my mother used to tell me about them."

I drop the letter off to the side and pull her into my arms, resting her on my chest. "The North Wardens still exist, though their numbers are greatly diminished. Their sanctuary is in Grimmwing. I like you reading to me."

She kisses my chest. "Perhaps I'll read more to you upon your return."

"I'm going to have to get used to sleeping alone again. I just got accustomed to sleeping in bed with you," I say with a heavy sigh.

She cuddles closer to me. "Is sleeping with me that bad?"

I laugh and brush her hair back from her face. "No, no, I'm just not used to sleeping in a bed at all."

She holds me even tighter. "Well, I'm glad I can share a bed with you. Where did you sleep before?"

"Usually, I sleep outside." I kiss her forehead, still ever aware of the approaching deadline to this moment. "I like to look at the stars."

"I'd like to try that sometime."

"What?" I sputter. "You want to sleep on the ground?"

"I'd be with you."

I shake my head at her. "It's cold and hard. You deserve to be in a bed. That's why I had this whole thing set up before I married you."

"You did this for me?"

"My princess deserved something close to a bed and a home." I wanted to provide what little I had to this marriage.

"I can sacrifice one night in my bed for a night under the stars with you." She kisses my chest again. "All I need is your warmth."

I groan. "You are making it impossible for me not to cancel my trip." I run my hand through my hair. "How have I become so addicted to you?"

She shakes her head. "I was about to ask you the same thing."

"So this need isn't one-sided?" I ask, rubbing her back as I kiss her head.

"Did I say that out loud?" she whispers.

I groan at the sound of my men getting ready to march outside. "They're going to come get me soon and steal me away from you."

Tears fill her eyes. "I'm not ready for that."

"Me either." Even as I admit that, I pull away, throwing my legs over the edge of the bed. I grab my breeches and pull them on.

She watches me as I get dressed, her eyes practically glowing. "Hello, handsome," she says, her voice husky.

"Hello, beautiful," I say, grabbing my lawn shirt and yanking it on before glancing back at her. Charlotte's hair is tumbling around her shoulders, her eyes hooded and filled with desire.

238

She flicks her tongue over her lower lip as if she is hungry for me. "You are making this impossible," I say on a low groan.

She drags her fingers along her collarbone. "I don't know what you are talking about."

"If I walk out of here as hard as a rock, I will never hear the end of it from my men."

She bites her bottom lip. "Well, that is the punishment for leaving me, isn't it?"

I find my boots and stomp into them, growling, "It's a punishment to leave you, period."

She arches her back, making the furs fall lower on her chest, barely clinging to her nipples. "Yes. I suppose you have two punishments then."

"Best cover yourself, wife." I shake my head and try to get control of myself before letting out a piercing whistle.

She frowns but moves the furs up, making sure she's concealed. Ben steps in and begins helping me into my metal armor. My leather training armor is already in one of the carts, but it's easier to wear my formal armor on the ride, though a lot less comfortable. He slips on my chain mail, not even breathing hard from the weight of it. The Boy is getting stronger every day.

"How is Eleanor?" Charlotte asks my squire.

The Boy ties my voiders on, buckling on my sword and my bow and arrows before answering. "She's still asleep, but she's not happy."

"I hope she hasn't given you too much trouble."

The Boy sighs, finishing my armor. "The only trouble was when she found out she has to go back to the castle today. I think Thalia stayed with her in the squire's tent last night."

Charlotte nods, and they continue speaking as if I'm not even present. "She must really like you."

The Boy gives her a soft smile. "She will be sullen today, Your Highness. I apologize in advance."

"I will tell her that you will return every so often to deliver my letters. Do you think that will make her happy?"

The Boy perks up, looking at me. "I will be?"

"You will be. Now go," I say, shooing Ben out of the tent.

His smile is bright as he leaves, and I turn to look at her in the bed. "Now, for my goodbye."

Charlotte picks up my discarded shirt off the floor and puts it on. She runs to me, wraps her arms around my neck, and kisses me hard. "Goodbye."

"You'll write to me?"

"I promise I will."

I look down at her and kiss her again. "Best get dressed. The Mountain will be here soon to escort you to the palace."

She releases me and finds her one intact chemise. She slips into a plain grey dress and turns her back to me. "Ties?"

I step closer and kiss her shoulder, pulling the laces tight. "Will you ride Snow while I'm gone? I would like to go on more rides together when I get back."

She nods. "I will."

Picking up her discarded chemise, I tuck it into the lining of my armor. "I want you to bond with her."

Her cheeks go pink as she watches me. "I think we are well on our way. She is a beautiful horse." I link my hand with hers, and we walk out of the tent together.

We stop beside the Black, and I turn to face her, brushing her hair back from her face. "You love me?"

She kisses me again. "I love you, and I will miss you, Evander."

I pull myself away from her and grab the mane of the Black, swinging up onto his back. "Snow is with foal, part of the reason it took forever for her to get down from Grimmwing."

She comes to my side, touching my leg. "I'll keep you updated."

I lean down and growl, "And make sure to scream loud so I can hear."

Her face turns red and she hits my leg. "Evander!"

I give her a hard, quick kiss, grinning as I pull away and sit up straight. "Stay safe."

240

My wife steps away from the horse, her eyes shining. "Goodbye."

I kick the Black off, my men following after me. The Boy rides to my left, Kian at my right.

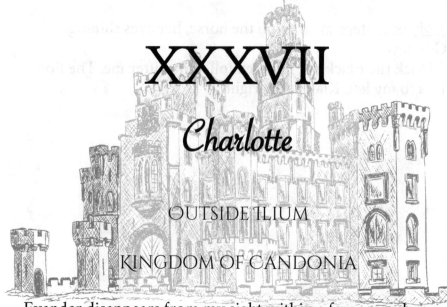

XXXVII

Charlotte

OUTSIDE ILIUM

KINGDOM OF CANDONIA

Evander disappears from my sight within a few seconds, leaving only dust in his wake. There is a tug on my soul the further away he travels, as if our hearts are bound. The connection feels stretched, wanting me to go with him, pulling me in his direction. I wish I could drop everything here, but I can't. My sisters need me, and this trip could be dangerous. *If I learn to fight, I'll be able to ride with* him, *at his side.*

Thalia walks up beside me, placing a comforting hand on my shoulder. "The Mountain is asking if we are ready to return home."

No. I'm not ready. I sigh before nodding. Eleanor is sniffling, heartbroken that Ben has left. It warms my heart that she has found a true friend. I take Eleanor's hand, leading her back toward the palace, Thalia and Demir following behind us. We make our way to the edge of the camp in silence until Thalia's laugh breaks the quiet. I turn to look at her, a grin tugging at my lips. She blushes when she notices me watching them. *Interesting.* I haven't seen Thalia genuinely happy since our mother died. Demir signs something, and she smiles. Thalia learned sign language years ago when she discovered her maid was deaf. Though she appears intimidating and judgmental, she is one of the kindest people I know.

"He is wondering if you would like to bring your horse to the palace," Thalia translates. I look toward the stable just outside of camp. Snow is pacing back and forth, her head moving side to side anxiously. *She misses them too.*

"Yes. I would like that," I say. Demir gestures to the stable, and we walk in that direction. Snow calls for the Black, and it saddens me. She doesn't understand that it will be a month before we see them again. Eleanor walks over to the mare, smiling softly.

"She is beautiful," Eleanor says.

"Evander gave her to me. You know, she might have a baby in her belly."

"She does?!" Eleanor exclaims, her eyes sparkling with excitement.

I nod. "So let's take good care of her. Alright?"

"Alright," Eleanor says, rubbing the side of the horse's neck soothingly as the stable boy tacks Snow.

I help Eleanor onto Snow's back as she continues to prance and neigh. I walk in front of her, pressing my forehead against her nose. She snorts and paws at the ground.

"I miss them, too," I say.

Snow breathes heavily in response, stomping her foot once more.

"She says she misses her brother. She wants to go with him," Eleanor whispers. Snow shifts restlessly beneath her. "She is very anxious. I can feel it."

Her tiny hands glow with a soft blue as she presses them against the side of the horse's neck. Eleanor's eyes change to a shimmering violet as she whispers something to the horse in an unfamiliar tongue. My body tenses and Thalia looks up at Demir, opening and closing her mouth. Eleanor knows better than to use her magic in front of others. Why would she do this now?

Snow relaxes beneath Eleanor's touch as Demir gapes at her. Eleanor rubs the horse's silky coat, unfazed and not realizing what she has just done.

I turn to Demir, my tone serious. "You tell no one of this. I have already told Evander, but I don't think he believes me."

Demir looks at Thalia, and he signs something to her. She signs back at him, laughing but not telling me what he says.

"I really need to learn this," I mumble under my breath. Thalia and Demir continue to sign, and I huff in frustration, grabbing the reins of my horse. Now I understand how Evander feels when I speak Candonian.

Sighing, I walk out of the stable. Eleanor continues to whisper soothing words to my horse while Thalia and Demir sign and laugh behind me. The walk back without Evander nearly breaks me. I already ache for him, and I don't know how I will endure the next month. How am I going to sleep tonight without his warmth? What am I going to do to make the time pass quicker?

A tear rolls down my cheek, and I quietly brush it away, hiding a sniffle. Eleanor is probably feeling the same, and I have to be strong for her. A heavy, comforting hand rests on my shoulder, and I look up to see Demir watching me with a frown. I give him a watery smile. "I know he will come home safe."

Demir turns, signing something to Thalia.

"He says that Evan will hurry back for you," Thalia translates.

"I hope so," I say with a small smile.

Demir snorts, signing once more, and my sister says, "He says Evan is willing to write letters to you. That should show you how much he will miss you."

"Does he not write letters often?" I ask. Demir frowns before signing to Thalia once more.

"He says never mind, forget he said anything," Thalia says.

I sigh under my breath, turning my attention back to the road.

We stop at the palace stables to get Snow settled before climbing up the long stairs to the castle doors. We get lucky, and the queen isn't here to greet us. Thalia takes Eleanor's hand, leading her up the staircase, and I can see Eleanor's shoulders droop. It only makes me sadder. With heavy steps, I make my way to my room, Demir following behind me. It seems darker in here, cold and empty. My bed has been untouched for days and looks unwelcoming. It makes no sense. I have only known him for a short time, but nothing feels the same without him. I wanted to return to my room with him and explore every square inch with his lips on mine. My stomach twists as I look up at Demir. His eyes soften with understanding, and he takes my hand in his. He traces a letter against my palm and then shows me the hand symbol.

"A?" I ask.

He nods and repeats the process with B. I am a quick learner, always have been, and soon I have the alphabet memorized. It makes me feel a little better that I have a way to communicate with him that isn't paper.

"Thank you for teaching me," I say, my shoulders relaxing.

"Just a start," Demir signs, spelling out the words.

I watch him carefully, trying to get a better read on him. When we first met, I knew he didn't like me much. Then there was the incident with the poison. I chew my bottom lip, my stomach churning with nerves.

"I don't want to be enemies," I say.

"We are not," he signs. I am surprised. From his facial expressions, I would have never guessed we weren't enemies anymore.

I smile softly. "We aren't?"

"If we were, you'd be dead."

I nod, going silent. I am not his enemy, but he is still unsure. The others in the camp continue to give me glares when I walk around with my husband. They don't trust me, and even Evander worries his men might harm me.

"The Boy convinced me to give you a chance," he signs.

"He did?" I say with a small smile.

Demir nods. *"I trust him."*

"He is a good kid."

"Is there anything else?" Demir asks.

I chew my bottom lip, thinking for a moment. Something has been on my mind for a few days now.

"I have a question," I say.

"Yes?"

I open and close my mouth a few times, trying to find the right words. "I see how the men look at me in camp. They don't like me much."

Demir's jaw tightens. *"Did they say something?"*

"I can see it in their eyes," I say, smiling sadly. My hands are shaking as I fiddle with a ribbon on my dress. A few times when I have been walking in camp, their glares have made my hair stand on end.

"Many still see you as the enemy. Most were sold in the market in Ilium," the Mountain signs.

The thought makes me sick, and I place a hand on my stomach to calm the nausea. "I want to give back to them."

"How?"

"I don't know," I say, shaking my head. My mind spins as I try to think. They were robbed of so much, stolen from their families, treated poorly, not fed enough, and they didn't get a chance at an education... The idea hits me, and excitement fills me. "Were they ever taught how to read and write?"

Demir considers. *"Not unless they had very generous masters. Many never held a sword before Evan. Most didn't even have names."*

I am surprised again at the horrors imposed on these people. I square my shoulders, determined to make at least this small bit right. "Do you think they would like to learn?"

"I can ask." Demir shrugs.

I nod. "If they would like that, then I can teach them. I also have to get approval for a festival for next month."

"Approval? From who?" Demir snorts.

I tilt my head. "My father. Although, I already know that he will approve it. He never says no to my ideas, which reminds me. I need to take care of a few things that Evander didn't get a

246

chance to handle before he left due to...um," I clear my throat, "a distraction."

Demir rolls his eyes, holding out a small piece of paper with sloppy writing and several spelling errors.

While I am absent, my wife is to be considered an extension of me. An order from her is an order from me.

Seeing Evander's handwriting makes my heart flutter. My fingers trail over the letters as I read his words and bite my lower lip before looking up at the Mountain. I smile at him. "We have some work to do then."

"At your service, my queen," Demir signs.

I smile up at him and begin to fill him in. "The first thing we must do is inform the villagers of their new home. There is abandoned farmland to the northwest that we will give to them. They will remain under our protection, and I will take twenty-five of my father's builders to help put up the new houses. Winter is a couple of months away, and I do not want anyone left in the cold."

Demir nods, and I sigh. "It might sound silly, but when everything settles, I was thinking of making that land a small city. A place that the soldiers can finally call home."

Demir grunts, signing, *"Evan hopes to give them homes."*

I bite my bottom lip, thinking of my husband. "He is a good man."

"There is a reason so many follow him."

I can see it now. I can see why Evander's men are so loyal to him, and why so many followed him rather than walk away. I fiddle with the piece of paper in my hand, smiling. "I am grateful he chose me to be his wife."

Demir snorts again. *"I said he should have picked Princess Lyra."*

I frown as doubt seeps into my mind. What would have happened if he chose her over me? Am I worthy to be married to a man who inspires change to many? Lyra bends the rules of her own Kingdom. The first out of all the countries to change the law of slavery. She managed to convince the Queen of Grimmwing, a woman of pure defiance, to change the law. Lyra being Evander's left hand woman is a much better choice than me.

"She would have been a better match, I suppose," I whisper.

Demir shrugs. *I'm not so sure.*

I look down at the paper, folding and unfolding the corners. "Would you mind sending word to camp about lessons tonight? I will talk to the villagers before the class about their new arrangements."

Demir nods, walking to the door. He stops just before exiting, looking back at me. *He cares for you.*

I blink back tears.

He huffs before walking out of the room, leaving me with my thoughts. Seeds of doubt continue to prod at my mind. *Am I the right match for him?* I square my shoulders and lift my chin because it doesn't matter. He is mine, and I am not giving him up.

XXXVIII

EVAN

OUTSIDE ILIUM

KINGDOM OF CANDONIA

Every step the Black takes is a step farther away from her. Each one forward is another I will have to retread if I finally give in and ride back for her. I've never felt this way about leaving anywhere. It is as if I am leaving a part of myself behind. A metallic taste is festering in my mouth, and no amount of water or mead seems to rid me of it. What kind of man, what kind of *Commander,* cannot ride away from a woman? Even if the woman happens to be my wife.

My lost little lamb. But I suppose that name doesn't fit her anymore, does it? She's not the lost one now. I am. I'm lost in a new world where my mind constantly circles around *her* rather than on the mission. It is the future of Aellolyn against the heart of a slip of a princess.

The Ancients of Fate watch the crown, turning over and over— heads, the world, tails, the heart. Heads and tails. Over and over. Though maybe it's arrogant of me to think the Ancients of Fate even concern themselves with me, or that I even register for them. Maybe I should stop believing that anything I do has an impact. *You think a slave can make a difference, boy? You think anyone will ever look at you as anything but a slave? A nothing? Vermin? Trash?*

I try to force that voice out of my head, but it keeps echoing in my mind.

He's exactly as I remembered. His hair is gray, and he's lost all his teeth. He would grab me with his bony, knuckled fingers and murmur, "Little Evander." Now I'm a man, and I'm here to make things right. Make a difference. Yet when I face the man who was my first master, I go back to being that terrified little boy again. I am that child who hoped that one of the other boys would be caught at night instead of me.

He coughs into a small handkerchief and shows me the blood. "You go by Evan now, don't you? You think that makes a difference? You think you'll make a difference? If anyone ever finds the truth, you'll end up back in chains, where you belong."

Once a slave, always a slave.

I am terrified and rooted to the spot, even as he lies dying in his bed. He opens his mouth to continue his hateful tirade of truth, but an arrow whizzes through the air, silencing him.

Wynonna.

She said nothing to me, even knowing my deepest shame, my darkest truth. She turns away from the scene, resting her hand on my shoulder. "On to the next."

On to the next. The next slaver, the next battle, the next conquest. Until Ilium, until Candonia, until Charlotte. That was when everything changed. I'm changing, and I don't know what I'm becoming.

I can feel the eyes of the other generals on me. Lorcan is frowning, his platinum hair flashing in the sunlight. He's not subtle in his dislike of my wife and takes every opportunity to make his opinion known. I might have to break his nose again, just for good measure.

Wynonna is at my left side, her bay horse skirting the Black anxiously, who's also on edge. We both left someone behind. He wants to go back and likely senses that I do, too, making him even harder to control. How do you manage a massive warhorse who wants to do the one thing you are trying to keep yourself from doing? The bond that makes us an unstoppable force on the battlefield makes it even more challenging to keep myself from turning around and going back.

I need to break this...*obsession*. I can't avoid the duties that come with being a Commander, a leader. Even without the future of Aellolyn in the balance, I have men who look to me for guidance, for wisdom. I can't let them down because I want to crawl into bed with my wife and never get out. People depend on me.

Why am I so entangled in her? It's only been a handful of days since we married, yet I feel like I need her to breathe. Every step forward is a step farther away. Perhaps this mission came at a good time. I can shore up the walls that once built me and break this obsession.

What is she doing right now?

Fuck! I sound like a woman, constantly fascinated with the movements and thoughts of another. When did I become so weak? So...*pathetic*.

The word whispers through my head, and I grit my teeth, keeping the Black on course for Grimmwing. It will take two weeks to travel with my army to Ravaryn, the capital of Grimmwing. Not to mention we will have to ride through Xiapia and Steodia to get there, neither of which are fans of mine.

Xiapia was our longest siege, and it took two years of surrounding their castle before they relented enough to hear our demands. They would have gone longer had we not burned their fields and poisoned their water supply, a necessity to make a stubborn enemy relent. Even when we sat across the table from the king, resentment continued to brew as he waited for my demands.

They outlawed slavery the next day, but I am not blind to the rumors that they support the black market trade, keeping it out of sight. We will not tolerate this. If I've learned anything from conquering and being married to my wife, it's that all countries have a weak spot, and it can be boiled down to simple export and import. Candonia sits in the middle of Aellolyn, and all trade goes through it. Everything from the Northern kingdoms, Xiapia, Grimmwing, Steodia, and Vruica, must pass through Candonia to reach the Southern kingdoms, Ciral, Vredour, and Kolia. I doubt that the Dynasty of Xiapia is pleased to hear that I am now the Crown Prince of the Jewel of Aellolyn. They are still stewing over losing a war that took place a thousand years ago. Xiapia's memory is long and bitter, and they don't forget any slight, no matter the time and severity.

Steodia was simpler. I had an ally on the inside. Kian's uncle reigns as king there and made it an easy transition from slavery to a more acceptable trade.

Yet, things are still not finished. Every time I conquer one, I am summoned to another. This was not supposed to keep happening. I was supposed to be able to settle in Ilium and allow my men to move on. I wanted them to have the home I promised them, the hope of land and a future. But here we are, riding for Grimmwing.

Kian comes up on my right side, his horse dancing. "You know it's alright to miss her."

His horse is a palomino and stands out just like him. When they need to blend in, Kian dyes its coat black. I have seen the two of them disappear into the shadows. Even though Kian always seems to call attention to himself, from his hair to his face to his horse, I know it's all an act. In a moment, in a breath, he can vanish before your very eyes. Something I wish he would do at this moment.

My head snaps to him, and I snarl, "It's also alright for you to have a broken nose to match Lorcan's."

Kian holds his hands up in surrender, but he continues to smirk at me. He's the mouthiest of all my generals, probably because he's one of the few that chose to join me rather than was found by me. Kian offered his services as a soldier eight years ago, worked his way up through the ranks to one of my hallowed generals. He is one of my closest advisors and friends. A very rare thing indeed.

252

"I'm just saying," he unwisely continues, "that we have all seen the way you and the princess look at each other."

Have they? Am I truly that obvious?

I glance at Wynonna for confirmation, and she nods in agreement, her head barely moving with the movement.

Fuck.

"My wife is none of your concern, and this conversation is over." I kick the Black forward, hoping to put distance between myself and the men, but Kian is persistent, catching up to me.

"You know it's alright to feel more for her than you thought?" he continues.

I don't give a warning this time.

I lunge off the Black and tackle Kian off his horse, landing on top of him in the road. The entire army pauses, waiting for this to be over.

I lift Kian by the metal of his armor, punching him hard enough in the jaw to split his lip and bruise my knuckles. Even more infuriating is the fact that he's still laughing.

Kian's eyes sparkle at me. "You are simply proving my point."

He spits the blood in his mouth onto the ground, smiling a red smile up at me. Releasing him, I step back and hold my hand out to help him to his feet.

Kian takes it with a smirk, pulling himself up.

"The more you fight what you feel for her, Commander, the more irritated and unpredictable you will become." Kian wisely drops his voice as he adds, "We depend on you to lead us, to guide us. We are fortunate to have her as our queen, but you need to get your head out of your ass."

My grip on his hand turns punishing, grinding his bones together. "Excuse me?"

Kian winces, his smile finally dropping. "Get your head out of your ass, *Commander*."

I release his hand and turn away from him. I get back on my horse and wait for him to get back on his. The other generals watch us with bored expressions. I frown at him as I think about the upcoming crossroads.

I need to find a way to prevent these uprisings from happening, and it comes down to money.

What would Charlotte suggest?

Even after such a short amount of time, I rely on her guidance. When we stop to camp tonight, I'll write to her and ask for her advice.

IXL

Charlotte

ILIUM

KINGDOM OF CANDONIA

I spend the rest of my day preparing for my first class. A part of me feels like no one will show. And why would they? They don't know me. For all they know, I could be a horrible teacher, or it could be a trap. My hands shake as I look at the grandfather clock. My eyes widen. I'm late. I never run late.

I quickly fix my dress and grab my papers before bursting out the doors. I run down the staircase, my hair wildly flying behind me as I bolt down the hallway to the front entrance. Demir is there, waiting for me. He is throwing his dagger in the air and catching the hilt with practiced ease.

"I'm sorry I'm late!" I exclaim, trying to brush my hair out of my eyes.

Demir looks up at me, spelling out the words, then showing me the proper sign for it. *"There is no rush."*

I clutch my paperwork against my chest. "I feel horrible for making you wait."

Demir snorts, patiently teaching me the signs for each word. *"I once spent three months in Grimmwing, in the snow, waiting for word from the Commander. You're fine."*

"What happened?" I ask, smiling at him.

"I got his message finally." Demir shrugs. I don't know how Demir was so patient with Evander. If I didn't get a message from my husband, I would go out looking for him.

I smile and nod toward the door. "Ready?"

Demir gestures me forward, and we exit the palace, making our way down the grand staircase to the stables. Snow paws at the ground, huffing as soon as she sees me. My bond with her is slowly growing, and she seems to know that I am a friend, not a foe. Demir holds his hand out to me, and I mount the magnificent horse. I rub her neck and croon to her before looking down at the general.

"Thank you."

Demir nods, mounting his own plump grey horse. I tap Snow's sides with my heels, and she walks forward, following behind Demir.

The camp feels a little emptier than it did this morning. There are fewer warriors here but more villagers gathered on the western side of the camp near our tent. I slide from my horse, landing hard on my slippered feet. I still need to get used to the height, and I might need some boots.

Demir takes Snow's reins and leads her to the camp stables. I turn to look at the villagers, and they all go quiet. They stare at me with their dirty faces. Some have bowls of gruel in their hands, while others have bread. A few of the adults have cuts and dried blood on their bodies. Probably from fighting the slavers when they were first taken.

Looking into their eyes, I notice something that I hadn't seen before. I see fear, curiosity, and hate. My throat clogs up, and my muscles tighten. The speech I had for them slips from my mind. I can't do this. I can't be their queen. How can I be a queen to those who hate me? I can never be what they need.

"I-I…um…" I stutter, wringing my hands together.

Demir returns to me, standing slightly behind. He snaps his fingers to one of the men and signs something to him.

"This is the wife of Evan the Black. While he is outside of camp, her word is to be considered his. Her actions, his," the warrior translates.

I gulp, my hands trembling. *Evander trusts me.* He trusts I will make the right decisions. Closing my eyes, I collect my thoughts and take a deep breath before opening them to look again at the villagers. A few of them are now looking at me with more curiosity than hate, though they are still unsure.

I let out a breath. "I am terribly sorry for what happened to your homes in Ghynts. It was foolish of me to believe that a law would protect my people from slavers, and I know better now. Before Evander left, we came up with a solution for those who have lost their homes. To the northwest of the city, there is abandoned farmland. We will give this land to you so you can rebuild. The land is fertile, and there are plenty of trees for wood. I have hired twenty-five men from Ilium to help get you into houses before winter. I hope that one day, this new land will become a town of its own."

After my small speech, the villagers murmur, and I hold my breath for a response. Was this a good idea? Will they resent me for having them move to a new place?

A little boy runs through the crowd of villagers toward me. He takes my hand while sucking his thumb, and it takes me a few seconds to recognize the child. His face has been cleaned, and his blonde hair washed, though his clothes are still dirty. I smile down at him as his mother steps out from the crowd. Her eyes are sunken into her face, and she has lines of stress across her forehead. The villagers all watch us as she stops beside me.

"Your Highness," the mother says, bowing her head.

"Yes?" I smile softly at her.

The woman blushes, curtsying before saying, "My little Liam told me how you brought him here and kept him safe. He doesn't trust many, so you must be something special."

Her words warm my heart, and I look down at the little boy. "Well, he was very brave. Without him, Evander wouldn't have been able to find you all."

My eyes brighten for a second as an idea strikes me. I crouch beside Liam, placing a hand on his shoulder.

I turn, looking up at Demir. "That kind of bravery deserves a medal. What do you think?"

He raises a brow, signing to me, *"A medal?"*

I nod. "A medal of bravery."

Demir thinks for a moment before pulling a dagger from his boot. *"This is all I have."*

"That will do," I say, holding my hand out for the knife. Demir places it in my palm, and I turn back to look at the boy. "For your bravery and assistance in helping save your village. I bestow this dagger to you, little warrior."

Liam gives me a toothy smile. His eyes sparkle with excitement before his mother gently takes the dagger from the boy, smiling at him.

"I'll keep this safe for you until you're older, Liam," she says.

I stand and brush the dirt from my dress before looking at everyone. "Tomorrow, I will send some soldiers and workers with you to your new home. I hope everything goes smoothly."

"Thank you, Princess Charlotte." The woman bows her head, speaking for the rest of the villagers. She gives me a warm smile. "Or would you prefer Mrs. Black?"

Mrs. Black. I like that. I am his wife, and that is how I want this moment to be remembered. This is something we did together. The first of many decisions we will make as a *team.* Building a future for those like these villagers.

"Either title is fine," I say, biting my bottom lip. "I do like the sound of the latter, though."

"I thought you might," she says, winking at me.

Liam pulls at me and, still sucking his thumb, leads me to a group of children who all look at me shyly. They are covered head to toe with soot. Their eyes all shining at me with curiosity.

"Are these your friends?" I ask him. Liam nods, and I lower to my knees, placing my hands on my lap. "How are you all doing this evening?"

The children circle around me, touching my hair and dress with fascination. One of the little girls places her hands on my cheeks and smiles softly.

"We are doing better now," she says.

I frown as I look at their clothing. They have lost all their possessions due to the slavers. I want to help them. I want to give back. These children deserve so much better than what they have had to endure.

"You know, my husband hired a tailor for all the warriors in camp. Would you like me to see if he can make you a set of new clothing?" I ask them.

A few of the children squeal in excitement while others stare in wide-eyed shock. They move closer to me, and a little redheaded girl, no older than three, tugs at my dress excitedly.

"If I get pretty clothes, I be princess?" she asks, her green eyes sparkling with excitement.

I nod, tapping her nose. "I don't see why not."

She squeals in excitement, turning to the child beside her. "Do you hear that? A princess!"

I smile, watching their excitement. Shadowy images of my future children with Evander pop into my head. They have their father's spirit and my determination. I imagine them always wanting to learn, whether it is something to do with books or sparring.

The children suddenly scatter, several letting out small cries, and I frown. There is a tap on my shoulder, and I turn to see Demir. He points to the sky, and I notice the sun is setting. It is time for class. I stand up, smiling brightly at him, feeling much more confidant.

"Thank you," I say, making my way to the tent. Now, for my second challenge of the night. Showing the men I am no longer their enemy.

XL

EVAN

THE BORDER OF CANDONIA

AND THE FOREST OF XIAPIA

Dear Charlotte...

That's not right. I never call her Charlotte. I scratch out the greeting, using too much ink and staining the parchment. Why is this so difficult? I crumble the paper, throwing it onto the ground where it mingles among the ten other letters I've started and stopped since we set up camp. There is so much I want to say to her, but yet quill to parchment, I come up blank. I'm used to observing, analyzing, watching others speak and communicate, making my own opinions. But I can't figure out what to write.

I am already struggling to make the precise letters in order to write to her. I check and recheck each tiny line on the page, making sure it's correct. Normally, I would have someone else read over what I'd written, make sure I hadn't misspelled something, or made an egregious grammatical faux pa. But this is a letter to my wife. That should be private. I have to be even more cautious with what I'm writing, as if I wasn't feeling enough pressure from this.

Should I ask how she is? If she's thinking of me? I want to ask any of the thousand other questions I've had, but seem to have forgotten the second I pulled out the sheaf of parchment. I even asked one of the men to lend me a small writing desk, setting it up for me in one of the tents.

Fuck! With a sweep of my hand, I wipe the small desk clean, knocking the inkwell onto the floor and staining the parchment that falls with it. I hit my head on the desk and try to organize my thoughts. Usually, I am so clear and decisive, but now I am a whirling pool of indecision. I can't figure out what to write to her.

What do I say? *I miss you already?* I've missed her every single step the Black took away from her. *Does she miss me?*

My head hits the desk again, hard.

I need to clear my thoughts, and then maybe I can figure out what the hell I'm going to write. I storm out of the tent, ignoring the sentries patrolling the perimeter we've set up for the night. Walking into the forest, I look up at the stars, seeking the comfort they usually give me.

Even as life changes, the stars always rise and shine above me.

Is she looking at the stars, thinking of me?

Fuck! What is wrong with me? This woman consumes me. A woman I stole. The woman I forced to the altar, a woman given no choice but to marry me. A woman who should despise me. Yet, she doesn't. I glare up at the stars as their light cuts through the forest's canopy. If only they could speak to me, guide me, give me the answers on what to do next with my wife. I shouldn't feel like this toward her. It's a weakness, and weakness gets warriors killed. If this continues, I won't be able to function. I'll let all the men who depend on me down because I can't focus on anything but her. There was a reason that Aesira never married. She must have known that in war, there can be no distraction, no love. Or people die.

I sigh and pull my gaze from the stars. I do not know how I got here and realize with a jolt that I'm proceeding into unknown territory with no weapons. *Ancients above, I'm an idiot.* I'd put my bow and sword down when I started writing and did not pick them back up when I left.

Which way was camp? Turning back the way I came, I look up at the stars again for guidance, navigating through the unknown terrain. Though the constellations may shift slightly depending on which country I'm in, I can usually use them as a guide. They are a map of the sky, almost as if Jarvaid is talking to me, telling me which way to go. A click of something metallic wrenches my attention from the sky to the ground. I look down at my right foot and curse loudly as the trap tightens around my ankle. A weight drops in the distance, yanking me upside down and leaving me dangling from the tree.

Great.

After a moment or two of hanging there, I close my eyes, relax my body, and wait for whoever set the trap to come look at their prize. At the moment, I need to figure out my next step. I can't dangle here for hours. A trap like this could be two things: a hunter or slavers. Either way, I'm no one's prey.

My hands stretch above my head toward the forest floor, a couple of inches away from the dirt. Whoever set this trap clearly wasn't counting on someone as tall as me. I open my eyes and look up, following the rope to the branch, then down to the weight that keeps me suspended. If they weren't counting on someone as tall as me, there is a good chance they weren't expecting someone as heavy, either.

I crawl up my body, my abdomen burning as I pull myself up to grip my boot, sweating profusely. I press down on my foot and notice the boxes lift ever so slightly off the forest floor before hitting again. The jolt from the weight landing makes me lose my hold, and I fall back.

Fuck. My head turns at the sounds of approaching footsteps, and I try to spin my body in that direction to face the oncoming threat. This is such an undignified way to die.

Five men emerge from the trees. One of them steps forward and smiles up at me. I scrunch my nose at the smell that comes from him as he taunts, "Kor, look what we have here."

He's missing a majority of his teeth, and his nose is bent at an awkward angle. Half of his head is shaved, and one of his ears is pierced. He would look terrifying to most, but even from this

262

angle, I can tell he would only come up to my chest if I were right side up. He is shorter than even my wife, though that does not mean less dangerous. Short usually means they have something to prove. A dagger never cares about the size of its wielder, only the cut it leaves behind. could kill as easily as I can if armed. My brows furrow at the thought, *I will kill all her enemies, so she never has to.*

"Certainly not basic hygiene." I snort, crossing my arms over my chest.

The second pokes me in the back with a dull sword. "You think this funny, do ya?"

"A little, if I'm honest," I answer, the small poke making me spin.

The second frowns. "You cracked in the head, boyo?"

I close my eyes on a hysterical laugh. "Me? I suppose I am. I can't stop thinking about her, and I know I shouldn't, so I suppose that does make me crazy."

The first one blinks in surprise. "Her? You sweet on a lassie?"

The others admonish him for asking a question, but he shrugs, clearly enjoying my ramblings. I attempt to maneuver myself again to look at the first man. I say, "Not just any lassie, a princess."

The third one snorts loudly before spitting on the ground. "A princess? He cracked in the head alright."

I shake my head. "She's amazing, gorgeous, intelligent, kind, and she makes me want to be more than I am."

The first frowns at me before letting out a big laugh. "And I'm sure she cares nothing fer yee."

This time I laugh with him. "That's the craziest part. I think she cares for me deeply. She even says she loves me."

"Then why haven't you made an honest princess out of her? Her da disapprove of yee?"

I shake my head again, sighing. "That's the other thing. We're married. But, I didn't give her a choice. She had to marry me."

The fourth cackles loud enough to make a couple of ravens take flight. "Had to marry ye? I thought princesses only married when they felt like it. Nothing makes a princess do what they don't want to do."

I drop my hands from my chest, my fingers touching the ground again. "Not this time. I invaded her kingdom and forced her to marry me. You see, I had to become a prince because I knew that the only way to make lasting change in Aellolyn was from a throne, and not just any throne, the throne of Candonia."

The first one looks down at me. "You must be behind the news, poor fool. Evan the Black has taken Candonia."

I smirk up at him and whistle loudly. "That I have."

The sound of the Black's hooves is enough to distract the first slaver, who had stepped closer to me during my diatribe. I punch him in the crotch with enough force to shatter his hip bone. As he collapses, I take his sword. "Thank you."

The three others lunge toward me, hoping to take me off guard with their numbers, but my weakness is now my strength. With the swing of the rope and my fingers touching the ground, I'm able to spin enough to stab the fourth one through the gut as he gets close. He clutches his stomach, the air whistling out of his mouth rapidly replaced by a torrent of blood.

I should have thought that through, because the rusty sword catches in his ribcage, and now I'm without a weapon. I push off the hilt, swinging back enough to miss the second man who comes running forward, an ax raised over his head. I brace myself for the swing and slam into the fourth man again, pushing him back.

That's going to leave a bruise. The Black rushes at the slaver with the ax, and the man spins toward him. As I swing back, I slam into him, grabbing the ax as he goes down.

With the ax in my hand, I continue swinging back and forth, trying to focus on the rope that is holding me up. If I would stop moving, I could cut myself down. The third slaver lets out a loud yell, charging for me. I hurl the ax, hoping to hit the rope, not having the chance to aim. I try to turn to face the last threat, but the Black gets there first. He slams the man with his chest, throwing him against a tree. He hits hard enough that his back breaks with a loud crunch.

I groan loudly. "The ax missed."

The Black bumps my side, spinning me again, before walking away to graze.

"Fat lot of help you are." The horse grunts in response, chewing on the grass.

I sigh and swing myself back and forth, trying to gain enough momentum to hit the tree that's holding me up. The blood is rushing to my head, and I need to get right-side-up before I pass out. My vision flickers, and when I slam into the tree, I have just enough thought to grab onto it. Finding the rope that connects to the boxes, I start to chew on it. I work at it until it's frayed enough for me to break.

All the air leaves my lungs as I land hard on the forest floor. All I can make out are the stars shining through the canopy. For a moment, I just lie there, thinking back to the reason I wandered out here. *My wife. My guiding star.*

XLI

Charlotte

OUTSIDE ILIUM

KINGDOM OF CANDONIA

I enter the largest tent and find several long tables inside. This must be where they discuss their plans with the rest of the warriors when it is time to implement. The room feels empty, with only five men sitting there. There are at least twenty thousand men still in camp, and only five showed up. It shows how little trust they have in me. Anxiety floods me, but I try not to let it take over my thoughts as I walk to the front of the room. I place my papers on the table before looking up and smiling warmly.

"Good evening," I say, trying to keep my spirits bright. The men grumble and nod back to me. Their lack of enthusiasm feels like a punch. I chew my bottom lip before turning to the chalkboard and writing the alphabet. The only sound in the room is the chalk scratching on the board. At least they are showing respect.

"Today, we will practice writing the alphabet. This will help you get used to holding a quill and strengthen the muscles in your hands that are needed to write," I say, turning back to face them. "I have prepared some outlines of the letters on pieces of paper. I have faith that you all will get the hang of it within the hour."

They grumble again, but I don't let it defeat me as I walk around, giving them their papers. The men pick up the large chalk, two of them struggling with their grip on it. I walk over and fix the chalk in their hand before making my way back to the front.

"First, we will start with the first letter of the alphabet," I say, walking over to the board and grabbing a piece of chalk. "There are two types of letters that we will learn today. A capital and the lowercase. For the capital, we make a line up, down, then across like this."

I demonstrate for them on the board before turning back to them. "Now, I would like you to try."

The men set to work, and it only takes them a few minutes to get the hang of it. Their writing is child-like, large, and shaky, but I am proud. They all seem determined to learn, even when they glare at me when I offer assistance. By the end of class, they have written the entire alphabet. It is an hour later than I expected the class to end, but they don't seem to mind. Most appear happy, showing each other their letters. It warms my heart when a few of them even show off their writing skills to me. I praise them, truly proud of their accomplishments. When I tell them that class is over, they grumble in disappointment before gathering their things. One of the older students, Jeremy, walks up to me.

"Princess?" he asks.

I look up from my papers, smiling at him. "Yes?"

Jeremy blushes. "Will you write a letter for me? For my family?"

"Of course!" I say excitedly. It is the first time any of Evander's men have asked anything of me. "What would you like it to say?"

"Former slave of Vruica, Jeremy of Irons, searching for his wife and two children, sold at auction three years ago. The boy will be nine next summer, and his daughter will be six in late winter. His wife's name was Lele when sold. Please send word to Evan the Black's encampment in Candonia," he recites before clearing his throat. "Will that be enough, miss?"

I write all the information down as he speaks. Only when I'm done do I pick up the paper and frown. His family is still missing?

"Do you know where they were last seen?" I ask, staring at the piece of paper.

Jeremy frowns. "The auction was in Ecten."

I write the information down before pulling out a new piece of paper. I write at the top in capital letters, *LIST OF MISSING PERSONS*. Then I create three columns: *Warrior, Looking For, Found*. Under *Warrior*, I write Jeremy's name, and in the column beside it, I write his wife's name, Lele. I look up at Jeremy. "What are your children's names?"

"The boy is Acton and the girl is Nini," he says.

I write their names beside Lele's before pulling out a third piece of paper. I write a letter to Lord Edmund of Ecten. He is an old friend of mine who was in favor of abolishing slavery. I know he wouldn't mind helping me look for those separated by the horrible trade. He has always helped when needed.

After writing my letter, I hold Jeremy's out to him. "We will find them."

"Thank you, miss." Jeremy's face softens as he nods. He turns to walk away but stops as he looks down at the letter. "Miss? Why do you want to help us?"

I tilt my head. "What happened to you all was unfair and cruel. I want to give you all a second chance at life with your families."

Jeremy shuffles from foot to foot. "Thank you."

"My pleasure." I smile. The warrior walks away, and I continue to gather my papers. Demir approaches as I finish up. He looks me up and down as the rest of the men leave the tent.

"*That went well,*" he signs.

I smile brightly at him, holding out the letter. "I hope so. Can you send a messenger to deliver this to the Lord of Ecten? He might be able to help find the man's family."

Demir takes the letter from my hand. *"Do you have something to send to the Commander?"*

My eyes brighten, and I pull out a letter for Evander. "I do."

He takes that from me as well before signing, *"You helping Jeremy will spread like wildfire."*

I smile to myself. "I only hope that something comes of it."

"Time to go back," Demir signs and offers me his arm, and I consider it a small victory as I take it.

"I'm ready." I giggle, and the two of us exit the tent. Before we leave camp, Demir hands my letters to a scout. I let out a long breath, looking up at the night sky. The sun set a while ago, and I wince. It hasn't even been a day, and I broke my promise to Evander. He is going to be upset with me, but it is not like I slept here.

The halls of the palace are quiet, the staff in their rooms preparing for bed. Demir drops me off at my room before taking his post, and I smile to myself. The day went better than I imagined it could, and the one person I want to tell is not here. I wonder if he is thinking about me as I think of him.

Evander's scent envelops me as I slip into his shirt and take a seat at my desk. Since my husband is not here, I will write to him. Maybe that will fulfill my need to speak to him. I spend some time writing, telling him how I feel and what I accomplished with the villagers. I don't mention the classes, wanting to surprise him when he returns. Once done, I melt some red wax onto the back of the envelope before pressing down on it with my seal. I smile softly before putting it aside.

I walk to my open window and look out at the stars. Is he looking at them as well? Is he thinking of me? I rest my head on the side of the window, my eyes watering.

"I miss you, Evander," I whisper. "Come home to me soon."

XLII

EVAN

THE BORDER OF XIAPIA AND STEODIA

It's another day moving forward, another camp set up, another night I'm lying under the stars missing my wife. I told them not to bother setting up anything resembling a tent for me tonight. I'm fine lying under the open sky, basking in the moonlight, thinking about the woman I left behind. We're almost halfway to Grimmwing, and I hate that I keep thinking about turning back around. I want to be in Ilium, crawling into bed and wrapping myself around her. I want to feel her every breath, as if I could force us into a single being. At least I have something of hers to hold. Her first letter made it to me, and I was relieved to see it. I read it again, hoping to shore up my need to turn back around and return to her.

Dear Evander,

I am missing you terribly today, and I know it won't get any easier. Is it foolish that I am wearing your shirt to bed? I wish it were you wrapped around me instead. I have told the villagers about their new home, and I think they are happy about it. There is much to do for it and the festival. I think I need more hours in the day. Anyway, how are you? What is it like where you are? Are you sleeping under the stars?

Love,

Charlotte.

I've memorized every curve and slope of her elegant script. Her flimsy chemise had turned into tatters under my armor, and I was forced to discard it before we even got out of Candonia. *I could ride back and get another one. Two, three, four days tops, and I could be riding into camp, my wife running to greet me, her hair flying behind her in a dark wave.*

I bump my head against the ground, hating how pathetic I sound. The dirt does nothing but endure my beating on it. Why do I think about her more and more the farther away I am? It is as if something is telling me, warning me, that I should be by her side instead of lying on the cold ground. I throw my arm over my face, trying to force myself to sleep, but I can't stop thinking. I got another letter from Ravaryn about the lack of gold and commerce throughout the country. The majority of their income was from the slave trade, they're floundering without it, and Princess Lyra is wavering in her commitment to the cause. I never thought to see the day.

No one was more impassioned about the end of slavery than Lyra, but her people are starving, and poachers are encroaching on her borders. She's stuck between her ideals and reality, a place I know well. I never thought it would be so complicated. I didn't know when I forced these countries to outlaw slavery that I would have to deal with the fallout, but I should have. It was so arrogant of me not to have planned for this. I thought there would be relief, and countries would fall in line, thankful to get rid of the loathsome trade. Now, I'm constantly called to enforce the law, to punish those who ignore it. But without something to replace it, people are becoming desperate. Even with the abolishment, slavers still have massive sources of wealth to pull from, and they will pay to get countries to turn a blind eye. I can't keep doing this for the next decade.

How do I replace centuries of trade? Fuck, what does Grimmwing need to survive? What can replace a massive hole in commerce? *Charlotte would know.* She used to serve as her father's advisor. If she was anyone but my wife, I would have brought her with me. She would have seen this coming, would have advised me on the way to stop it before it started.

I resist the need to get on the Black and ride for Ilium to ask her in person what she would do. She would have the answers I need, she would smile up at me, and the perfect solution would spill from her bow-shaped lips as if it was obvious to everyone.

And I would look down at her in astonishment, amazed at the way her mind works.

I lower my arm from my face and blink up at the stars, seeking the relief they usually provide me. I need the guidance of the Ancients to spirit me away from the present, giving me hope for the future. My lips twitch slightly, and I relax as I recall all the names I gave them as a child, the images that I used to find in them. I used to let them tell me stories, tales of faraway lands, and a family who would take me away from the master. That little boy could never have imagined this future. Never would I have dreamed that my life would include a princess with fathomless eyes who's wound herself so tightly around my soul that it has become impossible to distinguish one from another. That little boy would never have imagined that we stole her, that we took away her choice. That little would be so disappointed in me.

I watch the familiar constellations that once guided me through my darkest times. And then, between one blink and the next, they change, becoming something else. No longer is it the rabbit who hops freely across the sky. It's the curve of her cheek as she sleeps. The rearing horse is her hair falling down her back, playing against her alabaster skin. The fish that jumped through puddles my entire life are now her eyes sparkling across the night sky. Why now?

I've chartered my life with these stars. Every night they've been the same, no matter my wants and desires. No matter my thoughts or what consumed me. But now...

They're Charlotte.

My heart pounds as I push up on my elbows, looking at the sky in amazement. I trace the lines of her body through the stars, a shape I was blind to all these years. I need her, and I'm stuck on the cold ground, half a continent away.

"Commander!" Niklaus's voice snaps me out of my maudlin reverie, and when I look back at the stars, her image is gone.

I shake my head to clear it and sit up to look at him. "Yes?"

His dark hair is unkempt, and there's a growth of dark stubble along his jaw, very unlike him. Niklaus is almost always clean. Usually, it's Kian who's fighting a shadow on his dark gold face. His eyes are stark, and something that looks like fear is dancing within them. He never shows emotion. Ever.

Niklaus glances around, aware of how many other men have forgone tents to sleep under the open sky. We will be easily overheard. His voice is deep and rough, but his words are carefully considered and formed, much like Charlotte's. "We are approaching the border of Grimmwing."

"We are," I acknowledge, already knowing where this is going. Niklaus's eyes lock on mine. It's the same reason that he often stays behind when we go near Grimmwing. He's never stepped foot into the snowy wilderness since I first found him on the border. Eight years old, drenched in blood and close to losing his limbs to the freeze. "General, I'd like for you to take a platoon of men and ride for Vruica. There have been reports from the Mother Superior that slavers are encroaching on the North Wardens' haven. I would like for you to head there and cut off any caravans that hope to make it south."

Niklaus lets out a short breath of relief before bowing. "Of course, Commander."

On the utmost edge of Grimmwing and Vruica, the North Wardens are independent of either country, mainly because neither kingdom knows it exists. Niklaus has traveled with us before to the sanctuary, and I know it is outside his general distaste for the country. An impassable mountain range lies between the North Wardens and Ravaryn.

"When you've routed the slavers, send word. Depending on our status, I'll either send you back to Ilium or have you meet us in Steodia." I nod again, dismissing him.

Niklaus turns around, walking back to the men under his command. His shoulders relax, all coiled tension slipping from him. Niklaus is young, too young to be weighed down with whatever keeps him from crossing the border of Grimmwing. He was my first squire, my first *Boy*. To this day, I've never asked. I figure he'll tell me when he's ready, but until he does, I'll keep his secrets. I doubt anyone's truly noticed that he never crosses the border, and if they have, they were wise enough not to comment on it.

Niklaus is brutal and cold to most. The soldiers call him *Stone Wall* because he rarely expresses any kind of emotion. Even during battle, his face remains a blank mask. It has terrified many of the armies we've faced. I've heard rumors he's picked up the name *The Reaper* after one soldier spun a tale of Niklaus stealing someone's face in the middle of battle. Yet another tall tale that inspires obedience, more war is fought with words than with weapons.

I snort and lay back on the rough pallet, looking back at the stars, disappointed not to see her image.

XLIII

Charlotte

ILIUM

KINGDOM OF CANDONIA

It has been a week since Evander left. I have kept myself busy to make the time go faster, but today, I feel it. Each time I look at the clock, only a few minutes have passed. It feels like an eternity, and all I want to do is go back to sleep until he comes home.

Every morning I stand on the balcony and overlook the camp, hoping to see my husband's army returning. They never do. I have been counting down the days, tracking them on my calendar. Each day I mark off, my heart beats a little quicker. Just a few more weeks and he will be mine again.

With a soft sigh, I turn away from the balcony and make my way to my desk. The classes for Evander's men have been going well. I gain more and more students by the day, and each is excited to learn. Yesterday, I walked into the tent to find fifty men eagerly waiting for class. I will need to schedule a second one so everyone has a chance.

The missing person's list has continued to grow, but no one has been found yet. I know it will take some time. Aellolyn is a huge chunk of land, and it could take up to a month for the message to spread across the kingdoms. I keep my hope up for the men and the happiness they each deserve. I will never give up and will continue to help them write their letters to look for their loved ones.

A knock stirs me from my thoughts, and I tighten my robe before opening my bedroom door. Eleanor and Ben stand there. The boy's face is caked with dirt from his travels, and his hair is shaggier than when he left. Eleanor is wearing her pale blue dress with one big ribbon at the back and gripping Ben's hand as she smiles up at him. Her eyes sparkle with admiration and happiness. Eleanor has had a hard time, and the loneliness is getting to her. She often sneaks into my room in the middle of the night so it makes me happy that she has these moments with a friend.

"Ben. It's so good to see you," I say.

The boy smiles, holding up a letter. "He said to wait for your response, Your Highness."

I smile, taking the letter and looking down at my name scribbled on the front. *I love how he writes my name.*

"Can I show Benji around?" Eleanor asks, and I nod. She squeals in excitement before dragging the boy away. I smile, shaking my head at my sister's antics before closing my door.

I take a seat at my desk and run my fingers over my name. *Princess Charlotte.* I love his handwriting so much, and I can tell he put a lot of effort into it. His usual crooked misspelled writing is smooth and delicate. I gently break the wax seal, pulling out the piece of paper. I unfold it and grin at the sloppy and barely legible letter, knowing that this is indeed his writing.

Lamb,

We arrived in the province safely, and many were relieved to see us. Apparently, some of Grimmwing have fallen back to the old trade, and they need our help to roust slavers for good. It made me think. We need a new trade for the country to rely on. Grimmwing produces their legendary steel, but little else. Everything would have to be imported through treaties with other

276

nations. *I miss your guidance, and I didn't even think how complicated these types of politics could be. What would you suggest? I didn't think the slavers would be so tenacious. I'm sorry, I'm rambling, but I need your advice. Everyone looks to me for answers, and I'm a bit lost. And I miss you. I'm happy the villagers are excited about the prospect of a new world. I sleep under the stars, wondering if you're looking at the same ones. Are you?*

> *Your husband,*
> *Evander*

I place the letter on my chest, against my fluttering heart. He misses me. He truly misses me. The response has me giddy as I sit back in my chair. I giggle to myself, biting my bottom lip as I prepare to write a letter in return.

> *Husband,*
> *I look at the stars every night before bed and think of you. The days are getting harder without seeing your face. I continue to count down the days until you return. For Grimmwing, I know they have a coal mine and an abundance of fur from the bears and moose. Perhaps we can strike a new deal with them and add those resources to the trade. We can supply them with whatever they need in return. I can rework the trade agreement with Vruica, which is currently our primary source of coal. It shouldn't be too hard. There is a prediction that our winter will be cold and harsh this year, anyway. This could work in our favor. What do you think?*
> *Love,*
> *Princess Charlotte*

I fold the piece of paper, placing it into an envelope and sealing it with wax. There will be another two weeks until I receive my next letter from him, which makes me a little sad. I enjoy knowing he is well, and I love that he asked for my advice. We are starting to work as a team, and it gives me great hope for our future. If a king and queen can't communicate, then a kingdom can fall. Knowing he appreciates my guidance warms me. I wish I could go with Ben to see him. That would be perfect.

When Eleanor and Ben return, Eleanor's face is shadowed with sadness. She knows the time to say goodbye is upon her.

"Your reply, Your Highness?" Ben smiles. It is clear he is happy he got to spend some time with my sister.

I hold out the letter to him with a soft smile. "Here it is. Did you enjoy your tour?"

"Elle took the long way. I think she was hoping that I would end up not going back," he says, taking the letter. His face drops a little as he looks down at my sister. I doubt the boy wants to leave either.

"Well, I don't want you to go," Eleanor says, her cheeks turning pink.

Ben snickers. "Anything else you want the Commander to know?"

I think for a moment, wondering if there was anything I missed in the letters. My eyes brighten as I think of something truly evil. "Tell him that I do scream his name at night. Then when you return, I would like to know his reaction."

Ben looks at me in utter confusion, blinking a few times. "Um, alright?"

"He will understand." I bite back my giggle. *That will teach him to leave me.*

Ben frowns before bowing, still trying to figure out what I told him, I assume. "Your Highness."

He turns to look at Eleanor, reaching out to tap the end of her nose. "Elle."

Eleanor looks up at him, her eyes watering. "You'll be back soon?"

Ben nods. "I have a feeling the Commander will send me right back here."

"Good!" Eleanor squeals, clapping her hands together, and Ben turns away from us. He walks down the hall, and Eleanor runs to follow him. I smile at the children before going back into my room. It doesn't feel as dark in here as it did before. The light is shining in through my window, illuminating my bedroom brightly. I smile to myself before taking a seat at my desk once more.

Only a few more weeks until Evander comes home.

XLIV

EVAN

OUTSIDE OF RAVARYN

THE SNOWY KINGDOM OF GRIMMWING.

It's snowing again, which means the Boy will be delayed in his ride back from Ilium. He is supposed to be back today with a letter from my wife. I'm making a path in the snowbank as it melts under my constant pacing. My men are watching me surreptitiously, whispering and snickering behind their hands to each other. I know they are saying I'm being led around by a petite princess who has me turned inside out. I'm distracted, and that can cost my men their lives. But I can't stop wishing I was back in Ilium. That we didn't have to ride north to enforce these laws, and I had thought through the long-term effects of my pursuit of a free Aellolyn. The way things stand now, I might have to ride to the edges of the country every couple of days to enforce it. That would give me little time with my wife, in the home I want to build with her, in the life I want to give to my men. I want to rest, finally let my men rest.

Thankfully, we are not in a full-out war. Instead, we are picking off slavers who have encroached upon Ravaryn, and I'm supposed to be meeting with Princess Lyra today as an emissary of the throne of Grimmwing. I should be heading home soon, and the next time I ride north for a long period, I'm dragging my wife with me.

Lyra should be here anytime, and then we can sort this out. But I can't stop thinking that the Boy should be here any moment with a letter from my wife.

Focus. Lives are at stake.

A sentry blows the horn twice to announce Lyra's arrival, and the sound of her entourage forces me into the present. Lyra rides forward on a light bay horse. A long, fur-lined cloak trails from her shoulders, keeping her warm as the snow continues to fall. A gold circlet holds back her riotous red curls, exposing the delicate features of her face. Four armed guards ride at her side, all of them in full metal armor, halberds gripped in their hands. So much pomp and circumstance. Royalty.

You're royalty now, too.

Well, shit. That's something I'll have to think more about later.

Lyra's emerald eyes scan the ranks of men, her gaze searing, though analytical. Several of my seasoned warriors shift under her scrutiny. But when her eyes fall on me, her fiery brow raised, I still don't feel the need to confess everything like I do when my wife looks at me. Lyra is young and beautiful. I once thought to marry her, but her claim to the throne of Grimmwing is not one of birth. Her father married the Queen of Grimmwing after his first wife passed, leaving a young Lyra to a man who knew little about raising a child. So he did what most men would do. He tried to find a mother who could replace her dead one.

Lyra was adopted into the court, her father the new king, and she grew up immersed in the cutthroat life of royal politics. Somehow, even though she was not born to it, she is beloved by her people and became their emissary. Now, years after her father passed, she remains as the queen's ward because even her stepmother knows that she can't touch Lyra without a full revolt on her hands. I've never met the queen. All of my dealings have been with Lyra. She speaks with the full support of her nation at her back.

She smiles, calling out to me, "Blondie."

My lips twitch slightly in response. Lyra's the only person who calls me that. I bow my head slightly to her in a show of respect. "Princess."

Lyra dismounts, her long cloak falling around her ankles, the flash of her jewel-toned dress vanishing. She pats the side of her horse before handing the reins off to a member of her entourage. She pulls off her gloves and gestures to the tent set up for this meeting.

"So, you have something to talk about, yeah?" she asks, her lilting voice heavy with an accent, one that I will probably fall into the longer I'm in her presence. It's easy to slip back, easy to pretend I grew up in the nation of my birth.

I nod, moving into the tent. The dark mahogany table gleams in the light of the candles and torches. The wood is worn and scarred from the numerous times my generals and I have poured over it, plotting strategic moments, deciding the campaign. Lyra motions for her guards not to follow, leaving the two of us alone. I gesture to the opposite seat, sitting across the table from her.

"Sit."

Lyra lets out a snort, taking the seat. "Demanding as ever."

"I'm here as Prince of Candonia and emissary for the crown." My lips quirk at the title, still foreign to say out loud. I pass the scroll across the table to Lyra.

Lyra raises her brow before reading it over.

"I know your people are looking at a terrible winter," I add as she reads the new terms. "This will work to replace the commerce you lost."

Lyra looks up at me, leaning back in her chair, rubbing her chin. "It's a good proposal. I like it. Did you come up with it on your own?"

My body stiffens. *Why did she ask that? What does it matter if it wasn't my idea?*

My eyes narrow slightly. "No, my wife did. Why do you ask?"

282

Lyra smirks, shrugging before rolling up the scroll. "I will bring this to the queen, and if I have any say in it, we will accept."

"It's always good to see you, Lyra."

Lyra pulls out a small note from her cape, holding it out. "Give this to your wife for me?"

I blink, taking it from her hand. "What is it?"

"A note from me to her." She smiles. "Girl talk." My thumb trails over the wax seal, wondering at the contents. "It's nothing bad, blondie. I am quite happy the two of you are getting along. You're a changed lad."

I am?

"Changed? How?" I feel different, but I can't explain it. Maybe Lyra can help me figure out what exactly my wife is doing to me.

She looks me up and down. "You seem happier."

"Happier? I don't know if that's a good thing." I frown. What if a happy me is less alert? I would have never stumbled into that trap before being married. There are a lot of things I would never have done before I got married. My head starts to pound.

Lyra stands and moves around the table to pat my shoulder. "I think it is. You deserve some sort of happiness, Evan. You know that, right?"

Lyra is one of the few people who knows my past. When she was a young, spirited lass of ten, she caught my second master beating me. She stormed over and slammed her small fist into his stomach. When that did little, she kicked him in the shins. The slaver raised a hand to her in retaliation, but Lyra's personal guard stopped him before the blow could land.

I remember being astonished at this child doing what I couldn't do at fifteen. *Fight back.* A slave will never dream of freedom when he's known nothing but chains.

"She's too good for me." I pause. "You know who I used to be." *What I used to be.*

"Does she?" Lyra asks, scanning my face. I rub my neck, looking away. Lyra picks up her chair and moves it around the table to sit next to me.

"Drink?" I ask, hoping to change the topic.

She nods. "I'll need something strong if I am to go against the wench tonight."

I shout over my shoulder, "Boy!"

I blink in surprise when my squire appears. It takes all my considerable strength not to lunge at him for word from my wife. I can't show my attachment to Charlotte in front of Lyra. In front of others, I must remain in control. "Yes, Commander?"

"Will you get the Quipei from Xiapia? It's in the trunk in my tent and should be in the carved box."

He nods, leaving to retrieve it. Lyra snorts loudly. "I said something strong, not something to kill us!"

I shrug at her, looking up when my squire comes back with a dusty bottle and two goblets. He uncorks the bottle, pouring generous amounts in both.

"You have chores, Boy."

He nods. "Yes, Commander."

He bows before leaving again. I knock the edge of her goblet before taking a swig, immediately coughing at the burn.

Lyra takes a short sip. "So..."

My head drops back, looking at the ceiling of the tent. "Yes, she knows."

Lyra takes another sip. "And she hasn't petitioned for an annulment?"

"She hasn't." I choke slightly when I take a large gulp of the drink and then hit my chest several times to clear it.

Lyra laughs, then shakes her head. "So she has feelings for you then?"

"She says she loves me."

Lyra bumps her shoulder against mine. "Blondie! Look at you go."

I shoot her a look. "She can't love me, not truly. She doesn't have a choice and is just making the best of a bad situation."

Lyra scoffs. "I have known that lass for a long time now. She is as stubborn as they come. She wouldn't just say those words unless she felt them."

New topic.

"How are things here?"

The wood of her chair creaks as she leans back, and I turn my head slightly to look at her. "Fine. For now. I assume my time is running out."

"Why?"

Lyra takes another sip, shuddering slightly from the bitterness. "Don't worry about it."

I quirk a brow at her. "We're friends, Lyra, and allies. You can tell me."

Her fingers trace the shape of the cup. "It's nothing to be concerned about now. I will come find you when I need help, yeah?"

I nod, raising my goblet to her.

Hours later, I stumble away from the tent. I grab my squire, shaking him. "How come you didn't tell me you were here?"

He blinks. "I thought you knew? You summoned me earlier!"

"Letter!" I demand, slurring my words a bit more than I expected.

He smirks. "Oh, so that's what this is about?" He pulls out the letter, and I almost tear it in half when I snatch it from him. When he doesn't disappear, I ask, "Was there something else, Boy?"

"She told me to tell you that she screams your name every night."

My mouth goes dry, and I practically run to my tent to read her letter.

It has almost been two weeks since Ben arrived with the first letter. The thought saddens me a little. I didn't realize how slowly time would pass without Evander here. It is strange. These past few weeks have felt like an entire year. What happens if Evander doesn't return at the end of the month? Should I go to see him? The temptation to run away from the palace and look for his army in Grimmwing has gnawed at me. But I have duties here. Preparations for the festival began the moment my father accepted the proposal. He thought it was a magnificent idea and building is underway. It will be a way for the citizens of Candonia and Evander's people to meet on even ground. This will be a new beginning for all of us, and we can all feel at peace with our new lives. The festival will also spread awareness to other villages and cities that Evander is the future King of Candonia. If there is any illegal slavery still happening within the province, they will answer to him.

Getting up from my chair, I prepare for the day. Lately, I find myself getting ready on my own without the help of my maids. A part of me wants Evander to be here, doing up my ties and pressing kisses to my neck. It feels strange having the maids doing it now. Besides, I have forgone a corset since my marriage. Those things are uncomfortable, and they make it hard to breathe. I find my mind is clearer without that contraption sucking the air from me. The queen tried to insist I wear it, but I narrowed my eyes at her before walking away. Corsets are essential to a princess, duchess, and ladies. To not wear one would be a statement. Which is what I am doing. Showing the queen that I am in control of my own body and comfort.

My sisters and I are safe while Demir is with us. The queen is a smart woman and knows there will be consequences if she hurts us when he is around.

Once I am ready for the day, I exit my room and make my way toward the stairs. Today I will be working on trade agreements with my father before classes with the warriors. I never realized how many countries relied on slavery. The thought makes me sick, and it concerns me. These countries need money and supplies to care for their people. Hopefully, my new plan for trades will help lessen their need to rely on it.

I hear two young voices echoing down the hallway. Joy fills me as I turn the corner and spot the children walking up the stairs. Eleanor is hanging around Ben's neck, yelling something at him, as he smiles from ear to ear. I stop to wait for them at the top of the stairs, clearing my throat when they get close. Ben lets go of Eleanor, who lands on her bum. She shoots him a dirty look, but Ben doesn't look down.

"Your Highness." He bows.

I smile warmly at the boy. "I assume you have a letter from my husband?"

Ben nods. "I do, and he told me to tell you that *he heard you*. I suppose that means something to you?"

My cheeks burn and I giggle to myself. "Oh, that scoundrel."

Ben holds the letter out for me, and I take it before looking at Eleanor. "You know, I think the cook is making some cookies today. Perhaps you can take Ben and grab a few for himself and the generals?"

By the time I am done speaking, Eleanor is already pulling Ben back down the stairs toward the kitchens. I laugh softly before heading back to my room. Slowly, I open the letter and take a seat in my chair. I will never tire of reading his words.

Lamb,

You better be opening this in private so that I can scold you. You sent the Boy with a message that you screamed my name? I could barely focus for the rest of the night. I canceled all my meetings and stroked myself twice while thinking of you. I thought about getting on the Black and riding until I saw you. Cruel, lamb, very cruel. About renegotiating treaties, these are excellent ideas. Will your father go for them? Fuck, I wish you were here. If you were anyone but my wife, I would have you at my right hand for this kind of stuff. Your advice was just what I needed. I hinted at a potential new trade with Princess Lyra, and she immediately rejoined our cause with fervor. She was tapering off support as it was costing her citizens their livelihood. We'll be leaving Grimmwing by the time you get this letter, and I'll be on my way home to you. Two weeks, then I'll be home. How is construction going? And the festival? Did I mention I missed you yet?

Your Husband,
Evander

My heart flutters in my chest as I read his words over and over again. I trail my fingers over his name, biting my lip and wondering what he is doing now. He liked my advice. He would have chosen me to be his right-hand man. The thought warms my heart. Many of the suitors I met before Evander couldn't have cared less about my intelligence, but he values it. In the future, I will be at his side for these journeys, he will simply need time to adjust to the idea. Every great sword needs a hand to guide it. I press the letter to my chest, smiling brightly. He will also make it home in time for the festival. That was all I wanted. I want him to be home so we can celebrate together.

Placing the letter on the desk, I grab a piece of paper and my quill.

Dear Evander,

Yes, I suppose that was very cruel of me. It must kill you to know I moan your name every time I pleasure myself in my bed. I imagine your hands on every inch of my body. Your kisses in places only you get to see. I crave your touch. Perhaps you need to show me how much you missed me when you return home. In all seriousness, I have already spoken to my father about the trade proposal, and he has agreed. We will send word to the different kingdoms and work out the details while you make your way home to me. Construction on the new town is going well. Most of the foundation has been set, and the villagers appear very happy. My hope is that the village will one day become a city, and the other freed slaves will make a new life there. Start anew. What do you think? As for the festival, you should make it back just before it begins. Everyone is excited, and I think it will boost morale for everyone. Once enemies slowly become friends. I miss you dearly, Evander. I can't wait to see you.

Love,

Your Wife

I seal the letter with wax before getting up from my chair to look for the children. The hallways are busy with staff running back and forth, preparing for the festival, and working to keep the castle clean. Making my way down the stairs, I head to the kitchen. Eleanor is on Ben's back as he spins in place. My sister holds her arms out, her blonde hair flying behind her as she laughs. The cooks have wisely left the kitchen, leaving the children to their games. The smell of cookies and herbs fills the air, the scent one of comfort and home. This is one of Eleanor's hiding spots when she is trying to avoid the busy life of the palace.

As always, the kitchen is tidy, pots and pans are hanging from a metal bar above the island. The large stove has been recently cleaned, all the soot and ashes in a bag beside the door. Food is tucked away on the shelves and baskets lining the counters. Our cook has always had a knack for keeping her kitchen spotless. She is like a second mother to my sisters and me. She is one of the kindest women I have ever met.

I lean against the door frame and watch Eleanor and Ben. I dislike ruining their moment. They are only children for so long, and I know Ben will have to leave her in a couple of years.

I want the two to have as much time as they can with each other.

Ben notices me standing by the door and skids to a stop in front of me. His face goes a little red with embarrassment.

"Your H-Highness," he stutters.

I smile at the boy. "Did you enjoy the cookies?"

He nods. "Do you have more?"

Eleanor slides off his back and runs over to one of the wooden baskets on the counter. She reaches her delicate fingers into one of them before returning to Ben.

"Here!" she exclaims.

Ben takes the cookie, smiling at my sister before turning his attention to me. "Your letter?"

I hand my letter to Ben. "Thank you, Ben. For delivering the letters."

Ben tucks the note away before ruffling Eleanor's hair. "I mean, I have to make sure this one hasn't burned the palace to the ground."

"I would never!" Eleanor scoffs. Her eyes darken as she realizes Ben is preparing to leave, and she shifts from foot to foot. "My letter! Don't go yet!"

She bolts from the kitchen, and I look at Ben questioningly. He only shrugs, but I can see he is vibrating with excitement. His eyes are trained on the door that Eleanor just ran through. Their care for each other goes beyond friendship. Though, I don't know if they have realized it yet.

"Thank you for being her friend. I have noticed a difference in her. In a good way," I say.

Ben frowns, continuing to stare at the door. "A difference? She's perfect the way she is."

"She was sad before." I frown, remembering Eleanor before Evan took the city. She would always stare out the window, wondering if she would ever have a friend who would like her for who she is. "She was alone. Having you is a miracle to her, and you have made her very happy."

Ben looks down at his shoes, mumbling something under his breath. His shaggy hair falls in front of his eyes, making it hard to read his expression.

"What was that?" I ask, tilting my head.

"You make him happy, too," he says.

I know who he means. Since Evander's arrival, everyone I know has changed, including me. I smile to myself before whispering, "Well, it's only fair. He makes me happy. I think both my sisters are happier now. Strange, isn't it? I never thought I would be this happy."

Ben nods. "Both your sisters? Even the scary one?"

I laugh. "Even the scary one. She seems to be getting along well with the Mountain. I haven't seen her smile like that since we were kids."

Ben's big brown eyes bulge. "Is *he* smiling?"

"Yes. I think I've even heard him laugh," I say. Ben gapes at me in complete shock, and I giggle. "Does he not normally laugh?"

"No." The boy snorts.

"I guess all of us are gaining something positive from this," I whisper. Before Ben has the chance to respond, my sister comes sprinting into the room, out of breath. She holds her letter out to Ben, her writing larger and less tidy than my own.

"Remember. Only open it when you feel alone!" Eleanor instructs, sticking her finger in the air. Ben takes the letter from her and promptly opens it. Eleanor's eyes widen, and she jumps at him, attempting to grab the letter back. Her face turns bright red as she yells, "I'm serious, Benji!"

Ben only holds the letter up higher, reading her words, and Eleanor stops jumping. She sticks her bottom lip out at him.

"B-Benji… please," she whispers, her eyes misting. Ben finishes reading the letter before holding it to his heart and looking down at my little sister.

"You are my favorite princess," he says to her before looking at me. "No offense, Your Highness."

"None taken," I say, holding my hands up. "We should send you back to Evander. I have another message for him."

"Of course, Your Highness," he says.

"Tell him I will be waiting for him in my room when he returns. Once he is home, I would like him to come see me as soon as he can. We have some things to discuss," I say with a small smile.

"Will do." Ben nods.

The three of us head to the palace doors, tears filling Eleanor's eyes. *Only a few more days, dear sister. A few more days and they will be home with us.* I open the door, and Eleanor follows behind Ben for a few more steps before stopping. She stands there as Ben mounts his horse and rides away. Eleanor doesn't budge, and I walk over to her, taking her hand and squeezing it reassuringly.

"Come, El," I whisper. "We can work on the festival together."

Eleanor looks up at me with a watery smile before walking back with me into the palace.

XLVI

EVAN

OUTSIDE OF RAVARYN

THE SNOWY KINGDOM OF GRIMMWING

I hate that we're still here. I hate snow. I hate camp gruel. I hate the temporary tent I'm in. I hate Grimmwing. I hate pretty much everything that tells me I'm not home with my wife. We packed up the camp and headed south after I spoke with Lyra, but a snowstorm blew in and delayed our trip home. We are camped along the main road between Ravaryn and Ilium. It's buried deep in the stupid snow, and I'm about a moment away from taking my sword to the icy obstacle. Snow is dangerous, it covers the road, and a horse could step into a hidden hole and break a leg. There are too many risks and not enough benefits to pushing on, except for the obvious one. *Charlotte.*

A trumpet flare goes off, and I turn to see my squire riding into camp. The only thing that can keep me from hacking at the snow with my sword is a letter from my wife. I sprint to his side, uncaring that my men are watching with a bemused look. After this trip, they've all come to accept my fascination with my wife. I thought it would cause more problems in the ranks, but it seems they enjoy knowing that I am human after all. Not even letting my squire dismount, I drag him off his horse and pat him down for the letter, pulling out two of them.

"One is mine!" he demands, snatching one back. I tear open the other letter. The parchment is smooth, and I immediately recognize Charlotte's elegant script, though it takes me a moment to read the words.

Dear Evander,

Yes, I suppose that was very cruel of me. It must kill you to know I moan your name every time I pleasure myself in my bed.

My entire body stiffens, and I close the letter before I get too carried away. If I know my wife, she continued in the same vein just to torture me. She is set on punishing me for being gone this long, and this is a pain only she can deliver. I will admit that I've been reading in my spare time at night, forcing myself to work on perfecting the skills that help me communicate with her. I'm still a slow reader and likely will be for the rest of my life. But I'm getting better, and it is getting easier. Maybe, one day, I can read something to her without stumbling or falling over the words. I imagine us sitting on the banks of the lake, drying off after a dip as I read to her. I would choose something she likes, poetry or, knowing my wife, a catalog of the great moments in Aellolyn's history.

"Don't bother unpacking. We're heading home now," I snap to my squire, practically throwing him back into the saddle, whistling for the Black, and shouting orders to the men.

Wynonna looks at me, not bothering to brush away the snowflakes accumulating on her braid. "Commander? You know we can't go anywhere at the moment."

I frown down at her. The fur of her cloak is covered in snow, though she shakes it periodically to keep it from getting wet and freezing. "I don't know anything of the sort."

Wynonna sighs. "Evan. We all know that you want to go home."

My eyes narrow on my old mentor. If she's about to say something against my wife, I won't be responsible for my actions. I've spent over a month away from her. I rode North, renegotiated treaties, and kept my men safe, I'm allowed to want to get home. I'm allowed to want something for myself. "And?"

"It's simply not possible to move the troops back towards Candonia today." Wynonna points out, glancing at the snowbank that only continues to rise.

I look at the road, then back down at my mentor, then back at the road. I know she's right, it will risk lives to push forward today, but I can't stop this pull to be back in Candonia, to be back with her. Something is yanking me, tearing at me, insisting that I ride for her and don't stop until she's in my arms.

But the men have to come first. I can't lose the trust they've placed in me. They have faith I won't recklessly charge into battle at the cost of their lives. Faith I'm not sure I deserve anymore. What will I choose? My wife or my men?

The crown shines as it flips, end over end. Only the Ancients know how it will land.

I will not be another master. I have to be better, be stronger, and I have to resist this insistent pull. Sighing, I nod to Wynonna, dismounting. I pat the Black's side, who dances anxiously. "I know, I know you miss them too."

Since we left, the horse has been anxious to get back to Snow, likely sensing my own hopes. Our bond is deep, and we can sense each other's emotions. And right now? That's a terrible thing. We want to be home, and we're escalating the need in each other.

Walking side by side with the Black, I force myself to build a fire, setting up my pallet next to it for the night. I don't even bother with a blanket. If I stay close to the fire, it will keep me warm, and the snow won't be able to reach me while it burns. The grey clouds conceal the stars, making me even more irritable.

Wynonna comes to sit next to me, raising her hands to the flames. "Have I ever told you about Lorcan's birth?"

Where is this going? Wynonna never speaks about personal things, unless deep in her cups. What is it about this month away that is bringing out strange things in people I've known for a decade? Will I turn around to find Lorcan is dying his hair? Kian wearing pastels? Niklaus smiling?

"Only that your husband died right before you gave birth." Laying on my back, I blink as a snowflake lands on my cheek. I flick the offending drop away, shifting closer to the heat.

Wynonna sighs, picking up a stick and poking the fire. "Balderik was my childhood sweetheart. He was...everything to me."

Turning on my side, I prop my head up on my hand, watching her over the crackling fire. "And you lost him."

"I did." Wynonna pauses again. "Before, I was consumed with him. I couldn't leave for a day without this sort of panic festering inside me, demanding I return home. What if something had gone wrong? What if he changed his mind? What if he never loved me?"

Thoughts I have every day that I'm apart from my wife. My stomach turns. She had that and lost it? How did she continue?

She flicks her big braid over her shoulder as her lips form a half-smile. "He died in my arms. He made me promise to protect our children, be there for them, and make sure they grew into good people."

My eyes scan her dark ones, the fire highlighting grief the likes of which I've never known. "How did you do it? How did...how did you not give up?"

Her eyes lock on mine. "I think I gave up for a while. I wanted to forget and drifted for years in a fog. Lorcan took care of me. It shakes me to think how he became the parent and I the child during that time. Then, I met an eighteen-year-old sell sword in a tavern in Arcanum, with a fire in his eyes and a nobility in his soul that made him more than any king. He gave me a new purpose. He gave my son a new purpose."

My breath catches, humbled by this knowledge. "But what if I'm losing myself? Becoming lesser because of this...obsession with her?"

"What if you're becoming more?"

The fire crackles again, and I'm not sure how to respond. But Wynonna lays down on her palette, sighing, "Sleep well, Commander. You'll be home again soon."

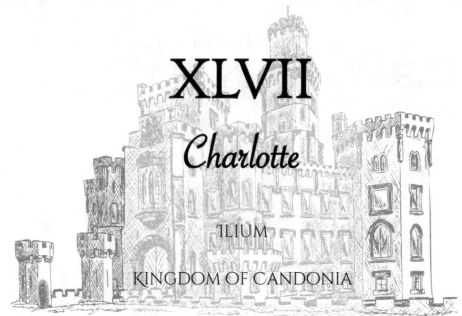

XLVII

Charlotte

ILIUM

KINGDOM OF CANDONIA

My husband will return any day now, and I can hardly wait. The temptation to get on Snow and ride out to meet him has become stronger over the past few days. I know he is on his way, which makes it harder. The wait has been agonizing. He could arrive home at any moment, and it makes it difficult to focus on my work. The next time he leaves me…well, I won't be letting him leave me again. The next time he goes, I will be joining him. He won't have a say in the matter.

Slowly getting out of bed, I wrap my nightgown tightly across my body. As hard as it has been, all has gone well since Evander left. With each class at camp, I see the warriors' demeanor toward me change. They are slowly starting to treat me with respect, not because I am Evander's wife, but because they value me as a person. It makes it feel like all my hard work the past month has paid off. I can't stop now, though. Even when Evander returns, I will continue with the classes and make efforts to improve their lives. They aren't just Evander's people. They are also mine.

I walk to the window to look for Evander, which has become a morning ritual. I stretch my arms over my head. My muscles ache, but not nearly as much as they did at the beginning of the month. Demir decided we needed some training. He has been teaching my sisters and me how to fight with weapons and hand-to-hand combat. Thalia is surpassing Eleanor and me by a landslide. She has always had an interest in martial training. There is something in sword work that calms her, even in her fits of rage. Demir has been giving Thalia extra sparring lessons, and it surprises me that the two are getting along so well without bickering. It truly makes me happy to see her content for once.

I smile and look out over the horizon where I last saw Evander. The northern road is still empty, undisturbed leaves scattered on the pathway. I sigh sadly. Not today. Perhaps tomorrow.

"Are you looking for someone?"

The deep voice takes me off guard, making me jump a little. My heart pounds as I spin to face him. *Evander.* He's back. I run to him, slamming against his body and kissing him as if I need him to breathe.

"You're home," I whisper against his lips. His familiar scent of vanilla and earth tingles my nose, and a part of me that I didn't know was tense, relaxes. He wraps his strong arms around me, his touch calming every single nerve in my system as I melt into him. I didn't realize how much I missed this until now.

"I missed you." His grip on me tightens. His words are genuine, and it warms me. I don't want to let him go, so I jump, wrapping my legs around his torso and burying my face against his neck.

"I missed you, too. When did you get home?" I murmur against him.

"An hour ago. I wanted to clean and eat before coming to you." Evander's lips brush over my pulse, sending shivers down my spine. I nuzzle my nose against his cheek, unable to get enough of my husband.

"Did you read my letter?" I ask as he lays me down on the bed.

"I got through a line before I ordered the men to break down camp and come home," he says, kissing my neck and shoulders. Each kiss warms a small part of my skin, leaving a tingling sensation with each touch. "I read another line every day I got closer to you."

"And your response?" I bite my lower lip, looking up at him. He grabs the back of my nightgown, ripping it down the middle, and I gasp.

"Is that not enough of a response?" he growls.

"I was hoping you'd show me." I giggle, arching my back. He doesn't respond as he slips off the ruins of my nightgown, kissing every inch of my skin. His warm lips trail between my breasts to my stomach, and I shift under him. Every part of my body aches and an overwhelming amount of emotions wash over me. "I love you."

He bites my hip before finally settling between my legs. "Say it again."

"I love you, Evander." I smile, looking down at him. He licks my clit gently, and I rest my head back on the pillows with a soft moan. Heat builds in my core with his every touch. My breathing quickens as I shift my legs, opening further to him.

"You didn't say it in your letters," he says between licks.

"I am so sorry, my love." I moan, my hips rolling against his mouth. My body continues to submit to every kiss, lick, and touch from him. Like a traveler walking in the deserts of Vredour in need of water, I need him. I feel Evander presses a finger inside me, and I moan once more.

"I thought you didn't love me anymore," he says, his voice a rough growl.

"My love has only grown stronger for you since you've been gone."

"Say it again," he commands, his mouth returning to my clit. He sucks hard and fills me with another finger.

"I love you," I moan louder.

"Scream it." He thrusts his fingers harder inside me. His tongue flicks faster, and the pressure builds quickly.

"I love you, Evander!" I scream, my walls tightening on his fingers as I come.

300

He smirks, pressing gentle kisses up my body to my lips. "I will never tire of hearing that."

I look at him with heated eyes. "I will never tire of tasting myself on your lips."

Evander growls, rolling onto his back. He tugs at his breeches and I roll over to help him. I pull his pants off, tossing them to the side before crawling on top of him. His chest flexes beneath my hands as I brace myself and press my entrance against him. I slowly slide down his thick length until I have taken all of him. His hands drop to my bottom, and I press my lips hard against his, moaning into them.

"Fuck," he groans. "My star."

"My prince," I moan, trailing kisses down his face and over his neck. I suck on his skin, leaving my mark on him as he has left his. We belong to each other. "Fuck..."

"I missed you so much." He hisses out a breath, his hands guiding my hips on him.

"I missed you so much, too. So alone..." Tears fill my eyes, and I kiss Evander's lips once more. "I love you."

I roll my hips against him, his cock hitting deep inside me. It sends waves of pleasure through me and I grip his chest. He shouts, arching his back, and I feel the throb of his release inside me. We both collapse onto the bed, and I roll beside him, trying to catch my breath. Sweat is dripping from our bodies, and I couldn't feel any more content.

"I never want to leave you again," he finally says, his breathing still heavy.

I move closer to him, placing my hand on his scarred chest. "Then don't."

"You know," his fingers trailing up and down my back, "I thought about sending for you almost every single day."

"I would have come," I say, rubbing my cheek against his chest. If he sent for me, I would have left without questions. Nothing would have stopped me from going. Nothing would have stopped me on my journey to him.

"It wouldn't have been safe," Evander says, kissing my forehead.

"Demir has been teaching me how to fight. I have been doing well." I sigh softly. My fingers continue to trail up and down his chest, his heart pounding beneath my touch.

He shakes his head. "I wouldn't have trusted anyone but myself to escort you, and that means I'd have to leave and come back."

"I understand," I whisper.

"You're precious cargo," he says, making my heart flutter.

"I love you." I smile, closing my eyes.

His body relaxes under me and he sighs. "I will never tire of hearing you say that."

Then I will continue to say it, Husband, because it is true. I love you.

XLVIII

EVAN

ILIUM

KINGDOM OF CANDONIA

"Now tell me what I missed," I prod, kissing her again. With her here in my arms, I can breathe again, my first real breaths since I left her. I don't have the sharp tinge in my side from being separated from her, and there's no metallic taste in my mouth. I'm home. The longer I rest in her arms, the more the memory of longing for her fades. It must have been my imagination, something manufactured in my head.

It isn't the palace. It will take me a long while for this massive structure to feel like home. The constant people underfoot, the sheer amount of paintings that stare at you while you pass by, all of it is overwhelming. It reminds me more of a mausoleum than a home. Yet, I feel that sense of belonging deep in my bones right now.

It's her. She's my home, the one I never dared dream I would have. I'd hoped to create a place for my men, of course. They long ago lost whatever ties they had to their countries of origin, and they deserved somewhere safe. Somewhere peaceful, where they could truly start fresh and put their lives as slaves and then as soldiers behind them.

But me?

I took Candonia out of necessity, and I married the crown princess strategically. I never thought to belong anywhere and never dreamed of having anything more than a strained relationship with my wife. Yet here I am, feeling more myself than I have in years, simply by being in her presence.

Her lips glide over my chest, and more warmth courses through me. "Well, what all have you heard, my love?"

Closing my eyes, I give myself up to the sensations with a sigh. "Only what your letters told me."

She picks up one of my hands, tracing the lines of my calloused palm. "Well, both kingdoms have agreed to the new trade deal."

My eyes blink open, watching her trail her long, elegant fingers along my scarred palm. "See anything interesting there?"

Some who were sensitive to the old ways could tap into the power of the Ancients and read the future in the lines of someone's hands. My squire's mother was one such woman. Her gift soon became a curse as a group of zealots who hoped to abolish the Church of Ancients burned her, believing in a single divine entity that rules over all. *Bunch of nonsense.*

My wife pushes my palm flat, focusing. "Eleanor has taught me a few things. She told me this is your lifeline." Her forefinger trails down the middle of my palm. "Looks like you'll be with me for a long time. Good."

I raise a brow at her. "Oh? A long time?"

A long time for a warrior was a couple of years. Men in my profession don't exactly live to see their first grey hairs. Though, I suppose I'm not of that profession anymore. I'm royal by marriage, and kings and princes always grow to be old and fat.

My wife points to the line above. "This is the heart line."

I know the answer to this. "My heart?" I reach out, cupping her cheek. "It's right here."

Her eyes shimmer as she moves her hand to my chest, resting it over my heart. "It's been broken quite a lot, hasn't it?"

My heart? No. No one has ever truly come close to touching it until her. But my spirit? My mind? My very soul? All have been broken and remade countless times. *Anyone can be broken.*

"It's healing now."

Her hand strokes over my chest, her scent of honey and chamomile making my body languid. I am completely sapped of tension. Her silky hair tickles my chin, splayed across my chest in a wave. "So, two new treaties. And I have something from Lyra for you."

She frowns and sits up, pulling the sheets with her. I don't understand her need to cover herself. It's just us, and I like her naked.

"Oh?"

I reluctantly roll out of bed and stride naked to my breeches. I find the small note in the pocket and hold it out to Charlotte. "She said it's for you."

She presses the sheets against her with one hand, reaching out for the note. "I haven't seen her in ages."

The sound of the wax seal breaking makes me tense, wishing I had read the letter before giving it to her. Lyra knows a lot of my past, more than I'm comfortable with. Has she spilled all those horrid secrets on the page? All the things I was forced to endure? I never want Charlotte to know those details. It is enough she knows I lived a life in chains, but knowing the whole truth would shatter her.

She smiles down at the letter, and I try to move around to see the words. "What does it say?"

"That she is an old friend of yours."

A breath of relief slips past my teeth. I slide back under the sheets with Charlotte and reorganize the pillows to support my back. "She is. Grimmwing was where I was born."

She places the letter on her side table, crawling over to me. "What happened?"

I exhale slowly and wrap my arm around her, allowing her to press up against my side. She rests her hand on my chest, and I am amazed again at how her touch soothes me. "It's not a pretty story."

Nor is it one I've ever said out loud before. But when she asks something of me, I'm helpless against it. If it's within my power, I'll give it to her. Even if it isn't, I'll find a way. She kisses my chest, unknowingly keeping the worst of the memories away. "I want to know."

I wrap a lock of her hair around my finger and sigh heavily. "I think it was a little village somewhere near the coast. It's been so long, and the memory keeps getting fuzzier. My Da paid the slavers to stay away. So long as he paid, they left us alone. But then there were no more fish, and my Da couldn't make the payments, so they came. I was five."

These were all new memories. Before I married Charlotte, I recalled none of this, but the calm she brings me has helped me reach into my mind. She blinks back tears. "Oh, Evander. I'm so sorry."

But I'm not done. I have to get through it all at once, or I never will.

"They took us in chains. My parents went to a different market. Me, I was young and expensive. With blonde hair and grey eyes, I was a desirable *commodity*. They brought me to the market where they could sell me for the most crowns." I pause, knowing this will devastate her. "They brought me to *Ilium*." Her body tenses against me, and I can't look at her. "I met Lyra when I was with my second master. She was visiting Vruica and punched my master for daring to harm me. She was ten. I had never thought to fight back. I didn't know there was another way until I saw her do that. I killed my next master, sold my talents as a sell sword, then I met Wynonna."

She crawls on top of me, tears rolling down her face, forcing me to look upon the devastation my words have wrought. She wraps her arms around me and shakes from the force of her sobs. "I'm so sorry… I'm so...sorry."

I rub her back soothingly as her tears wet my chest. I murmur, "Star, it's alright. It's alright."

"I-It isn't...it isn't. You were sold in my city, by *my* people. No wonder you h-hated me," she says.

Doesn't she know what she's done to me? How she's changed me? I kiss her head and press her face into my neck, reassuring her. "I never hated you."

Her hands dig into my hair, gripping me close. "W-Why? Why w-wouldn't you?"

I shift away from her to frame her face. "Look at me."

She sniffles heavily, tears welling in her jewel eyes. "It was my kingdom."

I brush the tears from her cheeks with my thumbs, shaking my head. She doesn't understand. "You changed things. You saved other children like me."

"You didn't know that when you first saw me. You thought I was like the rest of them."

Pressing my forehead to hers, I say, "You changed my mind."

She repeatedly blinks, trying to stem the tears. "I-I did?"

You changed everything. So much of my life was filtered in black and white, friend and foe. She's opened my eyes to the intricacies of grey. I'm better for it. At least, I like to think I am. Now, the weight of the future of Aellolyn, which once rested on my shoulders, feels lighter. As if I can trust others to share it.

"Your hands trembled that first night. You were terrified, but you still came to my tent. You didn't run." So brave, my little lamb. Even when she should have been frozen with terror, she would not yield.

She frowns at me, her tears drying. "H-How did that change your mind?"

"You showed no fear when we were married, even when I held your life in my hands. But when I had you completely at my mercy, you trembled. It made you more. More than just a pawn in a game I was playing. I hated seeing you scared." I didn't understand then, but I'm starting to. It isn't the king that is essential for victory. But the queen. She is able to move across the board freely, cutting in ways even the king cannot. My queen was disguised as a pawn. Now, she's checked the king.

"More than an emotionless princess," she says. "You choose me out of my sisters. Why?"

"Well, you are the heir, and you also tried to kill me."

She wipes more of her tears away. "I was close."

Snickering, I wrap my hands back around her, pressing her face back into my neck. It relaxes me to have her pressed against me, soothing even when she's distraught. "To killing me?"

She nods. "I'm a sneaky princess."

A short bark of laughter escapes me. "And what was your plan? You couldn't get the dagger out of the wall."

She lets out a laugh. "I would have run!"

My hands drop to her side, tickling her. "Oh, would you?"

She giggles, kicking her feet, trying to squirm away from me. "I would!"

"I would have caught you," I say, releasing her from my tickles.

She kisses me hard before saying, "Good."

XLIX

Charlotte

ILIUM

KINGDOM OF CANDONIA

Evander smiles down at me. The thought that he was sold in my city continues to be an aching wound in my chest. I would give nearly anything to be able to go back in time and keep him from having to endure his childhood. His kiss and touch soothe me, warming my skin as I move closer to him. His return home has calmed whatever ache I felt while he was away. I place a hand on his cheek, smiling softly at him.

"So, what else did I miss?" he asks. "Besides you changing the world?"

I bite my bottom lip, thinking of what else I have done. My eyes light up for a moment before I wince. There is one thing that I have been doing. Something that Evander would approve of if I had been coming home before sundown. I look up at him with a small smile. "I uh…I have been giving classes to your men."

"At night?" he asks, oddly calm. I know he is probably thinking of numerous ways to lock me in the palace while he is away.

"Demir was with me," I say, chewing my bottom lip. I know using Demir won't save me from my husband's disappointment and anger.

"At night?" he repeats, crossing his arms.

"I returned to the palace before midnight," I say, looking down at my hands.

"You were at camp. At night," he says, sitting up.

I wince, sitting up beside him. "Demir didn't leave my side."

"You. Promised. Me," Evander hisses out on a breath.

I grab his arm. "I didn't stay overnight."

"You know I said sundown." His jaw ticks.

"E-Evander..."

"I need to be able to trust your word," he says, letting out another breath. I can feel the anger radiating off his body, yet he hasn't yelled at me for breaking my promise. Something about his calmness makes my stomach twist. I rather he yell at me for being stupid and reckless. This disappointment burns more than ever, and I look down at my hands, trying to calm the guilt nagging at me.

"The men were really enjoying their lessons. I didn't want to ruin their excitement," I say.

"What were you teaching them?" he asks, taking a deep breath, calming himself.

"How to read and write," I mumble.

Evander pauses for a moment, taking in my words. "You did that?"

"Yes. I also, um..." I pause, getting up from the bed and grab the list of missing people, holding it out to him. He takes the list, frowning as he reads. I know it takes him a little longer, so I wait patiently. My stomach continues to roll as I wait for his reaction.

"What is this? Names?" he asks.

I nod. "Those families that have yet to be found...after being sold," I say.

He blinks at me in shock. "You're looking for them? Why?"

"Everyone deserves to have a second chance with their family," I say, looking at him.

He looks at the list once more. "And have you found any?"

I shake my head, my brows knitting. "Not yet. I sent a letter to an old friend of mine. He is finding as many as he can before he makes the trip here with them."

"He?" Evander narrows his eyes at me, his demeanor changing instantly.

I tilt my head in confusion. "Yes. Lord Edmund of Ecten. I have known him since I was a girl."

His jaw tightens. "An old friend?"

"Yes." I nod. "Is something the matter?"

"Nothing," Evander says, his body stiffening. "He's a lord?"

"He is." I nod again, watching him carefully. Something is bothering him, and I am going to try to figure out what the issue is.

"And he's going to just look for these people? No questions asked?" he asks.

"He was one of the lords who agreed with my law to abolish slavery," I say.

Evander shifts on the bed. "And he's older? An old man?"

"No. Edmund is only a few years older than me." I frown at him. He can't be jealous, can he? He knows my heart belongs to him, that I love him. "Are you sure everything is alright?"

Evander looks down at the list, ignoring my question. "This is very kind of you."

I lean over, giving him a comforting kiss on the lips. "Do upon others as you wish to be treated. My mother taught me that."

He kisses me again. "You are truly too good for me."

"I love you," I whisper against his lips. Looking out the window, I scoot closer to him. The fates tied our souls together for a reason, and I am finally starting to understand why. We both have the same goal, and both crave the love that no one else could give us other than each other. I take his hand in mine. "Should we head back to camp?"

"We should." He smirks. "I suspect your sisters are already there."

My brows furrow. "I figured Eleanor would be, but Thalia?"

Evander raises a brow. "Well, the Mountain was in camp looking suspiciously worn out with a cut on his cheek."

I laugh. "Did you know the first time they met, Thalia knocked him off his feet?"

"The Mountain?" Evander sputters in shock. I was surprised as well when it happened. My sister doesn't look very strong, so the fact she could knock over one of the strongest men in Evander's army would shock anyone.

I giggle, nodding. "I had to drag her off him."

Evander snorts, slipping out of bed and getting dressed. I do the same, jumping on his back and giggling. The two of us get ready together. He picks my clothes once more, and we settle back into our old routine. I step into the forest green gown with lace on the sleeves. Evander eases it up my body, his breath warm against my nape.

"I like this," I say. *I missed this.*

"I do too," he replies, pausing at the ties. "You should always let me dress you."

"Then you will," I say, sighing contentedly.

He tugs the ties closed, kissing my shoulder. "You like me being your lady's maid? Though I prefer to take it off you."

"Then you may do both," I say, looking over my shoulder.

Evander wraps a bit of my hair in his fist, yanking it lightly before kissing me. My heart races in my chest from the gentle pull, and my cheeks burn with heat. My mind is demanding more of the playful tug, but I clear my throat instead. "W-we should head to c-camp."

"Yes." He sighs, reluctantly releasing my hair. I bite my bottom lip, looking him up and down. "You keep looking at me like that, and we'll never leave this room."

I walk by him, whispering, "You were the one who tugged my hair."

He grabs me by the throat, yanking me back to him. His lips slam against mine savagely, and I moan deep in my throat.

"You were saying?" he growls.

312

"Fuck…" I whisper, my body heavy with lust. Evander lets me go, running a shaking hand over his mouth as he looks at me. My face only becomes redder. "Camp…we were going to camp."

"After you, my star." He nods, gesturing for me to walk out first. I keep my head low, heading toward the stairs. My mind is still fuzzy, and I am struggling to keep from turning around to look back at him. I am aching for him, need clawing at me, and my body is nearly vibrating with hunger. My heart pounds as I start down the stairs. We only make it halfway before Evander shoves me against the wall, his hand on my throat again. He fists my hair with his free hand and kisses me hard. I moan against his lips, my body submitting to the press of his. I grip his shirt and couldn't care less that my husband is about to take me in the middle of the palace. This man makes it hard for me to think logically. Evander's hands drop to my dress, yanking it higher. He only stops when he hears someone clear their throat behind him. He shifts to shield me from prying eyes.

"I hope you're prepared to die for interrupting," Evander growls.

I peek my head over his arm, noticing Demir standing there with a raised brow. I clear my throat before whispering to him, "It's the Mountain."

Evander snaps his head to look at him, snarling, "Leave now."

Demir blinks in surprise but spins on his heel, giving us his back. I squirm away from Evander, fixing my dress.

"Evander!" I hiss.

He takes a small slow step away from me, his eyes still glowing as he looks at the Mountain. "What did you need?"

"Her class. They're waiting for her," Demir signs over his shoulder.

I bite my lip, looking up at Evander. "I forgot my morning class."

"Cancel it," Evander snaps at Demir.

I look over at the general, sighing softly. "Tell them we can have a class at lunch. I will get Leonardo to bring pastries to make it up to them."

"Now. Goodbye," Evander says before Demir can respond. He looks back at me. His eyes are blown, and his breath is shaky. Once the Mountain is gone, Evander slams me back against the wall. He lifts me, his mouth bruising and hard against mine.

"B-Bedroom?" I moan, wrapping my arms around his neck. Evander shakes his head before tearing at his breeches. He lifts me, wrapping my legs around his hips. He slides his fingers through my folds, making sure I am ready for him before slamming inside me. I moan loudly, and he covers my mouth.

"You're mine," he growls into my ear, thrusting deep.

"Yours," I mumble into his palm. He slams back into me, vibrating my body from the motion. I moan into his palm, his hand heating my face. I lick and kiss his hand, his grip on my hip tightening as he groans.

In moments, my eyes roll back and close as my orgasm rips through me. My release triggers his, and I open my eyes to watch his face. My body feels weak, and I go limp against his chest, trying to catch my breath. He slips out of me, kissing my face as he fixes my dress. I look up at him, whispering. "So…"

"So?" He kisses me again.

"What was um…that?" I ask, still trying to catch my breath.

He blinks a few times, grabbing my hand and leading me down the stairs. "We should get back to camp."

"Evander…" I frown, pulling back slightly. He stops on the last step, looking up at me. "I um…"

"Yes?"

"I l-liked that."

"Did you?" he asks, his smirk turning wicked. A shiver runs down my spine, the look on his face making me weak in the knees. He knows just what to do to get me going.

"Yes. I did." I nod.

He yanks me down the stairs so I fall against him. I can feel his heart pounding under my palm. "Well, let's go back to camp so I can do it again."

314

"I like this plan." I giggle, taking his hand and leading him to the door. As we leave the palace and walk down the grand staircase, a thought hits me. Something magnificent happened while my husband was away, and I hadn't told him. Then again, he has been quite the distraction this morning. "I almost forgot! I have a surprise!"

"Forgot?" He snorts.

"Well, yes. You have been distracting me," I say, continuing to pull Evander along.

He laughs. "Where are we going?"

"You'll see," I say, leading him to the stables. I look up at him, pressing my finger to my lips as I point at the tiny foal standing beside Snow. Her fur is black with white spots resembling both the Snow and her brother the Black. She stays close to her mother's legs, shaking her head as we approach.

"Eleanor named her Moonlight because she was born under the moon," I say, watching the foal. "Cheesy, I know."

"Eleanor named her?" Evander sighs. "Then she should be hers."

"You sound disappointed," I observe.

He shakes his head. "No, it's not that."

"Then what is it?"

"Just reminds me that soon I'll lose the Black." He smiles sadly at the foal. "New life reminds me that life always has an end."

I take his hand, lifting it to my lips and kissing it. "We should live in the moment, my love. Celebrate what we have now."

He glances at me. "He shouldn't have lived as long as he has. I tried to retire him once."

I lean against his shoulder as the foal whinnies at Snow. "And what did the Black say about that?"

"He broke through the pasture and ran ten miles to find me." Evander laughs. "He spooked the horse I was riding, throwing me to the ground and on my back. All I could see was his big nose."

"Oh, that is true love." I smile, looking up at him. "We should take them to see him. I assume that it is his daughter?"

"No, he hasn't seen her for a while." Evander shakes his head. "Snow was in a herd."

"How did you find her?" I ask, walking over to my horse. I pat her nose before putting on her halter.

"We were in Grimmwing, and the Black suddenly lost his mind. He took off with me on him." Evander smiles at the memory. "He brought me to this clearing, and there in the middle was Snow. Of course, we can't be sure that they are related, but they certainly act like siblings."

"I love that." I laugh, leading Snow from the stables. Moonlight trots behind her. I can't help but think that the Ancients had a hand in all of this. That Evander finding Snow before finding me and then giving her to me is part of a bigger plan. Everything the Ancients do has a purpose.

"Hello, little one, would you like to meet your uncle?" Evander asks the foal as he pets the baby's neck. Moonlight whinnies again, and Evander turns, whistling loudly. The Black emerges from the edge of the courtyard. He charges over to my husband, his ebony mane flapping in the wind. When the Black notices Moonlight, he trots over, dancing on his hooves when he sees his sister. Moonlight moves behind her mother, snorting and stomping her foot. Snow looks down at her baby before using her nose to push the filly forward. I watch as the foal steps cautiously towards the Black, sniffing her uncle.

"They make a beautiful family." I sigh to Evander.

The Black leans his head down, nuzzling the foal's head. Moonlight neighs going back on her hind legs in excitement, and the Black does the same. I look up at my husband, biting my bottom lip. *I want children with him. I want a family with him.* Evander walks to his horse, rubbing his neck.

"Don't worry, they are coming with us this time," Evander says.

I smile, taking Evander's hand in mine. "Let's go. My class is waiting for me."

Evander nods, lacing his fingers with mine as we walk back to camp, with the horses following behind us.

L
EVAN

ILIUM

KINGDOM OF CANDONIA

The walk through Ilium is almost calming, and so different from when I first rode through over a month ago. I keep Snow's reins in one hand, though I doubt it is necessary. The Black follows me, and Snow follows him. Though the looks of suspicion and hostility are still present, they've significantly lessened, and instead of ignoring us as we walk past, several bow their heads in respect. Some even call us *Your Highnesses.* As in plural. Still strange to hear, though I suppose I'll have to get used to it.

The Candonian troop numbers were greatly depleted by the war, and once I feel settled enough in my role here, my men will filter into the royal army. Any who wish to forsake the way of the sword may. I'd promised them a home to call their own, not enforced servitude. Their lives and choices are their own. Several men have already requested to return to simpler lives as farmers and blacksmiths. Since Charlotte settled the people of Ghynts in my absence, I sent those men to help them rebuild and provide a layer of added protection. They will not be fodder for slavers again. Slowly, with my wife at my side, I feel the first stirrings of a future for our world. One of freedom and peace. One that be possible without her counsel and wisdom. Had I truly once thought her a pawn?

My arm wraps around her back, pulling her closer, kissing the side of her head. She looks up at me as we walk along the cobbled streets, her hand resting on my chest. "So, you never told me about your month away."

"I told you I missed you." She knew the only things of import, which were my meeting with Lyra and the new trade negotiations.

She wraps her arm around my waist, her hand gripping my belt as if she's worried I might slip away. "Yes, but what else happened?"

I shrug, pressing her closer. "That was the only thing that really mattered." I pause at a pastry shop, picking out one and paying for it. A month of camp gruel made me fantasize about the fare of Ilium, my mouth practically watering when the walled city came into sight. I take a huge bite, and my nose scrunches up at the taste. "I got captured, but nothing too exciting."

Charlotte's eyes go wide, and her body tenses. "You got captured?! And didn't think to tell me?!"

I take another bite. Maybe I just got a bad bit. I wince and glare at the pastry. "These are not as good as Leonardo's."

Charlotte's arms drop from my waist, and she moves to stand in front of me. She places her hands on my chest, digging her heels in to prevent me from walking forward. "I am not moving unless you explain what happened. Now."

I push the rest of the pastry into my mouth. Food is food, even if it is subpar. I look at Charlotte in confusion as I chew, swallowing enough to ask, "Explain what?"

"How did you get captured?" she demands.

I frown down at her. "I was careless. Do you think we have time to stop by Leonardo's?" I need to get the taste of this pastry out of my mouth.

She pokes me in the chest again. "How were you careless?"

"What's the matter? I'm fine."

Charlotte's eyes are stormy, her arms crossed over her chest, and her mouth turned down. "I love you, and I want to know what happened."

I let out a heavy sigh. Why is she so upset about this? It's not like it's an event. I've been captured so many times it is barely worth noting anymore. "Take me to get more pastries, and I'll tell you."

Charlotte nods and takes my hand, practically dragging me to Leonardo's. "So…?"

I lift her hand to my lips and kiss the back of it. "I was looking at the stars, thinking about you and not where I was going. I stepped right into a booby trap. The rope tightened around my ankle, yanking me into the air."

The baker pops his head out, most of his face covered in flour, his beard lost under it. "Lookie here, the prince is back."

Charlotte smiles brightly at the baker. "Could we get sixty baked goods, please? I need to make it up to my class."

Leonard nods before looking at me. "Anything for you, Your Highness?"

I kiss my wife's hand again and smile at the portly man. "I have all I need, but I will not object to a fruit tart."

"I won't be too long then," he says, slipping back into the bakery.

Charlotte looks up at me, her eyes snapping with concern. "What happened then?"

I tilt my head at her. Why was she so focused on this? "Slavers came. They didn't know who I was."

"Did they hurt you?" Charlotte asks, her sapphire eyes shining up at me.

I raise a brow. Does she have such little faith in my skills? "No, they did not."

She lets out a relieved breath. "You got them all?"

I nod. "Well, the Black got one."

"I am glad he was there."

My lips twitch. "You can tell him thank you."

She grins up at me, pulling away when Leonard and one of his sons bring out a box of sweets. "I will."

Charlotte pulls out a pouch of crowns and hands them to the baker as I gather up the boxes. I'll replace the money later when she isn't looking, which I've done every time she insists on paying for something. I already married her to gain a crown, and I will not have it said that I married her for coin as well. She smiles again, thanking the baker before we head back to camp.

When we are far enough away, I glance down at her. "He spoils you."

"Who, Leonardo?"

I nod. "And the tailor, the Mountain, the Boy." *Me.* "You have an effect on people."

Her cheeks turn red even as she smiles. "Oh, you flatter me."

Even as we wander down the street, my hands full of baked goods, I'm acutely aware of her presence and attuned to her every breath. "Since you walked down the aisle to me. You've had me under your spell."

"I have?"

We enter camp and I'm saved from going into detail about how I shook like an untried youth when she walked to me. "I have generals to strategize with, and you have a class to teach."

She holds her arms out for the boxes. "I will see you after?"

I hand the boxes to Charlotte and lean over, whispering into her ear, "I told you there would be more, didn't I?"

Heat flares in her sapphire eyes, and she bites her bottom lip. "You did."

"Hurry then."

She turns away from me, heading for the tent, shooting a hungry look back at me.

LI

Charlotte

OUTSIDE OF ILIUM

KINGDOM OF CANDONIA

The class goes well, and I couldn't be prouder. The men are eager for the knowledge, which is helping them learn faster. It warms my heart how quickly they have adapted. Once class ends, there are a few men who follow me back to my tent. They continue to ask about spelling and want me to look over their letters. I don't mind the extra questions. I know that the class doesn't last long and there are so many people attending now. Not all of their questions get answered during that time frame.

I pause at my tent, talking to one of my students and looking over his paper. The men are so excited to be learning, and I find it hard to break away. I feel someone watching me, and the hairs on the back of my neck stand up. I look up to find Evander behind the group. I can still feel his rough, possessive touch earlier. I want more of it. More of the barely concealed aggression in his glowing eyes. A shiver runs through my body, and his gaze intensifies. He wants me alone. Now. Turning back to the men, I smile softly.

"How about you join me in tonight's class, and I can help you with the rest?" I suggest.

The men nod, turning around. As soon as they notice Evander, they bow their heads before scattering, and I snort. He gestures with his chin, wordlessly ordering me into the tent.

I slip inside and turn to face him as he follows. "How was your meeting?" I ask, biting my bottom lip.

His hand fists in my hair, yanking my head back. "Who cares about my meeting?" he growls before kissing me hard.

He breaks the kiss, and I stare up at him in surprise. His free hand gently grips my neck, and he tips my chin up as he kisses down my throat to my shoulder. He tears at the ties of my dress, and I moan softly as my eyes drift closed. I squeak in alarm, and he growls at the sound of trumpets.

"Someone better be dead," he snarls.

I kiss him softly. "You realize you have me for the rest of your life?"

He frowns against my lips and winces. "About that…I have to leave after the festival."

"W-wait, what?" I blink, my heart dropping in my chest. The trumpet sounds off again, and Eleanor opens the tent flap. Her hair is braided down her back, and to my surprise, she is not wearing a dress but breeches and a shirt. She has a bright smile on her face as she looks up at me.

"Charlie! Come look!" she says before running back out. I raise my brow, staring after her. Evander sighs and takes my hand, leading me from the tent.

"What is it?" I ask my sister.

"Just look!" Eleanor exclaims, vibrating with excitement as she points down the path. I gape as at least twenty-five women and children walk into the camp. They are wearing rags, bedraggled and dirty. They move hesitantly, looking around at all the men. I blink a few times before realizing what is happening.

"What is the meaning of this?" Evander asks, frowning. I look up, opening my mouth to explain, when a man pushes through the crowd of gathered warriors.

"Lele?!" Jeremy shouts, his eyes wide with shock. I bite my bottom lip, holding in my excitement. Jeremy freezes, his hands trembling as a woman breaks from the group, tears making tracks down her dirty face. Her ebony hair is tied back into a high ponytail, exposing features sunken from years of work, but that doesn't take away from her beauty. Two children cling to the woman's skirts. The little girl looks just like her mother, while the boy looks a lot like Jeremy. The little girl squeals with shock, her own eyes filling with tears.

"Daddy!" she screams, running to her father. The girl jumps into Jeremy's arms, and he holds her tightly, his tears dripping onto his daughter's hair. His son and wife follow, and they cling to each other. My heart fills with joy for them. They can finally start their life together, the life they deserve.

"The missing people," I whisper to Evander as more women run to their warriors. Evander wraps his arm around my shoulder, smiling.

"You did this," he says and pulls me close. "I'm so proud of you."

He is proud of me? I blink back tears, not realizing how much those words would mean to me. I look up at him, happiness bubbling inside of me.

"You are?" I ask.

"I couldn't have stolen a better wife," he says, his lips twitching.

"This is worth it," I say.

He kisses my head. "You're worth it. To me."

Jeremy walks over to us, his daughter in his arms and tears rolling down his face. His son grips his hand tightly, trying to hold back his own tears.

"Thank you so much, Mrs. Black," Jeremy says. I nod and smile at him before he hurries back to his wife.

Evander looks down at me with a raised brow. "Mrs. Black?"

"It sort of stuck when one of the villagers called me that," I say, looking up at him.

"Not Your Highness?" he asks, his brow furrowing.

I rest my head on his shoulder. "Is it silly I prefer your name in camp?"

"No, I'm just surprised," he says.

"I like being your wife. Your name is an honor to have," I say, kissing his chin before turning to look around at everyone. My gaze catches on one man in particular. I smile, pulling away from my husband. "Is that Lord Edmunde?"

I run to greet my old friend as he dismounts from his horse. His raven black hair is swept back with some sort of gel, exposing his strong jawline. His piercing blue eyes are a shade darker than Kian's. He always wears his best clothes when traveling, and his navy blue traditional Candonian doublet with black breeches are immaculate. All the ladies in Candonia are madly in love with the young lord, and I can see why. Not only is he handsome, but he is a romantic as well. I know the true Edmunde, though. He has been one of my best friends for years.

"You're here!" I exclaim, pulling him into a hug.

"Of course. I wanted to ensure their safe travel." Edmunde smirks.

"That is so kind of you. Come! I must introduce you to my husband." I take his hand and walk back to Evander. "Lord Edmunde, this is my husband, Evan the Black."

Edmunde raises a brow at him before bowing. "A pleasure to meet the man who has been looking after my favorite princess."

"It has been my pleasure." Evander's voice drops dangerously low. I blink at him, raising a brow in confusion.

Edmunde looks back down at me. "I will be in the city for a while. We should find some time to catch up, Lottie."

"Of course." I smile. "Will you be coming to the festival?"

"Well, if you want me to go." Edmunde winks.

"Yes! I'd love it if you came," I say, clapping my hands together.

"I'm sure we would love it," Evander says, his voice lacking its usual warmth.

"Well, I should go settle in," Edmunde says with a charming smile. "I'm sure the queen will insist I stay in the castle with everyone. I will see you later?"

I nod at him. "Of course."

Edmunde grabs my hand, kissing it before walking back to his horse. I wave to him before turning back to Evander, who is already halfway to our tent. Following him, I enter to find him pacing back and forth. I watch him in confusion. What happened? I thought we were having a nice moment?

"Evander?" I whisper.

He turns to glare at me. "His favorite princess?"

"We have been good friends since we were children," I say with a frown. "He says it to both my sisters as well."

I see his jaw tick. "He wants you."

"Hardly," I scoff. "Besides, if he does, he is too late. I have you."

Evander goes back to pacing between our bed and the tent flap. "He's a lord. A blue-blood."

"So?" I frown. *What is the actual concern, Evander?* He ignores me, his jaw tightening. I step in front of him, forcing him to stop as his body pressed against mine. I place my hands against his chest and push to my tiptoes to kiss him. "I love you."

"I don't like him," he hisses into my mouth.

In between words, I continue to kiss him, hoping to relax him. "Hm, I couldn't tell."

"I don't want you to be alone with him," he says, his jaw tightening more.

I pull away. "You don't trust me?"

"No, I do." He shakes his head. "I don't trust him."

I sigh and kiss him hard. "I promise to always stay in the eyes of others when I speak to him." My husband is a complicated man. I take his hands and place them on my hips, trying to snap him out of his thoughts. "You know my heart belongs to you?"

Evander grunts. "I suppose I can't kill him."

"No, my love," I say, shaking my head.

He pulls me closer to him. "Are you sure?"

"I'm sure," I whisper, pressing soft kisses along his neck. "You know I only scream your name."

Evander huffs again. "I suppose I'll have to make sure you scream loud enough tonight that Lord Edmunde hears it."

I laugh softly at his jealousy before moving to whisper in his ear, "You might need to mark me as well."

Evander's eyes instantly brighten, and his hand fists in my hair, yanking my head to the side. His mouth goes to my neck. "A mark?"

"Yes. Like the ones I give you." My breathing becomes heavier as Evander sinks his teeth into my neck and sucks. My eyes close and a shiver runs down my spine. "Fuck, Evander."

He presses a kiss to the small bruise before covering it with his hand. I open my eyes and see the smug look of possession on his face as he walks me backward toward the bed. I keep my gaze locked with his until he tosses me onto the mattress. I laugh, flipping my hair back to give him a playful grin.

LII

EVAN

OUTSIDE OF ILIUM

KINGDOM OF CANDONIA

She bounces slightly on the bed, and my need to mark her, to *claim* her, is at an all-time high. I need more from her, enough so that it doesn't feel like I'm losing her. I feel like she's slipping through my careless fingers, farther and farther away. By the time I'm finished with her, we're panting next to each other on the bed, and her voice is a little hoarse from screaming my name. I was rougher than I've been in the past with her. But from the way she arched and begged for more, she loved every second. Maybe I'm waiting to do the thing that finally forces her to display the disgust I keep expecting. What will be that one thing that will cause her to push me away?

I have taken her three times today. She is exhausted, overwhelmed, and passed out on my chest. What's wrong with me? Why can't I get enough of her? Every time I think it can't possibly be that good, that I can't feel that much peace when I am inside of her, I prove myself wrong. With a soft sigh, I kiss her shoulder as she sleeps. She looks so peaceful. No nightmares plague her, or at least none that she's shared with me. There's so much I still don't know about her, so much I want to discover. But I can't seem to focus enough to get the words past my lips before I am jumping on her like a starving man at a feast.

Careful not to wake her, I slide out from under her and grab my clothes. I dress quickly before heading for the city, hoping to distract myself. It is fascinating to walk through Ilium without Charlotte by my side. The Candonians have no idea who I am. They know I'm an outsider, but they think I'm one of the men, not the conqueror. Not the man who besieged their city. They are openly cold to me, but I am used to it and ignore it. I weave through the streets from memory, finding Leonardo right as he's closing up.

"You're closing?" I ask.

"Your Highness!" the portly baker exclaims, and anyone close enough changes from cold to outright hostile. The whispers behind us gain a new intensity, and I smile at him.

"Leonardo, I'm looking to get some dinner for my wife. Do you have any recommendations?" I ask, picking up some of the boxes he had put on the ground as he locked his storefront.

He gives me a wide smile. "Come with me. There's a little meat pie place down the street that the princess loves. You can stop there."

"That sounds perfect." I walk by his side, again noticing the difference in people's attitude towards me. Leonardo must be well respected in the city because even those who overheard him call me by my title are watching us with confusion instead of hatred.

Leonardo glances at me from the corner of his eye as we walk. "I'm surprised to see you without the princess."

I raise a brow. "I do go places without her."

He laughs, his big belly shaking as he navigates us to the small store with a line around the corner. "This shop?"

He nods and takes the boxes from my hands, blinking when I step to the back of the line. "What are you doing?"

My brow furrows. "Waiting in line?"

The baker blinks at me for a moment before laughing. "Of course you are. I'm not sure what else I expected."

He gives me a short nod that almost looks like a bow. "Your Highness."

I nod back at him, waiting in line for my turn. Several people turn to look at me. A few open their mouths to say something, then think better of it and turn away. It takes the better part of an hour before I'm walking back into our tent. I find her sprawled across the bed, exactly where I left her.

Setting up the meat pies for her on the table, I pour each of us a glass of wine. She stretches slightly, opening her eyes and glancing over her shoulder at me. She sits up a little and asks, "What's this?"

Was this a mistake? I thought she would like it. I wanted to do something special for her, show her how much I care about her. But is this wrong? I shouldn't have done this.

"Dinner." I frown. "Are you...not hungry?"

She pulls the furs up to cover herself, smiling brightly. "I am starving. It looks so good. Thank you."

I cover a slight exhale of relief. I carry the food over and sit next to Charlotte on the bed, kissing the side of her head. "Of course, my star."

She picks up a piece of her pie, holding it out for me. "I love you."

I nip it from her fingers, sighing. "I like hearing you say that."

Charlotte kisses my nose before taking a piece for herself. She smiles again before going silent. She picks at the food but doesn't eat it, and I watch her in concern. Something's happened, and her mood has visibly shifted.

"What is it?"

She takes another small bite, shaking her head. "Do you love me?"

My entire body freezes, muscles locking down on bone. "What?"

She looks down at the food, tucking a lock of her mahogany hair behind her ear. "Do you love me back?"

The words I need dry up on my tongue. I blink at her and take a deep breath. "Is this because of earlier? Did I hurt you?"

Was I too rough with her? Is she finally pushing me away? Am I losing her? She shakes her head, continuing to look at the food. "No...it's just..."

A treacherous thought slithers across my mind, leaving an oily slickness in its wake. Turning on the bed to look at her through narrowed eyes. "Is this because of the lord?"

She shakes her head. "No!"

"Then why are you asking me that?" Are my deeds and actions not enough to prove how I feel? That I breathe for her? That I'd die for her?

"You never say it back."

I stare at her in shock, blinking blankly. Since when did the words matter?

"And?"

How can she not know how I feel? It's clear to everyone, but she needs the words? Why? Why now? She never asked before, not since she said it the first time. So what's changed?

"You...you don't feel the same?" she whispers, her voice breaking.

"No! No, of course, I do." *How can she not know?* Everyone has mentioned my feelings for her and how they've affected me. But now she's suddenly unsure?

"But you won't say it," she says, her eyes welling with tears.

I love you. But again, the words don't make it past my lips. Something is holding me back from saying it, something that refuses to budge, refuses to relent. It is building a divide between us.

"Does it matter?"

A tear slips down her cheek and she turns away from me. She brushes at her face and gets up, grabbing a shift. "Um...I have class."

Does she honestly not know? Does she doubt me? "You know how I feel about you." Why are the words so important? Don't I show I love her in every action, in every breath I take?

With her back to me, she slips on her chemise, staying silent.

"Don't you?" I ask as she picks up her dress and slips it on, fumbling with the ties. I stand up and touch her shoulder. "You do know how I feel about you?"

She takes a shaky breath before looking back at me. "I thought I did."

My eyes scan hers, looking for some hint at what's going through her head. Why is this suddenly coming between us now? "But...you need the words? My actions are not enough?"

She sniffles. "E-Evander..."

"Are they not enough?"

Am I not enough?

She nods and swallows hard. "They are." She fixes her dress. "I need to go."

I step back from her, my voice turning chilly. "Understood."

She walks around me and exits the tent without looking at me once. I grab the closest thing, a chair, and hurl it against the wall. It merely bounces before hitting the ground, with none of the satisfying sounds of it breaking.

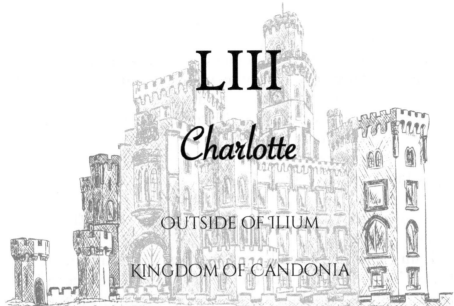

LIII

Charlotte

OUTSIDE OF ILIUM

KINGDOM OF CANDONIA

He won't say it. It is three simple words that I have said to him numerous times. Ones that he has wanted me to say over and over again, and he can't say it. It breaks me. I shouldn't care this much, but I crave to hear those words from his lips. *I love you.*

My class crawls by, and I can hardly focus after our fight. I am repeating myself and not processing what my students are asking. A few of them even ask if I am alright, and all I can do is nod absently. It is as if pieces of me are out of sync. He won't say those words. I know he won't. The only time I will be able to hear them is in my dreams.

The tent is empty when I get back. My lip trembles as I prepare for bed. Every part of me aches for him to return and hold me in his arms. He probably needs some time to think about it all and may not return tonight, leaving me to my own thoughts. I crawl into bed, curling under the furs, and eventually fall asleep.

It feels like only minutes have passed when I feel warm arms wrap around me and soft kisses being pressed along my neck. My eyes flutter open, and I shift in the bed, fitting myself closer to him.

"I'm sorry for earlier," Evander whispers.

"I love you," I whisper. Evander continues kissing my shoulder and neck before turning me to face him. "Is it so bad I crave to hear those words come from your lips?"

He sighs and locks his gaze with mine. "I've never said them before. Not to anyone."

"Oh," I say, moving closer to him.

He kisses me once more. "Ever."

I wrap my arms around him. "I didn't realize."

"I...feel it for you," he says, relaxing into my arms. "I thought you knew that."

I run my fingers up and down his chest. His scent and the heat of his body ease the cold our fight had wrapped me in. "I knew it, but you wouldn't say it. I thought maybe I was wrong."

"No. You're not wrong." He shakes his head. "Love is...a weakness for a warrior."

"And you don't want a weakness."

He brushes a strand of hair from my face. "But you are mine."

"Then why can't you say it?" I ask, looking up at him.

He closes his eyes. "Star."

I turn away from him and curl into a ball. I don't understand why this is bothering me so much. It really shouldn't. I know what my husband has been through and how it could be hard for him to admit it. Still, it makes my heart drop into my stomach.

"I'm tired," I whisper. Evander winces, but I don't turn around. His arms wrap around me as I sniffle. I don't want to talk anymore tonight. It hurts too much. Perhaps in the morning, I will feel better about it.

The morning light peaks in through the canvas tent, stirring me from my sleep. Evander's arms are still wrapped around me, and I sigh softly before slipping out of bed. The air is crisp, and I feel goosebumps pepper my skin as I leave the warmth of his body. The days are getting colder, which means winter will be a few short weeks away. I will need to prepare a winter wardrobe for myself after the festival tomorrow. There is still so much to do in preparation, and there is so little time. I open one of my chests, my fingers running over the silky materials as I ponder which one I should wear today. Behind me, I hear Evander shift on our bed.

"Star?" he mutters. "Come back to bed."

"I have to prepare for tomorrow."

"You don't want me to pick?" he asks, his tone hesitant.

My hand freezes on one of the dresses, and I turn to look at him. "I didn't want to wake you."

"Come here," Evander says, sitting up and holding his hand out for me. When I get close, he pulls me into his arms, wrapping them tightly around me. The hug comforts me, and I lose all motivation. This is what I needed. Him. His comfort.

"Evander...I have things to do." I sigh.

He kisses me deeply, and my mind is fuzzy when he pulls back to whisper, "You are my greatest weakness."

I smile softly. If this is his way of saying he loves me, I'll accept it. "I love you, too."

He frames my face with his strong hands, kissing me gently. I smile against his lips, not wanting this moment to end.

"I really do need to go, my love," I whisper.

"Nope, you stay here." He shakes his head, kissing every inch of my face. "With me."

I snort. "Are you going to prepare the market for the festival tomorrow?"

"Prepare the market?" He tilts my head to the side and kisses down my neck.

"Yes," I whisper, my breathing quickening. "That is where we will hold the festival. We need tables, chairs, and decorations."

Evander's mouth leaves a trail of heat across my chest before he nips the curve of my breast. "Uh-huh...tables and chairs."

"Y-yes." I bite my bottom lip. "And you have morning drills."

"Decorations," he says, pressing his face between my breasts. His warm breath on my skin sends shivers down my spine, but I can't let us get distracted. We have much to do today. I run my fingers through his hair.

"Once we are finished with our duties, you can ravish me all night. How does that sound?" I ask.

He frowns, not moving from my breasts. "Not now?"

"Think of it as a reward," I say. Evander growls and lifts his head to look at me. "Does that sound good?"

"Not as good as ravishing you now *and* later," he says.

"Come on, my love." I chuckle, pulling away from him. Evander's face contorts, trying to mimic my custom pout, and I have to hold back another laugh. There is something about a grown man pouting that is one of the most adorable things. I want to pinch his cheeks and kiss him, but I know that would only embarrass my husband. "How about you help me pick my dress?"

He sighs in defeat and wanders over to the chest. He rifles through the neat stacks before pulling out one of my plainer gowns. It is a grey one with a high neckline and long sleeves, with no jewels or lace. It is something a modest priestess would wear, and I raise my brow at him.

"How about this one?" he asks, holding it out to me. "I assume you'll be seeing that prick?"

"I wasn't planning on it," I say, not taking the dress. I don't even know why I have it in my wardrobe. It isn't flattering, and the material looks uncomfortable.

"Still." He narrows his eyes.

I tilt my head. "You truly want me to wear that? It is warmer this afternoon. I'll overheat."

"If there is a chance you're going to see him, I think we should risk it," he says.

I take his hand, placing it on my chest. "Who does this belong to?"

He mutters under his breath. My husband, the Commander of one of the biggest armies in Aellolyn, Evan the Black himself, is acting like a child. I shake my head at him.

336

"I can't hear you," I say.

"Me," he says, placing the grey dress down. He picks up a blush-colored one, the material thinner than the other. It still has a high neckline, but I don't mind it. The back is low on this, which should help keep me cool.

"I like that one," I say.

"I like it too. Hmm..." He nods before putting it down and picking up another one.

I snort at his antics. "What are you looking for?"

"One that makes you less gorgeous."

"Evander." I shake my head and pick up the pink one. "This will do."

"Fine, my star." He sighs. I step into the dress, smiling at the new nickname he has given me. Sliding it up my body, I slip my hands through the sleeves and wait for my husband to tie me up. He kisses along my back as he slowly tightens the ties, and a shiver runs down my spine. I am about to give in and turn to kiss him properly, but the horn for morning drills sounds off. Evander's hands tighten on my hips as if reluctant to let me go.

"They will miss me," he says with a deep sigh, his hands tightening on my hips as if reluctant to let me go.

"I suppose I can share," I say, kissing him softly. "I will see you later?"

He nods, nuzzling my neck. I kiss him one more time before walking out of the tent. It is time to prepare for the festival.

LIV

EVAN

OUTSIDE OF ILIUM

KINGDOM OF CANDONIA

Watching her leave is one of my least favorite things, even if I know that she's not going far. I want to pull her back to me. I want to make sure she's safe, and that she knows she's mine, especially with the new threat out there.

Lord Edmunde of Ecten.

Just his name makes my hands turn into fists. I saw the way his eyes lingered on my wife, the way he looked her up and down. He wants her. He wants what's mine.

Calm down.

I dress and strap my training armor on myself instead of waiting for the Boy to do it. Aggression is rolling off me in waves, and I need to get a handle on it before I see her again, especially if the *lord* is going to be present. I have never struggled so much to maintain my temper. From my first moments with her, all the emotions I keep brutally in check are fighting to be known, threatening to spin me out of control.

Everything about her makes me come undone. I command over ten thousand men, all of whom are willing to fight to the end for me. I've conquered over five nations, forcing them to enact a law to abolish slavery. My generals are all of noble birth, some even royal, and yet they follow me. With a swipe of my hand, my entire army will fall silent, waiting for my word. And one slip of a woman has me unraveling. She's the most powerful woman in the world, having done what kings, dukes, and assassins could never accomplish. She brought me to my knees. One word from her, and I'm a riotous whirlwind of need.

Fuck.

My squire nods at me as I come out of the tent, his hands behind his back. I shoot him a frown. "Would you like to join training today?"

I rarely allow my squire to join the actual training. Usually, his chores and duties keep him busy. But in two years, he'll leave me to go on a quest of his choosing. Ben will not return until he completes it and is ready to be officially knighted. Once he's gone, I'll choose another squire, and the cycle will continue. Though I do take time to train him, I know he itches for more, his eagerness coming off him in waves.

The Boy looks up at me, his dark eyes flashing with excitement. "Really?"

I nod, shooting him a rare smile and pointing to his tent. "Go get ready, Boy. I'll meet you on the training ground."

He spins, running for his own training armor. His feet barely touch the ground as he races for his tent. He will be the envy of the other squires for this. It is a rare treat for me to forgo training my army to focus on my squire.

I smile to myself and trek down the knoll. Many of my men are already going through drills. Kian is training a group of men to be assassins when we cannot march as an army and need a precise stroke. Niklaus teaches swordplay. Few have his level of skill, especially from horseback. Lorcan and Wynonna work with the archers and long-range weapons that are so important in sieges. The Mountain works with shield training, giving instructions on maneuvering and fighting with the bulky steel attached to their arms. My specialty has always been hand-to-hand combat.

I may go to battle with a bow and arrows on my back and a sword on my hip, but I rarely use them. I prefer to take my opponents' weapons, turning them against their owners, crippling them with their own hubris. It's too easy to find yourself disarmed on the field of war. You have to be able to turn a piece of wood into a deadly weapon if the occasion calls for it.

My squire reappears next to me, his leather-fitted armor breastplate a size too big on him, and he'd missed fastening a loop in his excitement.

I turn to face him and hold my hands out in front of me, crouching low.

"Alright, Boy, what's the key to fighting hand-to-hand?" I quiz him, even as I lunge forward, and he bolts out of the way. It's not enough to exercise the body. You have to exercise the mind at the same time. I don't train mindless brutes, or at least I like to think so. His chores aren't limited to just serving me. Each of them teaches him something, building up his strength and fortitude over years of practice.

"A low center." He tries to take advantage of me, overstretching to send a hit to my side, but I drop to the ground, sweeping his legs out from under him. The Boy is all limbs at the moment. He has sprouted a foot and a half in the last eighteen months and is still getting used to the extra inches. It's easy to topple him when he forgets to keep his center low.

He lands hard on his side, his eyes immediately watering and his breath hissing in and out. I get to my feet with a single press from my hands on the ground and hover over him. "And why is a low center important, Boy?"

I hold my hand out for his, and he takes it, allowing me to help him back to his feet. "On your back, you're dead."

I face off with him again. "Come at me."

He lunges forward, making it look like he's going for my torso but changes direction at the last second, going for my legs instead. Smart kid, except that he doesn't have enough weight to knock me to the ground. He loses his momentum, letting out a loud huff. My feet remain planted, and his body goes limp after a couple of tries to push me over.

I grab him by the scruff of his leather breastplate and place him back on his feet, putting both my hands on his shoulders. "That was incredibly well done."

His eyes shine at the compliment before he toes the dirt, dropping his gaze. "You didn't fall, though."

"If I were anyone else, I would have." I ruffle his hair, moving back in position. "You've got a couple more rounds to go before chores."

My squire rolls his shoulders, his eyes sparkling with excitement.

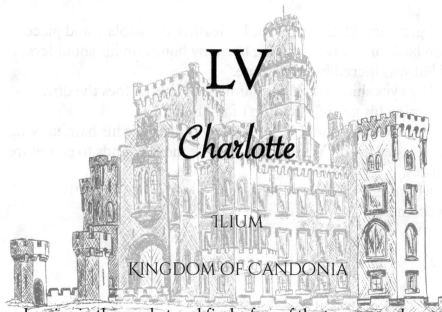

LV

Charlotte

ILIUM

KINGDOM OF CANDONIA

I arrive in the market and find a few of the townspeople already preparing for the festival. A small stage is being set up in the middle of the town square where bards will sing their ballads. A few well-known men and women will be performing, and rumor has it that each of them has created a song for the event. I am excited and can hardly wait for the music and dancing.

I place my paperwork down on one of the long tables and take a moment to gather my thoughts. I need to set up a few things before I can get to the fun stuff. Mostly, I need to make sure that the construction of the tables and booths is complete. I also need to make sure that those who are supplying the food will be ready for tomorrow. Since this is the first festival, I dipped into the palace savings and offered to pay for all the food. It isn't every day that we get to celebrate freedom, and I want to make this something to remember.

A few children run by me, their arms full of decorations, one of them holding the flag that Eleanor created. It is pastel blue, and in the middle are yellow, purple, and pink freesias, a round petaled flower that represents freedom. I thought it was the perfect idea, and my sister was so excited to show it to me.

I jump right in and help a few of the women arrange chairs around the tables. Leonardo brings us out some cookies, and we all take a break. The little boy I saved a month back approaches me, and I hold out a few cookies for him. He takes them excitedly before running over to his friends. I bite my lower lip, looking down one of the streets as I rock back and forth on my heels. A part of me wants to run back to camp and spend the afternoon with Evander. But I know he is probably doing drills with his men, and I must finish the preparations. I sigh and get back to work.

It's afternoon when I head back over to the stage, happy to see it is almost complete. Just a bit more, and it will be stable enough for tomorrow. I hear someone walk up next to me, and I smile, thinking to see Evander.

"You look happy," says a familiar voice, not my husband, but Lord Edmunde. To say I am a little disappointed is an understatement. I enjoy the company of my old friend, but I have been waiting to see my husband all day. I thought he might come to visit me during his break from drills.

"Lord Edmunde," I say, "I didn't expect to see you."

He smiles at me, picking up a box and taking it over to the stage. "And it's not a pleasant surprise?"

I shake my head and pick up the last box, following him. "It is. I am just surprised. I thought you would be at the palace."

It is a little strange for him to be out here with me. Edmunde was one of the lords who helped me make some dramatic changes to the laws of Candonia, but he is usually never out and about with the people. I place my box alongside his at the side of the stage. One of the bards is preparing a practice run, and Edmunde holds his hand out to me.

"Dance? For old times' sake?" He smirks.

"Oh, I couldn't." I laugh. There is only one man I want to dance with now, and it isn't him. I look around for Evander, hoping to see him emerge from the crowd, but he doesn't.

Edmunde bows deeply before taking my hand and spinning me. He dips me so low that my hair touches the ground. "Oh, come on."

"Alright." I smile. One dance between two friends won't hurt. Lord Edmunde spins me again before yanking me toward him. I fall against his chest, our bodies pressing close.

"I would like to speak with you," he whispers.

"What about?" I ask, pulling away from him and trying to compose myself.

"Your husband," Edmunde says, glancing around. If anyone heard him speak negatively about Evander, it could end badly for him. Evander has spies in the city.

I frown. "What about him?"

Edmunde glances around again before moving closer to me. "Runaway with me."

"What?" I ask, blinking.

Edmunde pauses for a moment, looking me up and down. "I love you. I have always loved you."

"I...I..." I open and close my mouth, trying to gather a single thought. I was not expecting this. To be honest, I knew the man was interested in me. He had pursued me a few times when we were younger, but I thought he was over it.

"I was waiting for you to be ready," he whispers, his eyes shining in the sunlight.

I press my lips together and then let out a long sigh before saying, "I'm sorry, Edmunde."

"Sorry?" Edmunde frowns. I open my mouth to reply to him, but someone grabs his shoulder, forcing him to the ground. My eyes widen in shock as they fall on Evander. Evander's grip on Edmunde is bone-crushing, and he yells out in pain.

"Evander!" I exclaim, grabbing his arm. Instead of releasing his hold, Evan tightens it, and Edmunde lets out another cry of pain.

"I wanted to surprise you," he growls, his steel eyes glowing as he stares at me. "But apparently, you don't need me."

Not true. I squeeze his arm, my eyes filling with tears. "Let him go, and we can go talk."

344

Evander snarls, glaring at the lord. He takes a few seconds before he releases Edmunde. "Stay away from what's mine."

Evander turns his attention to me, grabbing my arm and pulling me away. I can feel the anger radiating off him, and I prepare myself for the impending storm. He pulls me into an alley and pushes me up against the wall.

"The fuck was that?" he growls.

I close my eyes. "I was dancing with a friend! That is all!"

"You belong to me," Evander growls, one of his hands going to my throat and the other fisting my hair. "He touched you. Danced with you."

I open my eyes, looking up at him. "Evander, it meant nothing."

Evander yanks my dress off to the side. He kisses down my chest, his mouth wrapping around my nipple and sucking hard. I place my hands on his chest, my face turning bright red.

"Evander! W-We can't here!" I whisper.

He snarls in response, lifting my right leg to wrap around his hip. "You are mine."

A shiver runs down my spine, and my gaze connects with his. "I've always been yours."

Evander yanks at the ties on his breeches, pulling them down just enough to release his cock. He slams himself inside me as his mouth takes mine, and I scream into the kiss. He lifts me higher, wrapping my other leg around his hip, struggling to get deeper. I am suspended between him and the alley wall as he thrusts hard. He is rougher than usual, and yet, I don't mind. I want to be his. I want him to know I am his.

"Fuck, Evander." I moan loudly.

"Mine," he growls, his hand dropping to my lower back.

I lean forward, kissing him hungrily and biting his bottom lip. "Yours."

It is fast, hot, and primal, both of us muffling our moans of release in another kiss. I can taste the saltiness of Evander's sweat as I collapse against him and press a kiss to his neck. I wrap my arms around his shoulders, closing my eyes as I try to catch my raspy breath. *What was that about?*

LVI

EVAN

ILIUM

KINGDOM OF CANDONIA

Fuck. What was that? I lost control. Utterly. I saw his hands on her, and all I could think was *mine*. She trusts me not to lose control, and I violated that trust. I'm the monster they all call me, a beast who takes his wife in an alley in a fit of jealousy. I should be flogged for this. A proper lord would never do such a thing, and I'll never be proper. That prick, Lord Edmunde, would never do this to her. He would never degrade her like this, violate her trust in such a way. The thought makes me sick. They are right. They are all right. I'm a brute, a savage. No better than the men I kill. *Scum. Trash. Vermin. Slave.*

Even as she continues to hold on to me, her legs limp from pleasure, I brace myself for her reaction. She should shove away from me and tell me she despises me, that she never wants me to touch her again. I prepare myself to hear all the things she should have said to me when I forced her to marry me and after I took her on the ground. I've erred with her since our first night together, not knowing the treasure she is. Instead, I treated her like a common whore.

"I'm sorry...I wasn't thinking," I say through heavy breaths. I was only feeling, and the jealousy was eating away at me. The image of his hands on her, the ease of their conversation, how perfect they looked together haunts me. They are cut from the same cloth, and he is the man she should have married. If not for me.

She buries her face into my neck, clinging to me. I try to shore up my own emotions, preparing myself for when she spits in my face. Shame and self-loathing are simmering inside me, making my neck heat. "I hated seeing his hands on you. I lost control."

He's a lord, everything I'll never be. I changed fate. I took away the choice she should have had. The life she should have had, and the man that was meant to be hers. Some part of me wishes that I'd never set eyes on Ilium, that I hadn't returned here to execute poetic justice by taking the city where I was sold. But most of me is still selfishly clinging to reality, because as horrific as my actions are, I have her. She's still here.

She says against my skin, "You know I love you."

Even the words that usually calm me are only a painful reminder that if I hadn't stolen her, she would be saying that to him. The thought burns away the lingering shame, jealousy rising again. I welcome the emotion. It's the only way I'll be able to face myself in the morning. The only way I'll be able to move from this spot.

"And he loves you," I hiss.

"I was about to tell him my heart belongs to you," she says, pulling back to look into my eyes.

My body, once languid from release, immediately strings tight with tension at her words.

"He said he loves you?"

The words I can't seem to utter out loud to her. I feel them. A sensation of warmth and comfort suffuses my entire body when I am near her. I constantly think about her when I'm away, and I consider her opinion before anyone else's. I value her happiness above everyone else, even my own, but those words clog in my throat. Instead, I show her with my actions how much I care about her, but she cried when I couldn't say them to her. I know she did. And now? He said them. He did what I couldn't. Why wouldn't she go to him? He's everything I'm not. He can *say* the things I cannot.

She nods against me, and my hands fist at her back. "He leaves. Today. Or he dies."

The longer he's here, the more she'll notice the divide between him and me. She will realize that he is the man she should have married. The man she would have chosen.

She tenses, looking up at me, her sapphire eyes flickering with anger. "Evander."

"Charlotte." *Charlotte.* I never use her name. It's always been *Lamb* or now *Star*, never *Charlotte*. I can't back down on this. I can't lose her to this paragon of nobility that seems to have horned his way into our marriage.

She shakes her head. "It's like you don't believe that I love you."

"I don't trust him! Not you!" Or rather, I am afraid that she will see how wrong I am for her. Everything I do is the opposite of what he would do, what a man of noble breeding would do. The kind of man I would have never been, even if I hadn't been sold.

I trust her feelings for me, no matter how enraged or jealous I am. She has every reason to hate me and no reason to love me. I stole her from everything familiar. I kept her isolated from her family, hoping that she would cling to me, her loyalty switching to me instead of her father. I never believed I could feel more for her. I never thought I would love her, but I do, even if the words refuse to pass my lips.

"Trust me with this? I will put him in his place," she says, sliding down my body and stepping away, looking up at me sadly.

"He leaves. Today." I can't lose Charlotte. I can't. And him being here threatens my future with her.

She fixes her dress, concealing her body, and tidies her hair. She looks away, her voice laden with disappointment. "Fine."

She's upset with me, and she should be. My jealousy spun out of control, and now she wants nothing to do with me. She shouldn't. I'm everything the stories say about me.

348

Scum.
Monster.
Murderer.

"I have to go back to camp. I missed you, so I snuck away," I admit. She doesn't look back at me. Without another word to me, she steps out of the alley.

I watch her walk toward the square without looking back, and with a low growl, I storm back to camp, to my men waiting for orders, to everything that's familiar to me. I tried to exist in her world. Maybe I just don't belong there. I'm not smooth or refined, I can barely read, and I can't dance. I'm nothing that the royal courts revere.

I'm a conqueror. I'm Evan the Black.

But every step I take away from her makes me wish I was anything, *anyone,* else.

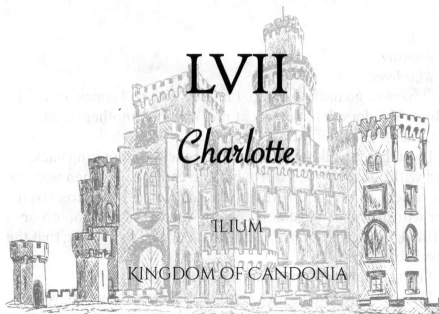

LVII

Charlotte

ILIUM

KINGDOM OF CANDONIA

My shoulders slouch as I walk back into the square. I feel the same every time we fight or have a disagreement. It is as if half of my soul is missing. I understand why he would want Edmunde to leave. If I saw Evander with another woman, I honestly don't know how I would react. Though the thought of it makes my stomach bubble with anger. Evander is mine. No one else's. I close my eyes, taking a few deep breaths to erase the silly image of my husband with another. I need to focus on the task at hand, asking Lord Edmunde to leave. It will not be a simple conversation. He isn't the kind of man to take no for an answer, especially if he thinks I am in danger. Perhaps if I share my true feelings for Evander and how well he treats me, it will be easier to convince Edmunde to go.

There are a few people who look at me as I walk up to the stage. They give me an odd look, which causes my cheeks to heat. After the scene Evander caused, I don't blame the concerned looks my people are giving me. But I ignore them and act like everything is perfectly fine.

I clear my throat. "H-how are the decorations coming along?"

"We are out of flags!" one child shouts, throwing his little arms in the air.

"Leonardo should have some more. Go check the bakery," I say, smiling softly as the child runs off. I let out a long sigh, but it doesn't calm the nausea that is threatening to overwhelm me. It was tempting to wait until the end of the day to speak to Edmunde, but something tells me I should get it over with and deal with it now. I want answers for his actions this morning.

The ball in the pit of my stomach only grows as I hurry toward the palace. I do feel bad for what my husband did to Edmunde, but he was out of line. He knows I am married and shouldn't be discussing such insane ideas like running away with him. Lord Edmunde knows of the rumors about Evander. He is capable of far worse things than breaking a bone. He could have killed him. Though, I am surprised that Evander is allowing me to handle this on my own. He could have gone to Edmunde himself and told him off, but he isn't. *He trusts me.*

At the palace, I head straight for the healing wards. It is no surprise that we have some of the best healers in Aellolyn, though none compare to those in Vruica. Edmunde is probably there now to get his shoulders checked. I head down the long hallway beside the throne room, taking a right before arriving at the healing wards.

There are multiple rooms used for the practice. Most of our warriors come here after battle or practice for medication and herbs to keep them in top shape. I opened the healing wards once to our people when an infection took over a third of the city two years ago. My father didn't like this plan since it put my sisters and me in danger, but we saved more of our people by doing so.

I enter one of the bigger rooms and find Edmunde being looked over by our head healer, Gregory Pietri. He is a shorter man with mostly grey hair now. His ocean blue eyes always sparkle when he shares his knowledge with others. He has taken on many students during his years at the palace, all becoming successful healers. Some say Gregory is over one hundred years old, but I find that hard to believe since he has hardly any wrinkles on his face. Then again, looks can be deceiving.

My focus turns back to Edmunde, and I wince. "We, uh, need to talk."

"Oh?" Edmunde snorts.

"What?" I frown.

He raises a brow. "After your husband almost broke my shoulder?"

I press my lips together before looking at Gregory. "Would you mind giving us a second?"

"Of course, Your Highness." Gregory bows before exiting. He closes the door behind him, and I stay silent for a few moments, trying to gather my thoughts.

"Edmunde, you need to leave," I say.

He laughs. "No. I am not leaving you in the hands of that...monster."

The word makes my blood heat. I will not stand for anyone calling my husband that.

"He is no monster!" I shake my head.

"Oh?" Edmunde frowns, pointing at his shoulder. His eyes narrow on me. "You deserve to choose, Lottie. Not marry someone because he threatened your family."

I purse my lips. Edmunde knows how much I value my freedom. My choice. It is why I have taken so long to marry. All the suitors I have met would want to control me and limit the freedom I have fought so hard to maintain. They only want to rule Candonia for power, and Evander was no exception. It is true, and I am not naïve to that fact, but things have changed after spending time with him. He values my opinion, asking for my advice and thanking me for it. He wanted to rule over Candonia because his people were wronged. Evander wants to give them the freedoms that we all have, and I do not think he is a monster for fighting for that. The only times he doesn't give me a choice is when it involves my safety. Other than that, he does not dictate to me.

"I would still choose him," I say.

Edmunde scoffs. "You would not."

My anger grows. "Do not tell me what I would and would not do. You do not know where my heart lies."

Edmunde stands, wincing. "Are you saying it lies with him? That...that...brute?!"

"Watch your tongue," I say, my eyes flickering.

"The church won't let you stay married. Not when they know the truth," Edmunde hisses. "They'll demand an annulment."

My entire body tenses at his words and I shake my head. "W-What truth?"

"His origins," he says, his eyes narrowing.

"His family is from Grimmwing," I say, trying to stay calm.

Edmunde crosses his arms over his chest. "He was a slave, Lottie."

Nausea overcomes me, and I try to keep my face as neutral as I can. *How does he know?* How did he figure this out? I could lose Evander forever if word gets out. I can't lose him.

"He w-was not," I lie.

"I did some digging when I found out he conquered here." Edmunde sighs. "Anything to figure out a way to get you free of him."

"You can't tell anyone," I whisper, my breath quickening. My eyes become desperate as I walk closer to him. "Please, Edmunde."

"Why shouldn't I?" He frowns.

Tears fill my eyes, and my hands start to shake. "Because I-I love him."

Edmunde snarls, "Him?! The monster?! He forced you to marry him!"

"He did, and I would allow him to do it again!" I yell, stomping my foot.

"Do you hear yourself?" Edmunde scoffs.

I cross my arms across my chest. "You don't know him like I do."

"Tell your *owner* that I'll be staying," Edmunde says, touching my shoulder. "And he can take it up with your father."

I hit his hand away, hissing. "Excuse me?"

"I'll see you at the festival, Lottie," Edmunde says, turning his back to me.

"No," I hiss again, "you won't. You will be gone."

"No. I won't." Edmunde waves.

"Fine," I growl, stomping my foot again. I turn away and storm from the room. I don't want to see that man again. Not for a while, at least. No one has ever made me this angry before. I do not enjoy this feeling, but the way he spoke about my husband made me want to punch him in the face. Tension is building up in my shoulders, and I move my head from side to side as I make my way back to camp. I need to see him. I need to talk to him. Make sure everything is alright between us. Seeing him always calms me. It's like my mind finally goes silent whenever he is around.

I head straight to our tent only to find it empty. Odd, I thought he would be back from drills by now. I turn on my heel, heading toward Ben's tent. If anyone in the camp knows where my husband is, it is his squire.

I am hardly surprised to see Eleanor standing outside Ben's tent. She is wearing a pair of plain breeches and a loose-fitted shirt. In her hand, she awkwardly twirls a sword. Sparring lessons? My lips curve in a small smile as Ben steps out of his tent with his own sword.

"Ben, do you know where Evander is?" I ask him.

Ben frowns, his face turning pink. "Um, I'm not sure you want the answer to that, Your Highness."

Eleanor winces at the thought, shaking her head.

"Why?" I ask, frowning.

"Nothing..." Ben hums, and Eleanor tugs on his hand.

I narrow my eyes at the boy. "Ben. I will not ask again."

Ben sighs. "He's injured. In the healer's tent."

LVIII

EVAN

OUTSIDE OF ILIUM

KINGDOM OF CANDONIA

It was dumb to pick a fight with the men. It was petty, childish, and stupid. Yet, I feel more in control. As if the beating I received somehow leveled the cosmic scales of justice enough to balance what I had done in the alley. Though I doubt it does. I can't have myself whipped without raising some brows. And it would only be enough if Charlotte were to wield it. I know my wife and doubt she'd consent to be a part of such a thing. Even with several broken ribs, a black eye, a split lip, and a broken finger, I still feel the burning anger lurking beneath my skin. I needed to burn off the lingering aggression from earlier, but it has not eliminated the source. *He's a lord. The man she would have married if she had a choice.*

"Evander?!" my wife demands, having found her way into the medical tent. I should have known she would find me sooner rather than later.

I sit up a little on the cot, wincing when it shifts my ribs. "Star?"

The ribs will be a suitable punishment, I suppose. I can't do anything until I heal. And though some Aellolynian herbs can accelerate the healing process from weeks to days, it will be days filled with discomfort. *Discomfort? You think that's enough to balance the scales after earlier? It's not enough.*

She runs to me, placing her hands on my face. "What happened?"

"Drills with the men." *I needed to forget about him dancing with you, touching you. I needed to forget how I violated your trust and treated you as less than you are. Mostly I needed to forget how I am not enough for you, not even close to being who you deserve.*

Her gaze runs over me, noting all the damage. "Oh, Evander..."

I shift on the cot, sitting up more. "I'm fine. I just needed to work off some anger."

She winces. "I..."

I open my arms for her, covering the hiss of pain the action causes me. "Come here. I'm fine."

She crawls into my lap, sniffling. "I don't like to see you hurt."

I deserve it for what I did to you. I wrap my arms around Charlotte and kiss the top of her head, the cot creaking beneath us. "It's my own fault."

She kisses my chest repeatedly, suffusing me with warmth. Perhaps, she didn't think that I had trespassed so egregiously on her trust. "Why? What happened?"

"I took on ten of my men this morning for drills." *Unarmed.* I thought maybe if I had injuries matching the way I felt inside, it would be enough. I should have known better. Wounds of the flesh healed. Wounds of the soul did not.

"It's my fault," she says.

"How?" If there is one person *not* at fault here, it's her. The blame rests solely on my shoulders. I made her marry me and took away the treasured choice she'd clung to for so long. My jealousy made me take her in the alley, made me force my men to fight me.

She looks up at me, her sapphire eyes still filled with tears. "If I hadn't danced with Edmunde, you wouldn't have been angry."

I look away from her, shame filling me. It's wrong for Charlotte to blame herself for even a moment, and it only makes me more disgusted with my actions. "It's not that."

356

She places a hand on my cheek, making me look back at her. "Then what is it?"

My voice cracks a little as I admit, "That he told you he loves you."

Before I did. Lord Edmunde once again proved to be more deserving of her. She frowns, kissing my chest again. "You know I'm yours."

"He's everything I can never be."

Titled. Blue blood. Rich. Powerful without an army at his back. The man you deserve.

"That doesn't matter to me. You are what I need."

New topic. I can't talk about this anymore. I can't keep highlighting the differences between us. Not when the foreign interloper is already driving a wedge between us.

"How did the rest of the setup go?"

She chews her bottom lip, her cheeks heating. "I um...left early." She glances around. "I went to tell him he has to leave."

My eyes narrow. Apparently, I didn't filter out enough of my aggression during training. I don't like the idea of my wife alone with him. This paragon of nobility who goes around confessing feelings for *married* women. "And?"

Her eyes squeeze shut, and I watch her brace herself. "He won't go."

Does he think he gets an option? Candonia is my kingdom now, my people, my *wife*. He doesn't get to ignore my demand. My body tenses, and I swing my legs off the bed, my hands fisting. "I won't give him a choice."

She grabs my arms. "Evander...he knows." She tugs me back. "He knows about your origins."

My breath freezes in my lungs. She told him? I had gone through great pains to conceal my past. I'd made sure that any records or history of it were burned to ash. The only reminder is carved into my skin. Only the people I trusted implicitly were made aware. Hurt blossoms in my chest as I search her gaze. "You told him?"

She shakes her head. "No! No, I would never! I don't know how he knows."

"Are you sure you didn't tell him?" How else could he have discovered the truth? Is there someone out there hoping to ruin my claim to the Candonian throne?

She settles me back on the cot. "I'm sure. I would never betray you like that."

I believe her. I truly do. Hissing out a breath of relief, I say, "I trust you, and I'm going to go visit this *friend* of yours."

She keeps me pinned with a hand on my chest. "You're injured."

Pushing her away, I struggle to my feet. "I've had worse."

She stands and places herself between me and the exit. "Let me come with you."

"Why?" Is she keeping that prick safe from my wrath?

"I don't want you to get hurt," she says, her gaze intent.

"Do you have no faith in me?" That sissy little lord won't stand a chance against me. He's lived a life of privilege, while I've lived one of survival.

"You're injured."

"It's a black eye and a couple of cracked ribs."

She glares at me, crossing her arms. "Fine." She turns away from me, sniffling. *Dirty tactic, very dirty.* She's using my own feelings against me.

I catch her arm, tugging her back toward me. "Star," I say with a heavy sigh. "Fine, I'll wait until after your festival."

She looks over her shoulder at me, her sapphire eyes heavy with emotions. "Is it so wrong for me to worry?"

I pull her gently into my arms and wrap them tightly around her. "About me?"

"Yes." Her hands slide up my chest as she kisses me softly.

I drop my hands to her hips, smiling at her. "You should trust me a bit more."

She covers one of my hands, pulling away, leading me out of the healing tent and toward ours. "I am allowed to fret over my husband."

"I don't think I've ever had anyone fret over me before." As she leads me through the camp, I notice how the men look at her. All the suspicion and mistrust have vanished in my month away. Now, they greet her with smiles and bows, and it doesn't escape my notice that she knows all of their names. How many have been attending her classes?

She glances back at me as we walk up the knoll to our tent. "Well, get used to it. You have a wife who loves you and will worry over you every time you leave her."

Shit.

"Speaking of, I do have to leave after the festival." I tried to tell her before, but we were interrupted by the families returning. I know she's going to be disappointed.

The tent flap closes behind us, and she turns back to me. "Why?"

"I have a man who infiltrated the Xiapia royal court, but we lost contact and need to check on him."

I watch the anguish build in her eyes, and I'm tempted to claw out my heart to get it to stop even as she kisses me and says, "I understand."

But from the blaze of determination in her eyes, I sensed immediately that my days off riding off without her were numbered. My wife was not a woman to sit idly by while I went off to war.

I press my forehead to hers. "You know if you cry every time I leave, you're going to make me cancel all of my trips."

Instead of the small laugh I expected, a tear slips down her cheek, and she lowers her gaze. "It's just...you *just* got back."

"It will only be for a few days, a week, tops."

"Promise?"

For her, I'll keep everything short. And soon, she'll be riding at my side.

"I promise."

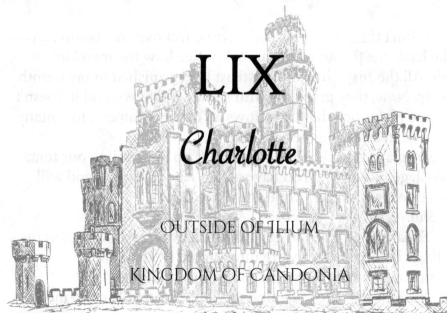

LIX

Charlotte

OUTSIDE OF ILIUM

KINGDOM OF CANDONIA

My heart twinges with pain when Evander tells me he has to go again. He just returned home after being gone a month, and he is leaving me again. Is there a way to freeze time? Live in this moment forever with just the two of us? Can I convince him not to leave? I move closer to Evander, pressing my body against his and brushing a kiss to his lips.

"Once you return, I want to spend time with just you," I whisper, my fingers running up and down his chest.

"How about we go away for a couple of days, just us?" he asks, with a wicked smile. I already know what kind of plans he has for us, and my heart flutters in my chest. There are so many places we can go, and if we are away from the palace, no one will disturb us.

"Truly?" I ask him, smiling brightly.

"I do have a place. Do you like the ocean?"

"I love it, and I haven't been since I was a girl," I say with a bright smile. I am already picturing our time there, walking on the warm white sands of the beach and the sun shining down on us as we swim in the seas.

"I have a small cottage in Ciral." Evander brushes the hair from my face. "Right on the coast. We would have to fish and cook for ourselves."

Most nobles would shudder at the idea of doing things for themselves, but it sounds peaceful to me. We could pretend for a moment that we aren't a conqueror and a princess. That we are both just normal people, and the only duty we have is to ourselves and each other.

"I would love that," I say, wrapping my arms around his neck and kissing him hard. "And while we are there, I hope that I finally..."

I close my eyes and look away, warmth creeping into my cheeks with embarrassment. Evander said he isn't ready to be a father, but all I have been doing since his departure is picturing a family with him. I see a little boy with his dirty blonde hair and a girl with brunette curls, big smiles on their faces. Their facial features are a mix of Evander's and mine. I want this.

"What do you mean?" Evander frowns.

"I ... I have been thinking a lot about our future while you were gone," I say. At night when I was alone, missing his warmth, I would picture us in the castle with my family...our family. I need this. I don't want to be alone again.

"Our future?" he asks, tilting his head.

"I-I want," I take a deep breath in, "children with you, Evander."

"Oh," he blinks repeatedly, "and, are you saying you're...pregnant?"

I shake my head. "No, not yet, but I hope our trip could help with that."

He blinks again. "I don't know what to say."

My stomach twists and I pull away from him. I knew I shouldn't have said anything. He has confessed to me that he is nervous about the idea. Yet, here I am, telling him how I want to start as soon as we can. I am a fool to think he would be open to discussing it now. I am a fool for trying to push him to be ready now.

"F-Forget I mentioned it."

He pulls me back against his chest. "You know that I have some fears about becoming a father."

I nod and pull away from him once more. Walking over to our bed, I slip out of my dress. Evander follows behind me, pulling off his breeches and tossing them to the ground.

"I-I know. It is foolish of me. I'm sorry," I say, my voice cracking.

"I want to explore it with you. You will be such an amazing mother. I think knowing that helps me feel less unsure."

"It's alright, Evander," I say, slipping my chemise off and getting into bed. I curl into a ball as he crawls into bed behind me.

"Charlotte. Look at me," he says. I turn, surprised he used my name rather than one of my nicknames. His brilliant steel-grey eyes lock with mine, and I can feel myself relax beside him.

"Yes?"

He kisses me hard before saying, "I want to have kids with you."

"But you want to wait?" I ask.

"No, no." Evander shakes his head. "I just don't think it's one of those things I will truly be prepared for."

I cuddle closer to him, kissing his cheek. "If it makes you feel better, I won't be prepared either. We will have to learn together."

"I'm happy it was you," he says, closing his eyes. My heart flutters in my chest, and I kiss him. Since our wedding night, I haven't wished to be married to any other.

"I'm happy you chose me." Evander kisses me hard, and I smile against his lips. "Promise to dance with me tomorrow?"

He nods. "I'm not very good at it."

"I'll teach you." I yawn, cuddling closer to him.

He yawns as well. "I love you."

My eyes flutter open, and I look down at my husband. Did he really say it? Those words I have been craving to hear from his lips. *I love you.*

"You love me?" I ask him. He snores softly, and I smile down at him, fixing a lock of his dirty blonde hair. "I love you, too."

I lay back down on his chest, and the smile remains on my face. His words continue to replay in my mind, my stomach doing tiny flips. I know I won't be able to fall asleep after hearing that. My heart and mind won't let me.

LX

EVAN

OUTSIDE OF ILIUM

KINGDOM OF CANDONIA

My head is pounding, and even the soft light coming into the tent makes me wince. The drugs that Kian gave me yesterday must be wearing off. Our assassin is also our best healer, and he didn't give me the option to refuse before shoving a bottle into my mouth. I don't like things that dull my senses. I hate drugs, and while I usually drink a mug of mead with lunch and dinner, I never over imbibe. For too much of my life, I was subjected to men and women who did so. I have the scars that prove what happened when they turned their attention to the slaves under their control.

I was small, too small and weak to escape their grasping hands. My first master liked little boys. Usually, I could run and hide, but I went to see the horse giving birth in the barn. I was outside the camp at night, and he caught me.

"Little Evander. All mine, now. Nowhere to run."

I wince, and my eyes flash open when a sharp pain radiates up my side. Charlotte is cuddling close, burying her face against my chest and pressing on a fresh bruise. Just like that, the memory of his stale breath and his hands on me slips away. I gasp as all my focus shifts to the present and Charlotte.

She quickly pulls away and sits up, realizing she's hurting me. "I'm sorry!"

I blink slowly, clearing my eyes of the instinctual tears that sprung to them when she touched my still healing ribs. "Sorry?"

Never be sorry, ever. Just her touch had yanked me out of the past. She so consumes me, I can think of nothing else but the present.

Charlotte moves the furs down to my waist, inspecting the large black bruise showing on my side. "I forgot..."

"It's fine," taking her hand from my side, I kiss the palm, "the drugs are just wearing off."

She frowns at me, lying down next to me again, careful to avoid my side. "They gave you drugs? What kind?"

I sigh and close my eyes, trying to relax, but my body aches with even the slightest movement. "Kian gave me something. It makes you delirious but speeds up your healing."

Even now, I can feel my ribs pushing back together, the cracks and breaks causing less pain. Some herbs were said to be blessed by the Ancient of Medicine, Etienne, and could cut weeks of healing down to days, even hours, depending on the healer's skill. However, there were always side effects. She tenses next to me, and I blink open my eyes to glance down at her.

"So, you don't remember?"

"Yesterday?" I search my brain, trying to figure out what she is talking about. She came to the healing tent, she told me about the prick refusing to leave, and then we fell asleep. What am I missing? "Most of it, why?"

She pauses and glances at my bruise. "You told me, um..."

My eyes are weighted, each blink almost sending me back to sleep. "Hm?"

She shakes her head, not answering. My limbs are heavy, and my mind cloudy. Too cloudy to press her or stop her from getting out of bed. "I have things to do. The festival starts at noon."

"You won't kiss my wounds?" I tease, my eyes drifting closed again. "I should probably sleep some more," I mumble. This festival is very important to Charlotte, and I can't sleep much longer, or I risk not waking up until tomorrow. She would never forgive me, which means I can't go back to sleep, no matter the need for my body to heal. I brace myself and grab a handful of my leg hair, ripping it out by the roots.

Fuck! Wide awake now.

The jolt of pain makes me more aware, combating the lingering grogginess from the drugs, and I manage to bite back the shout that rises in my chest.

She comes back to my side, gently kissing my ribs, then my cheeks and eyes. "I love you."

I will never tire of hearing that. It's still so strange to me. Charlotte has no reason to love me. I stole her and kept her from her family. She should hate me.

I press a gentle kiss to her lips and say, "Go get ready for your festival, and save me a dance, hm?"

She nods. "Promise to be there for the beginning?"

"Whenever you want me, star."

She slips on a shift, walking over to her trunk at the side of the tent. "Noon. I want you at noon. Is it alright if the men come to the festival after their morning drills?"

I yawn big. "Ask, and it will be done." I hold my hands up to her, closing and opening them repeatedly, as I'd seen her do. "Come here."

She walks back over to me, her gait an effortless glide. "Yes?"

I pull her onto my lap and wrap my arms around her. "You're amazing, and this festival will be perfect."

She smiles softly up at me. "Thank you."

"Would you rather I come early to help?" I can force myself to stay awake if she wants me to. The drugs will wear off faster if I'm moving around.

Her smile is dazzling. "I would love that! I thought that maybe the men could have the day off? So they can spend time with their friends and family."

"You want them to skip morning drills?" I've never given that order. The morning and evening drills are as certain as the sun rising and setting every day.

She bites her bottom lip. "More families are being reunited. It would be nice to give them a day to catch up."

I suppose today is a day for new traditions. "Tell the Boy, and he'll send the message out."

She kisses me hard, giggling against my lips. "Thank you, my love. I also have an outfit for you to wear today. It's a little traditional, but I think you'll look good."

My brows shoot up. "A little traditional?"

She scrambles off me, picking up her dress. It is a complicated looking confection of material and a strange circle contraption to give her a more bell shape. I hate the thing on principle.

"Yes, my love. Go look."

Ancients, she will have me a verified dandy by the year's end. But like always, I'm helpless to deny her. I stand slowly, concealing my wince of pain. I come to her side as she fiddles with the ties of her dress. "You might not like it."

"You picked it for me. I'll love it," I reassure her.

Charlotte smiles brightly over her shoulder, tightening the ties on her dress. She leans over and picks up the wrapped package, yanking the twine from it. "It has a cape."

"A cape?" I shudder, watching her pull out the separate pieces of clothing.

She holds up the black velvet cape. Gold silk lines the interior, and matching thread embroiders the edges, with the royal seal of Candonia hidden in the design.

"I think you'll look dashing."

I shoot her a droll look. "It's impossible to fight while wearing a cape."

Especially this one, as it will hit me at almost mid-calf, the yards of fabric making it impossible to navigate or move efficiently.

Charlotte puts the cape back down and picks up the white lawn shirt, its collar and cuffs also embroidered. She holds it out for me. "Well, you won't be fighting during the festival. You will be my wonderful, handsome husband."

"But what if someone else starts a fight?"

She kisses me softly, going on her toes to reach my lips. "Then I will hold your cape for you and cheer you on."

Taking the shirt from her, I pull it over my head, looking down at myself. I pick up the black breeches, finding that they have matching embroidery along the sides.

"Ancients above," I hiss.

She smiles up at me. "You're a prince, my love."

I pull the breeches up and tie them. "This can't be necessary."

She puts a hand on my chest, her eyes sparkling like gems. "Oh, please! For me?"

I groan and reach for the black doublet, but she takes it from me. "Let me help you."

I sigh and let her dress me. She attaches the cape to the hooks of my doublet, the gold buttons gleaming. She takes a step back, her gaze moving slowly up and down my body. "Oh, my…"

With the breathiness of her voice and the way her eyes are shining, I can tell she enjoys me all trussed up in finery. "You get this for one day."

"This is the best day!" She smiles, practically vibrating with excitement.

I point to my lips and demand, "Kiss."

She goes to her tiptoes, kissing me hard. I wrap her in my ridiculous cloak and sigh in frustration when her skirt prevents me from pulling her closer to me. Huffing, I ask, "How do you get anything done in these?"

She pokes my nose playfully. "You don't."

She holds her finger up at me and then lifts the back of her skirts. She unties the contraption, letting it drop around her ankles. Free of the encumbrance, she kisses me softly.

She laughs against my lips as I deepen the kiss, her arms wrapping around my neck.

LXI

Charlotte

OUTSIDE ILIUM

KINGDOM OF CANDONIA

The horn for morning drills sounds, and I pull away from Evander. His outfit has my heart fluttering, and if we had nowhere to be, I'd be ripping it off him. I can tell from the glint in his eyes that he is thinking the same thing, but I can't let temptation overcome me. The tailor did a wonderful job, and Evander is devastatingly handsome in his new clothes, but I can't just stand here admiring him. I need to finish the last details for the day. Preparing for this festival has taken up a lot of my time, and I am very excited about it. I can't miss it.

Evander growls, looking at the tent flap. "I am going to shove that horn up his ass."

I snort, kissing him softly. "We should go tell them that drills are canceled."

I turn away from him and pick up my crinoline. The thing is itchy and uncomfortable, but it is in fashion. So is the corset, but I managed to forgo it for this event. I want to enjoy myself, not worry about whether I can breathe or not. The queen would have my head if she were to find out. Evander grabs the crinoline from my hands, tossing it to the side.

"But, but…" I protest with a frown, trying to reach for it.

He frames my face in his large hands. "The only way I'm getting through this is if I'm able to kiss you."

"I dislike those things, anyway." He kisses me again, and I smile into it before taking his hand. "Come. We should go."

Evander sighs, looking back down at his outfit. "They're going to laugh at me in this."

"Give them one of your looks," I say, kissing him again and dragging him from the tent. "That will quiet them."

"My looks?" he questions, frowning.

"You know…" I look up at him, mocking one of his dirty looks as we walk over to the training grounds. He sends the look back at me, and I chuckle. When I first met him, that look had me trembling, but now I only laugh when I see it. He frowns slightly at me, and I smile at him before looking out at the training field. The warriors stare at Evander, and a few of them snicker. I tilt my head to the side, indicating to Evander that we are at the fields.

Evander snarls at me before raising his voice for the men. "In celebration of the first annual Celebracion la Libertade, there will be no drills today, so you have time to celebrate with your family. In honor of my wife and your future queen."

The men go silent, looking at one another in surprise before letting out a roar in cheers. They pat each other on the back before dispersing to their tents. Out of the corner of my eye, I see Jeremy run to his children. The kids jump into their father's arms in excitement. It feels good to give back to others.

"I like seeing them happy," I whisper to Evander.

"I like seeing you happy," he says, kissing my head. I spin to face him, my lips smash hard against his in a deep kiss. He pulls back, licking his lips as he looks down at me. "What was that for?"

"I love you," I say, smiling at him.

He smiles down at me. "Are you ready to go into the city?"

I nod in excitement, taking his hand in mine. "I am."

"Lead the way," he says. I pull him along, weaving through the camp. Excitement fills the air as we make our way to the city, and I only hope that I don't disappoint them with the festival.

I move behind Evander as we arrive at the edge of the market. I have to stand on my tiptoes to cover his eyes with my hands. He tenses slightly but doesn't remove my hands.

"Are you ready?" I whisper.

"I'm not a fan of the blindfold, but I trust you," he responds. My lips tingle as I press a kiss to his cheek and carefully guide him into the market. I remove my hands from his face and take a step back to see his reaction. The younger children run down the walkway with flags in their hands while the older children teach games to the newcomers. A few of Evander's men have arrived. They stand on the outskirts, shuffling their feet awkwardly. I grin when a few young women approach them. The men look at each other before allowing themselves to be pulled onto the dance floor. Smiles break out on their faces, and I can hear the laughter in the air.

To the right, I notice some of the villagers from Ghynts have arrived. They are chatting, and it is soon hard to tell who is from Ilium and who is from Evander's army.

The current band plays a new tune, and people partner up to dance. Colorful lanterns dance in the breeze above, waiting for nightfall. Freesias are scattered around the market, their scent hanging in the air. Booths selling food and other wares surround the square. Freed slaves have set up their own stalls, showing Evander's men and my people what they have accomplished since they gained their freedom.

"What do you think?" I ask him.

"It's beautiful." He gapes, looking around. His eyes suddenly narrow, and I frown, following his gaze. *Lord Edmunde.* Evander's fists tighten, and he starts to storm toward him. I stop him, entwining my fingers with his.

"Dance with me," I whisper. "Don't let him win."

His jaw visibly grinds, but he nods and stays with me.

"I'm yours," I whisper again, pulling him to the dance floor. Taking his hands, I place his palms on mine, and I hold my arms up high.

"I want him gone, star," he growls, rolling his shoulders. His gaze is not on me, but focused on Edmunde.

I sigh. "Please, Evander..." *I just want you.*

"Star, I don't want to ruin your event, but I don't like him here. He wants something, and with what he knows..." Evander sighs.

"He wants to make you angry," I say. "To prove to me that he is right."

His brow furrows and he looks back down at me. "Prove him right?"

"He wants to prove you are a monster," I say, continuing to dance with him.

"I am a monster."

My entire body tenses, and I shake my head. "You are not a monster."

"Not to you," he says, smiling down at me softly, "but too many."

I look around at all the happy faces. Does he not realize what he has done? He freed these men. He helped free these families, giving them all a second chance. How could he be a monster for doing that? I will show him he is not a monster, but a hero.

"Tomorrow," I finally say. "May we deal with him tomorrow? Or perhaps one of the generals can watch him. I just want some time with you."

Evander sighs again, his eyes searching for someone in the crowd. His gaze lands on Kian, where he is leaning against a wall. Kian nods at us before walking away, and I look back up at my husband.

"I'm yours now," he says. "Where to first?"

LXII

EVAN

ILIUM

KINGDOM OF CANDONIA

The festival is an overwhelming explosion of the senses, sights, sounds, and smells. Booths clog the streets, and many of my men are wearing the finery that the tailor worked overtime to create. Several of them are yanking at their collars, and I have to stop myself from doing the same. It's hard to adjust to the layers of clothing and stitching. Armor is different. Armor saves your life. This is just for looks and to suffocate you under fabric.

"Well, I know Leonardo has a stand set up somewhere, and I am quite hungry," Charlotte admits, biting her bottom lip. She doesn't even need the pleading look she adopts. I've accepted that when she wants something, I'll move the world to get it for her.

The looks I get from the Candonians are different again. Maybe it's the festival or that I'm dressed like a lord instead of a warrior, but they look curious instead of frightened. I wonder if Kian ever goes into the city dressed as a nobleman. It's an excellent way to blend in. At least better than in armor.

I lift her hand to my lips and kiss the back of it. "Must satisfy my future queen."

Her laugh is soft, the melodic and pure sound drifting over me, wrapping us in intimacy. She pulls me along the streets, navigating the crush of the crowd. People stop to speak to her or call out greetings. She knows them all, every name, every face, never ignoring them, always making time. How does she keep them all straight? Each time she introduces me, I see them flinch. She soothes them each time, refusing to give up until they are comfortable in my presence. We stop at Leonardo's booth, and the smell of baked goods makes my mouth water.

"Anything special for today?" Charlotte asks him. I can feel the eyes of other Candonians on us, and it takes everything in me not to spirit her away back to camp. I want her surrounded by people I trust rather than a city of unknowns.

"Of course, Your Highness. We have some blueberry danishes and some chocolate croissants," the baker answers with a twinkle in his eye.

Her hand tightens on mine, her eyes shining up at me. "What should we get?"

"What's chocolate?" I ask the baker. I've never heard of it before.

Leonardo chuckles, holding two of them out for us. I take it from his hand carefully, sniffing it before taking a bite. I'll try almost anything at least once. It's a side effect of being a slave, I suppose. You'll do whatever it takes to survive.

It takes a moment before the flavor hits me, and my mouth drops open at the taste. The bittersweetness plays havoc on my tongue. Is this something royalty consumes often?

"You cleaned him up good, princess," Leonardo says, watching my reaction with a smile.

I follow the first bite with another and then another. Before I am ready to be done, I am licking my fingers. "What is this?"

My wife laughs. "It's chocolate. It's a delicacy we only get once a year from the Kolia Kingdom. Leonardo thought it would be a wonderful idea to share it with everyone, so he lowered the price for today."

I blink and frown in shock at my fingers, disappointed to find there's nothing left on them. "This is amazing."

374

"I can give you another, Your Highness." Leonardo laughs, his big belly shaking with mirth.

I shake my head, even as I continue licking my fingers. "No, save that for the other guests, but this is without a doubt the second best thing I've ever tasted."

Charlotte walks over to me, feeding me the last bite of her croissant. "What is the first?"

I lick the remaining crumbs from her fingers and give her a wicked grin. "You."

Charlotte blushes, and the baker laughs, moving on to another customer. "Evander!" she scolds.

I give her a wicked grin. "It's true."

She scrunches her nose at me, her blush turning her ears red. A child comes to our side, tugging at Charlotte's dress. She looks down at the small child and does not hesitate to lower to her knees on the street. She smiles and says, "Hello, little one. How may I help you?"

The boy is around six, his hands covered in chocolate. "It's time for the flag decoration."

"That's right," she murmurs, standing. The young child takes her hand and leads her away from me.

I reach out to touch her back, but she's already too far away. I catch nothing but the barest feeling of her dress, and I drop my hand to my side, limp and useless. Without her next to me, I'm lost, a ship without mooring. I might rely on her too much. I used to know every step, the next, and the next, each with purpose. But now, I feel the echo of each step, and they are no longer simple. Now each move I make reverberates across all of Aellolyn. For the first time, I'm looking at everything with a bird's-eye view. This step will lead to another step to the side, yet another back, and so on. It is a crevasse constantly widening instead of closing.

A young girl stops in my path, looking up at me, blinking repeatedly. Her small body trembles as she locks her eyes with mine and stutters, "W-we need y-you!"

She takes a step back immediately after the pronouncement, and I ask, "Me?"

Another young girl appears at her side, slightly older, more sure. "Yes! We need your hand!"

Each of them takes one of my hands and drags me away, following the same path they Charlotte had taken. I'm so stunned by their lack of fear that I let them.

My wife is hovering over a table, surrounded by children. She looks up and smiles at me. "They found you."

"They just said they needed me."

They push me into a seat, gesturing my wife into the one next to me.

The posse of children stands on the surrounding chairs, taking my hand and dipping it in paint.

"Be careful of their outfits!" one of the older girls orders.

"I'm trying!" the other snaps back.

I blink at the bevy of children. "They're not afraid of me."

She giggles at me, resting her head on my shoulder as another child places our hands on the banner. "That's good."

"It's perfect!" one of them squeals.

"Mr. Black, can you help us hang it up?!"

"Yes!" another child demands.

A child wipes my hand clean of paint, and I nod. "Of course, and you can call me Evan."

The children cheer, picking up the banner.

"We want it above the stage," one little girl orders and pulls me to my feet while another picks up the banner.

"For everyone to see!"

I pick up the first boy who came to get Charlotte and place him on my shoulders. Together we tie the banner, making sure it is secure. I look down at the other kids. "How's that?"

The children cheer, "We did it!"

I help the boy off my shoulders, setting him carefully back on the ground, and he claps and jumps up and down. "Time for snacks!"

The children jump from the stage, running off. My wife wraps her arms around me and kisses my cheek. "They love you."

"It's strange," I say, blinking after the retreating backs of the children.

She pulls back, threading her fingers through mine. "What is?"

I lock my gaze with hers before kissing her softly. My future flashes through my mind, and at the center of it is the princess at my side. But now there's more, and it's no longer just us. "I'd like to have kids. With you."

She blinks at me in shock before jumping on me and repeatedly kissing me hard. "You would?"

I wrap my arms around her, keeping her feet off the floor. "I'm still nervous about it."

She keeps kissing me, practically vibrating with excitement. "That is fine. I'm just happy."

So long as she's happy, I can swallow my own nerves about children. So long as she's happy, I can do almost anything.

LXIII

Charlotte

ILIUM

KINGDOM OF CANDONIA

This day has been beyond perfect. I have spent time with Evander, and I have always dreamed of having a family with the man I love. Everyone at the festival appears to be getting along well. Old enemies are turning over a new leaf to create friendships that will last centuries. I am filled with contentment.

In the distance, a flare shoots into the sky, and horns sound off. I squeeze Evander's hand, frowning. Have I been too quick to judge? Has a fight broken out? No. The horn wouldn't have sounded so pleasant if that were the case. Someone of importance has arrived.

"Who's that?" Evander asks.

We move forward as the crowd parts for our visitor. Princess Lyra of Grimmwing stands at the other end of the market. Her bright red hair shimmers in the sunlight, her freckles prominent across her delicate features. There are at least ten soldiers with her. She waves them off, permitting them to go and enjoy the festival. Her elegant forest green dress trails the ground, and I know she is probably dying to get out of the thing. She is a lot like Thalia in the sense of hating dresses. They prefer breeches and shirts, claiming them to be more comfortable. To be honest, they aren't wrong.

Lyra approaches with a bright grin on her face. "Well, by the Ancients. If someone told me a year ago that you two would be the happiest looking couple in Candonia, I would have laughed in their face. But look at yah!"

Evander smiles at the princess, bowing his head. "Your Highness. You've met my wife, Princess Charlotte."

"You know how I feel about titles, blondie," Lyra scoffs before turning to look at me. "It's been what, a year now?"

"Two." I laugh. "I've missed your visits, Lyra."

Lyra pulls me into a hug, and the smell of strawberries and vanilla wafts off her. Most Grimmwing royalty are taught to fight, and though Lyra looks as soft and fragile as a lily, she is stronger than most princesses. She prefers it that way, enjoys surprising her victims with her knowledge and strength.

"As happy as we are to see you, Lyra, I am surprised. I just left you in Grimmwing," Evander says.

Lyra pulls away from the hug, her expression shifting ever so slightly. As princesses, we have both been trained not to give away our true emotions. So, I am surprised to see her demeanor darken. It concerns me.

"Yes, well, something has changed." Lyra looks up at Evander seriously. "I was hoping to speak to Kian. Is he around?"

Evander's brows furrow. "Kian? He should be watching the prick."

"Which prick is he watching now?" Lyra snorts, looking around.

My husband looks down at me. "Care to explain?"

I open and close my mouth, trying to figure out an explanation but failing. Finally, I just say, "Lord Edmunde."

"That wanker still sniffing around your skirt? I thought he would have given up his pursuit by now." Lyra snorts, still looking for Kian.

"Pursuit?" Evander asks, his brow raised.

I look up at him, chewing my bottom lip. Lyra knows most of the stories. There were times Lord Edmunde would hint at a proposal or mention the possibility, but I would always deny it.

"Do you not know how many times your wife has said no to the lad? I'll give him one thing. He is a stubborn ass. I could just put him out of his misery," she says.

"Lyra!" I exclaim, my eyes widening.

I feel Evander tense beside me as he points into the crowd. "There's Kian."

Both Lyra and I turn our heads to look. He is standing by the wall, talking with Niklaus. Both men seem oblivious to what is going on around them, but I know better. Men who are well trained know everything going on around them, even if they appear distracted.

"Blondie," Lyra's voice lowers, "who is that standing with Kian?"

Evander crosses his arms across his chest. "Niklaus. He is one of my generals."

Her eyes flicker with recognition as she stares at him. It was the same when I first met the dark-haired man. He looks so familiar, yet I can't figure out where I have seen his face before.

"Where is he from?" Lyra asks, frowning.

"I met him on the border of Steodia, but he doesn't know his origins. He was a child," Evander says.

"If you'll excuse me," Lyra says, turning away from us.

The Princess of Grimmwing walks to the two men. Something feels wrong, and I have a tingling sensation at the back of my mind, urging me to ask her more questions. I like Lyra. She is different compared to the other princesses in our neighboring kingdoms. Her father married into the royal family when she was only a girl. It was around the time the late King of Grimmwing and his family passed away in a tragic accident. The king's sister married Lyra's father so she could claim the throne. Lyra's father passed away a few years ago. The queen had no children of her own and kept Lyra in the castle, allowing her to stay the princess.

"I feel like something is wrong," I say to Evander.

"As do I." His voice is grim.

"Should we get involved?" I ask.

"No, I'm sure…" Evander trails off, and I look up at him. His eyes are narrowed on Edmunde, and I kiss his chin to bring him back. "I'm sure it will be fine. This is your festival. Let's enjoy it."

I smile, kissing him once more. "I want to go listen to music. May we?"

"Lead the way," he says.

The rest of the day goes by smoothly. There are plenty of games, delightful food, and wonderful music. Many Candonians have approached Evander to shake his hand and introduce themselves to their future king. It is a start and so much better than the fear and outright hostility. I think in time, they will see what I see. Evander is a man who cares about freedom and is willing to fight to give his people a better life.

We make our way to the edge of town, where the men are preparing the fireworks I managed to trade from Xiapia. The dynasty is known for its experimentation in explosions, and I thought everyone should have the chance to experience the colorful lights that explode in the sky. The sun has finally set, which means it is time. Evander squeezes my hand before kissing the back of it.

"I love you," he says.

I look up at him, my eyes widening. He said it. My husband hasn't been drinking, and the drugs should be out of his system. That means he is aware of what he said. *He said it.* My heart flutters in my chest and tears fill my eyes.

"You do?" I ask.

He smiles at me, pressing his coarse palm against my cheek. "I'm sorry it took me so long."

I place my hand on his chest, a tear rolling down my cheek. "It's alright. I'm just happy to hear you say it."

Unbelievably happy.

There is a loud bang, and we both look up. Blue and green sparks light up the sky.

"It's beautiful," I say in awe.

"To a new future, a new world." Evander smiles down at me, his eyes softening. "To you, my guiding star."

I wrap my arms around his neck and press myself as close as I can get. "And to you, my prince. Without you, this wouldn't be happening."

Fireworks light up the sky as Evander pulls me into a kiss, sending warmth curling in my belly. I will never get enough of this man.

He pulls back just enough to say, "I hate that I have to leave soon."

"Let's enjoy the rest of the night. Just the two of us." I press my breasts against his chest, giving him a wicked grin.

"The rest of the night." He nods, his arms wrapping around me tightly. "I'm so proud to have you as my wife."

I melt in his arms and kiss him again. "I am so glad you found me. It will be you and me forever. Right?"

"Just you and me," he says. I press my lips hard against his, giggling. He pulls away slightly, his lips curved in a rueful smile. "We should mingle."

I move my lips back to his before shifting from foot to foot. "I need you."

He looks around. "Now?"

"I'm uh…really um…" I whisper, my face turning bright red. I can't say the words, but Evander knows what I mean. He takes my hand, yanking me away from the crowd. They don't seem to notice us, their gaze transfixed on the fireworks. He pushes me up against the wall in an alley, kissing me hard, and I moan softly.

"I love you." I nip at his lower lip, tugging at his breeches.

He starts lifting my skirts, huffing in exasperation, "So many layers!"

I smile, helping him with my dress. His steel-grey eyes connect with mine, sparkling from the lights of the fireworks. He slams himself inside me at the same time the next firework explodes. His hand grips the back of my neck, keeping my focus on him.

"You'll bear my children?" he asks.

"Yes," I moan, my nails digging into his back.

"You'll be my queen?"

"As long as you are my king."

"You love me?" he asks.

"I love you, Evander," I say breathlessly, pressing my forehead to his. *And I always will.*

XLIV

EVAN

ILIUM

KINGDOM OF CANDONIA

The fireworks continue in the background, but all I care about is my wife. I hold her in my arms, both of us panting. A slight sheen of sweat covers my brow, and I wipe it off on her skin. There is a chaotic culmination of sound as the sky explodes, the festival concluding. There is a feeling of rightness, of *fate* settling in.

We take a few more moments to settle our breathing. Charlotte's hands are gentle as she fixes my breeches and adjusts her skirt. Unless someone looks closely, we appear the same as we did earlier. "We should go back before they look for us," she says, her voice still shaky.

I kiss along her shoulder and up her neck. Even having just taken her, I'm already thinking about the next time. "Yes."

She kisses my cheek, nuzzling me. "Come."

Once, I would have balked at anyone giving me such an order. But from Charlotte? It's an entreaty I am helpless to deny.

I roll my shoulders, stretching in bed next to her. My ribs are almost healed, the benefits of mystical herbs speeding along my natural regeneration. It's time for me to leave again. I kiss her face, ears, nose, cheeks and whisper, "Star? It's time for us to go."

She doesn't open her eyes. Instead, she just pulls the furs over her head. "A few more minutes, my love."

Is she always going to make it difficult for me to leave? I pull the furs away from her face. "You have to go back to the palace."

She shakes her head, her eyes fluttering open. "Not without you."

I let out a heavy sigh and brush a lock of hair out of her face. "We talked about this." She doesn't say anything, trying to pull the furs back up. "It's only for a couple of days."

She pouts. "I don't like this."

"I don't like it either."

She sits up and kisses me before asking, "You promise you'll be back in a week?"

I nod at her. If I can make the trip shorter, I will.

She gets out of bed and grabs her chemise, slipping it on. "Are all the generals going with you?"

"The Mountain and Niklaus are staying behind."

Her lips curve in a small smile, though it's tinged with sadness at seeing me leave. "So I can continue my classes?"

"Of course, Star."

Charlotte goes to her tiptoes to kiss me. "Will you pick my dress?"

I walk to her trunk and rummage through the ridiculous amount of material and lace until I find the one I want. It is a pale lilac dress with shorter sleeves. It is made with a light fabric but not too thin, enabling her to go without a corset.

She bites her bottom lip, watching me with warmth, her sapphire eyes glowing. "That is one of my favorites."

Does she think I don't know that? That I couldn't tell her which of these dresses she's worn in front of me? On which days? I could even tell her the ones I've ruined. The same ones I've secretly replaced through the tailor in the city. I'm becoming more familiar with her clothing than I am with my own.

"I know."

She tilts her head to the side, her hair falling in a silken wave. "How?"

I brush her hair back over her shoulder, smiling as it falls forward again. "I know you."

I study you. I know your every breath in and out because if you're close, I can't seem to keep my eyes off you. Charlotte takes the dress from my hands and slips it on, turning away to allow me to lace up the back. I take my time, slowly kissing up her spine, worshiping her skin before it is concealed. My task complete, I linger at her shoulder, resting my cheek against her silky skin.

She shivers and glances back at me. "Why'd you stop?"

I nuzzle her neck and whisper, "I'm sad that I'm going to leave you."

It seems we are stuck in a constant loop of me leaving and returning. She's been diligent in her training with the Mountain, perhaps with more time, she'll be able to ride at my side. Charlotte turns to face me, wrapping her arms around my neck. "You'll have a part of me with you."

I place my hand over my heart. "I will."

Charlotte runs her fingers down my chest and sighs. "I'll...meet you outside?"

I nod in answer, and she kisses me one last time before leaving the tent. I take a moment to get dressed, as if that will somehow keep me from having to leave. Maybe if I take my time, word will arrive that our contact in Xiapia has gotten in touch and this trip is no longer necessary. But things don't work out for me like that. Outside of war, I'm not a lucky man. Though I suppose I am fortunate that it was her and not some other princess.

When I exit the tent, Charlotte is waiting for me, her hands clasped in front of her. She smiles at me. "I love you, Evander. Stay safe?"

I tilt my head, watching her. "Of course, my Star. What's wrong??"

Her smile turns down at the edges. "I am going to miss you."

Stepping closer, I wrap my arms around her, resting my chin on her shoulder. "How about I promise to make this my last trip for a while?"

A promise I'm not exactly sure I can make, but while she's gazing at me, her big eyes welling with tears, I'll promise her anything.

"Really?" she asks, kissing my cheek.

"Commander?" Lorcan asks, clearing his throat.

I shoot him a lethal glare, pulling away from my wife. "Yes?"

"It's time." Lorcan shoots a not-so-subtle look of mistrust at Charlotte. I dismiss him with my hand.

I kiss the side of her head. "The Mountain will escort you to the palace. Last trip for a while, I promise."

I whistle for the Black, and the horse trots closer. Charlotte steps away from me, watching as I mount.

"I love you," she says.

In lieu of responding, I lean down and kiss her before kicking the Black and riding off. I've said the words once. She knows to trust them.

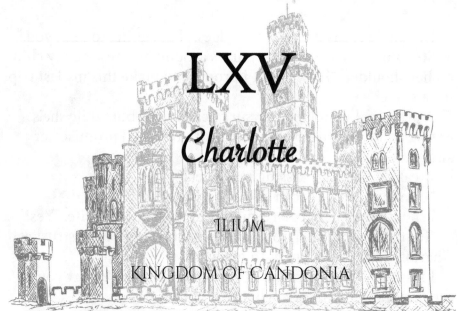

LXV

Charlotte

ILIUM

KINGDOM OF CANDONIA

There is a part of me that feels like it goes missing the moment Evander is out of sight. It happened the last time he left as well. Like I have a hole in my chest. I place a hand over my heart, ensuring that there is no wound. There isn't, but the feeling doesn't fade. I assume it won't until he returns and I am back in his arms.

I turn to Demir, who stands nearby holding our horses. He appears happier than usual, and there is a slight curve to his lips that I have never noticed before. He's always seemed like a stone wall, often unreadable, but never happy. The first time I saw him truly smile was at the palace, the last time Evander was away. Why would he be smiling when he is stuck watching over three princesses?

I decide not to question him about his smirk. If I do, it may fade, and I prefer to see people happy. We mount and ride in silence as I think about the events of last night. The fireworks were spectacular, and Evander told me he loves me. The night couldn't have gone better. Well, it would have been better if it never ended.

Niklaus rides up as we arrive at the castle. As usual, he appears stiff and mysterious. Every time I see him, that sense of familiarity nags at me. If I have a talent, it is that I have a memory like the Ancient of Knowledge, Skender. I can remember faces, places, dates, and history like they are written on the back of my hand. Yet this man and his resemblance elude me. Perhaps I can pass the time that Evander is away by solving this mystery.

Demir signs to the other general while dismounting his horse.

"Evan asked me to stay behind," Niklaus says, frowning as he looks up at the palace. "He insisted I stay inside while he's away."

"Is there a reason?" I ask, sliding to the ground. I know by now that Evander always has a reason.

"No, Your Highness," he replies.

"Strange, there must be a reason." I frown, leading my horse to the stable. When I can't think of an explanation, I look up at Demir to see if he can give me some insight.

"Evan did not explain," he signs.

I sigh, turning to Niklaus. "Well, I'm happy to have you here. The more, the merrier."

Niklaus slides off his horse and hands it off to a stable hand. He scowls and storms into the palace. Wonderful, I was only trying to find positives in this situation. If I were him and Evander left me behind with no explanation, I would be frustrated as well.

"This will be fun," I say, looking up at Demir.

"Niklaus does not like to be ordered around. Even by Evan." Demir snorts.

I snort. "He will not enjoy being in the palace."

"There is a reason Evan never ordered him to stay behind. He despises royalty," Demir signs.

I frown. "Why?"

"No idea. He never told us. He was Evan's first squire, you know? The first Boy."

"Where did Evander find him?" I ask, tilting my head to the side.

"Before my time." Demir frowns.

"That makes me curious," I say, chewing my bottom lip.

Demir waves me off before signing, *"He won't answer questions, even if you are Evan's wife. The warriors call him Stone Wall."*

Aren't all you men a stone wall filled with secrets? I think to myself. Sticking my bottom lip out, I sigh. "Hm."

"Don't even think about it." He frowns.

"What?" I ask, pouting.

"Lia gets the same look on her face when she's about to launch a sneak attack on me."

Thalia. Is that why you are so happy, Mountain? I raise my brow at him. "My sister, hm?"

"She has asked for...training." He sighs.

I nod, smirking at him. "You should probably go see her then."

Demir gives me a hard stare and grunts before turning away. I stay behind a bit longer, grabbing a brush and grooming Snow. Her foal comes to her side, rubbing her body against her mother's, trying to calm her. Snow is anxious, dancing from foot to foot. We are the same in some ways. As soon as Evander and the Black go, the two of us become an anxious mess. I rub the bridge of her nose gently, soothing her with a hush.

"Soon. They will be home soon," I say.

To my surprise, the week practically flies by as I keep myself busy. It is a bit easier this time around, but not by much. Late at night, when the day ends, I find myself staring out the window at the stars. Some nights, I wouldn't sleep until early morning. It isn't the same without him, and I miss his comforting warmth. It is becoming a need, a necessity. Hopefully, tonight is the last night I have to go without it for a while.

There is a knock on my door, and I turn toward the sound. I am not expecting anyone at this hour. It is past midnight, and everyone should be asleep. Then again, it won't surprise me if it is Eleanor. The girl has had nightmares every night Ben has

390

been away. Something about how the sea swallows her love whole, and there is no way for her to get him back. I allow her to stay with me in my room until she feels better, which usually means she stays the night.

I tighten my robe around my body and pick up a candle before opening the door a crack. My entire body tenses when I see who it is.

"Lord Edmunde?" I say, surprised.

He tilts his head at me. "Are you going to let me in, Lottie?"

"What are you doing here?" I ask, squinting at him. Edmunde pushes the door open and slides into the room, closing it quietly behind him. "Edmunde!"

"Lottie," he says, looking around.

"You cannot be in here," I say, tightening the robe around me.

"We used to always spend time in each other's rooms," Edmunde replies, raising a brow.

I tense. "Things are different now. I have a husband who I love very much."

"Who doesn't love you back," Edmunde says cruelly. Before, I would have gone silent and doubted my husband's intentions. But now, I know that is a lie.

"He does love me," I say. "Now, I suggest you leave before I call for the Mountain."

Edmunde crosses his arms over his chest. "Call him. I'm sure word will get back to your husband that I was in your room at night."

I open and close my mouth, my eyes wide as anger takes the place of irritation. As much as I want to summon Demir, I know he will tell Evander. Then Edmunde would be a dead man, and I can't watch him die.

"I thought you were my friend," I say on a low growl.

"You are not thinking clearly, Lottie," he says. "You think love is the same as hate."

I shake my head. "No. I'm thinking perfectly clearly, Edmunde. He cares for me. He loves me."

"How can you choose him?!" Edmunde frowns. "He forced you!"

"Leave," I say, angry tears filling my eyes. I know my husband forced me to marry him. I am no fool. But this bond that I have with him tells me it was meant to be. I will allow no one to make me doubt him.

"Give me a chance, Lottie," Edmunde says, cornering me. "I've loved you since I was a kid."

I press my back up against the wall, looking up at Edmunde. "Please…"

Edmunde sighs, pulling away from me. "I don't want to be a monster."

"Then trust me," I say, holding his gaze. "You know how stubborn I am. If I didn't love him, I would have run away with you."

"I can't believe I'm losing you to…a savage." Edmunde growls with disgust.

I frown. "I will not tolerate that sort of talk about my husband."

Edmunde scoffs. "You know he is."

That's it. "Leave," I hiss.

Suddenly Edmunde leans forward and presses a gentle kiss to my lips. I blink a few times, my shoulders tensing. I push against his chest and he pulls away.

"Goodbye, Lottie," he whispers.

"Goodbye," I say harshly.

He turns away from me, exiting my bedroom. As soon as the door closes, I place a hand on my chest, trying to grasp what just happened. A sick feeling fills my stomach, and my lips sting from the kiss as if my body is rejecting Edmunde's touch. I rush to the sink and wet a cloth before scrubbing my lips. The feel of Edmunde's lips on mine lingers, and a surge of anxiety comes over me. I need Evander.

Exiting my room, I look for Demir. He was supposed to be close by, watching the door. How did Edmunde get past him? I turn down the right corridor, stopping when I see Demir exiting Thalia's room. His hair is disheveled, and his shirt buttons undone. I raise a brow after examining him.

"What's this?" I ask. Demir turns to look at me, his face flushing red. Just as I open my mouth to ask more questions, he bolts down the hallway. "Stop!"

Demir doesn't stop, and I let out a breath before chasing him. I am not as quick as him, and I do not have as much stamina. One thing I do have to my advantage is knowing the layout of the palace. I pull down one of the light fixtures, and a secret door in the hall opens. The door closes without a sound behind me as I sprint through the passage until I reach the end of my shortcut. I pull down a lever and slip out from behind the wall. Someone slams into me, and I fall to the ground, groaning and rolling to my back. Demir is standing over me, his face still glowing red.

"Stop. Running," I pant, trying to catch my breath.

"Excuse me," he signs before holding his hand out for me. I take it, getting up onto my feet.

"Are you going to tell me what happened?" I ask.

He shakes his head. *Stubborn.* I think I know a way on how to get him to talk.

I shake my head. "I wonder how Evander will feel knowing Lord Edmunde got into my room in the middle of the night because someone was busy."

Demir blinks. *"Did he hurt you?"*

"No, but he…" I shake my head. The feeling of nausea returns to the pit of my stomach, and I can't finish my sentence.

"He what?"

I look away from him for a moment. "He tried to convince me to run away with him."

"And you said no?" he signs.

"I did." I sigh.

"Why?"

"What do you mean, why?" I frown at him, surprised he is asking that question. Does he not know that my loyalty lies with Evander? I thought it was obvious by now.

"I have seen how he looks at you." Demir shrugs.

"I'm in love with Evander. Not him," I reply.

"*Good.*" Demir nods. *"Evan returns tomorrow. Are you going to tell him?"*

"Yes. I don't want any lies between us," I say. I have seen what it does to people when secrets are kept. They fall apart, lose their trust in the person they love the most. I don't want that to happen between Evander and me.

"I could kill him," Demir signs before crossing his arms over his chest.

"No! He is still my friend," I say.

"Are you sure?" he asks.

"I'm sure. I will stay in Eleanor's room for the rest of the night."

I don't want to take the chance that any unexpected visitors might decide to come back. Demir nods before escorting me down the hallway to my sister's room. On the way, he fixes his shirt and smooths his hair. By the time we arrive, he looks a little less disheveled, but I notice some red marks forming on his neck. *Damn Thalia.*

"Your sister is...very confusing," Demir finally signs.

"Which one?" I smirk to myself, feigning innocent.

"Thalia."

"How so?"

"She wants things I can't give."

"And what can't you give?"

He frowns. *"Evan will tell you."*

I nod again before placing my hand on my sister's door. "You're a good man, Lord Demir. Thank you for watching over us."

Demir nods before walking down the hallway, and I enter my sister's room.

My brow furrows when I find my sister not in her bed, but out on her balcony. The wind gently blows the curtains forward, and I see her long blonde curls flying behind her. She has changed since meeting Ben. I have never seen her happier than when she is with him, but she is sadder than ever when he is gone.

I let out a long sigh before joining her. "Aren't you supposed to be asleep?"

Eleanor gasps, turning to look at me. Her blue eyes turn wild as she jumps into her bed, pretending to snore.

"You know, that only worked when you were little." I laugh, sitting on her bed. "I'll be staying with you tonight if that is alright."

Eleanor opens one eye and nods. I frown in concern. The whites of her eyes are pink and the under-eye puffy. She has been crying. My heart squeezes in my chest.

"What's wrong, El?" I ask her.

"I...I miss Benji," she whispers.

"Well, did you hear?" I ask her. She shakes her head, and I smile. "Ben will be back tomorrow."

Her eyes light up. "Really?!"

I nod. "The sooner you fall asleep, the sooner he will be back."

Instantly, Eleanor lays back down, and I giggle before crawling under the covers beside her. I kiss my sister's forehead before falling asleep myself.

LXVI
EVAN

ILIUM

KINGDOM OF CANDONIA

The horn blares in the morning air, announcing our approach, but I barely hear it. I'm carrying my injured squire in my arms, galloping toward the palace. I rode ahead of the rest of the troops once we found out he was injured. He moans with fever as he sits in front of me, his head lolling. We skid to a stop in the courtyard, and I jump off the Black. I pull the into my arms and rush up the steps of the palace. I can hear my men's horses catching up, riding through the streets. All are concerned for the boy.

I kick in the palace doors and shout, "We need a healer!"

My squire mumbles in my arms, his torso covered with gauze. He had said nothing, didn't even hint that he was injured. Not until he fell from his horse and hit the ground just as we crossed into Candonia. There is no other healer between the border and Ilium, at least not one that I trust to heal the Boy.

I see the little princess, her pale hair whirling around her in a halo as she races along the landing above. Her bright smile morphs into horror when she sees the boy. "Benji!" she screams.

Charlotte appears behind Eleanor. She runs down the steps at the commotion and quickly takes charge. "This way!"

I follow Charlotte down the hallways to the healers, even as my squire's head rolls back weakly, his eyes half-open. She shoves open a door, making the healer jump in surprise as we crowd in. My men have caught up and are flooding the palace behind me, all crowding to check on the boy. When he sees the boy in my arms, he points to the table. "Put him there, please."

I carefully place my squire on the table, and my men close ranks around him. An impenetrable wall of some of the best warriors in Aellolyn, fretting over a fourteen-year-old boy.

The healer grabs herbs, smashing them with a mortar and pestle, and my voice drops to a hoarse warning, "He dies, so do you."

The healer gulps nervously, mixing the herbs faster. I distantly hear the little princess trying to order my men to move, no doubt trying to get to the boy's side. A harsh wind blows through the room, and it takes me a moment to realize there are no windows. My hair rises on end, the only warning I get before my men are thrown back by an invisible force. Most hit the wall hard, and several fall unconscious. Their armor will protect them from any real injury. I'm spared by being on the other side of the table, only able to watch as my men crumple. My eyes land on the culprit with shock. Eleanor's white hair is whipping around her head, her eyes glowing a bright, unnatural purple. With the obstacles cleared, she moves to the boy's side, whispering to him. My eyes bulge even more when I catch the language she is speaking.

A language long dead. The Language of Ancients. The Divine Tongue. A language you can only understand if you've been blessed by the Ancients. But this...she...she was more than blessed. The Blessed were only able to channel specific abilities of the Ancient who chose them, but not like this. *Never like this.* This was something else, *she* was something else, something supposed to be extinct.

My squire's eyes flutter open, glazed and unseeing, trying and failing to shove the young princess away. "No, it will kill...you."

I snap at her in the Ancient language, *"Listen to him."*
Only those Blessed know the Divine Tongue, something wound into our mind the moment we are chosen by the Ancients. The only other Blessed were up North, and none of them contained

this kind of power. *She's death and destruction in the body of a tiny twelve-year-old.*

Eleanor ignores the squire and me, the air crackling around her. The hair on my arms raises, the electricity and magic in the room calling to me. The glow from her eyes leaks down her face and into her arms as if slipping from her. She places her hands on his wound, power dripping from her palms into the boy. I put steel into my voice and order, "*No!*"

I can feel Charlotte's eyes on me, but I can't look away from Eleanor, not when she is performing magic without training. Charlotte asks, "What is going on?"

I don't have time to explain. The boy pushes at her again, and I circle the table. I grab her hands, yanking them behind her. "You will kill yourself."

Eleanor cries, wailing and fighting my hold. "I don't care! Let me heal him!"

The healer struggles to his feet, Eleanor's magical push having knocked him to the ground. He cautiously gathers his herbs and mixes them before packing the boy's infected wound.

Eleanor is still fighting to get back to him. Keeping her arms locked at her sides, I carry her away from the table. When my back hits the wall, I pull her down with me, allowing the healer to work. In the Ancient language, I assure her, "*He will be fine.*"

The healer glances at Charlotte as some of my unconscious men slowly start to wake. "I need some clean towels and warm water."

Charlotte nods, leaving the room to get the supplies. Eleanor wails, blood dripping from her nose. "I can save him! I can!"

I release her arms, and she curls against me like a child. I rock her back and forth, pressing her face into my chest. My squire hisses and passes out, muttering in Candonian. Charlotte returns with the towels and buckets of water. She wets a cloth and places it on the boy's forehead. "We've got you, Ben. We've got you."

The healer applies the mixture to the infected wound on his back and wraps his torso with fresh gauze. He glances from Charlotte to me. "If he makes it through the night, he should survive."

The little princess tenses in my arms, trying to fight my hold. To my men, I snap, "Back to camp. I'll take it from here."

They slowly file out, several making the sign of protection when they pass Eleanor. I can't blame them. When the room empties, I slowly stand and put Eleanor on her feet. I place my hands on her shoulders, ready to restrain her if necessary. She lunges toward the table, and Ben's eyes blink open again. He looks at Eleanor and then his gaze locks with mine. "Keep her away from me."

His eyes roll up as he passes out. Charlotte chokes back a cry, fixing the boy's hair, and Eleanor looks up at me, her eyes flickering from purple to blue. "W-What did I d-do?"

I lower myself down to her level, brushing tears from her cheeks, saying in the Ancient language, "*I don't know, little moon. We'll stay here until he wakes up, alright?*"

Eleanor wraps her arms around my neck, clinging to me. I stand and wrap my arms around her, lifting her against me. The healer bows his head and leaves the room. Charlotte comes to me and rubs her sister's back. "I'll go get us some food."

I nod at her, keeping my arms around Eleanor as Charlotte leaves. I switch back to the common tongue and say, "It's alright, little moon, he'll be fine. I promise."

She sniffles against my shoulder. "I-I love him. He is my best friend. I-I can't lose him."

I hush her and move to the chair. "I know. We won't lose him. He insisted he needed to get back to you. We didn't even know he was injured until we crossed the border. He fell from his horse."

She sobs into my shoulder. "S-So you don't k-know what happened?"

I shake my head. "No, he was hiding his injury. He knew we would have to stop until he healed, and he wanted to come home."

Eleanor pulls away from my shoulder, one of her small hands wiping her tears. "It's m-my fault?"

It's mine. The Boy knew how much I wanted to get home. He must have been injured during the ambush in Xiapia. He kept it secret, so we could both get home. His injury, his life, is on me. Another death to add if he doesn't make it through.

"You don't know that," I say.

"If he stopped to heal, h-he wouldn't be like this," she says, her eyes solidifying blue.

"Yes." There's no point in denying it.

She pulls out of my arms, stumbling toward Ben, reaching out to touch his head. I move fast, covering her hand, reminding her. "No magic."

She blinks up at me, asking, "C-Can I hug him?"

I stare down at her, my tone serious. "Of course, but no magic. You are too young to control it properly."

Eleanor nods and crawls onto the cot with the boy. She wraps her arms around him, holding him tight as she cries.

My heart breaks for Ben. He is a good kid, and the fact he was injured so seriously burns me. Eleanor is struggling, but I can see in Evander's eyes that he is worried too. I know he is hard on Ben, and he continuously tells me how he has to leave in the next few years, so don't get too attached. But I know my husband cares deeply for the boy.

In the kitchen, I wrap some bread, cheese, and fruit in a cloth. With everything going on, I know neither Evander nor Eleanor will feel hungry, but they need to eat. They need to keep up their strength and stay strong for Ben. He is going to make it through. Our healer, Gregory, is one of the best in Candonia. Even if the weapon used to hurt the boy was dipped in nightshade, Gregory should be able to save him. Though Ben's injuries seemed unusual. When I was helping Gregory, my knowledge of healing and its magic seemed to elude me as I tended to the cuts.

My cousin Demetrius, Prince of Vruica, taught me most of my healing skills. He is the most talented healer in Aellolyn. People come to him from all over if their illness is unknown to the common healer. Demetrius enjoys expanding his knowledge and has even made a few medical breakthroughs in the past few years. If Ben doesn't get better, I will send for him.

Worry nags at me as I walk back to the healing quarters. The hallways appear darker even though the sun is high in the sky. All the lanterns are out, and I can feel the magic in the air flowing toward Ben's room. I don't have the powers my sister does, but I can still sense it. It is a light hum of energy all around us. It is rumored that my grandmother from my mother's side practiced the mystic arts, but I will never know for sure.

I enter the room, noticing Eleanor cuddled up beside Ben on his cot. Evander is sitting on the chair in the corner, his eyes on the children. I walk to him, wiping the tears from my eyes.

"I've got some food," I whisper. Evander holds his hand out to me, and I take it. Unfolding the cloth, I pick up a piece of bread and offer it to him. "Eat."

He takes a bite of the bread, nipping my fingers. "I'm not the injured one."

"That doesn't mean you shouldn't eat," I scold, before looking at Ben and Eleanor again. There is a light snore coming from Eleanor, her blonde hair covering her circular face. "She has never lost control like that before."

"She's always had power like that?" Evander asks, his brows furrowing.

I nod. "I thought I told you."

"You said she had abilities. I thought you meant she was sensitive," Evander says, shaking his head. "Not...this. This is something else, star."

I agree with him. Before, Eleanor would only use her powers for seeing soulmates, seeing auras, and even spirits. She had never knocked back five men using her mind. I didn't even realize she could do that. Taking Evander's hand, I lead him out of the room in case my sister is still awake.

"What is this then, Evander?" I ask.

He frowns. "Where's my kiss?"

I give him a small smile before kissing him softly and then resting my forehead on his. "I missed you."

402

"I missed you, too," he whispers, cupping my cheeks with his hands.

I kiss him once more before pulling away. "Are you going to tell me now?"

Evander pauses, closing his eyes. "She's a High Sorceror."

"What? I have read about them, but...I didn't think," I whisper, stepping away from him. My mother used to tell us stories about the High Sorcerors when Thalia and I were little. I thought they were just stories. If they were true, then they would have been long gone or in hiding.

"They're supposed to be extinct," Evander says, hissing out a breath. How he knows so much about them only adds to my building questions. "She will have to go away."

My eyes widen and I look up at him. "W-what?"

Evander only shakes his head, pressing his forehead to mine. "Later, when the Boy is up."

"Evander, she won't go easily," I warn.

"I know." He huffs.

I close my eyes, kissing him again. "That will be tomorrow's problem."

"I missed you so much," he says, wrapping me in a tight hug. It feels good to be back in his arms, and although I ache for Ben, the hole in my heart is whole. As soon as I saw Evander, that strange, empty sensation disappeared.

"Promise not to leave me for a while?" I ask, wrapping my arms around his neck. *I don't want to feel empty again.*

"I promise." He nods, kissing me.

I let out a breath of relief before whispering. "There is so much to tell you."

"Later," he says.

"Alright," I whisper, kissing him again. Evander entwines his hand with mine before pulling me back into the room. We walk over to the wooden chair, and Evander takes a seat, pulling me onto his lap. I curl up beside him, grabbing a piece of bread from the cloth I left on the table. Eleanor shifts slightly and looks up at Ben.

"You have to wake up, Benji," she whispers. "There is so much I have to show you."

With a soft sigh, I look up at Evander and hold out the piece of bread for him to eat. He takes a bite before looking over at Eleanor.

"You know you have to be careful, little one. You could have killed yourself and him earlier," he says.

Eleanor lifts her head slightly to look at Evander. "I-I could h-have?"

He nods, kissing my fingers. "Yes. Your magic is wild. Without training, you could cause great destruction."

My sister looks back up at Ben. "What do I do?"

"There's a place I can take you where you can learn. Safely." My grip on Evander tightens at the thought of Eleanor leaving. I have always been protective of her. Even though I am busy most of the time, I still find time in the day to take care of her. Would it be the right thing to send her away?

"W-with Benji?" Eleanor stutters.

He shakes his head. "No, little moon, you will have to go alone."

"I... I..." Eleanor chokes up, tears rolling down her face. Her grip on Benji tightens, and I know she is struggling. Who would want to be alone again?

Evander glances at me, his eyes showing a hint of sadness. He looks back at Eleanor and says softly, "You are a danger to everyone if you don't get training."

"C-Can I wait until Benji wakes up?" Eleanor asks.

"Of course." Evander says, smiling softly.

"W-will I b-be able to see my sisters?" she asks.

"Yes, you just need to be somewhere safe while you learn," he replies, running his fingers through my hair.

"And when I'm done... Benji can still b-be my knight?" Eleanor asks.

"Your knight?" My husband blinks. I look at her, confused as well.

404

"He promised," she whispers.

Evander tilts his head. "He leaves for his quest in two years, and then another two years on the quest. If you still want him as your knight then, he can be."

My sister goes quiet for a moment, looking up at Ben. His chest is rising and falling at a steady pace, which is good. No fever. No infection. He is going to make it.

"Then I will train," Eleanor finally says.

Evander looks down at me with a smirk. "We will head for the North Wardens when Ben is on his feet. I'll confirm the details with your father, so he is aware."

I kiss him, nodding. "Promise she will be safe there?"

"Of course." He nods. "You can't even find the North Wardens unless you are blessed by the Ancients."

I breathe out a sigh of relief. "I trust you."

I will always trust you.

LXVIII

EVAN

ILIUM

KINGDOM OF CANDONIA

"I'm exhausted," I admit, settling into the chair, keeping my wife pressed against me.

Charlotte cuddles closer to me, whispering, "Then sl—"

A knock on the door cuts her off, and I glare at the wood as Lyra steps in. Her lilting voice is soft, conscious of the sleeping squire. "I heard about the lad."

I tense at the sight of the redhead. "Lyra? You're still here? I would have thought you left already."

It was a long ride back to Grimmwing, and soon the snow would make the way impassable.

She sighs audibly. "I've been trying, but the one person I need won't come with me." A faint snore comes from the cot, and the little princess drools slightly on my squire, finally having passed out.

I glance down at my wife. "You should put her in another bed so that the Boy can heal."

Charlotte sighs at me and gets off my lap. She walks over to the table and gently pries Eleanor's fingers off of Ben. She shoots me a look. "Eleanor will not be happy when she wakes up."

"I know. Come back to me once you get her settled?"

Charlotte nods and gives me a small smile before asking a

footman to carry Eleanor into a connecting room. Charlotte follows behind him, leaving me alone with Lyra.

"This is terrible timing, really," Lyra admits.

"Whatever do you mean?" It's never good timing for someone to be grievously injured.

She sits heavily in the chair, bracing her hands on her knees. "I need one of your generals to return to Grimmwing with me."

Over the years, many, and I do mean *many*, people have requested my generals. It was always urgent, always life or death. But I'd never said yes. Each of my generals came to me to escape something, and I will never hand them back to the things they once ran from.

"Absolutely not."

Lyra winces, running a hand down her face, exhaustion showing in her eyes. "Please, Evan."

I can't remember once in our long friendship the word *please* ever crossing her lips. Whatever it is, she must truly be desperate.

"Why?"

My wife walks back into the room and sits beside me, taking my hand in hers. Lyra looks down. "Do you know Niklaus's history?"

"No. Nor do I need to." If he wanted me to know, he would have told me sometime over the last eleven years. I have never asked, and I respect my men's privacy. I only pry when it could present an issue to the army. Otherwise, it's none of my business.

"Well, you really should. Niklaus is the rightful King of Grimmwing." My brows go up in surprise. I had pegged him as noble long ago. The way he spoke, read, and ate, even as a child, reeked of a privileged upbringing.

"That is why he looks so familiar," Charlotte says under her breath.

My hand tightens on hers. "There is already a Queen of Grimmwing."

Lyra's stepmother and a pernicious shrew who made Lyra's life miserable. But it matters not to me who sits on the throne, so long as they work to abolish slavery.

"And you know what she is like," Lyra hisses. "She is engaged to Lord O'Connor. You know who that is?"

My entire body stiffens at the name. Lord August O'Connor made his fortune on the backs of slaves, and I know he has been actively petitioning the upper nations of Aellolyn to unite their forces against me. Kian has already routed several assassins sent by him within the walls of Ilium. He hopes to reinstitute the old trade. I cannot let that happen, even if I must break my own rules to prevent it.

"I don't decide for Nik. If you can get him to agree to go, then you have him." Lyra is one of the few that I would ever make this allowance for, though I know Nik won't go happily. He hasn't crossed into the borders of Grimmwing in over a decade. Even if he goes with Lyra, she will struggle to get him to Ravaryn.

She smiles to herself. "The last thing I needed was your permission. Thank you, Evan, and you, Charlotte. You both have been very helpful."

She rests her hand on my shoulder before getting up and leaving the room. Looking back at my wife, I lift her hand to my lips, kissing the back of it.

She crawls into my lap, resting her head against my chest. "Our world is changing more and more by the hour."

I wrap my arms around her and settle my back against the wall. "Oh?"

"Ben is injured. Eleanor is going to leave us and so is your general. Thalia and the Mountain are *something*, but I'm not sure what." I blink down at her in shock. She glances at the door, then back to me. "I found him sneaking out of her room last night."

"He is not subtle."

She laughs. "I had to chase him down!"

"And you caught him?" Despite his size, the Mountain is agile.

She smirks up at me, but then frowns. "Yes. Though, I am confused."

"Confused?"

She nods, her blue eyes filled with concern. "She wants things he can't give. He told me to ask you what he means by that."

Figures he would give me that task.

"He's married."

She winces, squeezing her eyes shut. "Oh, no."

"He doesn't talk about it." When he lost his voice, he went home to his wife, and she told him never to return. The only reason he told me was so I would know that if she ever came to camp, she was to be turned away. She was dead to him. Not that I can blame him.

She sighs, pinching the bridge of her nose. "And I thought the two of them were perfect together. You know, I haven't seen my sister truly happy since our mother died."

"The Mountain let her touch him, and that never happens. *Ever.*" He usually goes out of his way to avoid contact unless it's in combat. It is as if he understands violence but not affection.

She blinks open her eyes. "He was a little disheveled when I saw him. Like I assume they were…"

That wouldn't surprise me. "Likely, he would be um…"

"What?"

I clear my throat. "Resisting going all the way. Because he can't make an honest woman out of her."

She blushes when she understands. "Is there anything we can do for them?"

"No, my star, there isn't." As much as I wish there were.

She looks down at her hands sadly and goes silent.

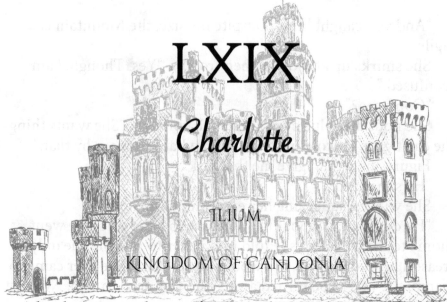

LXIX

Charlotte

ILIUM

KINGDOM OF CANDONIA

A loud scream wakes me from my sleep, and I almost fall off Evander's lap. He wraps his arms around my shoulder, pulling me back against his chest, and I blink in surprise. When did I fall asleep? The last I remember, we were discussing Demir and Thalia. The day must have really tired me out.

Eleanor runs into the room, crawling onto Ben's cot. She curls into a ball, her arm wrapping around Ben's chest. I blink a few times, how long have I been asleep?

"W-what's happening?" I ask Evander.

"Your sister woke up alone." Evander shakes his head, his hands gently running through my hair. He sighs before turning his attention to my sister. "Little moon…"

Ben groans and his eyes blink open. Sweat beads on his brow as his body works hard to heal. His once pale face is flushed with some color, but Eleanor appears oblivious as she holds him tighter.

"I'm not leaving him," she says, her eyes swollen and red from crying.

Ben looks down at her with a raised brow. "Elle? You're hurting me."

Eleanor's eyes widen as she looks up at Ben. "You're awake!"

Ben touches his injured side, and I notice his breathing become labored. His fever is spiking. I get off of Evander, rushing over to one of the water buckets and soaking a new cloth. I hear Ben mutter something in an Ancient language. One that my mother used to know before her passing. The dialect sounds similar to the songs she used to sing to us. Eleanor responds in the same language. I have so many questions, but there will be a time and place for answers.

I wring out the cloth and walk back over to Ben, who has passed out again. I take the original towel, which is now warm, and replace it with the cooler one.

"I'm going to get a cot brought in for me." Evander groans, standing up slowly. He stretches his arms, allowing them to pop, before walking out.

Eleanor looks up at me with big eyes as I press a hand to her cheek, urging her off the cot so I can change Ben's bandages. After my mother died, I studied the art of healing. Then there was Demetrius, who expanded my knowledge. Not to the extreme, but I have learned enough to tend to someone until a healer arrives. If I knew the tricks I do now, I might have been able to save my mother.

I unwrap the bloody gauze and toss it into a laundry basket before grabbing fresh gauze, more ginseng, and chamomile. A strange combination, but if it is mixed with the spring waters of Vruica's waterfalls, it gains the magical ability to help drain any infection. I walk back to Ben, looking over his wound. When I first saw it, green puss dripped from the cut. I knew then that whatever hit him was covered in poison. It is a slow-acting one, by the looks of it, but I don't have enough knowledge to know what the enemy might have used. Gregory did, and his quick actions probably saved the boy's life. The wound itself has already stopped dripping puss, and the blood has finally clotted. We only have to ensure he makes it through the night.

I look down at Eleanor as I wrap up Ben's wound, her body sagging with stress and exhaustion. "I should grab us some lunch," I say, hoping to engage her.

Evander walks back in with a cot, placing it on the wall beside the door. I open my mouth to ask him what he would like to eat when someone slides into the doorway. General Niklaus. He doesn't even acknowledge that he hits the door face first before rounding on Evander.

"You said I could go?!" Niklaus yells. His icy blue eyes are blazing with anger and confusion. Evander's eyes narrow on his general, and Niklaus apologizes. "I am sorry, but, Commander, you are siding with Lyra? I thought I was essential to you?"

"You are essential, Nik," Evander says, standing straight and crossing his arms. I finish with Ben's bandage and walk over to the bucket of water to wash my hands. My focus is on the two men, but I turn to watch Eleanor as she crawls back onto the cot.

I walk to Evander and kiss his cheek. "I'll go get us some food."

He nods to me, and I exit the room. Their voices are a low hum as I turn the corner. The kitchen staff has a stack of sandwiches already prepared. I take three and smile my thanks to the cook before making my way back to the healing quarters. Niklaus and Evander's voices are a little louder when I return, and I catch the end of their conversation.

"Don't be such a woman. You can deal with a challenge." Evander's voice rings in my ears as I enter the room. My eyes narrow on my husband as I place Eleanor's sandwich on the table beside Ben's cot. Evander must feel my glare because he looks up, confusion filling his tired eyes. "What?"

"Not all women are stubborn, you know," I say with frost in my tone. Both men snort, and I frown at them. It is true. Not all women are stubborn, and if they are, it is because they are fighting for something important. Besides, men can be just as stubborn, if not more so. They just prefer not to admit it.

I narrow my eyes at both of them. I stuff the sandwich in my face, talking with my mouth full. "Well, I'm not sharing my food."

Evander protests, "Is that any way to treat your beloved husband?"

"If he is sassing me, then yes," I say, continuing to chew.

"Good luck." Niklaus shrugs, hitting Evander on the shoulder. He appears calmer now than when he first stormed in. Whatever my husband said to him seemed to work. The general walks out of the room, and I give into Evander's face as he makes his eyes all wide. I hold a slice of cheese out for him, and he grins. He takes a bite of the cheese from my hand, and I smile.

"I love you," I whisper.

"Oh?" he asks, raising a brow.

"I do," I say, kissing his forehead. He nips more cheese from my fingers, and I smile at him. "I have a few things I need to do today. Will you be able to handle Eleanor on your own?"

He frowns at me. "I just got home."

"I would ask you to come with me, but I think someone should be here in case he wakes up," I whisper, fixing his hair.

"Here I was, hoping to steal you for an hour or two...or three." His eyes go hooded, and I can't say no to that heated expression on his face.`

Looking over at Ben and Eleanor, I shift from foot to foot. Maybe I could steal him for an hour. If anything happens, Eleanor will be here. She will know who to grab, and I assume Gregory isn't that far away.

"Would you like to join me for a quick walk in the garden?" I ask him.

He holds his hand out for me, and I take it.

LXX

EVAN

ILIUM

KINGDOM OF CANDONIA

It's only been a week, but I'm craving her. She only has to hint, and I'm hard as steel. My wife giggles softly, the sound making me feel more at home. She takes my hands and looks back at Eleanor. "If anything changes, you come to find us, understand?"

Eleanor nods, holding tighter to Ben. "I understand."

I brush his hair back from his forehead, eyeing Eleanor's hold on the Boy. The closer they grow, the more it will break them when they are torn apart. It will be even sooner than him leaving for his quest. The North Wardens are deep in the mountains of Grimmwing, perched on the side of a cliff. The Boy won't be able to visit her, and she won't be able to leave.

I walk out of the room with Charlotte, my hand still locked in hers. She takes a deep inhale of the fresh air, and her smile is bright. "So, tell me about your trip. Was it successful?"

I grab her around the waist, lifting her and kissing her hard. "You don't really want to hear about my trip."

She shakes her head, locking her legs around my waist. "No. I want you."

I smirk against her lips, carrying her deeper into the gardens. I've never truly explored the immaculate area around the castle, and the hanging gardens of Ilium are rumored to be enchanted.

She wraps her arms around my neck, giggling. "Where are you taking me?"

I kiss her again, continuing along the paved path. "No idea."

She nips my lower lip and says, "I have a spot where we could be alone."

"Where?" I growl, my hands tightening on her as I resist the need to strip her out of her clothes.

She pulls back from my lips, pointing down a pathway practically overgrown with shrubbery. "If we continue down there, there is a hidden rose garden."

I follow her directions, keeping my lips locked on hers the entire time. I hold her tight against my body, refusing to let her down. When the pathway narrows, she points. "To the right." I turn, my hands finding the ties at the back of her dress, tearing at them. I am desperate to get her out of it, to be inside her, to know she's mine. She moans when my mouth finds her neck, and she tugs at my shirt. "We're here."

Fire licks through me as I let her slide down my body. I try to rip the ties holding her dress on, muttering, "These will be the death of me."

Charlotte laughs again, pulling my shirt over my head when I lean down. She tosses it to the side, her voice a low purr as she says, "I've missed you."

I frame her face with my hands. "Not as much as I missed you. It killed me to leave." I kiss her hard, forcing her mouth open, demanding access.

When I break the kiss, she blinks, covering my hands. "I wish you didn't have to leave again."

I hadn't given much thought to the implications of having to escort Eleanor to the North Wardens, but it meant another long trip away from home. I can think about that later. Finally getting the ties of her dress undone, I watch as it pools at her feet.

Impatiently, I turn her around, goosebumps forming on her skin. She smiles over her shoulder at me in nothing but her chemise. "Just you and me?"

"Just you and me." I slip her chemise off her shoulders.

I toe off my boots and toss them to the side before untying my breeches. I kiss the silky skin of Charlotte's shoulder, trailing my lips down her spine and nipping her ass lightly.

"Excuse me!" She jumps, turning to look down at me.

I smirk up at her and stand. Guiding her forward, closer to the nearest tree, I growl into her ear, "Hold on to the tree tight, Star."

She shivers, obeying. "Yes, my prince."

I tip her hips back and bend my knees. I press inside her slowly, my hands on her ass. "Fuck."

"Evander," she gasps.

"You're so tight." My hand stings as I smack her ass hard, pulling out at the same time.

"I was made for you." She whimpers, her fingers digging into the bark.

I lean back, so the angle allows me to hammer inside her, knowing the grip I have on her hips will leave bruises. "Yes, you were. All mine."

She spreads her legs more, allowing me to hit deeper. "All yours."

I need her more than I need to breathe. Even as I take her, I want to be closer, meld myself into her. I am never letting go. My spine tingles, and I grip her tighter. "I love you."

I can feel her leaning back, meeting my thrusts, and I know she's close. "I love you, too."

"Come for me."

She climaxes, robbing me of my control as she moans my name loudly. I shout as I come, hollowing myself out inside her. She collapses against the tree, closing her eyes and panting. I hiss as I slowly pull out of her and kiss down her back. "I missed you."

She looks back at me, her eyes hooded beneath dark lashes. "I missed you, too."

"We should get back." I sigh, looking around for our clothes. My legs are still shaking from the force of my release, and I wish we could stay here, just the two of us.

She nods, turning to face me, glancing at the garden. "It's so peaceful out here."

"I prefer our meadow by the lake."

"Oh? Not the alley?"

I can't help the wicked smirk that plays across my lips. "The meadow is sentimental."

"Is it because that is where you took me for the first time?" Charlotte presses closer to me, wrapping her arms around my neck.

"It is." I brush back an errant lock of hair from her face before disentangling from her. She picks up her chemise and slips into it. I find my breeches and yank them on, followed by my boots.

"It's strange to see how far we've come."

"Oh?" I ask, pulling on my shirt.

"Don't you remember our first meeting?" She looks around for her dress, stepping into the pool of material and pulling it up.

I wince. "I prefer not to."

Charlotte slips her arms into the gown. "That first night...you could have taken me. You could have left me in a tent on my own, surrounded by your men, but you didn't."

"I would never."

"But you could have. When you didn't take advantage of me, when you comforted me, that's when my opinion of you changed." She walks to me, holding her dress to her chest. "It gave me hope for our marriage."

I move around her to lace her dress. When I finish, she turns and places her hands on my chest. "What did you first think of me?"

"When you first walked down the aisle, I thought you were the most beautiful thing I had ever seen."

She smiles. "And when did you realize you cared for me?"

My brow furrows in thought. "A single moment?" She nods. "Our first night together."

"Really?" She draws a shape on my chest.

"You were so nervous, your hands shook. But you didn't run. When you cried into my chest, I hated the sound so much that I vowed not to be the cause of it again."

She goes to her tiptoes, kissing me passionately, her fingers tunneling into my hair. I laugh against her lips. "Star...we have to go back."

She shakes her head. "One more kiss."

I give her a quick peck on the lips. "Satisfied?"

She nods, releases me, and takes my hand. "Very."

Walking by her side, I pull her close and kiss her head. "What did I miss?"

She tenses ever so slightly. "Um...Lord Edmunde."

Prick.

She looks up at me, her smile and glow gone. "He asked me to run away with him."

I sway as if I just took a physical blow. "And you said?"

She faces me fully, taking my other hand. "I told him no. That I'm in love with you."

"And his response?" I can't imagine he took that well.

"He said his goodbyes," she mumbles something indecipherable, "then he left."

"What was that?"

She blushes. "He kissed me."

My jaw locks and a vein in my forehead threatens to burst.

"I'm sorry, I didn't want him to kiss me." She chews her bottom lip, dancing from foot to foot.

"Where is he?" I growl, pulling away from her, prepared to flay the man alive.

She grabs my arm. "I-I don't know."

I close my eyes, trying to get a handle on my jealous rage, even as it demands that I hunt and destroy. "Go inside. I need a moment to myself."

She releases me. "I'll be with the children."
The moment she is out of sight, I lose control.

LXXI

Charlotte

ILIUM

KINGDOM OF CANDONIA

It's strange how the good moments between Evander and I always end up ruined. Either by him leaving or some other miscommunication. In the end, I always feel that hole in my heart. Like there is a puzzle piece missing, and the only thing that will fix it is him. When did I become like this? When did I become so attached to another being? The only people I have ever depended on are my sisters and my father. Even then, I was perfectly fine being alone.

Is it wrong for me to want to spend a few days with my husband and not worry about the world? From the moment he left the first time, I have felt this shift inside me, and my need for him only grows by the day. In our time together, there hasn't been a week without something critical happening. Either he leaves, we argue, or something happens within the kingdom.

I take a seat on the cot, looking at Ben, who is still passed out. When I'd returned to the room, I'd convinced Eleanor to go clean up and feed herself. It was a bit of a struggle, but I don't blame her. If Evander was injured and unconscious, I wouldn't want to move either.

Demir has joined me in the room. He is sitting in the corner cleaning one of his swords, the metal already sparkling in the light. He is deep in thought and must be struggling with a few things. I don't know all the details of his relationship with Thalia, but I fear it won't end well for either of them. I have to restrain myself from asking more questions about his life and his intentions toward my sister. They are both stubborn, private people, and neither talk much about themselves or their struggles. Maybe when Ben is better, I can get Thalia to speak to me.

Another hour passes before I hear Evander enter the room. He looks calmer than when I left him in the garden, though there is still some tension in his shoulders. Demir senses Evander's frustration and quietly leaves the room.

"How is he?" Evander asks, glancing at me.

"He is well, and I managed to convince Eleanor to take a bath and eat. She should be back soon."

Evander lets out a long sigh and pulls a chair close. He opens his arms to me, and I quickly crawl into his embrace. His scent alone soothes the ache in my chest.

"You aren't mad at me?" I trail my fingers along his jaw.

He shakes his head, kissing the top of my head. A weight lifts from my shoulders, and I cuddle closer to him. We sit there in silence for a minute, and I listen to the steady sound of his breathing. It's a comforting sound. While he was gone, I dreamed of him almost every night, and in those dreams, there would be things missing. The warmth of his touch, the sound of his breath, and his scent all remind me that this isn't a dream, and he is truly here with me.

"I'm sorry I get jealous." He pulls me closer even as he says the words.

I kiss his chest before looking up at him. "It's fine, my love."

"It's not." He shakes his head. "I married you, and you're mine."

"I am yours," I reassure him. There were moments when he was away that I had anxieties over the same thing. What if he found another woman? What if all those sweet words he whispered to me were lies? But then he returns, and I feel our connection and those anxieties slip away.

Evander buries his face into the crook of my neck. "It's still hard sometimes."

"What is?" I ask, running my fingers through the soft gold of his hair.

"He's a lord." Evander pulls away from me and rests the back of his head against the wall.

"And?" I look up at his closed expression, wondering where he is going with this. Bloodline has never been an issue for me. It has mattered to the court and others, but never to me. I believe in love, in soulmates. If I were going to marry for status, I would have done it on my eighteenth birthday, as tradition states. But no, I waited. I waited for him.

"Nothing," Evander says, shaking his head. "Did Ben wake up?"

"No. He mumbles some things in his sleep, but that is it. His wound was clean when I changed the bandages. It appears he is on the mend," I say.

"Mumbles some things?" Evander asks, tilting his head.

I nod. "I couldn't understand what he was saying. It was the language you and my sister were speaking earlier. I am not familiar with it."

From the corner of my eye, I see Eleanor enter the room. She has changed out of her poofy dress and into a pair of brown breeches and a loose-fitted shirt. Her hair is tied back into a traditional Candonian braid, starting at the top of her head and weaving its way down. She crawls back onto the cot with Ben, cuddling up against him. Demir appears at the door, leaning against the wall and looking over at the kids.

"Little moon, you know he can't heal with you next to him," Evander says. Eleanor ignores him, keeping her body turned away from us. *She is going to put up a fight, and when Eleanor is determined, nothing stops her.* Evander blinks a few times. "Little moon—"

"How come you guys can stay in here, and I can't?" she asks, finally speaking up. "It's not fair."

422

"Because it's not proper." Evander rolls his eyes.

Many things that have happened the past few months haven't been proper.

Eleanor scoffs. "The Mountain visits Thalia in the middle of the night, and they are best friends."

Demir chokes, and I turn to look up at him. His face glows as red as a tomato, and I can't help but laugh into Evander's shoulder. Demir pushes himself off the door frame and walks away without another word.

"I want to stay here," Eleanor says as soon as he is gone.

"No." Evander shakes his head. "You can't sleep here."

"Evander." I sigh as Eleanor's tiny arms tighten around Ben in a silent protest.

"I will not repeat myself," he says, his eyes narrowing.

Eleanor sits up, her eyes glowing violet. "You are not my father! You are not in control of me!"

"I will get your father, and then you won't be able to see him at all," Evander snarls, his own eyes glowing at her. "Don't take advantage of my lenience."

As Eleanor's eyes return to their normal sea blue, they fill with tears.

"I hate you!" she screams, running from the room. I wince as her sobs echo down the hallway.

It is going to be a long night.

LXXII

EVAN

ILIUM

KINGDOM OF CANDONIA

I close my eyes and rest my head on the wall behind me, trying to relax. My wife sits up, and I can feel her eyes on me. "Evander."

I force my eyes open and look down at her. "Yes?"

Her eyes are stormy, and disappointment lines her features, but she didn't contradict me in front of her sister. "He is injured and not well. I think it is alright for her to be here until he wakes."

I narrow my eyes on her. "I won't have them forced into a marriage because they get caught in a compromising situation." My lips twitch slightly. "I'm saving that for our kids."

She frowns. "Excuse me?"

Her entire body stiffens against mine, her demeanor changing from disappointment to something far worse. My smile dies. "What?"

She shakes her head, her voice filled with horror. "We are not going to force our children into a marriage. They need the option to marry for love."

Like you forced me.

I stole her. How could I forget? I never earned her. I never asked her. She would change things, wouldn't she? Given a chance, she would go back and make it so we never married. I thought we were past this, that we could finally appreciate the love that is blossoming between us. I must be wrong. Her sapphire eyes, the ones I treasure and adore, are shimmering with determination. It is clear that she would not see our children in the same *situation* as us. She thinks I would do the same to them, doesn't she? She believes I will take that choice from our children because I took it from her. She is mine because I surrounded the city and stole her. I never earned her. She never chose me, and she wouldn't have. I thought we could appreciate what we have, no matter how it came to be. The way she speaks, it is as if such a fate is worse than death. It makes me ill.

"Like the option I never gave you." I shift her off my lap and slowly stand, shocked I am able to with the way I feel. The world tilts, yet I see no difference around me. How could I have forgotten? How could I have gotten so comfortable that I forgot how we began?

I stole her. She didn't choose me. Even if she could have, even if I stood in front of her and asked her to be mine, she would have said no. She would have chosen a thousand other men before she even considered me. I'm not noble, well-educated, elegant, or refined. I'm more comfortable sleeping on the ground under the stars than I am in the palace. No, she would have never picked me to be hers.

"Evander?" she calls, reaching out for me.

I won't look at her. I can't because if I do, I'll go back to forgetting. Those sapphire eyes will pull me in, and I'll forget how we began all over again. How I poisoned us from the start, no matter how we grow, no matter how much we love each other. I can't change the past, and somewhere, deep down, she will always hate me for it. How long until that hatred festers and grows inside her? A year? Two? Soon she'll be unable to look at me without seeing the man she wished she married. And I'll hate myself even more for not being him.

"You know, I've been deluding myself."

She reaches for my hand, but I pull away. If she touches me, I'll give in. I want her that much. I *need* her that much. But as much as I want to, I can't keep her. She doesn't belong to me. She never has. "What do you mean?"

"You will never forget that I forced you into this. That if you had a choice, you would never have chosen me." Saying the words aloud breaks me in such a way that I doubt I'll ever be whole again.

"That isn't true!" she protests, but it falls on deaf ears. She can insist all she wants, but I saw her reaction at my poor joke about our children. The way she recoiled. She may lie to herself and me, but she can't conceal her own response.

"You think I would put our children through this. And you said it as if it were a fate worse than death. I'm not your first choice or even your five-hundredth." I shake my head again, trying to keep my emotions in check, even as they fight to make a fool of me. They want me to beg, to forget, to take the scraps offered. It's not enough. I need more from her, and I'm never going to get it. "I'm going back to camp. When the Boy wakes up, I'll have him brought to me." Despite my best efforts, tears fill my eyes even as I bow deeply to her. "Your Highness."

I spin on my heel, leaving the healing quarters, but she runs after me. "Where are you going?"

I don't look back. I can't. The tear has fallen down my cheek, and so I continue forward, pretending not to hear. This is it. When I leave this palace, I will leave my heart behind. I can already feel the creeping numbness crawling over me, the void I used to embrace as a slave, to detach from the present. It's a survival tool, and I'll need it once I leave because everything in me, every inch of my body, is screaming at me not to go. My heart begs for me to forget and pretend like this is enough. But I swore once that I would never beg for scraps again, and I won't now. I can't. She grabs my arm, and pain clogs her voice as she says, "You'll come back, won't you?"

I pull out of her hold and walk out of the palace, refusing to look back.

LXXIII

Charlotte

OUTSIDE OF ILIUM

KINGDOM OF CANDONIA

It is pitch black by the time I arrive at Evander's camp. Our fight from earlier has left me unsettled. We have fought numerous times before, but something about this feels different. He called me *Your Highness,* not *lamb,* not *star,* not even Charlotte. He has never done that before. Not since the first day we met, and not even when extremely frustrated with me. Something is different. Even as he walked away, the tension in his shoulders seemed tighter than before. I have never seen him like this, not even the day we met.

Each step closer to our tent has my stomach twisting, and my thoughts are in turmoil. *What if he is done with me? Will he leave me?* After everything we have been through so far? All the challenges. He wouldn't just go. He couldn't. Then again, he was beyond upset earlier. It seems as if he is struggling with the idea that he wouldn't be my first choice, and there is some truth to his fears. It had never occurred to me to think of Evan the Black as a suitable choice of husband. He was our enemy, *my* enemy. The rumors that circulated around Evander were the only sources of information I had on him. They had me hating him with a passion, but then I got to know him. I saw the man he is, the man he wants to be, and I fell in love.

Now, I am worried I'm losing him because he believes I would never choose him. I wouldn't have chosen anyone. If there were someone else, I would have married them by now. I didn't know I was waiting for Evander, but now he is my only choice.

Rain pours from the sky as I open the tent flap. Evander is sitting at his desk, his head low as he focuses on his writing. The tent feels heavy with tension, and his back still looks stiff. I wring my hands together, my throat closing.

"E-Evander?" I say, able to hear the fear in my voice.

His back snaps straight, but he doesn't look at me. "Your Highness."

My stomach twists again, and I squeeze my eyes shut. "W-why are you calling me that?"

"Can I help you?" he asks, going back to writing. *Strangers.* We have gone back to being complete strangers. No, that isn't right. We started as enemies, but even in that, there was passion. We have never been cold like this, and we were never truly strangers. This hurts, and I don't like it.

"You n-never came back." I choke back a sob as I walk to his desk.

"Is there a question in there?" he asks, his tone frigid. His eyes finally connect with mine, and all I see is a dark grey storm. There is none of the warmth or love that softens his eyes when he looks at me. They are dead. My heart stings as if a thousand needles are poking me over and over again.

"I-I..." I sniffle. "What's going on?"

"I'm giving you what you want," he says, holding out the letter. "A choice."

I frown and open the letter. I quickly scan it, a tear rolling down my cheek and onto the piece of paper. His handwriting is messy, but all the words are spelled correctly. I have to read it a few times to ensure I am understanding it right.

"A petition for annulment?" I choke out. My hand goes to my mouth as more tears stream down my face. "E-Evander?"

"Goodbye, princess," he says, turning his back on me. I reach my hand out to touch his back, but stop. I am not sure I can take it if he rejects my touch again. My heart feels shattered, broken in two, and pieces of it permanently destroyed by this letter. The tent walls close in on me, and I can't breathe.

I can't breathe.

I back away from him and stumble out of the tent, gasping for air. The rain is pouring from the sky, soaking my hair and cloak. I tuck the petition into the front of my dress before I run toward the palace. The city streets are empty, and the lanterns light my path as I weave through the market. I can't stop crying, my tears mixing with the rain.

I lose my footing on the steps leading to the palace door, bashing my knees on the slick marble. I don't feel the pain in my legs or hands. The ache in my heart is an overwhelming agony that I have never felt before. It is like someone reached into my chest and ripped it out, squeezing it until it turned to dust.

I carefully get to my feet and stumble up the remaining steps, pushing the grand doors to the palace open. Luckily, the main hall is empty. I have never lost my composure in front of my people. I have been trained to always look proper and hide all of my feelings. Tonight, I do not care. I am broken.

My sobs are quiet as I tiptoe up the stairs to my room. Water drips from my gown, leaving a trail behind me. I hear a door open, but I don't turn around, unable to face anyone.

"Charlotte?" Thalia's voice echoes behind me.

Don't stop. Don't look.

I keep walking, crossing my arms over my chest. Numbness settles into my body, and I realize I'm shivering, though I don't feel cold.

"Charlotte?" Thalia grabs the back of my dress.

"Yes?" I whisper, my tone flat.

"Why are you soaked? Where is Evan?" she asks, not letting me go. I remain silent, my gaze focused on the carpet. I will lose it if I face her, but I know she won't let me walk away without an explanation. "Charlotte?"

I sigh, and my sister moves around me, placing her hands on my face and lifting my gaze to hers. I feel nothing as she rubs her thumbs on my cheeks, trying to warm me from the cold.

"What happened? Who hurt you?" she demands, her eyes glowing in the dark.

Looking around, I take my sister's hand and lead her to my room. As soon as I close the door, I break down and collapse to my knees. She drops beside me, wrapping her arms around my shoulders. My cries are ugly as I let my emotions go. Thalia helps me from the ground, brushing my hair from my face.

"I'm here. I'm here." Thalia walks me into my bathing room. I stand there shivering as she leaves, returning with hot water. No maids follow her as she works to fill my tub. Thalia helps me from my dress as I cry, placing the letter that I'd hidden in my gown on my desk. She leaves the bathroom as I warm myself in the bath. The pain grows more intense as the water brings life to my body. I prefer the numbness and the cold.

I don't know how long I stay there, but my fingers and toes are pruned when Thalia returns. My sister has changed into her nightgown, her hair tied back into a braid and her golden eyes shimmering with her own tears. My duty as the eldest is to be strong for my sisters, and they have never seen me cry like this before. I never wanted them to.

Thalia gives me a sad smile before helping me from the tub. She wraps a warm towel around me, kissing my forehead before leading me into the bedroom to dress. I manage to put on my nightgown before breaking down once more. My knees hit the ground, and I cover my eyes as my sobs echo in the room. Thalia loops her arm around my back and leads me to the bed. She stays silent the entire time, not asking questions as she tucks me in. I curl up into a ball as my sister lies beside me. She wraps her arms around me, resting her cheek against my head.

"It's alright, Charlotte. We will figure this all out."

LXXIV

EVAN

ILIUM

KINGDOM OF CANDONIA

I'm numb.

My mind has retreated to the haven that I once used to survive my life as a slave. I am detached, cold, and unfeeling. It was a tool I'd used for survival and one I never thought I'd need again. Yet, here I am, falling back on it in order to follow my own routine. I calmly walk to the palace, my eyes trailing sightlessly over the steps to the entryway. I am moving by rote, not hearing the sounds of my boots or the Black in the courtyard, nickering for me to return.

I'm gone.

She would never have chosen me. Now, she won't have to stay in a marriage with me. She can file the petition with the church and be free. She'll announce my origins to do so, and then I'll know we are done. There will be no coming back from that. No reconciliation. Nothing. I'll be without her. Forever.

But she'll be free. She can choose who she wants to be with, even if it will never be me. She needs to be free to make her choice without my influence, which means I'll be taking the Boy back to camp. I don't need to be in the palace while she is deciding. I'll make a tactical retreat to my camp and continue feeling vacant.

I hear the Boy and Eleanor arguing the moment I step into the hallway. I haven't slept in two days, and I can't eat or train, feeling hollowed out from the inside. There has to be a way to fix that. I have to find a way to survive without my heart and still function. Right now, it seems impossible.

"I had to do something!" The little princess shouts, and I can already imagine her pale hair flying, her hands clenched tightly in anger.

"I don't like you doing stuff like that for me," my squire insists. He is finally awake. He's been in and out of consciousness for a while, and it's good to hear his voice. Though it does nothing to infringe on my numbness, nothing to warm the cold.

"You're my best friend! I can't let you die on me!" she insists.

I pause in the doorway, surveying the state of the room. There's a broken bowl and the remains of soup on the ground. The Boy is finally sitting up, the little princess at his side. Their fight is consuming them, neither even looking up as I enter the room.

He scoffs and swings his legs to the side of the bed. "I would have been fine! It's just a scratch."

"I'm taking you back to camp, Boy," I announce coldly. This argument would have gone on for days if I hadn't interjected. The Boy pales, his eyes swinging to me. "And we'll talk about what exactly a *scratch* is."

Eleanor tears up as she gazes at me. She jumps to her feet, trying to stand between my squire and me. "B-But he isn't fully healed! He has to stay here!"

I move forward, holding my hand out to the Boy. He takes it immediately, allowing me to help him to his feet. "We have healers in camp."

And I don't want to be in the palace, not when I know she's here somewhere. Not when she hasn't made her choice. Not when I know if I see her it might crack the detachment I'm

432

sheltered in. She's always found her way inside me, past my every defense and wall, breaking through as only she can.

Eleanor's breath comes faster and faster as she tries to come up with a reason for me to let the Boy stay. She stutters out, "B-But...but..."

Eleanor's eyes flicker, and her hair glows, signaling that her control over her volatile powers is slipping. She needs to head north as soon as possible, but for now, I ask, "Would you like to come visit him there?"

The tension in the room eases, and her eyes return to their normal blue. Eleanor nods, wiping at her tears. "Yes."

"He won't be far, little moon." I wrap my arm around the Boy, supporting his weight, and glance back at Eleanor. "Would you like to come with us to help settle him in?"

She nods again, coming to my side and taking my free hand. "I'm sorry for yesterday."

I smile down at her, moving with the pair of them. "I will always do what's best for the Boy and you, little moon." My hand tightens on hers. "No matter what happens between..."

She tilts her head at me. "Between what?"

I shake my head, continuing to support my squire as we depart the palace. "It's nothing."

She squeezes my hand again. "Where is Charlotte?"

I hate that I want to turn back and find her in the palace. Was she already planning her next marriage to the man she gets to choose? "I don't know, little moon."

She pauses at the base of the steps, looking back up at the palace, before looking back at me. "I'm happy you're here. Charlie always seemed sad when she was alone."

I don't know what to say to her, and I can't look at her. I stop at the Black and carefully lift my squire onto his back. Ben is pale and gritting his teeth, holding back a hiss of pain. I steady him before holding my hands out for the little princess. She frowns and grips my forearms, allowing me to settle her behind the Boy. "You'll stabilize him?"

She nods, wrapping her arms around his torso. "Yes, Commander."

I mount behind the small pair, kicking the Black's sides and heading for camp. My heart is still inside the walls of the palace, beating for the wife I might never see again.

LXXV

Charlotte

ILIUM

KINGDOM OF CANDONIA

It has been five days since I last saw Evander, and I am not doing well. I haven't been able to get out of bed, and I have barely eaten. Thalia has told the maids not to tend to me. Instead, to save me from gossip, she spends the mornings with me, making sure I have some breakfast and getting me to walk around the room. Then she returns at night to brush my hair, feed me again, and help me bathe. I hate feeling so weak, but I can't do much about it. My heart is broken. I have never felt this much pain and emptiness before. I want to curl up into a ball and stop existing until I am healed. But I am afraid that without him, I will never be better.

Thalia informed me a few days ago that Ben was awake, and Evander had taken him and Eleanor to camp. I am surprised. If he wants nothing to do with me anymore, why care for my little sister? I curl into a tighter ball on my bed. First, I've lost him, and I assume he will take Eleanor to the North Wardens soon. My world continues to change by the day, and I wish it would stop.

I pull the blankets up to my trembling lips, tears rolling down my face as I stare at the stack of unopened letters on my desk. The one on the top is special. It is to tell me the location of someone dear to Evander, but I can't find the will to open it. I haven't found the will to do anything other than stay in my bed and cry.

There is a soft knock at the door, and I debate on whether I will ignore it. Then again, I have hidden long enough. I wrap my robe tightly around my figure and make my way slowly to the door, opening it a crack. Ben is standing outside, looking down at his feet. A spark of warmth pierces the fog of pain. Knowing the boy is alright and on his feet makes me feel a little better. I don't know what we would do without him. I don't know what Eleanor would do without him.

"Ben," I whisper, my voice raspy from my sobs, "how are you feeling?"

"Better now," he says. "But I wanted you to know that Evan is, um...gone."

My world shatters. My room becomes smaller, tightening around me, and my breathing is shaky. I grip my chest as everything around me becomes dark.

"F-For good?" I stutter.

"No!" Ben exclaims, shaking his head. "No, he took Eleanor."

My free hand grips the door, and I look down at the ground. I was so closed off that I hadn't realized when Eleanor came to visit me the other day that it was her last at the palace.

"She visited me the other day. I didn't think..." I whisper, my throat closing as tears roll down my face. Ben coughs awkwardly before patting my shoulder. It only causes me to break down more, sobbing between breaths. "I-I don't know w-what to do, Ben."

Ben winces. "About the Commander?"

My body shakes with the soul-wrenching sobs, and I nod. "I'm s-sorry, Ben. I-I..."

The boy looks at me for a second before pulling me into a hug. He holds me against his gangly body as I cry and try to catch my breath.

"I don't want to lose him," I finally say.

Ben rubs my back comfortingly. "You can't. He loves you."

"Then why is he pushing me away?" I whisper.

"I don't know," Ben says, shaking his head. "I don't know."

"I need to get him back," I say, looking up at Ben and trying to pull myself together. "Come in."

"Alright." Ben's brow furrows and he steps into my room, closing the door.

I walk to my desk, rifling through my paperwork. Over the past few days, the papers have been piling up, but I have had no motivation to go through them. Thalia has been helping me with my duties, and luckily my father hasn't pushed me by trying to figure out what is wrong. I am blessed to have a family that is supportive and understanding. I pull out the annulment Evander wrote and clasp it in my hands.

"Evander gave me a choice," I say. "To annul our marriage or keep it. I have been trying to figure out why he would do this. I thought he loved me." It has been the only thing on my mind. I have been trying to understand what Evander truly wants. Does he truly love me? Even Ben looks confused by my husband's actions.

"Well, do you want an annulment?" Ben asks, blinking at me.

I shake my head. "Of course not! Yet, I know Evander. This will continue to bother him for the rest of our lives."

The choice. The thing he stole from me. It doesn't bother me anymore. I am glad that he stole me and that we fell in love. If he hadn't done that, then I wouldn't have found my soulmate. But he thinks I would never choose him in a million years. I need to prove him wrong.

"He always told me he wanted me to have a choice. That most of his life he didn't have a choice," Ben says, looking away.

I chew my bottom lip. "Evander is a wonderful man. I do choose him, but I'm afraid he may never truly believe it."

"Maybe you need to show him." Ben shrugs.

"You're right." I frown, thinking for a moment. It would need to be a grand gesture in front of everyone, something to show him that I do not regret my choice. It can't be done behind closed doors, or this issue may arise again in the future. I don't want this to be on the back of his mind anymore. But how to implement it? How to show him? I look at the desk and spot the letter I have been dreading opening. An idea sparks in my mind.

"I am?" Ben frowns.

"Yes, you are," I say, picking up the letter. I close my eyes. "I have an idea, but I need you and the Mountain to help me."

Ben blinks again. "Of course."

I push the overwhelming feeling of anxiety from my mind and open the envelope. Although Evander told me not to, I have been searching for his parents. I'd written the letter as if I was searching for a guard family. That way, no one would know the truth of his origins.

Everywhere I'd made inquiries had turned up empty. It was beyond frustrating, and I'd started to lose hope until I received a message from a duke in Ciral. Something about his response seemed different, and I'd been waiting for the right time to open it. I unfold the neatly written letter, a smile tugging at my lips as I scan the words. Excitement fills me, and I give Ben a bright smile.

"There are two things we must do," I say.

"Is this going to get me into trouble?" Ben asks, blinking a few times.

I shake my head. "Any order from me is like an order from Evander, correct?"

"Yes." The boy gulps.

I smile softly at him, the pain in my heart easing a bit. "Then if anyone is getting into trouble, it shall be me."

"Then I am at your disposal." Ben sighs.

My eyes light up, and I look back down at the letter, my fingers trailing over the words. "Do you know the village Tarrin in Ciral?"

He nods. "Vaguely."

"Evander's parents are there." I chew my bottom lip, my brain ticking with ideas. The villages there are still overrun by slavers. I don't think Evander's men had a chance to conquer that section of Ciral yet. The kingdom is southeast of us and wouldn't have been on Evander's path to Ilium. That is why he hasn't found them yet. Now is our chance to get them back for him.

"His parents?" Ben sputters. "He has actual parents?!"

I nod. "He didn't want me to find them because if people find out his origins, then they will annul our marriage."

"And?" Ben blinks in confusion. "I thought you didn't want an annulment."

"I don't, but I don't want Evander to have to hide who he is," I say, shaking my head. If I show him and the world that I can love him for who he is, then the doubt in the back of his mind about who I would choose will fade. Besides, there are loopholes, and I think my plan will work as long as Evander still wants me at the end of this.

"But, if they know?" Ben frowns.

I give him a small smile. "Well, I can marry a duke."

"Should I even ask?" Ben says.

"You'll find out soon enough," I say, shaking my head. "I need the Mountain and the rest of Evander's army to invade the village of Tarrin and free the slaves there. Then I need you to send some runners to the Lords and Ladies of Candonia and neighboring kingdoms to come for an event in a month's time."

Ben nods. "Are you sure about this?"

"I am very sure," I say, nodding.

Ben gulps. "I'll let the Mountain know on my way out."

I nod at the boy, and he exits the room. *It is time to get my husband back.*

LXXVI

EVAN

THE NORTH WARDENS

KINGDOM OF GRIMMWING

I slow the Black on the treacherous mountainside. The edge of the trail crumbles, the rocks falling into the crashing sea below. I forgot how out of the way the sanctuary is. It has been years since I stumbled upon it. The only path cuts into the side of the cliff, its entrance hidden from all but those who know where to look. The waves crash against the rocky shore far below us, and looking at the plummet from the path to the sea makes any man green. The trail wraps around the mountain, making it appear that we are heading nowhere, nowhere but into Visha's embrace.

Eleanor sits in front of me on the Black. She is wrapped in my lined cloak, with her face burrowed against my chest. I'm not sure if she's frightened of the drop or merely asleep. Either way, her clinging to me sends a pang of regret through my body. I'll never cradle my children like this. I'll never experience this again. When I go home, or rather, back to Ilium, I'll be returning to a wife who doesn't want me. I gave her a choice, and deep down, I know she's going to realize what a blessing it is to be free of me.

We make the final turn around the cliff, and the plateau flattens out, revealing the North Wardens. The sanctuary is ancient, rumored to have been built almost a millennium prior.

Four towers spiral up to pierce the sky, each of them glowing slightly with magic. They are interconnected by closed hallways and rooms surround the center. From each tower, an arch hovers over the middle of the courtyard, the four joining to form the astronomy tower. It appears to hang suspended high above. Trotting forward, we ride through the arched entrance. The runes and spells of the warding glow as we pass.

Snow falls lightly to the left. In the center of the courtyard, the sun shines warmly. One part of the monastery has trees falling, and the other has them blooming. All four seasons occur at once. It is a magnificent sight, and an air of magic and wonder surrounds us.

Eleanor shivers against me and peeks her head out from under the long fur cloak wrapped around us both. Her silver hair is tangled and matted on one side. "Is this it?!" she asks, excitement filling her voice. She sits up, rubbing her eyes and scanning her surroundings. I tighten my arms around her when she nearly topples off the Black as she tries to look at the astronomy tower above us.

I nod at her. "Welcome to the North Wardens, princess."

The sun continues to shine brightly while the snow remains outside the walls, except for the winter tower, which retains a light dusting. I dismount and hold my hands up for Eleanor. My men slide off their horses, their mouths gaping.

Eleanor takes my hands, looking around in astonishment, her eyes wide. The main doors open, drawing our attention away from our surroundings to the four nuns hovering in the hallway. Though their habits vary, each wears a dark color that indicates which Ancient has touched them. Their sleeves are embroidered with their various specialties. The mother superior steps forward, looking me over. Her sleeves are covered with symbols of all the Ancients, but she wears the color of Kalliste, Ancient of Magick and Beauty.

"Welcome, Commander," she calls.

I give her a short bow. "I bring you a student, mother."

She smiles at Eleanor, her eyes softening. "Another hoping to be welcomed into our order?"

I shake my head as she glides closer, tightening my hand on Eleanor's. "You misunderstand, mother. I bring you a *student*."

She pauses, looking at me, then back down at Eleanor. Her brown eyes shimmer and her dark skin pales as she comes closer. She stops a foot away from us, dropping to her knees in front of the little princess, her eyes filling with wonder. "This...this is impossible."

Eleanor presses closer against my side. I wrap my hand around her back, sheltering her. "Evan said you'd be able to help me."

The mother superior cries, crystalline drops falling heedlessly from her face. She inspects Eleanor, her hands shaking. "Is it true, child? Are you a high sorceress?"

Eleanor nods, hesitantly stepping closer. "Yes. It is."

The mother superior cries more. "I have trained for this day my whole life."

Eleanor eases her hold on me, moving away from my side. "Does this mean I won't be alone anymore?"

The mother superior smiles even brighter through her tears, trying to get a hold of herself. "Never again, little one."

Eleanor's smile is brilliant as she looks up at me. "Did you hear that?! I'll never be alone again!" The mother superior stands, offering her hand to Eleanor. The little princess accepts, and the nun turns to lead us into the sanctuary. Sadness touches Eleanor's voice as she says, "I'll miss you and Ben and the Mountain and my sisters."

"We can all visit." So long as I guide them, anyone can find the North Wardens and visit her. I have no intention of just abandoning her to a group of strangers. I won't leave a child to that fate, no matter what happens between her sister and me.

"Really?"

"Of course," I say.

The mother superior frowns at me over Eleanor's head. "Your men and guests are welcome here, but you know the rules."

442

I nod. "Yes, out by sunrise."

An ancient warding prevents those who aren't members of the sanctuary from remaining longer than twenty-four hours.

The little princess looks back and forth between us before whispering, "Can you stay with me?"

I lean down, whispering back, "For the night."

She nods, squeezing my hand again. "Have you been here before?"

The mother superior answers for me, "The Commander is sensitive to the Old Ways, but he has yet to take his holy orders."

I can't help the laugh that comes at the idea of me taking orders. "A life of celibacy and non-violence would never suit me."

Eleanor blinks up at me. "Does that mean that Benji will have to take orders?"

The mother superior frowns. "Benji?"

"My squire." I glance at Eleanor. "Only if he wants to, and I doubt you would want him to."

"I wouldn't?" she asks.

"He could never marry," I say, sending a victorious look at the mother superior when she scrunches her nose.

"Who is he? Your squire?" she asks, and I open my mouth to respond, but Eleanor beats me to it.

"Benjamin Wolfsbane of Ghynts, he's going to be my knight."

The mother superior gasps loudly. "A Wolfsbane? You know a Wolfsbane? A Wolfsbane built the sanctuary. They founded our order! He belongs here! Not as a squire!"

My eyes narrow on her. "That is not your call or mine. When the Boy is of age, he will make his own decisions."

The mother superior glares at me. We fight a silent battle over Eleanor's head that Eleanor interrupts when she yanks my hand. "I want to see the whole place!"

The following day, I am rubbing down the Black as the rest of my men prepare for the trek back. The sun will rise any minute, and we need to head home...not *home*, Ilium. I don't have a home anymore. I hear the frantic footfalls as someone approaches, and Eleanor shouts, "Wait!"

I turn with a smile. Eleanor has sprinted down in her nightgown, her big eyes sparkling with excitement and a twinge of fear. "Hello, little moon."

Eleanor doesn't stop her headlong race. She collides with me, wrapping her arms around my waist. "Thank you."

I pick her up, hold her tight, and whisper, "You know, no matter what happens between your sister and me, I will always protect you."

Eleanor pulls away, her eyes shimmering with tears. "You promise?"

I nod solemnly. "I promise, little moon."

She whispers to me, "Don't give up on my sister, alright? Who will look out for her if I'm not there?"

I gently put her back on the ground. "She will always have someone."

She pouts, shaking her head. "But you are her special someone."

I clear my throat softly. "Not for much longer, but don't worry about that right now, little moon. You have magic to learn."

She hugs me tight again. "I love you, Brother."

I gently tug a lock of her hair. "Behave, or I'll have to bring your father to visit."

She nods, looking up at me as I straighten. "I will! Tell Benji he has to come to see me too, please?"

"Of course, we should be back in a few months."

She releases me completely, stepping away so I can mount the Black. "I will see you all then!"

I smile down at her. "Learn everything you can."

"I will!"

444

I smile one last time before turning the Black away. My smile drops the second I leave her gaze, knowing I'm going home to nothing.

LXXVII

Charlotte

ILIUM

KINGDOM OF CANDONIA

Evander arrives home today. My stomach twists and turns as I pace the grand hall, waiting for him to walk through the front doors. I have been planning for this day for a month. My anxieties grew with each passing day, and I have no idea how he will react to this plan of mine. Will he hate me forever? Is this going to be the last straw for him? I place a hand on my stomach, trying to settle the nausea that has taken over.

Ben has fully recovered from his injuries and left the palace yesterday to meet Evander. I told Ben that he is to bring Evander straight to the castle as soon as they return, so I can give him my answer. An answer I hope he will accept. I hold my breath, counting to ten before releasing it, repeating the action over and over. My hands are shaking from the nerves that are bubbling in my stomach.

Behind me are the doors to the grand hall where the lords and ladies wait. Not only am I going to be giving a speech in front of Evander, but I will be doing it before all of Candonia. I pray it goes the way I have been dreaming.

The front doors of the palace open, and I see Evander along with Ben. His face is paler, dull, and lifeless. I can see dark circles around his eyes, and his blonde hair looks a little longer than usual and a tad messy. To my surprise, he is wearing the formal Candonian attire I had custom-made for him two months ago. I look at Ben beside him and know that it was the boy's doing. Thalia, Demir, and Ben know bits and pieces of my plan. Only I know the whole thing.

I clutch the annulment in my hands, picking at the sides of it. I want to rip it in two, jump into Evander's arms, and repeatedly tell him how much I love him. But I can't. Not yet. First, I need to do this.

The doors behind me open, and everyone in the ballroom goes quiet, their attention falling on Evander and me. My husband blinks at them, hurt shining in his eyes.

"What are these people doing here?" he asks, his voice dull.

"They are here to witness my choice," I say, raising my chin. *Keep it together, Charlotte. You can do this.*

Evander's jaw tightens, and I realize he doesn't know what is about to happen. "This seems unnecessary. You could have just filed the papers with the church."

I shake my head and raise my voice, so the words ring clearly for all to hear. "I choose you, Evander."

The words shake him, and he blinks his brilliant steel-grey eyes at me. A glimmer of hope shines in them as his features come back to life. "You...what?"

"I choose you," I say, biting my bottom lip. I glance down at the papers and let out a long breath. This is it, the moment I have been waiting for. I look up at Evander and smile. "When I first met you, I hated you. I believed the rumors that you were a filthy barbarian who stole from others. But on the night of our wedding, you showed me a different side of you. A kind and caring side that few people see. You continued to show me who you are as a person, and I fell in love with every part of you."

I open and close my mouth, gathering the courage to speak the next part. My hands tremble as I fiddle with the annulment in my hands, and I let out a breath. "The day you told me you were sold as a slave in my city, I was ashamed. Not because I married a former slave, but I was ashamed of myself and my ancestors for allowing slavery to happen. No one should ever have to go through that. No one should ever have to be separated from those they love and treated like animals. We are all so much more than that."

Looking up at him, I give him a small smile. "I am so proud of how far you've come, Evander. You never fail to surprise me. You are one of the most determined people I know, and when you love, you love with your whole heart. Your smile and your laugh never cease to warm my heart. Now, I know that by admitting your origins to all of Candonia, our marriage is not recognized by the church. That is why I am announcing you as Duke of the new city, Oploria. The city of your people and where they can live in peace and prosperity. All thanks to your determination and bravery."

Tears fill my eyes, and I choke up as emotions overcome me. "And if you'll have me, I'd be honored to marry you again."

Evander blinks at me, his eyes glistening with unshed tears. He is silent for a few minutes, and my lungs start to close up. Will he accept me? Will he continue to love me?

"You," he clears his throat, "you're choosing me? In front of everyone?" Evander chokes out.

I nod again, allowing the tears to flow down my face. "I choose you. Every part of you."

"You want to marry me? Even though you don't have to?" he asks, still in disbelief.

"I do," I whisper, nodding again. Looking down at the annulment, I rip it into small pieces before allowing it to flutter to the ground. Evander watches the papers fall before looking back up at me. He holds his hand out, like the day of our wedding. I was foolish not to take it then, but I know better now. My heartbeat settles as I entwine my fingers with his and step forward. "I love you, Evander. I always will."

He lifts his free hand to my cheek. "I love you, too."

I press my lips to his, the warmth of him bringing my entire body to life. Just like that, the numbness and icy ache in my heart are gone. I can feel again. The crowd erupts in cheers as he wraps his arms around my back and lifts me into the air. His kisses are warm, soft, and passionate. Love. That is all I feel for this man. Evander pulls away from me, smiling brightly. I have never seen him smile with such happiness before, and it fills me with joy.

Evander turns and waves at the crowd. I rest my forehead on his and smile. There is still one more surprise I have in store for him, but this moment is everything I need. His smile, his touch, his joy, it is all I needed to jump-start my heart and feel genuinely happy.

I chose you, Evander. I always will.

LXXVIII

EVAN

ILIUM

KINGDOM OF CANDONIA

I broke the chains which held me prisoner at sixteen. I thought I was free then, but I was wrong. Oh, so wrong. No, those chains followed me, binding my hands and feet. I hadn't understood then, but I do now. I put those chains on myself.

She chose me in front of everyone. Without coercion or threats, without an army circling her home. There is no reason for her to pick me, to claim me publicly. The world now knows my history, and she still chose me. The slave. Her husband. Her prince. It's hard not to cry from the emotions battering me. I'm overwhelmed that she didn't do this in secret, just the two of us. Charlotte paraded her choice in front of all the nobles of Candonia. She wanted there to be no question that given a choice, she still would have chosen me. She presses her forehead to mine. "I have one more surprise for you."

My laugh is shaky as I put her on her feet. "I don't know if I can take another."

She smiles at me and shifts to the side. "You'll like this one."

An older couple steps out of the crowd, their eyes on me. A memory tugs at me as I focus on the man and woman. They look familiar, but I can't place them. The man seems worn, his skin is tan even under his well-kept beard, and I can tell he wants to pull at the formal clothes he's wearing. I meet the woman's eyes. They are a clear grey and so familiar that my body freezes with revelation. *Crashing seas and storms, ice and hail, fishing from the cliffs, the smell of sea brine, coarse sheets against my skin. My mother's hugs, my father's boisterous laugh that shook his entire body.*

She walks closer to me, reaching up to touch my cheek. Her grey eyes mist, welling with tears. Her face, a deep bronze, like Kian's. No doubt her parents hailed from Steodia. *Connections and histories I never considered. Lineage and heritage are nothing when you live as a slave. But everything is different now.* Her accent is thick with emotions, but I have no trouble understanding her. "You've grown so much."

I blink, looking at the pair. "Ma? Da?" I continue blinking, trying to hold back the tears. So I do what I'll always do when I'm lost, I look for my wife. I glance at Charlotte, holding my hand out to her. "This is my wife."

My Da nods and his smile shines through his beard. His own eyes are misty. "We know, Son. She found us."

I laugh waterily, shaking my head. I need to explain, but I don't have the mental capacity to do so. "This... She chose me. She chose me." I kiss her head. "She chose me."

Has any man ever deserved her? She chose me. She found my parents, and I will spend every day of my life trying to be the man she needs. "I chose you." She looks up at me with such love that I can't help but believe her.

My ma pulls me into a tight hug, even though I don't let go of my wife's hand. I need the mooring, the anchor. My ma chokes on her words. "We are so proud of you."

My Da places a hand on my shoulder, and the tears of happiness finally break free. Once, I remember him being as tall as a mountain. Now he's a couple of inches shorter than me, but his voice is exactly as I remembered, coarse and rough. "We thought of you every day."

"You've grown so tall," my ma says, looking up at me.

My eyes flicker between them. "I thought you died."

The last time I saw them, they were being dragged away. I knew that older slaves were less likely to survive. My Da clears his throat and says, "Your wife sent for us. She helped free us."

"Freed?" I look down at Charlotte, frowning.

"Your handsome friend came to the village and helped free us all." My ma smiles softly, blushing slightly. If her hands were free, I think she might fan herself.

Handsome friend? "Kian?"

My Da rolls his eyes, sending a look at my ma. "The big, silent one."

I gape at them. "The Mountain!?"

My ma nods. "And the cute little lad."

My eyes narrow, and I look over my shoulder at my squire. "Boy! You knew about this?"

He pales and then vanishes without answering, leaving nothing but a vague outline of where he once stood.

My ma reaches up and grabs my ear in a punishing grip and Charlotte giggles. "Be nice to him."

I bat her hand away. "You still have hands like a vice, Ma." I rub my ear, glaring at my wife. "I'll remember you laughing at that, lassie."

She bites her bottom lip. "Will you?"

My ma pinches my cheek. "You be nice to her, too. She is a keeper."

I gently knock her hand away. "Ma! Stop! I'm a grown man now."

She pinches both of my cheeks before I can stop her. "You are still my wee lad. Do you remember the one time you were running around with nothing but a pot on your head?"

My ears turn red.

"Margaret, you're embarrassing the lad," my Da admonishes her.

"Ma!" I add before kissing both her cheeks. "I'm happy you're here, but I will have you tried for treason if you continue with these stories."

She scoffs at me before looking at my wife. "I will tell you more of those stories later, lassie."

Charlotte giggles again, looking up at me. My ears only burn hotter. I sigh and say to my parents, "I'll speak with you both later. I want my wife to myself for a moment."

They give us knowing looks before walking away to speak with the king. Charlotte gazes up at me. "Yes?"

I take one of her hands, moving it to cover my heart so she can feel it racing against her palm. "You did all this for me?"

She nods. "I didn't want there to be any more doubts. You are the only one for me, Evander."

"I can't believe you did this." I doubt I'll ever believe it. Likely I'll wake up tomorrow with a racing heart, convinced I'm alone, and she wants nothing to do with me. I'll just have to hold her until the fear dies.

She wraps her arms around my neck. "I love you."

I pull her close. "I love you, too," I smirk down at her, "Mrs. Black."

EPILOGUE

Charlotte

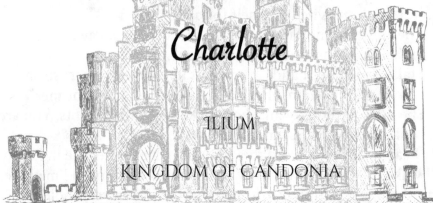

ILIUM

KINGDOM OF CANDONIA

It has been two months since my declaration of love for Evander, and things are finally settling down in the Kingdom of Candonia. Evander and I were remarried a month ago. A little last minute, but we did it the traditional way. He insisted it be that way. Since then, we have not spent a day apart. We have moved into the palace with the rest of the family. It has taken a bit of time to get used to, but I like this new life. Evander has been helping the villagers and his men settle into Ilium and Oploria. Oploria still has a long way to go until it becomes a large city, but everyone there appears content and happy to be getting their second chance at life.

We have reunited more families throughout the months, and our people couldn't be happier. Candonia is prospering more than ever, and Evander doesn't know this, but I believe he will make a wonderful king.

Evander's parents, Leah and Ian, have been a wonderful helping hand. They stay in the palace with us while having access to a cottage at the edge of town. They want to spend as much time with their son as possible, and I can't blame them. Leah spends time with Thalia and me during the day. My sister looks up to the lady like a second mother. She has been teaching us things the queen never taught us, like sewing and cooking.

When Eleanor was here for the wedding, I found her spending time with Evander's ma. She told my sister more stories of the high sorcerers and other tales of her childhood. Eleanor loved every minute.

Ian is a quiet older man, but he and my father have been getting along well. The man is very good at chess, and occasionally I will find the two of them in the library playing the game. It is one of the few times I see actual life in my father's eyes. Our families are at peace with our marriage, and I couldn't be happier.

Now, for one last thing. I have been waiting a few weeks to confirm my suspicion. I would hate to give Evander false excitement, and honestly, I am nervous about his reaction. Will he be happy and excited like I am? Or will he be disappointed? I pace back and forth in our new bedroom.

After we moved into the palace, I decided we needed a new room where we could start our new life together. We are not going to be what everyone expects of a conqueror who stole a princess. We are going to be a happy couple who are madly in love.

I run my fingers over my desk as I hear the door to our bedroom open. I turn on my heel to see Evander. His hair has been recently trimmed, though it still falls across his brow. I love him and his mess of hair. He looks rejuvenated compared to a few months ago. *Happy.* He smiles at me, and I run to him, jumping into his arms. He makes an oof sound as I smother his face in passionate kisses.

"I wasn't gone that long." He laughs.

I giggle, my eyes connecting with his brilliant steel-grey ones. "I have something to tell you."

"Something bad?" He blanches.

I still see the worry in him at times. The fear that he will lose me. When that happens, I kiss him and remind him that my heart is his.

"No!" I shake my head, smiling brightly. "Not at all!"

"Tell me then," he says, kissing me again.

"I'm um…" I pause, unable to say the words out loud. I take his hand and place it on my stomach, hoping he gets the clue.

"Full?" he asks, frowning.

I snort. "In a way, guess again."

"Hungry?" he asks.

Shaking my head, laughing. "No, no! I'm pregnant!"

Evander's eyes practically bulge from his head. "W-what?"

"We are going to have a baby," I say, biting my bottom lip. His reaction is the only one that matters to me, and right now, he is unreadable. My hand shakes slightly, tightening on his. It takes a few seconds before a smile breaks across his face and he lifts me in the air to spin me around.

"We're going to have a baby!" he exclaims.

I laugh and kiss him. "We will have to make preparations. Do you think your ma will mind helping me?"

"No." He smiles, shaking his head. "She loves you more than she does me."

I laugh again, kissing him. "Are you ready for this?"

"With you, I'm ready for anything," he says, pressing his forehead against mine. I kiss him deeply, feeling as if I can't contain my joy.

Just you and me.

RETURN TO
THE WORLD OF
AELLOLYN IN

The Mountain's

Princess

COMING SOON

CPSIA information can be obtained
at www.ICGtesting.com
Printed in the USA
BVHW040816041121
620777BV00011B/193